KINGDOMS AND CHAOS

KING'S DARK TIDINGS

BOOK 4

KEL KADE

This is a work of fiction. All characters, places, and events in this novel are fictitious. Opinions and beliefs expressed by the characters do not reflect the author's opinions and beliefs.

This book is intended for adult readers. It contains graphic violence, creative language, and sexual innuendo. This book does not contain explicit sexual content.

Dark Rover Publishing, L.L.C.
Allen, Texas, U.S.A.

ISBN: 978-1-952687-05-1

Also available in audiobook produced by Podium Publishing 2018

Written by Kel Kade
Edited by Leslie Watts
Interior Illustrations by Kel Kade
Cover art by Chris McGrath

BOOKS BY KEL KADE

MAP OF EASTERN ASHAI

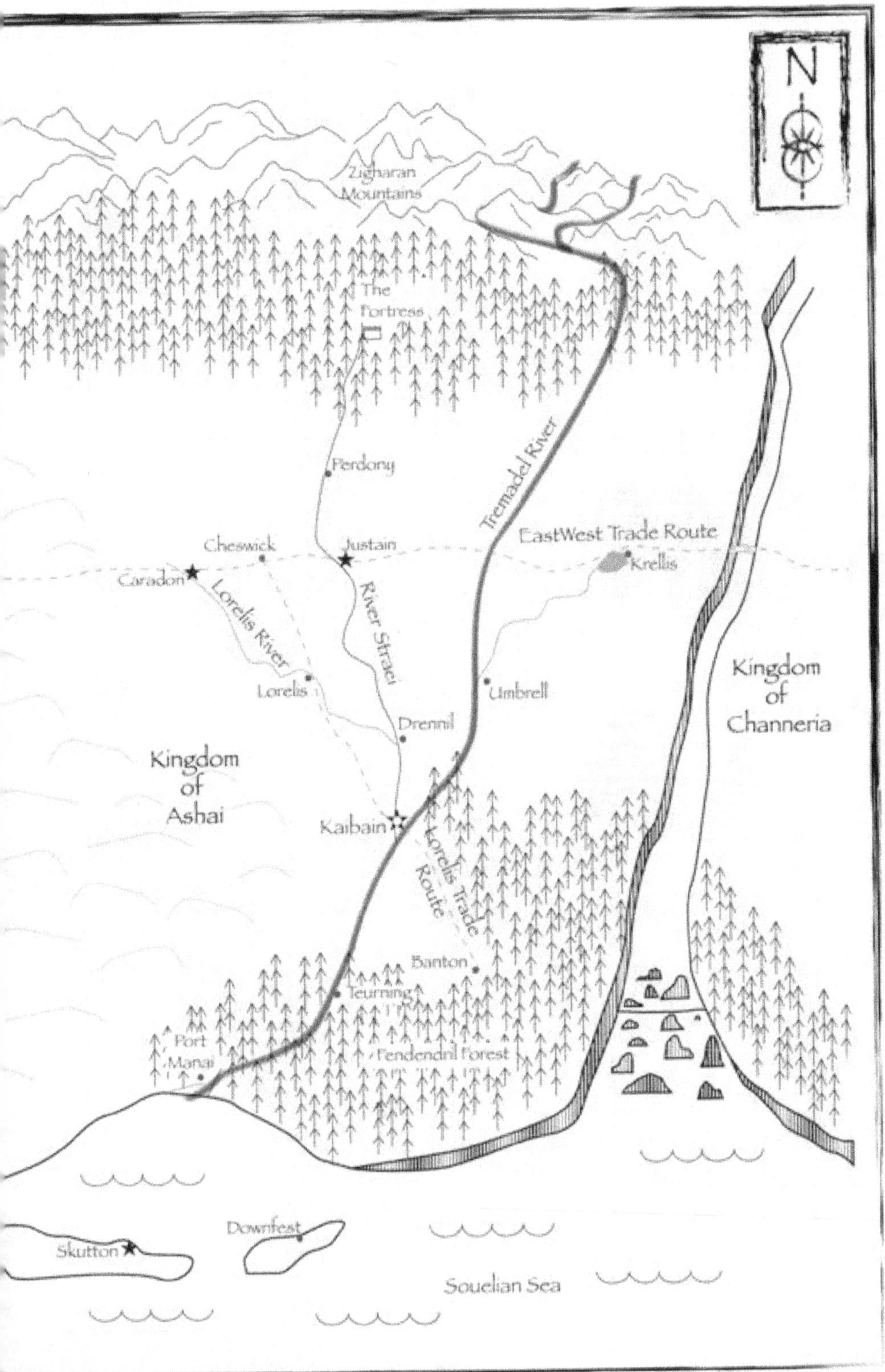

REGIONAL MAP OF THE SOUELIAN SEA

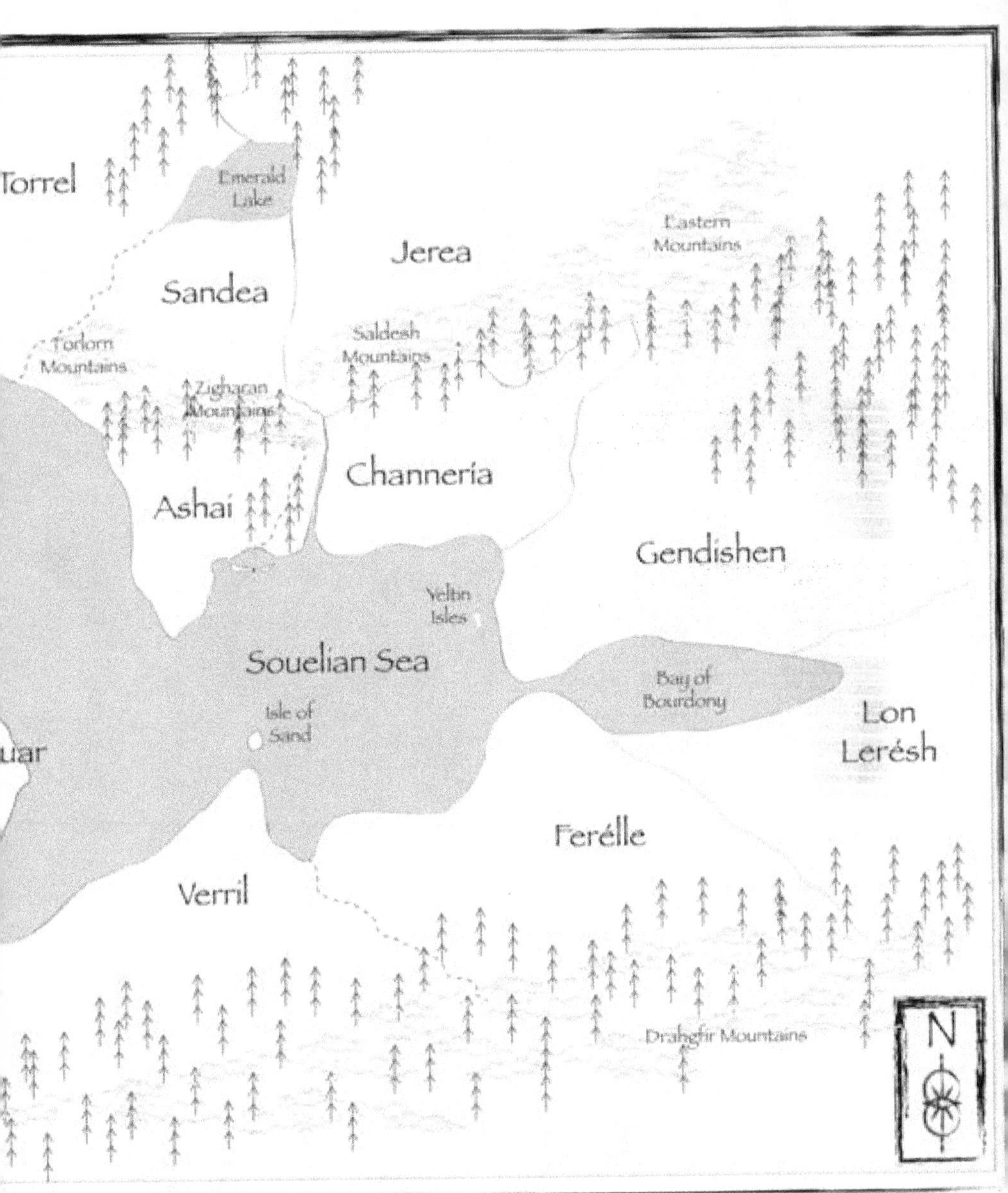

MAP OF THE EASTERN SOUELIAN SEA

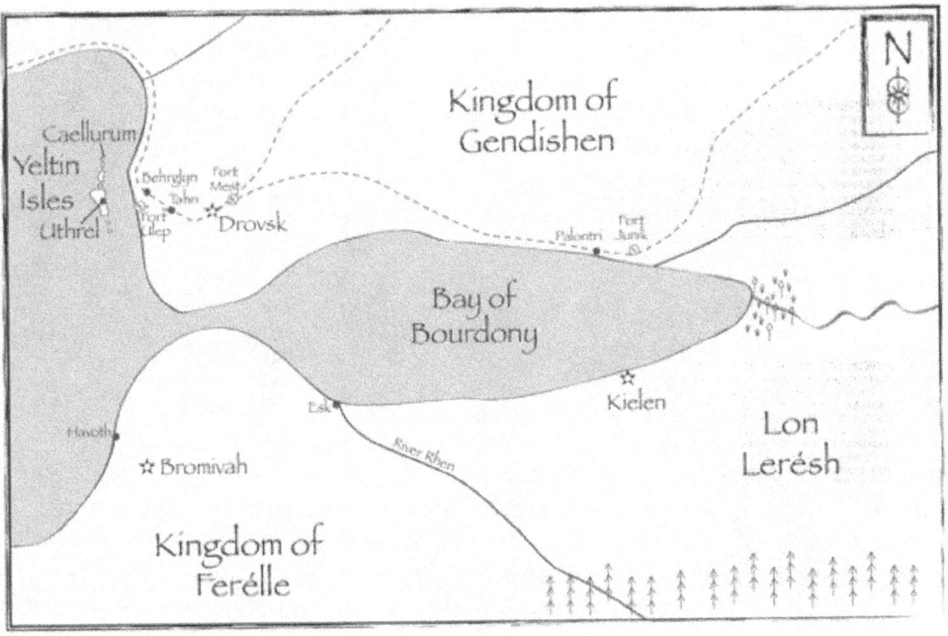

1

Rezkin tightened the strap securing his pack behind the saddle and then took the reins. Leading Pride forward, he looked over his shoulder to make sure the others were with him. He did not want their presence in Gendishen announced, so all but one of the landing party were dressed as mercenaries, a guise they decided would not raise suspicion since bids for mercenary companies were rising in every kingdom. It was a lucrative profession *if* one could survive the war that would follow. Only the priest, Minder Finwy, appeared out of place. While the Gendishen extremist views of the Purifiers did not adhere to the tenets of the Temple of the Maker, and, in fact, the collectiare openly condemned their actions, the people of Gendishen respected and honored anyone who served the Maker—so long as he or she was not a mage.

Rezkin's party had come ashore midmorning, far from any settlement, sacrificing time for secrecy. By foot, it would take the travelers half the day to reach the trade route and from there another three days to the nearest city. Rezkin hoped they would not have to walk the entire distance. Gendishen was known for good horse breeding, and King Privoth, like his ancestors before him, had vowed to create a breed to rival the battle chargers of Ashai. The Gendishen *reds* were no battle chargers, but they were fast. Since his was the only mount, Rezkin hoped to procure some reds for the rest of his party. He had dusted and painted Pride's coat, mane, and tail to make the horse's appearance less striking, although it was unlikely anyone would recognize the battle charger for what he was. As far as Rezkin knew, no battle charger had ever trod upon Gendishen soil. Even so, he had covered the majestic stallion in a worn and muddy brown caparison that hid the impressive armor underneath.

Kai cleared his throat, the gruff sound barely discernable over the sound of the waves breaking against the rocks on the desolate shore. "You should ride," he said. "You are the king. No one would begrudge the king his mount."

Rezkin checked the dinghy one more time and then waved to the crewmen who would return it to the ship. He looked at Kai and said, "To what end? We can go no faster than the slowest walker. I would grow bored in the saddle. I prefer to be active. Besides, while they may not resent me for riding, they *will* respect my decision to join them in the walk."

Kai hefted his own pack. "Perhaps, but it is unseemly for a king to be trudging through the dirt like common infantry."

As Rezkin scanned the horizon, he said, "Remember we are mercenaries. Besides, Cael is a warrior kingdom led by a warrior king—one that fights with his men, *walks* with his men, and dies with them if necessary."

"Is that right, Rez?" Farson said as he strode up to Kai's other side.

Rezkin had struggled with the decision to bring the estranged striker but had concluded that he would rather keep the man in his sights than allow him to run amuck in his new kingdom. He stared at his former trainer, waiting to hear his latest resentful accusation. Farson did not disappoint.

Farson said, "Would you die with us if we came under attack from an undefeatable force? Or would you be on that horse and away to safety?"

"I follow the *Rules*, same as you," said Rezkin.

"Not like me. We are not the same. *You*—as king." Farson huffed with contempt. "You will drop this role as soon as it becomes inconvenient."

Rezkin paused, and Kai and Farson stopped beside him. He glanced over his shoulder to see that Jimson and the others were far enough back to lend them privacy, all but Minder Finwy. The priest was scrabbling over the detritus at a respectful distance, but he was still close enough to hear the conversation.

Rezkin lowered his voice. "What would you have me do, Farson? These people have need of me. Ashai has need of me. Should I abandon them now? To do what?"

Farson scoffed. "Are you doing this to serve their needs, or are you using them to serve your own?"

Exasperated, Rezkin said, "What needs have *I*?" He closed the distance between them, inciting Farson to palm a dagger from his sleeve. He made no effort to hide his distrust.

Rezkin said, "I have more money than I could spend in a lifetime. I am trained to become anyone, to do almost anything. I am not like them. That is clear, as is *Rule 257*. Have no doubt that I understand. Yet, without *them*"—he nodded toward Malcius, Brandt, and Yserria—"I cannot heed *Rule 1.* Without *them*, I have no reason to *be* anything. Without *them* I have no purpose."

He knew that arguing with Farson was futile, so he did not wait for a response. He instead tugged at the reins and headed inland at a brisk walk.

Kai turned to Farson. "I have not heard of a *Rule 257*."

Farson followed in his former pupil's footsteps, calling over his shoulder, "*Be one and alone.*"

The terrain between the shore and the trade route was rough, covered with sharp rocks, pits, and hollows that could collapse under the weight of a careless traveler. Brandt and Malcius were surprisingly quiet, keeping most of their anguished grumbling to themselves. Jimson and Sergeant Millins were good soldiers, suffering in silence and making sure the others navigated the treacherous passage without injury. Yserria danced over the rubble with ease but tended toward the opposite side of the group from Malcius. Rezkin had hesitated to bring her since swordswomen were even more uncommon in Gendishen than they were in Ashai. She was a capable fighter and spoke fluent Leréshi, though, which would help to disguise their party's origin.

Malcius huffed as he caught up to where Rezkin waited for them with Wesson. He said, "We should not have left so soon after the battle. What if there are more demons? What if those white creatures attack again?"

"You had the option to stay behind."

"You know I could not," Malcius said with a nod toward Yserria. He tugged at an amulet that had been fashioned to hold her life stone. "Not since you hung this burden around my neck."

"It is only temporary," said Wesson.

"You cannot know that. I was talking about the attack, though. What of the creatures?"

Rezkin said, "I cannot be everywhere, and the war will not wait. I delayed this trip long enough. It has been two weeks, and we have seen no signs of aggression from the creatures. If anything, they seem eager to please. Shezar and the mages are keeping an eye on them. The shielreyah insist they will be able to prevent them from becoming a problem again."

"They could not the first time," Malcius said.

"That is because the shielreyah are not fully conscious," said Wesson. "Their souls reside in the Afterlife. They could not detect the threat because their vague awareness could not conceive of it. Now, they are aware of the potential danger."

"I harbor no trust for them either," Malcius grumbled. "And it makes no sense. The shielreyah were created to protect the fortress. If a threat exists on the island, they should know of it."

Rezkin said, "The shielreyah refer to the creatures as *ictali*. Apparently, the ictali were utterly loyal and devoted servants when the shielreyah lived. They would not have recognized them as a threat. I believe the only reason they attacked was because of the demon's control."

"And Healer Aelis? Was he under its control as well?"

"I have reason to believe he was already possessed when he joined us in Skutton."

Wesson said, "I have seen only a few references to demons, most of them warnings in introductory texts. They all agree that demons can only possess a person with consent."

Malcius looked at Wesson aghast. "Why would anyone do that?"

Wesson shrugged. "For power. Some even think they can use it for good. My master told me a story about a healer who wanted to cure his wife of some terrible ailment. He did not have enough *talent* on his own, so he made a pact with a demon. It did not end well for either of them. They think they can control it; but, in all the stories, the demon ultimately overcomes the person's will. I am not sure if the ritual we interrupted in the forest was a form of forced possession or some other kind of demonic control. We do not have enough information. Truthfully, I never completely believed the stories. I thought demons were myths. Surely, if they were real and so powerful, they would have consumed the world ages ago."

"All the more reason we should have stayed in Cael," Malcius grumbled. He sighed with exasperation as he stumbled over another loose rock. "I do not understand why we could not bring at least one earth mage. It would have made our passage far easier."

Rezkin said, "I told you the *talent* is not tolerated in Gendishen. All forms of magery are outlawed."

Wesson added, "The *talent* is referred to as the *scourge*, and those *afflicted* with the scourge are put to death. A special division of the king's forces called the Purifiers are dedicated solely to the investigation and elimination of the afflicted."

"But *you* are here. You could do something about this," Malcius said as a stone shifted beneath his foot.

"We do not wish to attract the attention of the Purifiers," replied Rezkin.

Wesson said, "It is unclear how the Purifiers identify the afflicted, since only those with *talent* can sense it in others. Still, if anyone witnessed my actions, they would certainly report us."

Brandt, who had arrived on Malcius's heals, said, "It makes no sense to me. Most people would kill to have the *talent*. Why would an entire kingdom spurn the gift?"

"People often fear what they do not understand, and they tend to hate what they fear," Rezkin said. "No ruler of Gendishen has possessed the *talent*. The king rules with strength of arms alone. A mage class would threaten the ruling family's power."

"So they just kill anyone they think is a mage?" Brandt said. His irritation was compounded as he snagged his pant leg on the razor edge of a boulder.

Rezkin navigated around a steep slope of talus, leading Pride to stabler ground. He said, "The surrounding kingdoms are glad to accept *talented* refugees, which has always been a major point of contention between Gendishen and its neighbors, Channería and Lon Lerésh. To keep the peace, the other kingdoms begrudgingly agreed not to assist in an escape, but they will provide sanctuary if someone makes it across the border."

"Why is Mage Wesson here, then?" Brandt asked. "He will be killed if caught."

Rezkin paused to dig a rock from Pride's hoof as he answered. "According to the *Interkingdom Accords*, rulers and dignitaries from foreign kingdoms are exempt from the anti-scourge laws for the duration of a sanctioned visit. I doubt King Privoth will extend us the courtesy without first recognizing me as an independent monarch. Therefore, we could not bring any mages. Journeyman Wesson, however, insisted on attending despite the dangers. He knows his strength and also speaks fluent Gendishen."

"I am willing to hazard the risks," Wesson growled in a heated tone unlike his usual easy-going demeanor. "What they are doing is wrong. People should not be persecuted for being born different from others. The Gendishen believe the *talent* is a choice—that wielders have made pacts with demons or the like."

"But it is a blessing of the Maker," Malcius exclaimed. "Mages can do great things!"

"And terrible things, too," Sergeant Millins muttered as Malcius stumbled into him.

"Come now, Sergeant, how can you say that?" Malcius said, shrugging off the soldier's assistance.

"The sergeant is right," Wesson said. "I know more than most that the power can be both a blessing and a curse—not in the bearing of it, but in the use. For one with my affinity, it is easy to destroy and infinitely harder to create."

"I think you will find that is true in all things," Rezkin said, "not just with the *talent*."

Rezkin wondered if Wesson's true reason for attending was to keep an eye on *him*. Rezkin had been better about keeping his emotional—and often paranoid—*episodes* under control, but the strikers still treated him warily. He had overheard Kai asking if Farson had noticed a difference in Rezkin's behavior, and his former trainer had laughed. Farson had said that if they were observing a strangeness in Rezkin, it was because he wanted it to be so. Farson's assertion had been a relief, since Rezkin would not want his potential enemy to perceive the weakness.

After finally reaching the road, the travelers took a short respite and then walked for another hour. Gendishen was a large kingdom. Far to the east were forests and to the north, mountains, but it was otherwise dominated by flat plains. Even the smallest bump in the landscape was a notable topographic feature. As such, most of the residents were farmers, ranchers, and plantation owners. The countryside seemed to go on endlessly, and everything in sight was tall grasses, clumps of bushes, or short, scraggly trees, feasted upon by herds of grazing animals. Occasional disturbances in the grass, usually caused by a fox or wild cat, would incite a frenzy in the grassland birds, which took to the air in a noisy flurry. The buzz and snap of insects was only overshadowed by the hollow drone of the breeze wafting through the sea of wispy green and gold stalks.

Eventually, Rezkin came to a halt. "We shall stop here," he said.

"Why so early?" Malcius said. "We have at least a few hours before sundown. We should push ahead and get to civilization sooner."

Rezkin nodded up the road and then to the meadows surrounding them. "This is unknown, possibly hostile territory, and we travel light. Are you capable of hunting in the dark?"

Malcius said nothing but furrowed his brow in frustration as he followed his pack to the ground.

Brandt turned from surveying the landscape and said, "I am not questioning your decision, Rez, but I *am* wondering why you chose *this* spot. It looks identical to everything else around here."

"True," said Rezkin, "there is little to distinguish it." He pointed to a spot a short distance away and said, "Those grasses are slightly greener than the rest. Do you hear that bird song? It is bouncy and quickens at the end. It is a sedge wren. They are often found in wet areas."

"You think we will find fresh water here?" said Brandt.

Rezkin shrugged as he untied his pack. "Possibly. It is no guarantee."

"Did you teach him that?" Malcius said, as he stared at Farson.

Farson paused in the searching of his pack and glanced between Malcius and Rezkin. People generally avoided bringing up their past connection since it was obvious their relationship was less than conciliatory. Malcius seemed to be in a foul mood, though. Farson finished fishing in his pack and set to stringing his bow before answering.

"No, that was probably Beritt. He was good with birds—most animals, really—and he was an excellent tracker."

"So where is Beritt now?" Malcius asked.

"Dead." Farson turned and disappeared into the tall grass, and Malcius looked to Rezkin for answers.

Ignoring the unspoken question, Rezkin said, "I go to scout the area." Then he, too, vanished.

Malcius was not satisfied. He looked to Kai, who was brushing down the disgruntled stallion. "What happened to Beritt?"

"How should I know?" said Kai without pause. "It is none of my business."

"You are a striker. Is it not your business to know what happened to your brother?"

"As far as I am concerned, Beritt died twelve years ago on a mission. Such was the official position of King Bordran. Beyond that, it is neither my business nor *yours*."

"But he obviously did not—"

"Perhaps he asked too many questions," Kai snapped. "Leave it be, Lord Malcius. No good can come of dredging up *his* past."

"You mean Rez—"

"You and Brandt will start clearing the area for a fire pit. Unlike your little fiasco on the beach in Port Manai, this will require some forethought. We do not wish to burn down the field with us in it."

"But the soldiers can—"

"Stop arguing. You are not lords in a plush estate. You are mercenaries. Act like it."

Since Farson had gone south, Rezkin headed east and then turned north. The scent of horses and unwashed bodies reached his nose as he pressed through the grasses, some of which were taller than he. Quickening his pace, he turned back toward the road. After a cautious circuit of the group, he moved to crouch within the brush at the side of the road. It was a noisy bunch of twenty-seven rough-looking men with an assortment of mismatched weapons and armor. Each wore about his waist a black sash bearing a white crescent moon at one end. Only five of the men led horses, and all but one of the mounts were loaded with equipment. Several casks and trunks were piled into a rickety mule-drawn wagon from which the company's standard flew atop a tall pole. A few boisterous fellows trod at the front, setting the pace, while the rest dragged their feet behind. Some wore bandages, and the lone rider appeared as if he might not see the dawn.

Rezkin waited for the company to pass and then skirted back the way he had come. Upon arrival at the camp, he silently approached Farson from the rear. The striker turned too late. If Rezkin had intended it, the striker would have been dead. Farson graced him with a scowl, and Rezkin replied with a grin. The effort was rewarded by Farson's obvious disconcert. Rezkin could not remember ever smiling at Farson, outside of an act.

"Find Kai," he said.

Without question, Farson shouldered his bow and vanished into the grass.

Rezkin surveyed the camp and was fairly satisfied with their progress. A broad patch on the side of the road had been stamped down, and the group was huddled around a pit that had been cleared for the fire. An unoccupied perimeter separated them from the tall grasses, although it was still too narrow for Rezkin's comfort. They would have at least a few seconds' warning before an ambush, assuming their assailants were not carrying crossbows. Brandt crouched over the pit attempting to light the fire, and Jimson and Millins plucked a couple of unidentifiable fowl, while Yserria hovered at the far perimeter with the appearance of keeping watch. Wesson was, with crossed legs, weaving his fingers through the air over a palm-sized lump on the ground as Minder Finwy watched.

Wesson glanced up as Rezkin neared. "Can you feel it?" he asked.

"Only since entering the circle," Rezkin said.

"You are a mage?" Finwy said, genuinely surprised.

"No," said Rezkin.

Wesson glanced at him dubiously but did not comment. Instead, he said, "I have been working on narrowing my vimara bleed." He dangled an object in the air that looked like a black stone carved into an intricate knot. Tiny runes were marked along each curve, and a smaller red stone was set in the center. The object hung from a leather lace strung through a hole in the knot. "This amulet should help. You are particularly sensitive to it." He raised his head and narrowed his eyes at Rezkin. "I wonder if you use a method similar to the Purifiers …" Without finishing the thought, he went back to his ministrations.

When Farson and Kai arrived several minutes later, Rezkin said, "We will have company soon. Mercenaries are heading our way from the north."

"Trouble?" said Kai.

Rezkin said, "They have injured and may wish to avoid conflict. That being said, we will implement the plan." He looked to Brandt and Malcius. "Remember, do not speak. If you must, keep it short and slur your words. Neither of you sound like mercs." He paused, giving them a once-over. "And slouch."

"Got it. Pretend we jus' returned from a bender," Brandt mumbled. Malcius punched Brandt in the arm. "What? Palis would have laughed."

"Shut up," Malcius grumbled, but his expression softened at the thought.

Rezkin shook his head. "If you must, but stop smiling. You have a terrible hangover."

"Well, that shucks," Brandt said in his best drunkenese, eliciting a genuine smile from Malcius. The expression abruptly vanished behind a scowl directed at Yserria before he went back to poking at the ground with a twig.

"What about you?" he muttered. "You do not sound like a *merc* either."

"I am capable," Rezkin said as the sounds of the troop finally reached his ears. He checked his longsword that was strapped to his back, shifted the shortsword at his hip, and then plopped down on the ground practically on top of Wesson.

The mage looked up in alarm. “Wha-what are you doing?”

Rezkin drew the hood of his worn brown cloak over his head and sprawled out on the flattened grass as he lounged against Wesson’s side. “Yer too purdy to be on yer own, boy,” he said in Ashaiian with a heavy Gendishen accent. “If one of us don’t claim ya, one of *them* will. Best it be me.”

“B-b-but Yserria! I mean, she is a *woman*! Why do you not claim *her*?”

“Yserria’ll put ’em in their place. *You* can’t or ye’ll expose yerself as a demon-bound afflicted, and then we’ll have to kill ’em all.”

“Wait. You would *kill* them? But, they have done nothing to us. We could find another way. I could—”

“Can’t have no rumors gettin’ ’round, Wes. You show ’em, we kill ’em.”

Wesson was visibly upset, and Finwy pursed his lips in disapproval. The others said nothing as they shared a surprised and uncomfortable silence. The strikers and soldiers, who were trained for combat, did not appear to share their distaste for the brutality of war—or at least accepted it as necessary. Farson dashed into the grass while Kai, Millins, and Jimson moved to intercept the incoming company at the road. The others stared at Rezkin as if he had just grown a second head, and he supposed he had, in a manner of speaking. Wesson quickly hid the amulet he had been enchanting and then sat stiffly under Rezkin’s weight. The clink of armor, creak of wood, and snorts of men and horses were nearly upon them when a small, furry creature darted out of the grass to roll in the mat and dirt at Rezkin’s feet.

He spied the beast curiously, and Malcius blurted, “Is that your cat?”

“I s’pose …” Rezkin drawled.

“I do not remember it being in the dinghy when we rowed ashore.”

“Nor do I,” said Wesson, “and we have not seen it all day.”

Rezkin shrugged. “Cats be mysterious. Quiet now or the jig’ll be up as soon they get here.”

As the troupe came into view, Kai called out in a traditional Gendishen greeting. “Hail to the travelers. May we meet and part in peace.”

Given the Gendishen penchant for violence, Rezkin thought it sounded more like a plea. The mercenaries plodded to a halt, and the lead man, a black-haired, hefty fellow with dark eyes and a braid dangling from his chin, spat off to the side.

“Peace? You don’t look the sort is lookin’ fer peace.”

Kai grinned and shook with a hearty laugh. "We ain't lookin' fer trouble neither—not 'til there's silver and gold weighin' down our purses."

"Then we're of a like mind." The man surveyed the group and added, "You lot ain't much to look at. About eight of you, not including' the priest? You got some hidden in the grass?"

Kai mirthlessly chuckled. "What we be lackin' in numbers, we're makin' up fer in skill."

The leader said, "Ha! Next, you'll be tellin' us yer all swordmasters." His men burst into uproarious laughter, slapping their armor and jeering.

"And ya got two women!" shouted another fellow who was missing a few teeth.

"That one's a lad," Kai said with a nod toward Wesson, whose face was flushed. "You prob'ly don't wanna be challengin' his friend there." With a nod toward Yserria, he said, "That one's a lass, though, and I'd wager she'll lay any one of you out."

The men laughed and a few stepped closer to get a better look at the tall, red-headed beauty. She set her stance and patted her sword hilt. Her distaste for the men was obvious by her determined expression. She lifted her chin in defiance and spoke in Leréshi. "*Presh tuar duevinua.*"

Rezkin snorted and remarked, "*Duarvashkatin conjuhotu.*"

Yserria looked at him with surprise and grinned.

The black-haired mercenary hawked a glob of phlegm at Rezkin's feet. "A Leréshi, then? The lassies don't often carry the swords, but I'll not be messin' with one who does. Which of you has she claimed?"

"He's dead," said Kai.

"That's fitting," the man muttered. Seemingly satisfied, he waved back toward his men. "Kingdom pays more fer large companies. If yer as good as you say, you'd be best signin' with us. We'll all get more at the end."

Kai grinned again. "Aye, but the fewer of us is at the end, the more we all get?"

The man scowled furiously. "We don't stand fer traitors."

"Maybe not, but ain't none of *us* is really one of *you*, eh? You get a bigger contract fer the extra swords and then stab us in the back."

The mercenary leader said, "He that wears the crescent *be* the crescent."

The other mercenaries nodded and barked their agreement.

"Seems a better deal," replied Kai. "Mayhap we'll march together. See if we can come to an agreement."

The man grunted. "We'll get yer measure." Then, he turned and waved his hand in the air as he began barking orders to his men.

The mercenaries set their camp on the opposite side of the road. They had little in the way of comforts, but they made due with their wagons and battered gear. About an hour after sundown, Rezkin stumbled into their camp carrying a jug of ale he had snagged from their supplies. His arm was slung over Wesson's shoulders, and Wesson looked as if he would crawl into a hole and die.

"What do you want?" said one mercenary whose hair had thinned by half, the remaining strands hanging past his shoulders. "No one invited you to our camp, and ain't no one gonna be givin' you their drink. You get back to yer side of the road afore we make sure you can't come back."

"See?" Rezkin said in Gendishen as he slammed the jug into Wesson's chest. Then he thrust it back into the air with a slosh. "I tol' ya they'd be interested in a story."

"I really don't think they are," Wesson muttered in the same tongue.

The black-haired leader rounded the fire. "I know yer kind—saw you earlier, lazin' about with your pretty boy while the others worked. You prob'ly think you should get the same take as us is workin' hard, don't ya?"

Rezkin laughed and pushed Wesson to the ground. Wesson scowled up at him, his frustration genuine. Then, he ducked his head and played the part of the cowed young man with no choice but submission. He was ashamed to admit that it was not so far from the truth. He had never tried his power against Rezkin and wondered if it would be as ineffectual as the power wielded by the other mages. Rezkin tumbled gracelessly to the ground beside him, nearly losing the contents of the jug in the process.

"They don't want me doin' none of that. I gotta stay rested, ya see? In case any of you decide to make trouble."

The men burst into laughter, but the leader was having none of it. "You had best be able to put your sword where yer mouth is."

Rezkin laughed boisterously, slapping his knee. "If I did that, I'd not be talkin' no more, would I?"

"We'd all be better off," said the mercenary leader. He turned to Wesson. "And you? What good are you? Yer too puny to lift a blade, and I doubt you got a scar on ya."

Wesson was saved from answering when Rezkin jabbed an elbow into his ribs. "He polishes my weapons."

The men snickered and groaned as Wesson's face heated. He decided that whenever they were away from the mercenaries, he was going to give Rezkin a piece of his mind—even if it killed him.

Turning back to Rezkin, the leader said, "What's this story yer talkin' 'bout?"

"First, Boss, what be yer name?" said Rezkin as if the alcohol were taking its full effect. Even Wesson was inclined to wonder if he had truly been drinking.

"The name's Orin, commander of the White Crescents."

Rezkin said, "Commander, eh? Army man? What kinda name is *White Crescents*? Don't sound like no merc comp'ny to me. Blood Moon, maybe, or Black Eclipse, but White Crescents?"

Orin kicked Rezkin in the side and then grabbed his chest plate. With a hard yank, the mercenary leader lifted Rezkin toward his face. He then leaned over them both, and Wesson could smell the man's putrid breath as he said, "On the night of an eclipse, the white crescent is the last vestige of light ya see before all goes dark, and it's the first ya see if yer lucky to see the light again. It's what they calls a *metaphor*. It's fer battle, fer life."

Rezkin stared at the mercenary for entirely too long and then burst into laughter. He shoved the man back with surprising force. "How poetic. Now let's get to the story."

Orin waved off the men who had jumped to defend their leader, or perhaps just his pride. "What story is it yer tellin'?"

"What?" said Rezkin, blinking up at the man as if he couldn't see through the ale drowning his mind. "No. Can't say as I've got no stories worth tellin'. I's wantin' to hear yers. Why are half yer men injured and one looks to be makin' a deal with the Maker? The way I sees it, y'all must've been the victors, seein' as how yer still alive. I ain't heard about no battles, though."

With a wave toward his men and a grumble, Orin sat down on a saddle draped across a mound of grass. He pulled a knob of crass root from a pouch at his waist, gnawed on the stalk a moment, and then shoved the whole thing into his cheek before answering.

"Weren't no battle of men. Was the drauglics—come down from the mountains, I suppose."

"Drauglics?" barked Rezkin. "I ain't buyin' it. We ain't nowhere near the mountains, and ain't no one ever seen one on the plains."

"Can't say as I blame ya," said Orin. "I wouldn't neither but for the rumors. You must've heard 'em. Been goin' round for months. Drauglic sightings, peasants in the outlands disappearin'. Some say they been findin' pieces of people—*eaten* they say—slaughtered. I didn't believe none of it myself—least not 'till we was attacked. A day and a half ago to the north. We was huntin' fer game not far from the trade route when they just appeared outta nowhere. We counted about twenty bodies at the end but don't know how many done run off. Took us by surprise, nasty suckers. Before the attack, our company was forty-two with as many horses."

"So they was after the horses," Rezkin said.

Orin motioned for one of his men to chuck another log onto the fire and said, "I don't think they cared if they got man or horse, only the horses didn't have swords."

"And the drauglics? What'd they have?"

"Crude weapons and farm tools, mostly—a few swords and knives they prob'ly took off their victims."

"Drauglics carry weapons?" said Wesson "I thought they were small, primitive creatures."

"So he *can* speak," said Orin with a chuckle, but his humor faded quickly. "These weren't small things. They was nearly as big as a man … well, a small man, maybe. They wield weapons, but I hear they ain't smart enough to forge metal. They make their weapons from sticks and stones, and some of 'em got wood or leather armor. The better stuff is what they find or steal. They looked kinda like men from a distance, but they was lizards—got purple and orange scales over parts of their flesh."

"They sound awful," said Wesson.

"Don't you worry 'bout it, boy. Yer *friend* there seems to think he can take on an army!" He and his men laughed and jeered.

Rezkin rose unsteadily, motioning for Wesson to stand. He leaned heavily on Wesson's shoulder as he said, "Only thing I'm plannin' to take on is this here ale."

Orin grunted. "Seems to me you've had enough, but at least you'll be rested if we decide to attack ya. Maybe even you'll kill a few of us, eh?"

"Sure, and the purple lizard men, too," Rezkin said with a drunken gurgle.

When they got back to the camp, Rezkin slumped to the ground in front of the fire and called loudly for Malcius to dish up the grub. Having already removed much of his armor, Malcius shuffled forward, leaving his sword with his pack. Rezkin grabbed him by the shoulder and shoved him back, causing him to trip and tumble into Millins who was trying to sleep before taking his turn as lookout.

"What was that for?" Malcius hollered, his anger getting the better of him.

"Don't be stupid," Rezkin said, switching to the highly accented Ashaiian trade dialect. "You leave yer sword unattended, and it won't be tendin' you when ya need it. I don't care whether your pissin' or bathin', you keep that blade on you *always*."

"Like *he* bathes," Brandt said with a snort, dutifully playing his role of debaucherous mercenary.

Malcius's response died on his lips when he saw Brandt's gaze flick to a place beyond the firelight. A movement in the dark, the crunch of a footfall, and the jingle of buckles betrayed the mercenary hovering at the road.

Attempting to mimic Rezkin's style of speech, Malcius said, "I don't need to, seein' as how, unlike you, I don't go rollin' about with swine." Rezkin, Kai, and Brandt burst into laughter.

Yserria huffed, and the trade dialect so common in Skutton rolled off her tongue like liquid silk. "You're all swine, and if ya don't lay off the ale, you'll be spitted like swine, too."

Malcius cinched his sword belt with an angry tug and said, "You'd best hope that don't happen since none of us'd be around to save you this time."

Yserria squared her shoulders. "No, I can see that honor don't run in the family. You forget that I don't need your help."

Alert to the shift in tone and the silent watcher at the road, Rezkin interrupted the exchange. "The woman's got a point."

Malcius looked at him flabbergasted. "*You're* questioning my honor?"

Rezkin turned a sharp gaze on his friend and slurred, "No, ya idjit. Ain't no honor to be had by the likes of us." Malcius's mouth snapped shut, and his shoulders dropped as he resumed his mercenary role. Rezkin continued. "I was talkin' 'bout us getting' spitted." He slapped Wesson on the shoulder and motioned to the roasting meat. "Since Mal can't keep his head straight, you get the food." As Wesson crouched over the fire muttering incomprehensively, Rezkin said, "Them over there is sayin' there's lizard men goin' around eatin' people."

"Lizard men?" Brandt said hesitantly, as though hoping to avoid becoming the butt of a joke.

Kai, the presumed leader of the group, leaned forward from where he sat atop Rezkin's saddle, "You mean drauglics?"

Rezkin nodded. "That's what they's sayin'. They was attacked less than two days ago. Drauglics killed 'bout a third of their men and took most of the horses."

"We'd best be on high alert," Kai said, meeting each of their gazes. "It'll be easy fer those creatures to sneak up on us in this high grass."

"You mean *real* drauglics?" Brandt exclaimed. "You're serious."

Rezkin nodded. "Their scales are hard. A sword can get through with enough force, but it ain't easy in a heavy battle. Got scales on the sides of their necks, so you gotta jab straight for the throat. Same with the torso. The middle's soft, but they usually cover it with some kinda armor. Yer good to go fer the inner thighs, groin, and soft spot under the tail."

"They have tails?" Brandt said with too much enthusiasm.

Kai grumbled, "You'd best hope we don't run into any."

Rezkin nodded toward the others, silently indicating the man at the road had returned to his camp.

"You sound like you've battled 'em before," Brandt drawled, still wary of being overheard.

Rezkin nodded. "About two years ago, a large band of 'em took up in the Zigharans. We went in a cleared 'em out."

"You and your trainers?" Kai said.

"Nah, just me and my men. Men like them," Rezkin said with a nod toward the party on the other side of the road.

Kai narrowed his eyes. "I thought you said you'd just left yer trainin' when we met."

"Right, but I weren't always at the fortress." He met Kai's suspicious gaze and said, "Didn't go near no settlements. There was trainin' to be done. Battles to be fought. Wars to be won."

"You fought mock battles?"

The others watched him with hawk-like gazes as he spoke. Even Millins had given up on his attempt at sleep. Despite the attention, Rezkin realized that he was no longer inundated with the persistent paranoia that had plagued him since landing on Cael. He said, "Only thing mock about 'em was the reason for fighten 'em. Men was captured or hired to fight on both sides, and none of 'em knowin' why. Turns out, weren't no reason fer it but *me*. I even went on campaign with a King's Army unit called the Scavengers."

"*You* were part of the Scavengers?" Millins exclaimed, his expression soured with disdain.

"Who are the Scavengers?" Malcius said as he took a bowl from Wesson.

With a glance toward the other camp, Millins drawled, "Not all men make good soldiers. Some cause trouble—fightin' in the unit, problems with the locals, offendin' the nobles, deserters. Those men go to the Scavengers. Nobody *wants* to be a Scavenger. They get the worst assignments, the worst pay—most or *all* of it levied for fines before it even reaches their purses. As a reward for their sadism, the strictest officers are assigned to whip the Scavengers into shape." Millins looked to Rezkin. "So, you were placed in charge?"

"Nah, I was a green recruit. I got caught for desertion," he said with a half grin. "My job was to fit in—to learn the ways of the army. It ain't so convincin' to fake if ya've never experienced it. I'll tell ya, the deserters is treated the worst. The vilest degenerates in the army got too much honor … or fear … to abandon their posts. Even the foulest of the lot spit on the deserters. I had to work my way up the ranks—without exposin' my trainin'."

Malcius said, "Who were you battling?"

He looked angry, and Rezkin could only guess as to why. Rezkin shrugged and said, "Bandits, mercs, insurgents. We was at peace, but that peace was kept by maintainin' close watch over the borders. Northern forces prod for weakness. We made sure no one survived to keep proddin'. Anyway, I made sergeant—"

"Wait, you made sergeant in a *year*?" said Millins.

Rezkin grinned. "Commander said I was the fastest learner he ever seen. After I made sergeant, I weren't gonna get no more promotions in that unit, and I couldn't transfer. I was there fer a reason, after all. So, we was sent to battle an army of four merc companies. We was outnumbered three to one, and I had to pretend to be an average soldier, except without gettin' killed. The mercs killed most of our men, but we took out a lot of theirs. I had orders, though. When it looked like we was done for, I killed the rest of our men."

Leaning forward so he could see around Wesson, Minder Finwy looked at him with horror. "You killed your own men?"

"Well, I let a few live—the ones that was loyal to me. Then, I challenged the merc commanders. They was confused and didn't wanna accept. I killed 'em anyway, along with a lot more of their men. Eventually, the others accepted that I'd won the challenge, and I took command of what was left. That's when we went to face the drauglics—a horde of the beasts. The rest of the men died."

"But *you* lived," said a deep voice from the grass. Orin stepped into the firelight and kicked dirt over Rezkin. "Yer full of it. That's a bloody fish tale if I ever heard one. Takin' out army units and merc companies like they was children."

"I wouldn't kill a bunch of children," Rezkin protested. "No challenge in it. Senseless killing, that."

Orin spat. "Weren't no battles. Weren't no missin' army units or merc companies. I'da heard about it. Men like you is what gives mercs a bad name. Makin' people think we're all soulless bastards."

Rezkin grinned. "You wouldn't be the first to call me that."

"You brag like yer some kinda god of war. When the real fightin' starts, we'll see who holds the torch and who runs crying into the dark."

As Orin stomped back to his side of the road grumbling about fish tales, Farson emerged from the grass near where the mercenary had been hiding. He nodded at Rezkin's questioning glance.

"You knew he was there," said Brandt.

Malcius exhaled in a whoosh. "You had me going. I thought you were serious."

Rezkin got up to unroll his blanket and sleeping pad, ignoring Kai's stare. Eventually, the striker turned his gaze to Farson who had bent over the fire to collect his dinner.

Farson sighed and looked up at his comrade. "What?"

"I'm tryin' to figure out which parts are true."

"You mean some of it was?" said Brandt.

Kai looked at Rezkin and said, "The best stories always got a bit of truth."

Farson looked to Rezkin who merely shrugged as he laid back to rest his head on his pack.

"It was all true," Farson said. "Except he left out a few parts—like the reinforcements."

Millins turned to Rezkin. "So, you had reinforcements against the mercenaries?"

Farson said, "The mercs had the reinforcements—a cavalry unit from Jerea. It was probably the horses that attracted the drauglics. They said they'd been harried for more than a week as they rode and were already down by a third when they joined up with the mercs. By the time the battle between the Scavengers and mercs was over, the ground had become a bloody soup with body parts floating in the muck." Nodding toward Rezkin, he said, "He killed the rest of the Scavengers and took over the mercs, like he said. Then, drawn by the scent of blood, the drauglics came down from the mountain. They fought off the ones that attacked and then chased the rest into the mountains. Only *he* returned."

The others silently pondered the revelation. Finally, Millins said, "He really killed his own men?"

Farson scoffed. "They were never his men. We put him there for the experience, but they were always meant to die. *He* might not have cared about the circumstances, but *we* did. You know who we are. We're men of honor. We wouldn't send him to kill a unit of our own men without good cause. What he didn't mention was that the Scavengers had gone rogue. What would you expect to happen if you put the worst of men together with weapons and a semblance of order? There used to be a mining village at the base of the Zigharans near the Tremadel. The Scavengers raided the village—killed all the men and children. They saved the women until they were spent and then killed them, too. The soldiers he didn't kill were the new recruits that had arrived in the unit with him afterward." He narrowed his eyes at Rezkin and rubbed his chin. "We didn't tell him to do that—to spare them. I suppose those few died honorably in service to the kingdom."

"It sounds like he *did* care about the circumstances," said Brandt, eyeing Rezkin sideways. "I mean, he left the good ones alive."

Farson glanced at Rezkin as well. While he appeared to be ignoring them, he could obviously hear the entire exchange. "They all died in the end."

"You can't blame him for that," said Yserria. "It was the drauglics." She fisted her hands on her hips and leaned over the striker. "You made him live with those horrible people for a *year*. He was what—sixteen?"

Farson scowled at the woman. "Yet he's the one who lived."

Wesson turned to Rezkin. Of everyone present, he had seemed the least fazed by the story. He said, "How do you do that? How do you deal with all the death?"

Satisfied that everyone had been fed, Rezkin snagged the remainder of the roasted meat. Settling back down beside the mage, he said, "You have to remember, besides Farson, everyone I ever met before leaving the fortress is dead. Everyone. Ever."

2

"He should have been taking us with him," said Chieftain Yuold.

Frisha sighed. "Chieftain Yuold—"

"Gurrell," he said.

With a placating smile, Frisha clasped her hands and said, "Gurrell, I know you're concerned, but he had his reasons."

"Reasons that I am not understanding."

Tieran stepped forward. "Chieftain Yuold—"

"Gurrell," he said again.

"Chieftain Yuold," repeated Tieran. "King Rezkin explained to you that he did not want his connection with the Eastern Mountains men to be apparent until he knew which way King Privoth was leaning. It is in your best interest, and ours, to keep our cooperative agreement to ourselves for now."

Gurrell pulled the green strip of fabric from his bicep and held it before Tieran's gaze. "It is not being a *cooperative agreement*. He is our chieftain. Until he does become defeated in challenge, he is being our leader. We are the knives at his side. We are the axes at his back."

Tieran said, "Ah, I am not sure that phrase translates well. In any case, he ordered you all to stay here and help us make this city livable."

Gurrell lifted his chin as a trickle of pride burned in his chest. "We are great builders." Then, with frustration, he added, "But nothing is needing to be built here."

Tieran said, "Then you may join the patrols exploring the bowl."

"Gah! There is nothing to be fighting in the bowl. We have been traveling to the far mountains and back, and we have been mapping the caverns."

Frisha said, "Gurrell, perhaps you would help us with something of great importance."

Gurrell looked down at the small doe-eyed beauty and grinned. Finally, they were getting somewhere. "What is this great task we are to be doing for you, Lady Frisha?"

She said, "You and your men are great warriors." Gurrell grunted in agreement, and she continued. "Rezkin …um …*King* Rezkin wants Cael to be a warrior kingdom."

Gurrell smacked his armor with a meaty fist. "As should all great kingdoms be."

"Yes, well, perhaps you could assist in training our fighters to be warriors."

From beneath thick, harsh brows, Gurrell stared at her. His steely grey eyes were intense and unblinking. Frisha was suddenly concerned that she might have offended the very large foreigner.

He said, "You are wanting the Farwarriors of the Viergnacht Tribe of the Eastern Mountains to be teachers?"

Frisha tilted her head to look up at the beastly man. "Um, it was an idea—"

Gurrell grinned broadly, his teeth bright in contrast to his bushy dark beard. "This is being a great honor!" He turned to his men who filled the remaining space in the room behind him and raised a fist in triumph. "You are hearing? We are to be the bringers of strength and courage to the lost people, the people of our chieftain. The farwarriors will be teaching the ways of our ancestors, the greatness of the way of the Viergnacht! The strongest chieftain in history will be leading the Viergnacht Tribe and the Kingdom of Cael, two supreme warrior nations!"

The rumble that followed blasted through Frisha's head, an explosion of mountain man enthusiasm. She peered up at Tieran who stood at her side. "I'm sorry. I didn't think—"

"No, that was nicely done," he said, his words nearly lost in the revelry. "It will keep them busy, anyhow."

Gurrell turned back to them and pointed at Tieran with the butt of a hand axe. "We are to be starting with him."

Tieran's eyes widened. "*Me*? No, I do not—"

"You are being the chieftain's kin and must meet the challenge if our chieftain falls."

"No, I told you and everyone else that I do not wish to be king."

"Then you will be meeting the challenge as champion for the queen."

"What queen?" said Tieran.

"Queen Frisha," said Gurrell. "She is being the betrothed of the chieftain. As his kin, you must be standing for her."

Frisha shook her head. "No, I'm not—"

His massive paw gripped her shoulder. He said, "And you will be training with us."

Frisha's heart jumped. "What? But, I am a woman, and you only have men!"

"Ha! Yes, this time the farwarriors are being only men. The women are being the protectors of our home while we are farwalking. Our women are the fiercest warriors. We do leave knowing our women will be fighting with the greatest strength and heart against any who do threaten our people. They are also having the strength of the other men who are not farwalking."

Frisha wrung her hands anxiously. She had already tried training with Rezkin and had decided being a warrior was not for her. "So, your women are warriors, too? Do you have women chieftains?"

"No, our women do not be sharing in chieftain. The men are not to be fighting against our women. The women are being half of the council, and they do decide which women share in the council. The men are not being involved in this. The Viergnacht Tribe Mother is Auria."

"Is she your wife?" said Frisha.

Gurrell laughed. "No, Auria is being Olfid's wife. We are not kin. The women did choose her as tribe mother. After the chieftain wins a challenge, the council does vote to decide which will lead—chieftain or tribe mother. I was selected to be leader, and Auria is my second. While I am away, Auria is being leader." He motioned over his shoulder to a dark-haired man with matching scars on each of his cheeks. "When I am with the farwarriors, Myerin is my second."

Frisha hesitated to ask, but her curiosity would not be deterred. "So, if the council is unhappy with the way you are leading—"

"They will be voting for the tribe mother to lead. Auria is a good leader. Our new chieftain must be joining the council. They must know him to make the vote. I am defeated, and now Auria will lead. I will be her second while the chieftain is away. Once the council does vote, he may be leader."

Inwardly cringing, Frisha said, "So, if the tribe mother does not have to be the chieftain's wife, then why must I train to be a warrior?"

"You did say that King Rezkin is wanting for Cael to be a warrior kingdom. You are to be his queen. You must be a warrior queen." Behind him, Myerin grumbled something in their native tongue, and Gurrell stroked his beard thoughtfully. He said, "You are thinking it is not good for you to be learning the fighting of men."

Frisha was suddenly very pleased with Myerin. "Yes, it does not suit me."

Gurrell nodded. "You are being right. The women of the mountains tribes do fight differently from the men. Myerin is knowing more of this. His three older sisters did use him for practice as he grew. One of his sisters is now on the council."

Myerin grinned with pride and slapped his chest.

Gurrell said, "We will be waiting for you in the training grounds."

The men filed out, and the space suddenly seemed to expand infinitely.

Frisha looked at Tieran who stared at her in defeat. "I'm sorry?"

He shook his head. "Unbelievable."

Kai strode up beside Rezkin. "May I speak with you?"

The two paused to distance themselves from those ahead, and Jimson pulled the followers back to give them space to talk.

"What is it?" Rezkin said as they resumed walking.

Kai waited a moment and then switched to Leréshi since it was likely only Yserria, and possibly Farson, could understand them. Farson was out scouting, remaining hidden from the mercenaries, and Yserria was too far away to hear. Kai turned to Rezkin and said, "I know you have been confused."

"About what?"

"Everything. *Outworlders*. I have been watching you for months now. Your mind is always churning. You observe everything. You think too much. You have been trying to figure them out—*us* out." Rezkin nodded, and Kai continued. "What I do not understand is how you can be so confused when you were with the army for a year."

Rezkin glanced at the others, his gaze lingering on Millins and Jimson. He said, "The army was not the outworld—at least, not in the greater sense. I was trained to understand the army, the regulations, its functions, its people. It was the same with the mercenaries. I was also informed of the kind of men with whom I would be engaging. I knew they would not follow the *Rules* because they were degenerates. I played a role, and they played theirs."

"They were not playing roles," said Kai.

"Perhaps not, but it was all the same to me. As I said, we never went near any settlements. The men lived, ate, slept, and fought together. They also died together. That was all there was. *These* outworlders," he said with a nod over his shoulder, "they are not like the soldiers and mercenaries. They are strange to me, but I do understand one thing clearly. Farson is right. I am not one of them. I will never be one of them."

"We are not all like them. You were trained by strikers. You are like us."

"No, Kai. You are more like them than you think."

"How is that?"

"You have ideals. You speak of good and evil as though they are measurable things. You believe in honor and hold it in high regard, whereas I have none."

"That is untrue. You have spoken often of honoring your friends."

"Only because it is *Rule 1*. If not for that, I would not bind myself in such a way. I would have dismissed them as irrelevant—and absurd. But, I must adhere to the *Rules*."

Kai did not speak for several minutes. Rezkin watched as a kite swept the sky in lazy circles overhead, and his gaze shifted to the drifting grasses surrounding them. The mercenary company led the procession with one less member than the previous day. The severely injured man had succumbed to fever in the night. Wesson had berated Rezkin for not offering his healing services but had finally accepted his assertion that the man had been too far gone for help. It might have even been true.

The silence that loomed between the footfalls, tromp of hooves, and rickety creaking of the wagon at the front was eventually shattered by Kai's gruff voice. "You have a sense of right and wrong. I have heard you speak at length about noble duty."

"It is a role, Kai. If one is to play the noble, he must conduct himself by noble standards."

"But you understand how those standards came to be. You must value them."

"Only in that they provide structure to a society that would otherwise endure chaos. The outworlders accept them, so they must live by them. It is their own standard of *Rules*. When I play the part of the noble, I conduct myself as such. It is not who I am."

"I do not believe you."

"It is fact."

"Oh, I believe that *you* believe what you are saying, but it is not the truth. I think you underestimate yourself and the connection you have with these people. If you are not the man you profess to be, then who are you?"

Before Rezkin could respond, Farson appeared at his side. "You are free with your words—last night and today. You reveal much. What has loosened your tongue?"

Rezkin ran a thumb along the warm metal of a knife he kept up his sleeve. He had done the same many times as a small-man to remind himself that words could be as dangerous as a blade. He watched the kite swoop in ever tightening circles. He wondered if the citadel's power was still affecting him and shifted his focus to feel for the warmth of the small stone resting against his chest.

Kai interrupted his thoughts when he blurted, "Is that your cat?"

Rezkin looked down to see the small tortie sitting in the middle of the road staring at him. It flicked its tail and then ran into the grass on the west side of the road. Rezkin's gaze flicked to the sky, and he followed the kite as it swept around again.

"Raise the alarm. Prepare for battle. Kai, check the rear—Farson, the sides."

Rezkin yanked the packs from Pride's back and then threw himself into the saddle. Heavy footfalls tore up dirt and rocks as the horse pounded down the road toward the front of the procession. Men scattered amongst angry shouts but not fast enough. In his urgency, Rezkin was forced to direct Pride into the grass where the chance of a misstep was greater. He had to stop the convoy before they waded into the trap. He was too late.

Rezkin's furious arrival at the front inspired the drauglics to attack early. Their company had not yet been surrounded, but the horde emerging from the grass was so great it would make no difference. The White Crescents would be overrun.

A horn blared just as the first of the drauglics jumped for Rezkin. Although they were the size of an adolescent child, the creatures were capable of jumping half again their own height. The drauglic crashed into Rezkin's side, its scaly arms wrapping around him as it gnashed at his throat with its sharp teeth. Rezkin held tight to the saddle as he thrust a dagger into the soft tissue beneath his attacker's arm. Another drauglic jumped at the stallion's head, and Pride reared, crushing the creature beneath his massive hooves. Rezkin held tight as the drauglic that had attacked him lost its grip, giving him enough time to draw his sword. The injured drauglic leapt at him again, its perseverance rewarded with a blade through the throat.

Pride gnashed his teeth at another of the creatures and broke through the purple scales on its shoulder. The drauglic shrieked and swung a sharpened stone hatchet at the horse's neck. Kingslayer took the creature's arm off as Rezkin drew Bladesunder. He gripped the saddle with his legs as the blades flashed through the air at his sides, scoring scaled flesh and rending armor. One drauglic latched onto Pride's hindquarters, and Rezkin was glad they had been traveling as mercenaries. The creature's talons tore through the shabby caparison that hid the quality mail cruppers beneath. Rezkin twisted in his saddle and slashed at the drauglic's worn armor. As he drew back his blade again, Pride unexpectedly bucked, tossing the drauglic into Rezkin's back. The creature wrapped its arms, taut with wiry muscle, around Rezkin's chest, its claws digging into his brigandine.

Rezkin's muscles clenched as the horse trampled another drauglic, but the thrashing and the weight of the drauglic on his back eventually forced Rezkin from the saddle. Pride kicked out at exactly the wrong time, smacking Bladesunder from his grip in midair. Rezkin landed atop the drauglic, the air knocked from his lungs. He inhaled sharply and then swept Kingslayer across his own chest, amputating one of the creature's hands. The creature screamed in his ear as Rezkin drew his serrated belt knife. He threw his feet over his head and rolled backward to crouch above the drauglic's head. He plunged the dagger into the lizard man's throat, and blood and ragged flesh spewed across his face as he withdrew the wicked weapon.

Rezkin looked up to see a gangly drauglic in patchwork leather armor grinning at him as it collected Bladesunder from the bloodied dirt at his feet. The drauglic's yellowed, pointed teeth dripped with saliva, and it hissed. With the hilt gripped in both hands, it raised the sword over its head and then shrieked in pained horror. Its hands came down, but it seemed unable to release its grip. The air filled with the scent of charred meat as the flesh beneath the creature's scales began to glow red and smoke erupted from its hands, which crumbled like blackened soot. Bladesunder toppled to the ground as the drauglic's scream was silenced by the blue-swirled steel of the sword's kin.

Rezkin could hear the discordant crescendo of battle, but he had no time to check on his friends. They were at the rear of the convoy, while he was in the thick of the enemy. Pride stomped and thrashed as drauglics jumped at him, slashing with stolen blades and stabbing with primitive spears. Some of the creatures threw stones, and Rezkin was grateful they had no arrows and crossbows. The battle was fierce, and it did not sound like the other horses were faring as well as Pride.

Wesson stood in the center of the circle with Minder Finwy, his sword wielding companions fending off the enemies advancing on them. From where he was standing, he felt as though the enemies were targeting him, but he knew that was absurd. Everyone was fighting except him and the minder, and the minder, at least, gripped a dagger. Wesson had never acquired any skills with mundane weapons, believing the curse of his destructive power was terror enough. He knew that using that power could expose him and potentially attract the attention of the Purifiers. A part of him, the part that dwelled deep within, the part he kept locked behind a fortress of mental barriers, was fighting for release. It wanted out. It wanted to spew flame and render flesh from bones. It wanted to burst the bodies of his enemies in a bloody rain, a glorious red swath painted across everything in sight. And he wanted to let it.

No, he reminded himself. *Beauty before bane*, his personal mantra. *Quell the storm.*

A drauglic lunged at Yserria with a stone club while another raked her across the back with vicious claws that scored so deeply into her armor that a trickle of blood seeped from the wound. She ducked as the club sailed toward her head, and the creature smacked his own comrade in the jaw. The injured drauglic screamed, his jaw hanging limp, and then leapt at the one that had struck him. While the first drauglic was distracted, Yserria threw her weight into a mighty upswing that cleaved the stone-wielding drauglic from the groin, upward through his buttock, to finally lop off the tail. The creature fell writhing to the ground, and the other landed atop him shortly after with a gushing jugular.

Wesson suddenly stumbled as he was shoved from behind. He turned to see Malcius fighting off a drauglic bearing a rusted, broken sword. The creature, which wore an ill-fitted metal helm and chain mail over its torso, was a few inches shorter than Wesson. Although it was strong, it seemed to be having difficulty under the weight of its stolen armor. Its movements were sluggish, but between the metal armor and its natural scales, it was difficult for Malcius to score a fatal blow. Wesson itched to heat the armor until it glowed yellow and burned through the creature. A moment later, Malcius finally prevailed with a jab straight through the drauglic's mouth into its brain. Wesson's mind cleared long enough for him to be sickened by the bloodthirsty thoughts. Malcius immediately turned to engage two more of the creatures who were less armored but equally less encumbered.

Beside Malcius, Brandt blocked a swipe of claws with a buckler he must have claimed from one of the drauglics. He slammed the buckler into the creature's protruding snout and then sliced his sword across the abdomen exposed below the fragmented wooden armor. The creature doubled over as its entrails spilled over its talonned feet, and Brandt kicked it in the head. As it toppled, Brandt spun to attack one of the creatures assaulting Malcius. He sliced the artery of the inner thigh, grabbed the fiend by the tail, and plunged his blade up through the soft tissue into the creature's torso.

Wesson forced his eyes away from the liquid red curtain to survey the field beyond his protective circle. The mercenaries were enduring the brunt of it. Only one of the horses besides Pride still stood, and the beast that had been pulling the wagon was long since gutted. He could not see Rezkin, but he could still hear the furious shrieks of the battle charger, which he hoped was a sign that the elite warrior was also still alive. Kai and Farson fought between them and the swarm of drauglics that had gotten past the mercenaries, and Jimson and Millins were battling the creatures that flanked them through the tall grass. It was obvious that he and his circle were enduring barely a trickle of the overall assault, and he was frustrated he was the weakest among them without use of the power he so often scorned.

Wesson was about to turn when he saw a drauglic leap at Millins who was manning the rear. The soldier was already engaged with two of the fiends, and his back was left exposed. The lizard man's talons dug into Millins's lower back, and it wrapped its muscular arms around his head. Without a second thought, Wesson released a stream of raw power, a graceless spell lacking substantial form. The three drauglics and two more beyond simultaneously exploded. Loose flesh, shards of bone, heads, and limbs were ejected several paces in every direction. Those pieces that had sailed upward came raining down with satisfying thuds, and the prostrate Millins was buried under the shower of bodily debris.

Rezkin felt the shock of the spell just as it was released. He had but to wait a breath before it activated. From where he was, he could not see the effect, but he knew that if Wesson had taken the chance on using his power, his friends had to have been in grave danger. He was sure that Wesson would protect them if the situation became dire, but he hoped the mercenaries had not seen the action. The fact that they might have born witness to an act that in any other kingdom would have been respectable did not seem like a satisfactory reason for killing men who had martial value.

It had been some time since he had been in a battle this brutal. These drauglics had little or no concern for their own lives, and they attacked with ferocity. Although drauglics had always been fierce foes, they tended to retreat when it appeared they might lose too many. Rezkin had not yet found the *ukwa*, the leader or chief of the drauglic clan who would sound the call for retreat. While their language was primitive and seemed to have few words, the ukwa held a position of such importance as to be graced with a drauglic title.

Rezkin finished off the five closest drauglics with a flurry of Sheyalin slashes and thrusts and then rushed into the tall grass from which the creatures were attacking. Several of the lizard men scattered upon his approach, startled into running rather than fighting. He hacked through a number of others, leaving a bloody trail in his wake until he finally fell upon his prey. The ukwa was standing on a crudely constructed mound of dirt, stones, and hay so that it could see over the swaying grasses to the battlefield. It appeared to be caked in dried green mud that Rezkin knew to be the dried feces of its followers. The scholars and mages who studied such things posited that doing so allowed the drauglics to scent their leader. Luckily for Rezkin, it was also easy for anyone else to scent the ukwa, particularly if the ordure was fresh.

The ukwa saw Rezkin approaching before he could reach the creature. It screamed a senseless cadence, and the half dozen lizard men who surrounded him echoed his call. The dwindling horde of creatures that were engaged in battle shrieked in unison and then began to retreat. Many flew past Rezkin without even attempting to strike at him, although that did not stop him from hewing down those within his reach. Within minutes, the entire clan had retreated into the grass, and the tousle of stalks continued beyond his view of the horizon.

After searching the immediate area for any stragglers, Rezkin strode down the path of detrital gore that he had paved through the pasture. When he arrived at its end, the remaining men and one woman were gathered at the epicenter of the battle where Rezkin had made his stand. Everyone was keeping a safe distance from the battle charger whose eyes were still rolling as he snorted and stomped on the bodies of dead lizard men. The mercenaries and his friends were covered in blood, much of it their own. Of everyone, Wesson was the cleanest, and he stood pensively hiding in the rear. Farson and Kai were speaking quietly several paces from the others. Their injuries appeared to be minor, but it was always difficult to tell with strikers. Like Rezkin, they were trained to hide their weaknesses. Malcius, Brandt, Yserria, and Minder Finwy all had deep cuts on their limbs and torsos, Millins was laid out on the ground, his shoulders propped against the wagon, and Jimson gripped a dislocated arm, seemingly unconcerned with the seeping gashes across his cheek and jaw.

The mercenaries had fared far worse. Of the twenty-seven from the previous day, only twelve remained, and all their horses were lost. Orin stood in the center of the mounded ring of drauglic bodies. He was slathered in gore, his left hand wrapped in a blood-sodden rag. Rezkin guessed the man had lost a few fingers.

The mercenary leader spit a glob of bloody phlegm and said, "Ya see that line over there by the wagon?"

Rezkin surveyed the area. A number of drauglic and mercenary bodies were concentrated in the location. Rezkin nodded.

"My men and yours fought over there—on the other side." His gaze roved over the surrounding mounds. "I'd say more than half of the dead lizard demons are on this side. On this side of the line was *you*. You and that beast you call a horse." He glanced past Rezkin down the bloody path. "Who knows what ya left out there?"

Rezkin adopted a feral grin. With a sloppy Gendishen drawl, he said, "Whether you run cryin' or bear the torch, I'm there. I *am* the darkness." Orin looked at him like he was mad. Satisfied, Rezkin lightened his tone. "I didn't kill them all, if that's what yer askin'. They run off into the grass. Thing about drauglics is, if ya sneak up on them, they'll run. But, if they get all hyped up to fight, they don't stop—not 'till the ukwa calls them off."

Blood dripped from Orin's braided, black beard, but he did not seem to notice or care. "The *ukwa*?"

"Their chief," Rezkin said as he stepped over bodies to reach Pride.

Orin never took his eyes off Rezkin. "Couldn't help but notice over half my men are dead and all yers are still standin'. Well, save that one"—he nodded toward Millins who appeared pained but awake—"but he don't look to be checkin' out."

Rezkin said nothing as he examined a few of the drauglic bodies on the ground.

"I guess I'm startin' to believe yer fish tale," said Orin. When Rezkin neglected to answer, the man said, "What's yer plan now?"

Orin's face was pale, and Rezkin realized the mercenary was probably in shock or he would have been seeing to his wounds instead of asking questions. Rezkin muttered softly to the horse and stroked and petted his neck and sides as he examined Pride's injures. Once the stallion was calm enough to be led, Rezkin took the reins and started toward the rear of the convoy where he had left his packs.

"Hey!" Orin said as Rezkin made to pass. "I asked what yer plannin'."

Rezkin shrugged. With a nod, he said, "Ask the boss."

Orin glanced toward Kai who was watching the exchange with a sharp gaze while maintaining quiet conversation with Farson.

"You still expect me to believe he's in charge?"

"Don't matter who's in charge. He's the one ya gotta speak to. I'm busy."

Orin turned to his men. Those who could stand were helping the less fortunate move to a clear area where they could tend to their injuries. The mercenary leader held his hands out to the carnage in disbelief. "He's busy, he says."

As Rezkin passed, Farson looked at him deadpan and muttered, "Seriously? *I am the darkness*?"

Rezkin grinned. "Outworlders enjoy theatrics."

He was in the midst of cleaning, stitching, and bandaging Pride's wounds when Malcius approached.

"What are you doing? Can you not see that people are injured? You care more for the welfare of the horse?"

Dipping his fingers into the ointment, Rezkin answered quietly. "We cannot afford for his wounds to fester. It would be much more difficult to tend to a feverish battle charger without the aid of a healer or life mage. Also, right now he is worn from the effort and energy of the battle. Later, he will be rested and churlish. Trust me when I say that we do not desire for him to turn his ill temper on *us*."

Malcius glanced back to the evidence of Pride's brutality. "No, I should say not. But you *will* see to the others?"

"None of you look to be dying."

Malcius scowled. "This will surely scar," he said, pointing to the gash on his neck.

Rezkin said, "I believe warriors enjoy showing off their war wounds." He did not mention that if the laceration had been a thumb's width to the left, Malcius would have bled out within minutes.

Malcius huffed. "Millins is the worst. Those horrid talons ripped into his back and hips. Kai has already seen to Jimson's arm. We can all use some stitches and ointment."

"You already know I intend to assist you, Malcius."

"Do I? What about the mercenaries? You let that one die last night."

"To aid him would have been to risk exposure for what was likely a lost cause."

"You might have saved his life," Malcius replied.

Rezkin met the young lord's angry gaze. "And he would have lost it today."

"You did not know we would be attacked. Or did you?"

Shaking his head, Rezkin said, "No, of course not. Do you think that if I had, I would not have planned for it?"

"What now, then? Will you help the mercenaries, too, or let them suffer and die?"

"I will assist. Let them think I picked up some few healing skills in the army. We shall not mention which army."

Malcius nodded, seemingly satisfied, until Rezkin said, "Hold this," as he pulled together split horse flesh. Cautiously, Malcius approached the deadly equine and placed his hands as instructed. A massive black head snaked around, and Malcius yelped as if the horse would bite him. The beast merely rolled his eyes in challenge.

After seeing to the worst of Pride's injuries, Rezkin cleaned and stitched Millins. Someone had started a small fire, and the mercenaries were busy cauterizing the worst of their wounds. It was a primitive technique, one used by men with no knowledge or skill in the proper stitching and dressing of wounds. Unfortunately, most who did not die from the wound succumbed to infection. The survivors were left with unsightly and possibly disabling scars. In Gendishen, where even mundane healers were often accused of cavorting with evil spirits or demons, people were willing to risk infection over outright blood loss.

Rezkin was in the midst of stitching Millins's wounds when Wesson squatted beside him in the shadow of the wagon.

"Do you think any of them saw?" the mage asked.

"I do not believe so. If they had, we would surely know of it by now."

Wesson glanced at the mercenaries pensively. One of them, in particular, was staring at them. "Perhaps, but it could be that they are pretending not to know until they find a purifier. Maybe they are afraid that if I know that they know, we will kill them."

"We will," said Rezkin. At Wesson's disapproving glance, he said, "It is not my preference either, but if allowed to live, they will betray us."

"You cannot know that. I cannot believe that everyone in this kingdom is so cruel and hateful. They should be given a chance."

Rezkin gave him a disparaging look. "A chance to betray us?"

"No, a chance to prove themselves."

Rezkin shook his head. "I recognize your conviction, but if they fail and behave exactly as we expect them to, *we* will be the losers."

"He's right," said Millins. The sergeant was damp with sweat, and his eyes were glossy, but he was aware enough to follow the conversation. "These people … the sentence for harboring or aiding the afflicted is torture and death. They will not risk that for you."

Rezkin did not wish to continue the discussion where they could so easily be overheard, so he ordered the mage to check on the others. Although Wesson had no innate healing ability, and he could not have used it if he had, he did have some education in anatomy and mundane treatments. Wesson stood and bumped into Minder Finwy as he left to do Rezkin's bidding. Rezkin felt the minder's gaze as he finished the final suture. He applied additional ointment to the wounds and then sparingly applied the bandages. The others still required treatment, and he had no idea if they would be attacked again before he was able to replenish his supply.

As Rezkin collected his supplies, he said to the minder, "If you were hoping to aid the sergeant in his passing, your services will not be required."

Millins gave the minder a wary look and shook his head.

Finwy smiled and said, "No, it seems you have done well enough to prevent that." He glanced up to see that the mercenaries were still gathered afar and said, "This is not the behavior I would have expected of the dark warrior who defied Ionius in his own throne room."

"You were there?" Rezkin said.

"I was."

"Then you should know already that my concern was for my people. Sergeant Millins is one of them."

Finwy dropped his gaze to the listless soldier. "Ionius also believes his concern to be for his people, but I doubt anyone would ever find him administering to their needs personally."

"I have the *Skills*, we are few, and many are injured. Ionius has plenty of people to see to the needs of others in his stead."

"You defend him?"

"No, I concur with your conclusion. It is unlikely, however, that he would ever be put to the test."

"Yet you would not hesitate to kill others who have done no wrong."

"Would you kill someone to prevent a terrible injustice that has not yet occurred but that you know will happen if you do nothing? Or will you allow it to happen and then punish others for the offense? If you know it is going to occur, are you not also culpable for doing nothing to prevent it?"

"I see your point. It is a most difficult conundrum. I would look to the Maker to guide me."

"And if the Maker is silent?"

"When the Maker is silent, it is because the experience of making the choice is more important than the outcome."

"If the Maker denies his counsel when it is requested, then how can one be held accountable for making the wrong choice?"

Finwy tilted his head. "Perhaps neither decision is wrong. Perhaps it is about how we deal with the effects of making that choice."

"One of those effects being the judgment of others?"

"You will be judged no matter the choice you make."

"Which is why I do not concern myself with the judgment of others."

Finwy looked at him doubtfully. "Is that so?"

"I follow the *Rules*, and so I prevail. Eventually, I will not. The opinions of others concern me only in so far as they either aid or obstruct my plans."

"Whose rules are those?"

"I do not know who made the *Rules*." He turned to check the status of his friends as he said, "Perhaps it was the Maker."

Followed closely by the minder, Rezkin meandered between the corpses to where the mercenaries were tending their wounded. They rejected his offer of aid, insisting that they were as capable as any field medic. They were not, but Rezkin had no desire to argue the point. His friends were assuaged that he had tried.

"We'll need the horse to pull the wagon," Orin said for the seventh time.

"No," Rezkin replied, for the seventh time.

"Yer a selfish bastard, thinkin' that beast you pass off as a war horse is too good to be pullin' a wagon. We've got half the wealth of the White Crescents in that wagon."

"I've told you. That horse won't pull a wagon," Rezkin said. "You try to hitch him up, and you won't have a wagon left to pull."

"You whip him good, and he'll learn," Orin groused.

Rezkin scoffed. "He's a finely trained war horse. Ain't no one gonna break him to pull a damned wagon."

Kai said, "You try to whip that horse, it'll be the last thing you do."

Orin spied the stallion out of the corner of his eye. He shouted to his men to gather what they could carry and then push the wagon into the grass, covering the tracks as best they could. As he turned away, he muttered, "Bloody horse killed more drauglics than I did. I don't know how you got such a beast, but he's as ornery as you. The both of you—killin' things and doin' whatever the hells you want. You deserve each other!"

A strange sound erupted beside Kai. Rezkin had never heard Farson laugh, but he was laughing now. Rezkin had no idea what was so funny. He and Pride were both trained to be efficient and effective in battle. They were a matched pair, as they should be.

Those well enough for the task dug shallow graves for the fallen mercenaries and then put as much distance between themselves and the carnage as they could. With a single camp, the healthiest kept watch in shifts while the injured fell into fitful, feverish slumber. When Orin became too delirious to reject the healing draught, Rezkin poured it down the mercenary leader's throat. Although Orin's death would have been an opportune time for Rezkin to claim his men, he was disinclined to suffer the trouble. He was satisfied to let Orin keep the other mercenaries in line, and Rezkin was reasonably sure the man knew where he stood.

The following day was worse. The wind whipped across the prairie, and every inch of skin not covered suffered its ill effects. Seeds and pollen danced on the breeze like tiny pixies, and every time the travelers were forced to leave the road, the grasses lashed at their arms and legs. The aches from the previous day's abuse had set in, and no one had slept well during the night. They were all too aware that an unknown number of drauglics had escaped and could attack again at any time. Eager for the safety of walls and other men, they trudged forward, injured and without horses, forced to carry their own supplies.

Just after midday, a plantation came into sight. It was far from the road, but the dirt wagon trail had been well maintained. The main house was a large, one-story affair, the kind that wrapped around an inner courtyard. The trim and sills were painted yellow, and white lace blew in the breeze from the open windows. Several outbuildings dotted the property, including quarters for field hands, a barn, smokehouse, and drying shed, along with three squat silos. A trail of large stepping stones led through the shorn lawn to a rustic gazebo that stood in the shade of a few cultivated trees beside a small pond. With autumn near, the cool breeze swept over the short stone wall, still warm from the late summer sun, and insects buzzed and snapped a soothing cadence. It was a tranquil scene, designed and sustained by the loving care of a tender heart, except for all the blood.

Bits of bloody hooves and tufts of fur were scattered in the pens. Smeared across the front porch and along the yard was a dry, rusty trail, and scraps of shredded clothing were strewn over the dirt and grass, some still containing body parts. Carrion birds squawked as they fought over the remnants. Pride snorted and stomped over the debris toward a low trough to one side of the barn. The horse vigorously expressed his displeasure as he was forced to wait while Rezkin inspected the water.

Meanwhile, Kai motioned to Brandt. "Check the well," he said. "Mal, watch the field by the house." He switched to Leréshi when speaking to Yserria, instructing her to keep an eye on the road. He then followed Farson toward the other outbuildings while Orin and his men prepared to enter the house.

Rezkin drew Bladesunder and stepped into the barn. It was dark inside, and his eyes required a moment to adjust, but his nose had already told him what he wanted to know. Once he could see properly, he checked each stall for confirmation. Rats scattered upon his approach, screeching their displeasure with his arrival. Everything that had been kept in the barn at the time of the attack had been killed. The carcasses of the larger beasts remained, mutilated and divested of their flesh. One did not have to study the plethora of vaguely manlike tracks and deep gouges to know what had happened.

A pained shout sounded from the yard, and Rezkin rushed to meet the foe. When he arrived, though, he saw only his party rushing toward Brandt who was tugging something heavy from the well. Tears streamed down Brandt's face as he gripped the pale, sodden lump in his arms. It was a small-man, a *child*, Rezkin reminded himself. The boy appeared to be around nine years old. He could not have been dead for more than a few hours, and he bore no visible injuries.

"He was tied to the rope," Brandt said through choked sobs.

Rezkin scanned the grasses in the distance as he spoke. "This attack appears to have occurred a few days ago. His parents probably lowered him into the well for protection. The water is cold, though, and he likely lost consciousness before drowning."

Malcius frowned down at Brandt, obviously disturbed by the sight of the boy but also concerned for his friend. "He is not Alon. Did you hear me, Brandt? He is not your brother."

Brandt squeezed his eyes shut and took several deep breaths. He lowered the child to the ground and turned away as he regained his feet. "I know. I, ah, need a moment."

"Do not go far," Rezkin said. "We know not what dangers lie in wait." He motioned to Wesson. "Cap the well and mark it. We should not drink the water. We can get what we need from the troughs for now."

Malcius's face screwed up in disgust. "You want us to drink from animal troughs?"

"The one by the barn looks clean enough, or would you prefer to drink from the well of the dead?"

"No, the trough will do," Malcius said begrudgingly.

Orin came tromping from the house with a dagger in hand. "What's all the fuss about out here?" Then he noticed the lifeless boy. "Ah, I see. We'll get him buried. Yer priest can say a few words." He cleared his throat and motioned back at the house. "It's a bit of a wreck, but looks like most of the blood's on the outside. It'd be better to take up in the house tonight than risk the fields. If we start early, we'll be in Behrglyn before sundown."

The mercenary was looking at him, but Rezkin glanced toward Kai. The striker jumped at the silent instruction. "A'right, sound like a plan. Let's see what food stores they've got. Don't think we'll be huntin' 'round here."

Orin grumbled, "Like as not, we'll be the ones is hunted."

Hours later, the sun had not yet met the horizon and the group had already reinforced the doors and windows. They had just finished eating their meal when one of the mercenaries came rushing in to alert them of the new arrivals. A mounted Gendishen military patrol was moving up the road toward the house. Rezkin and Kai shifted to the nearest window, and Malcius and Brandt ducked in beneath them for a view. Dozens of soldiers rode Gendishen reds—at the front, a *dergmyer*, an army rank roughly equivalent to an Ashaiian major. Beside him was a *myer*, which was similar to a captain. Behind them were two older men and a young woman in brown robes. Each was adorned with a snakeskin baldric upon which glinted numerous small metals and talismans. The woman carried a wooden pole with two iron rings holding multiple sets of chained shackles dangling from the top.

"Who are *they*?" Brandt said.

"Those in the brown robes are purifiers," Rezkin replied.

As they filed into the yard, the mercenaries partially blocked their view of the approaching convoy.

Kai hummed under his breath. "It is unusual to see a dergmyer on patrol."

Rezkin stepped away from the window and turned to see Wesson staring toward the blocked window. The young mage's expressive face bore a mixture of fear and anger.

"You should stay as far from them as possible. We do not know how effective your amulet will be against whatever method they use to identify the talented."

"Then we should test it," Wesson said.

Rezkin glimpsed the large patrol. "This is not the best time."

Wesson said, "What? We should wait until we are confined to a city, surrounded by people?"

It was completely unlike Wesson to so openly express his disapproval of Rezkin's decisions, but Rezkin knew the mage was sensitive about the issue. Rezkin glanced toward Minder Finwy who stood silently watching from the doorway that led to the next room and then looked back to Wesson. "If we test it, and it does not work, we will have to kill everyone out there—the purifiers, the soldiers, *and* the mercenaries. Can you live with that?"

Wesson turned away and huffed in frustration. "No, I do not want that."

Kai said, "We have trouble."

"What is it?" Rezkin said as he moved back toward the window.

"They are moving in to seize Orin and his men."

"Do you see any of ours?" Rezkin said, since Farson, Jimson, and Yserria had been keeping watch outside when the patrol arrived.

"No."

"I pulled them back," Farson said as he suddenly appeared from behind.

Rezkin rested a hand on Brandt's shoulder. "Keep an eye out the window." He turned to Farson. "Why are they detaining the mercs?

"They think we had something to do with the destruction here. Orin has been trying to explain, but the dergmyer does not believe the drauglics exist."

Brandt called out, "They are coming."

Rezkin wrapped his worn brown cloak around him and pulled the hood over his head. To Farson, he said, "The others?"

"They are in position."

"In position for what?" Malcius asked. As Rezkin moved away, Malcius called, "Wait, in position for what?"

"Be quiet," Kai huffed. "They are in position to attack if need be. Come with me, and I will position the two of you as well."

"We are going to attack a double army patrol?" Malcius exclaimed.

"If necessary," Kai said. "Would you rather be executed for murders you did not commit?"

Rezkin stepped through the doorway onto the front porch but stopped when he noticed a small black and brown splotched cat lying in his path. He made to step around the cat, but it gained its feet quickly then wound itself in figure eights around and between his feet. He wondered if it was a sign that he should wait. He looked to the patrol that was gathered in the road and side yard. Since he stood in the shadow cast by the setting sunlight, they had not yet seen him. Orin's men knelt in the dirt in a line, and a soldier was preparing to bind their arms.

"Get them," the dergmyer said.

Orin got to his feet and then turned toward the house. He glanced up to see Rezkin as he stepped into the shade of the porch.

"I'm s'posed to bring y'all out. They think *we* attacked the plantation, and they won't listen to reason."

"Why are they here?" Rezkin said.

"They said they was sent to investigate reports of killings and people gone missin'. They ain't seen the drauglics yet. They says if we give up without a fight, they'll take us back to Fort Ulep for a trial." He glanced back to see his men kneeling in the dirt. "Between us, I don't think they plan to wait. Yers is in good shape, mostly. I wouldn't blame you if you take yer men and run."

Rezkin met the mercenary's determined gaze. "Yer prepared to die with yer men."

Orin looked at his men again. "I must."

"They're yer friends then?"

"As close as I got, I guess."

"Are you prepared to fight fer 'em?" asked Rezkin. Orin looked at him in confusion. Rezkin said, "Yer not supposed to fight unless ya have to, but yer not supposed to get captured or die neither. You protect yerself first, except when it comes to yer friends. You gotta take care of them. Now, yer supposed to retreat when ya can't win, but this ain't one of those times."

"What do you mean? There's a double cavalry patrol out there. We got less than two dozen and most of 'em is injured or captured or both. We try to fight, and we'll all get killed."

"Some of 'em, maybe, but we can win. I know our abilities."

"That's ridiculous. Even if we did win, that's the king's army. We'll be hunted fer treason and murder."

"Drauglics'll probably take care of the evidence," Rezkin said. "Besides, we need horses, and they've got horses."

"They've taken our weapons."

Rezkin unstrapped the small crossbow he had hidden beneath his cloak. He handed it and a leather roll of bolts to the mercenary. "I expect these back when we're done."

Orin took the weapon, looking at Rezkin cautiously. "I don't remember seein' these on you."

Rezkin shook his head. "That's the point."

Intentionally scuffing his feet in the dirt, Rezkin strode across the road with an indolent swagger, his cloak slapping against his legs. "A'right, I'm here. What do you want?"

The dergmyer ignored him completely as he supervised the delivery of the horses to the vacant animal pens.

"Take him into custody," said the myer.

Rezkin pushed his cloak back to reveal the sword hilts at his hips. "I'll warn ya, I don't intend to go peaceably."

The myer huffed. “If you cause trouble, we will not hesitate to kill these men.”

With a lazy sweep of his gaze over the haggard faces of the kneeling men, Rezkin shrugged. “Don’t matter to me. Ain’t my men.”

“You are not with them?” said the myer. When Rezkin gave no answer, he pointed to Orin and said, “Well, I know them to be his men, and he might not appreciate your causing their deaths.”

Rezkin said, “Way I see it, you kill them, it’s you is causing their deaths. Don’t matter no how. He’s already decided his men are as good as dead. He don’t plan to go peaceably neither.”

Orin raised the crossbow with his good hand to aim at the myer from where he stood a few paces to Rezkin’s right.

The myer gave Rezkin a look that thoroughly expressed his dismay. He waved to the several dozen armed men behind him and said, “Do you not see that the two of you are outnumbered nearly forty to one? There is no need for you to go down fighting. If you surrender, we will take you to Ulep for a trial.”

“Why would you do that? You ain’t even investigated yet, and you’ve already decided we’re guilty.”

“It’s obvious what happened here,” the myer huffed.

“It is,” Rezkin agreed, “if you care to look. It was drauglics.”

The dergmyer walked up behind the myer who respectfully ceded the position. “Why have you not captured this man?”

“He says he intends to fight,” said the myer.

The officers’ attention was diverted when Minder Finwy approached from Rezkin’s other side. Finwy said, “Sir—”

“Dergmyer.”

Finwy tilted his head. “Dergmyer, I am Minder Finwy, assistant to Minder Barkal of the Temple of the Maker in Serret. I have been traveling with these men, and I assure you, they had nothing to do with the deaths on this plantation. None were living when we arrived.”

The dergmyer glanced from the minder to Rezkin to Orin and back to Rezkin. The dergmyer raised a hand and flicked a finger. “Shoot them.”

The lead archer raised his bow, and seven others followed. Before the first arrow was released, Orin had already shot off a bolt and Rezkin had drawn his swords. The silver blades flashed in the waning light as each arrow was knocked aside or cleaved in two. The minder and Orin, for all his bluster, both dove behind Rezkin for cover, but the mercenary was not fast enough to avoid an arrow through the leg.

As soon as the commotion started, Kai and Farson began picking off troops from the rear. The shouts initially went unnoticed, since Rezkin was keeping the closest troops and most of the officers busy. The unbound mercenaries responded quickly to fight for their lives. They attacked the nearest soldiers, collecting weapons as soon as they became available. One of the mercenaries was rendered unconscious before he even gained his feet but was saved from a killing strike by his comrade.

From the field on the right, Yserria danced into the fray, each of her graceful movements ending in a bloody swath. Jimson was at her side, and Malcius and Brandt were farther down the line. Most of the horses were gathered in the yard or were already in pens, but those still in the road were spooked. Some of them trampled the soldiers in their escape to the fields, likely to be eaten by drauglics if they did not return quickly.

While the soldiers, mercenaries, and Rekzin's friends were fighting, the purifiers huddled around their pole of shackles. As Rezkin waded closer, he began to feel the tingle of mage power, and he realized that it was emanating from all three of them. Heavily engaged with a practiced opponent, Malcius was suddenly smashed against an invisible barrier, as if a wall stood between him and the purifiers. The female purifier reached into her robe and withdrew a long dagger. With a hateful glare, she lunged for him. Although Malcius was unaware of the attempted assault, he rolled out of the way just in time to avoid both the dagger and the sword strike aimed at his head. His opponent's blade collided with the ward, deflected unexpectedly, and he stumbled. Malcius took advantage of the error and plunged his sword into the man's exposed back.

Rezkin realized the barrier only blocked objects from passing in one direction when the woman suddenly charged through to attack Malcius from behind. Rezkin grabbed for a dagger, but before he could release it, an arrow sailed into the woman's heart. Malcius and Rezkin both glanced to see that Yserria had liberated a bow and arrows from one of the dead archers, and she was apparently an excellent shot. Yserria lowered the bow just as Kai crashed into a man who was approaching her from behind. Farson swept across the road, making quick work of the remaining soldiers in the surrounding cluster. The surprise attack on the troops had been swift and efficient. Before long, soldiers began throwing their weapons aside and laying prostrate on the ground as a sign of surrender. Those that remained lost morale when they realized their officers had been the first to fall. The mercenary company lost another member and a second was severely wounded, but they had killed all but ten soldiers and two purifiers who were taken prisoner. They had also gained a little over sixty Gendishen red cavalry horses.

Orin groaned as he hobbled over to Rezkin. "What've we done?"

"Saved our lives," Rezkin said.

"We'll be lucky to be hung for this," the mercenary mumbled.

"They were going to kill us anyway."

Orin nodded. "No way to win."

"We did win. The problem is *them*," Rezkin said, pointing to the prisoners. Jimson and Kai were binding the soldiers' hands while the others searched bodies and gathered horses.

Orin limped up to the prisoners, a broken arrow protruding from his calf. He leaned toward them and yelled, "I told yer commander we had nothin' to do with it! They was gone or dead when we got here. But he had to blame me and my men! Now these're all dead"—he waved toward the bodies scattered over the ground—"and we're stuck with you lot! What do you expect us to do now?"

The prisoners glanced at each other, and one of the younger soldiers said, "You could let us go?"

Orin frowned at him. "Let you go? So you can get another patrol—or a *battalion*—and come after us?" He limped and huffed and growled and then kicked a rock in frustration. It thudded off the temple of a fresh corpse, which sent him into another juvenile tirade.

Yserria watched the rugged mercenary with fascination and muttered to Rezkin in Leréshi, "*Men are too emotional.*"

Orin stopped in his tracks and said, "What did she say?" He took a few steps forward and raised a finger along with his voice. "What did she say?"

"You should not let down your guard."

"Ah," Orin said as he released a breath. "Well, the Leréshi's right. Enemies are all around." He narrowed his eyes at the prisoners and motioned for Rezkin to step aside. "We've got drauglics—*drauglics*! And now our own army. But *you*, you could've left. You don't know us. Why'd you stay and get yerself into this mess?"

Rezkin shrugged. "We needed the horses."

"Bah, Behrglyn's a day away. You coulda gotten horses there without makin' an enemy of the king. Why'd you help us?"

Rezkin glanced at Kai who was selecting the best horses. "Boss says we fight, we fight." Orin gave him a dubious look. Rezkin grinned. "We coulda killed *you* and taken *yer* horses when we first met." With a nod toward the house, he said, "My friend in there don't like senseless killin'."

"The pretty one? I noticed he weren't out here fightin'. So he's the conscience and yer the sword?"

Rezkin tilted his head. It was an idea he would have to consider later. He shrugged and said, "Somethin' like that. Besides, it woulda been a waste of resources. Yer men came in handy durin' the battle with the drauglics. No tellin' how many more we'll meet."

"Maybe, but now we've got *them* to worry about. Once they blab, the king'll have an army after us."

"Dead men can't talk," Rezkin said. Finwy looked up, obviously paying attention despite his preoccupied appearance, and Rezkin's friends shared an uncomfortable glance.

The young soldier scrambled forward on his knees and exclaimed, "But we surrendered."

Rezkin looked at the man with an icy gaze. "The mercs surrendered earlier, and your dergmyer woulda had them killed anyway. You'd've done the killin' when he'd ordered it."

Tears welled in the young man's eyes as he shook his head. "No! I mean, I have to follow orders, but I wouldn't *want* to."

"Well, I don't *want* to have to kill you," Rezkin replied, "but yer a threat."

The older purifier interrupted. "We are servants of the Maker. We do his bidding. You cannot kill us."

Orin limped over to the man. He pointed back at Minder Finwy and said, "*That's* a servant of the Maker, and yer troops tried to put an arrow through him. Damned purifiers—think they can go around takin' and killin' anyone they please who ain't done nothin' wrong."

The purifiers both looked at the mercenary with fury in their dark gazes. The eldest said, "The afflicted have made pacts with demons. What could be worse?"

"Says you!" Orin said. "I don't trust the scourge no more than you, but the rest of the world is sayin' they're blessed of the Maker." He waved at the minder who was wandering about mouthing silent words over the dead. Finwy looked up and nodded then went back to his ministrations. "It always felt kinda wrong, but truth is, I didn't care much before. I ain't sayin' I want anythin' to do with the scourge. I don't like no one havin' that kind of power so as I can't fight against it; but now I know what it's like being accused of something I didn't do and havin' people gonna kill you fer it. That's wrong!"

The sun had finally descended below the horizon, and Kai and Farson delivered a lamp and a few hastily made torches. Farson came to stand at Rezkin's side.

"*What do you intend to do now*?" he asked in Pruari, since it was unlikely anyone present would speak the language. "*We cannot keep prisoners. Will you kill them*?"

"*It is what you taught, yet I feel it is not what you want*," Rezkin replied.

Farson was silent for too long, but Rezkin waited. Finally, the striker said, "*It would be a mistake to let them go.*"

"*If I kill them, I will lose the respect, and possibly the loyalty, of my people.*"

"*You are at war. They will have to learn that there are difficult choices to be made.*"

"*We are not at war with Gendishen*," Rezkin said.

"*We could take the horses we need and run off the rest. It will take them some time to report and without the use of a mage relay, they may be unable to get word ahead of us.*"

Rezkin shook his head. "*That may not be true. The purifiers are mages.*"

"*You are certain*?" Farson said with genuine surprise, "*Mages are killing their own?*"

"*I am surprised the strikers were not aware of it*," Rezkin said.

"*We have never been able to infiltrate the purifiers, and I am not sure Privoth even knows how they do what they do. It makes sense, though. Only one with the talent can sense them, and they would sense someone with the talent who is not of their order.*"

Rezkin's intense gaze was dark in the flickering shadows of the torch light. "Only *those with talent*?"

Farson looked away, but, for once, he did not avoid the question. "*I have no answer for that. I know not how you do it. Your masters said you are not a mage, and all the talented strikers confirmed it. Somehow Peider and Jaiardun trained you to fend off mage attacks and walk through wards, and I never knew what to believe. I truly thought you had the answer, but I am no longer certain.*"

Rezkin could appreciate the sentiment. The only thing he could be certain about with Farson was that he could never trust the man, and his former trainer would be disappointed in him if he did. He put those thoughts aside and said, "*We need to consult with Wesson, but we will have to separate the purifiers from the others. I still do not want his abilities exposed to Orin and his men. Place the purifiers in their own shackles. They are enchanted with runes to prevent mages from using their powers.*"

"*So what do we do with the others*?"

Everyone waited in silence during their exchange. Rezkin could feel his friends' eyes on him. He needed more time to come up with a plan that could protect his friends and preserve their honor. "*Move them to the courtyard for now.*"

The purifiers were placed under guard in the outbuilding that had once housed the ranch hands. It was safest to keep everyone together in case the drauglics returned. The scent of the carnage in the yard would surely attract their attention if they were near. For this task, though, they had to maintain secrecy.

Wesson stepped through the doorway into the small front room of the lodging. A table was pushed up against the far wall, and each of the purifiers sat on the floor tied to a table leg. Dressed as he was, Wesson was not the most convincing mercenary, but no one would have guessed he was a powerful mage. The purifiers barely gave him a glance. Wesson noticed a small furry animal dart into the building behind him. It strutted into the corner and then sprawled lazily on the ground, blinking large yellow eyes and flicking its tail.

Wesson glanced at Rezkin. "Is that your—"

"Get on with it," Rezkin said.

Wesson glanced at the cat one more time and then slowly approached the purifiers. They did not react until he was within six feet of them. At that point, both of their heads came up, each bearing an expression of contempt.

"*Afflicted*," growled the eldest.

Wesson spoke in Gendishen so the purifiers would not know they were Ashaiian—just in case Rezkin decided to let them live. For once, Wesson thought he would not mind if Rezkin chose death. "They are still bound by the shackles?"

"Shackles and mage rope," Rezkin replied.

"Interesting. What kind of mages are you?" Wesson asked.

"We are not *mages*," the eldest said. "We purge the scourge from this realm, back to H'khajnak where it belongs."

"How do you know I am a mage?" Wesson asked.

"We can see and feel your filth. It spreads from your core to infest every inch of your being. By now it has surely suffused your mind. Let us rid you of its taint so that it does not consume your soul as well."

Wesson squatted in front of them. "How do you propose to do that?"

The purifier stared at Wesson intently, appearing as though truly concerned. "We take what is pure for preservation. We would rescue your soul from its afflicted vessel."

"I see. In other words, you would kill me."

"It is the only way. Any death will do, but purification by fire will surely cleanse the deepest desecration."

"You want me to volunteer to be burned at the stake?"

"Many of the afflicted understand the terrible curse they bear. They choose to sacrifice their plagued corporeal vessels and preserve their family names. A true self-sacrifice is the only way to ensure the curse is not carried on in the blood."

"If they do not?" Wesson asked.

"They are burned anyway, and their families with them, along with anyone else believed to be aiding them." The man turned his attention toward Rezkin and said, "Anyone who turns in an afflicted may be granted a stay of execution in exchange for a penance."

"You should not bother with him," Wesson said. "He has extreme methods of negotiating. I do not think you would like them." The purifiers looked at Rezkin uncertainly, and Wesson changed the subject. "What do you see when you look at me?"

The one who had been speaking snapped his mouth shut and looked away. The younger one stared at the elder, silently urging him to answer. He glanced anxiously at Rezkin and then looked back to Wesson. "We cannot see the scourge while wearing the shackles."

"If we remove the shackles, you can actually *see* it?" Wesson said.

The younger nodded vigorously. "Yes, I can tell you what it looks like. If you could see it, you would understand how it infests the body. It is everywhere. It seeps out and stretches to touch others. Those of us blessed by the Maker to be able to see it can feel it as well. I can feel it in you now, but it is muted."

Wesson said, "They are readers. The purifiers are *readers*." He looked to

Farson who stood beside the table behind the purifiers. "Would you please unshackle him?"

"Are you sure? He could use his powers to attack or escape."

"I can handle him," Wesson said.

Farson did as asked while Wesson stepped across the room and removed the stone amulet, surreptitiously handing it to Rezkin outside the purifiers' view. The older purifier watched Wesson intently, his expression becoming furious once the amulet was removed. Wesson returned to stand before the prisoners. The younger purifier was still tied to the table, but the shackles were removed.

"What do you see?" he asked.

The young man glanced at his companion, who was still scowling. "He should be told," he said. "He must be given the opportunity to make the right choice. If he knows, perhaps he will choose the right path." The tingle of vimara filled the space, and the young man stared into Wesson. "I see the normal colors. Strands, some of them thick, others thin. But, there is so much of the *other*. The darkness overwhelms. I have never seen so much darkness."

Wesson frowned. "You can see the vimara, but you do not know how to interpret it."

The young man frowned. "There is nothing to interpret. It is all evil. You are beyond redemption."

"When you look at each other, do you not see the power?"

"Ours is special," the young purifier said. "The Maker has twisted it for his own use. We are blessed with the ability to identify the accursed bearers of the scourge."

"So *you* claim to serve the Maker with your power, but everyone else must be evil? Why are you so different? You can perform spells, same as anyone else."

"No! We cannot, we do not."

"I saw your ward," Wesson said.

The young man frowned and glanced at his companion, who now appeared to be sulking. "Yes, some Purifiers have sacrificed a small piece of themselves in service to the Maker. It is a foul taint, to learn the art of demons, but they do so to protect the rest of us. They, too, become afflicted, and each of them will be burned before it fully infects them. It is a foul practice. I would never sully my soul in such a way."

Wesson turned to the older man. The man would not meet his gaze. "It was you, then? You learned the spell for the ward?"

His voice was gruff as he said, "Yes, I made the deal with the demon inside me."

"Now that you have felt it, you must know that is not true. The sensation—it is not one of evil."

The man scowled. "I know nothing of the sort."

Wesson looked at the younger man. "You could perform the spell, as well, if you learned."

The younger man lifted his chin defiantly. "No, I cannot. My power is blessed of the Maker. I will not let the demons in."

"How many have you helped to kill?"

The young man's eyes shimmered with pride. "I have participated in twelve purifications. We cleansed the afflicted and their families. All of those communities are now safe from the putridity of the scourge."

Wesson felt anger and sorrow welling within him in equal amounts. "The *talented* are not born evil. Learning spells does not make us evil. How we choose to use the *talent* is what makes us heroes or monsters. You choose to use yours to hunt down and kill innocent people. You cannot blame your actions on demons. You are humans, humans choosing to do evil."

His senses overwhelmed, Wesson turned away. Rezkin stepped forward and started to speak, but the mage whipped around and shouted, "Have you ever even *seen* the power in use? I mean, more than your meager ward? Have you seen someone use it to create a beautiful statue, construct a building, draw water from the earth, or to make a plant grow? How about healing? Have you ever watched someone returned from the edge of death?"

"All tricks of the demons to entice you into giving over your soul," said the younger man. He glanced at his partner and said, "Even the enticement of protecting your brethren."

The old man pursed his lips then spat with ferocity. "It is true, but it was a sacrifice I was willing to make to continue the Maker's work and to protect others who do so. I hate myself a little more each time I feel the filth spread through my body, but I would do it again."

Wesson's face heated, and he spun on his heal. "They are a lost cause."

"What do you wish to do with them?" said Rezkin.

Startled, Wesson said, "What? You are asking *me*?"

Rezkin tilted his head. "You are my mage. They are your responsibility."

"I am *your* mage? You mean I am the—"

"Of course."

Wesson glanced at the two interested purifiers. "May we speak elsewhere?"

Rezkin nodded to Farson to replace the shackles, and he waved Wesson through the door.

Once they were outside, Wesson hissed, "I am only a journeyman. I cannot be the king's mage."

"According to whom?" Rezkin said.

"The king's mage should be an archmage. I am not even a full mage, much less a master mage, and I will probably *never* reach the level of power and skill required to be an archmage."

"*I* am the king, and I decide who is the king's mage. It is you." Rezkin tilted his head and said, "Unless you are tendering your resignation?"

"What? No, but I have not even sworn fealty to you."

"I do not require it. If you are not resigning, then you are the king's mage. What do you wish to do with the prisoners?"

Tears welled in Wesson's eyes. "I am not cut out for this kind of position."

Rezkin's cool blue gaze seemed to glow in the moonlight. "You are exactly the kind of person the king's mage should be."

Wesson blinked away the moisture. He choked down the tightness in his throat and said, "They have confessed to their crimes. They have hunted, tortured, and murdered, but we are not in Ashai or Cael. In Gendishen, these are not crimes."

"So long as they are committed against the *talented*," said Rezkin. "Should their actions perpetuate just because it is accepted in their culture?"

"Of course not, but *you* are trying to create a kingdom that depends on being in Privoth's good graces. If we start making trouble, at best, he will call us murderers. At worst, he will consider it an act of war."

"Actually, the second scenario would be better," Rezkin mused.

"How is declaring *war* better?"

"Because that would mean he recognizes us as an independent kingdom." Wesson scowled at him, and he said, "As far as making trouble, we have already done that. We killed fifty soldiers, including several officers who are probably members of noble houses and will suddenly become *valued* once they hear the men are dead and that we killed them. It would be easy to cover this up. We could kill the survivors and mercenaries and then travel cross-country to avoid encountering anyone on the roads who might make the connection. Or, we could kill everyone we encounter, but I think that would be counterproductive."

The light of the moon and the few torches still scattered around the yard was enough to expose Wesson's horrified expression.

"Be calm, Journeyman. I have no intention of doing those things. I know you and the others would be uncomfortable with such actions."

"*Uncomfortable* is an understatement," Wesson said, "and I have concerns that it seems to be the only thing holding you back."

Rezkin shrugged. "What do you want to do with them?"

3

"What is wrong with *him*?" Malcius asked.

Rezkin glanced at the mage who had been sulking in the corner all night. His mood had not improved, and he looked haggard in the morning light. His present drab countenance mirrored the functional and austere Gendishen style of the room.

"His emotions have won the battle for his mind. Eventually, rationality will triumph. For now, he has a job to do, and so do you."

Malcius looked at Wesson doubtfully. "Do you really think this is the best solution?"

"We can do it this way, or we can kill them all. Letting them go is not an option."

"Alright, but I am still not convinced. It is disconcerting," Malcius said with a shiver. "I think I might prefer death."

"I may agree with you," Rezkin said. Actually, the thought disturbed him deeply. These were outworlders, though, and they lived by different rules. He said, "Do you believe we should give them a choice?"

Malcius was silent for a moment and then said, "No. They will probably choose death on principle alone. It would be better to do it and hope they appreciate our mercy later."

"Very well," Rezkin said before stepping into the adjacent room where Orin and one of his men were finishing their preparations. They had collected additional healing supplies, food, and perhaps a few valuables during their short stay. "It is time for you to leave."

Orin's head came up. "You're not joinin' us?"

Rezkin glanced at Farson who was covering the fact that he was spying on the mercenaries by grumbling as he appeared to be mending the "broken" straps on his armor.

Rezkin said, "I'll catch up. We have unfinished business here."

Orin's expression darkened. "Ah, the soldiers. What, uh, exactly do you intend to do with them?"

Rezkin flicked the pommel of the sword at his hip. "You let me worry 'bout that. Can't have no witnesses, so unless you wanna join them, you'd best be gettin' along. The boss and the rest of the men'll go with you, except for Wess."

"You sure the boy can handle that sorta thing?" Orin said. "He seems a bit weak in the stomach. I heard him mutterin' all night over in the corner."

"He'll survive."

"Well, let's hope we don't get attacked by drauglics before you catch up."

Farson coughed, and Rezkin glanced over to see his former trainer's telling look. It was one he had seen often as a small-man—one that meant he had forgotten something. Mercenaries liked to gloat.

"I ain't yer nursemaid," he said, "I seem to remember you sayin' I was the kind to give mercs a bad name."

Rezkin was never in the mood for banter, but on this day he was feeling uncomfortable with his chosen course of action. He knew he should just kill the prisoners. Letting them live was to leave enemies at his back. It was a mistake, but it was one he had to make if he desired to preserve his friends' honor—and their respect.

"Yer a right cocky bastard," said Orin, "but I guess you got reason to be." The man collected his pack with his one good hand and limped toward the door. He paused and said, "You just remember, the bigger yer head, the easier the target."

Rezkin grinned and nodded appreciatively, but Orin scoffed at the perceived sarcasm. He followed the two mercenaries and Farson into the adjacent room, and they all continued out the front door while Rezkin remained behind with Wesson. He watched out the window as his friends mounted their newly acquired horses and started down the road. Farson did not go with them. He waited at the edge of the property with Pride and Wesson's mount. Rezkin had thought the journeyman, who had once aspired to be a life mage and had shed tears for a donkey, would have wanted to choose his own horse, but Wesson had shown no interest.

Once they were gone, Wesson looked up at him. "I don't like this," he said.

"I know, but the alternative is death."

"This might be worse. I do not know for sure what will happen. I have never tried this spell, and normally I would never test a spell like this on a person. Actually, I would never *use* a spell like this on a person even if it were tested and accepted."

"You are the one who suggested it," Rezkin said.

"Well, yes, I know, but it was just an idea. I did not think you would approve."

"You have seen the spell used before on other things?"

"No, not exactly," Wesson replied as he glanced away. He sighed heavily and said, "I made it up. I have been studying the structure of the citadel and considering the shielreyah. I mean, this really has nothing to do with that, but it was what gave me the idea. The mage academy would say it is impossible. It requires mixing two affinities in a way they are not supposed to be combined."

"But you think you can do it?"

"I … um … maybe. It might work, but not necessarily in the way I expect —or they might explode."

Rezkin raised an eyebrow. "Explode?"

Wesson scratched his head and wrung his hands since he could not fidget with his robes as usual. "It uses mostly constructive power, and it is new and probably a little beyond my ability to control, considering my affinity for nocent. Also, I will be performing it on living beings who are not willing participants."

"That makes a difference?"

"Yes, it can. Mundanes also bear the power of *will.* Even healers have trouble treating patients who do not desire aid. It is one of the reasons life mages are not great in battle. Can you imagine? Besides battle mages, they would be the most powerful on the field if they could simply change a person's body in the midst of a skirmish."

"I see your point. Are you ready to perform the spell?"

Wesson nodded. "Yes, I have been practicing all night. If these men can avoid the fate of the purifiers, I will do what I must. It is worth a try."

The courtyard was an outdoor space in the center of the building with a perimeter of potted plants and flower boxes. In the center was a swirling design made of flat paving stones. Although it was open to the sky, it was partially covered by an overgrown trellis. The splash of color from the fragrant red blooms was the most vibrant ornamentation they had seen in Gendishen thus far. The tables and chairs that had previously occupied the courtyard had been stacked in one corner, and the ten Gendishen soldiers were tied in a line down the center.

Rezkin paced around the group once and then said, "We are going to allow you to live."

There was a collective sigh of relief, and the younger soldier's shoulders shook as he began to sob.

"We cannot let you go now, obviously, since you will return to your fort and report this misunderstanding in your favor."

"No, we wouldn't," said one of the men closest to him. "We'd tell them what really happened. The dergmyer messed up. We know it."

"It no longer matters. Whatever you tell them, they will come after us, and we do not have time for that. It would be equally tiresome to have to needlessly kill more of your comrades. So, you all need to consent to what we are about to do so that you can remain alive."

"What are you gonna do?" the man asked.

"It does not matter. You choose, alive or dead."

The youngest soldier sobbed harder, and Rezkin wondered how he had ever made it through basic training.

Rezkin shook his head and said, "Here is what is going to happen. We are going to untie you and give each of you a sword because you may need them later. If you make trouble, I will kill you, and believe me when I tell you that the two of us are more than enough to handle the ten of you."

The men appeared to contemplate the claim and seemed to accept that Rezkin could do some damage, but they glanced at Wesson doubtfully.

"Give them a demonstration so they do not do anything foolish," Rezkin said.

Wesson nodded and then snapped his hands through the air. A raging stream of fire burst over the soldiers' heads, singeing the leaves on the trellis as the golden flame exposed the terror on their shadowed faces. Shouts of *scourge* and *afflicted* and *demon* could be heard under the thunderous roar of flame.

Rezkin looked at the mage and said, "That was a little dramatic."

Wesson grinned and met the most determined soldier's anxious gaze. "Sorry, I tried to rein it in, but I got excited."

"Where are the purifiers?" shouted one man.

Wesson glanced at Rezkin and then said, "The purifiers are dead. They were given a chance to repent, but they could not be swayed."

Rezkin and Wesson untied the soldiers, who each hurried to put distance between himself and the mage. They were instructed to collect a sword from the pile and then stand in a circle in the center of courtyard facing outward. Once the men were in place, Wesson began weaving the difficult spell. Rezkin watched him with interest, the process seeming needlessly complicated. To the mundane soldiers, the mage appeared to be erratically waving his hands in the air as he muttered; but, when Rezkin focused, he could see the complex tapestry of vimara that started with Wesson's hands and then expanded outward and around the entire room. Wesson began cinching it inward, the weave getting tighter as it wrapped around the soldiers.

"Uh, Rez? You might want to leave," Wesson said, the waver in his voice baring his concern.

"What is the problem?" Rezkin said.

The men began to panic, even more so once they realized their feet were rooted to the ground.

"Well, um, you kind of got wrapped in the spell, and … um … I am not sure you can get out of it."

As Rezkin stared, he noticed a small splotched cat had come to sit beside the mage. It watched the proceedings with interest and did not seem concerned in the least by the commotion.

"It will be fine. Continue," Rezkin said.

"I appreciate your confidence in my abilities," Wesson said through gritted teeth, "but this would not be the spell with which to test yourself."

Wesson threaded the last strand into the spell, splitting it into multiple lines and attaching one end to the trickle of vimara within each of the men. The soldiers' vimara began to seep into the spell, keeping it powered as Wesson withdrew his own. He breathed a sigh of relief and looked at Rezkin, who was wrapped in threads as well.

"Alright, it is tied off. I can activate it when you are ready."

"Wait, what are you doing to us? We deserve to know," shouted one of the soldiers.

. . .

Wesson looked at the frightened faces of the men on his side of the circle. "Did your mother ever tell you not to make an ugly face because it would freeze that way?"

The one who had asked said, "Yeah, I guess so."

"Well, that is about to happen—to your whole body."

Rezkin grinned and said, "So strike a daring pose."

Wesson frowned. "It will be temporary," he said with an anxious glance at Rezkin, "but it will keep you from reporting to the fort while we go about our business. The drauglics should not even take notice of you if this works, but we do not know the circumstances in which you will find yourselves when it wears off—hence, the swords."

"Wait, you can't do this—"

"It is better than death," Wesson said again, more for himself than for them, since he was uncertain they would survive the spell.

Rezkin nodded, and Wesson ignored the men's shouts as he activated the spell. A silent concussion of power swept outward from the center and then was just as suddenly sucked inward in a bone jarring implosion. Panic surged through him as he worried over his potential mistakes. When he was not showered in gore, he finally filled his lungs with the air he so badly needed.

Wesson watched as the spell began to take hold, and the men yanked furiously at their failing limbs. "They are going to hurt themselves," he muttered.

Rezkin glanced at the cat and then focused, pressing his will on the men who were already under the influence of a powerful spell. "Attention!" he shouted.

The combination of Wesson's spell and whatever power was behind Rezkin's will produced the desired effect. Like the well-trained recruits they were, their frantic motions ceased, and each of the men abruptly came to attention, a ring of soldiers bearing arms. Their skin and hair became pale and then turned white as their breathing slowed to naught. Their clothes and swords were changed as well, and within seconds, the soldiers had become phenomenally detailed statues, their exquisite forms refined by the imperfections of ten unique individuals.

Rezkin felt the spell slither over his skin, but with each grasp and tug, its tendrils failed to gain purchase, slipping away ineffectually. The stone pressed against the skin over his sternum turned cold, and a sense of alien anger invaded a small and distant part of his mind. His gaze urgently sought the cat, but it was no longer resting at Wesson's feet. In fact, it had penetrated his space without him noticing and was sitting only a pace away, glaring. Its attention was not on him, though. It was on his chest—exactly where the stone lay hidden beneath his shirt and armor on the lace around his neck. The cat stared intently, and then its yellow eyes flashed orange. Seemingly in response, the stone heated to an uncomfortable burn. Then, the cat met his gaze and blinked, its accusatory expression becoming haughty and judgmental.

Rezkin tore his eyes from the cat to see Wesson watching the strange, silent exchange between man and tiny beast. Ignoring the cat, Rezkin dragged his fingers down the face of one of the statues and found that it felt like any natural stone carving.

"Are they aware?" he asked.

"I do not believe so," Wesson said as he stared into one soldier's empty gaze. "They are stone throughout, mind and body."

Rezkin ran his finger along the stone that used to be a blade. "How is this temporary, then?"

Wesson's expression was worried. "I am not sure that it is. I tried to tie the aura to the spell. I am no necromancer, but I thought maybe I had achieved a connection with the chiandre. The spell was supposed to mimic the properties of stone while maintaining the body's ability to support the soul and also preserving the soul's connection between the body and the Afterlife. *This*"—he looked deeply into the eyes of the statue—"is so complete, it is amazing. I have never heard of anyone transforming a living being into stone." Then, remembering his subjects, his eyes began to tear. "I can no longer sense the power of the spell, though. I think I messed up. I am afraid I have killed them."

"Time will tell, Journeyman," Rezkin said. "The drauglics will not be interested in stone, and they will be armed when they awaken."

"If the spell has already dissipated, then they are surely done. I designed it to become unstable as their vimara drops. When it dipped below a certain threshold, the spell would no longer receive power, and it would collapse. It is why I could not have used it on the purifiers. Their wells were deep. They would have remained embedded in stone for centuries, maybe longer. With these mundanes, it should have lasted a month or two at most. If the spell has already ceased, though, and they have not changed back, then they are dead."

"We tried," Rezkin said. "Remember, any one of them would have killed you had he known what you are. They would have killed the rest of us on the unfounded assumption that we killed the residents of this plantation."

"I know," Wesson said with a nod. "Really, I do."

"Then what distresses you?" Rezkin asked.

Wesson turned. He looked like he wanted to say something, but the words were not strong enough to pass his lips. Finally, he whispered, "Another time, perhaps."

~

After days of plodding down the busy road that led from the coast through Behrglyn and Tahn to the inland capital of Drovsk, the dark smudge on the horizon took form. Orin and his men had elected to travel separately, hoping the physical distance between the two parties would be enough to detach them from the events at the plantation. Luckily, it appeared the drauglics had either avoided or had not yet reached the somewhat more populated south.

The long approach to the King's Seat gave the travelers ample time to survey the city's unusual architecture. For those who had been graced with the sight of it, nothing could compare to the splendor of Caellurum, but anyone besides the Gendishen would agree that Drovsk was ugly. The surrounding landscape was hidden by crops and wild fields—no mountain, forest, or sea in sight. It appeared as though some weary traveler from long ago had given up after weeks of trudging through endless plains and decided to build a city where he stood. Without the luxury of natural defenses, a monstrous wall had sprouted to surround the castle at the center. As the city grew, more walls had been built, but rather than surrounding the entire city over and again, as in Serret, each consecutive wall encapsulated only the newly built structures. Rezkin imagined that if he could view the city as a hawk, it would look like a senseless mosaic. The only entrance was through the gate at the end of the road. Once inside, travelers had to navigate a nonsensical maze of gateways, each with guards determining who was permitted into the respective sector.

Rezkin's group stopped long before they reached the city, though. A blockade manned by soldiers had been erected across the road, and picket lines of tall, sharpened posts and crossbeams had been planted along the sides of the road leading to the gate. Some travelers and merchants were permitted passage, but the mercenaries and young men hoping to enlist in the regular army were sent to camps on either side of the road. The mercenary camp was far less orderly, but the men there strutted with greater confidence and seemed to be thrilled with the prospect of war. Fights broke out between the different companies and sometimes among members of the same company, and veterans often jeered at the green army recruits who wandered too close to the road.

Kai led the party to hide amongst the tallest grasses they could find, using the grazing horses to break the line of sight to the road. Once there, they quickly changed out of their worn attire to something more suited to a king's entourage. Rezkin donned the guise of Dark Tidings, and the others wore tabards bearing the green lightning bolt on a black field. Wesson quietly muttered to himself about the fact that he was unable to wear the robes he had painstakingly earned as he brushed down the pants and tunic befitting the king's manservant.

"Remember," Rezkin said, "you are all warriors now. You are the king's warriors."

"We are too small in number to be convincing," Malcius said as he plaited his hair.

Farson nodded toward the stream of travelers on the road who were attempting to reach the capital. "While our party is small and lacks the typical fanfare of a royal arrival, our sudden and unannounced appearance at the capital's gate should have an impact."

Malcius tied the ribbon at the end of his braid and said, "I suppose that makes sense, but what if they just arrest us?"

Farson glanced from Kai to Rezkin. "That would not be in their best interest."

Malcius scowled, an expression that had, of late, nearly replaced his previously untroubled visage. "Two strikers, a swordmaster, and a … whatever he is"—he waved toward Rezkin—"are not enough to take on a kingdom."

Brandt said in a forced whisper, "Do not forget the battle mage."

"Who will surely be found out by these purifiers. What can one mage do?"

Farson shook his head as he began stuffing his items into his pack. "I have not seen Mage Wesson use his *talent* in such a way, but even a weak mage with a natural affinity for destructive magic can cause significant damage."

Yserria, who had been pointedly avoiding direct interaction with Malcius, finally snapped, "If you do not wish to be here, why did you come?"

His fiery gaze struck the woman. "No one wishes to be here. I want to make sure things are getting done."

Yserria laughed. "And what do you think to do if they are not?"

"It is *your* fault we are in this mess!" he said as he closed the distance.

Yserria met the lord's hostile approach in kind and yelled, "How is it *my* fault that we must prevent a war with Gendishen while claiming their land?"

"If it were not for *you*, Palis would be alive. We could return to Ashai and lead a campaign against the tyrant in the name of House Jebai. I could stand before my father with honor. *I* was responsible for him! How am I to return now, having lost my brother?"

Rezkin was glad that Malcius was finally putting voice to his festering resentment, but the circumstances at that moment were not ideal. "Yserria is not responsible for Palis's death, Malcius. He was his own man, and he made his choice."

"If she had done what she was supposed to, he would not have gone back for her, and he would not be dead."

Yserria thrust a long, slender finger in Rezkin's direction. "I did what I was supposed to do. I protected my king!"

"Who *ordered* you to return to the ship," argued Malcius.

Kai interrupted Yserria's response. "*I* gave her the order to stay with Rezkin no matter what. She is a member of the King's Royal Guard. It is her duty to protect her king with her life."

"But the *king* ordered her to leave!"

Kai dropped his pack and turned to Malcius. "It is the responsibility of the royal guard to ignore such orders if it appears the king's life is in immediate danger. Rezkin was alone on the beach with an army bearing down on him. If I had not been otherwise engaged on the ship, I would have been there, too. Yserria acted with courage, not just in facing the enemy, but also for risking the wrath of her king for doing so. By tradition, her act of bravery would have been recorded in the *Book of Honors*, placing her one step closer to official knighthood. As it is, she has endured only the guilt and resentment associated with your brother's death—the death of her potential betrothed, no less."

Malcius's nostrils flared. He glanced between them and then turned and stormed farther into the grass. Since there was no place in which to find privacy, he had to settle for distance.

As Farson stood to follow, Rezkin said, "Keep an eye on him, but give him some space."

"What do you know of space?" Farson snapped. "You would not have required it."

Rezkin shook his head. "He has not learned to separate from his emotions.

Outworlders must be permitted time to battle with their feelings before they can be expected to function with sense."

"An astute observation," Farson said cautiously.

Rezkin picked up the black sword from the wrap that lay on the ground and thrust it into the scabbard strapped to his back. "It is inefficient and needlessly draining of energy, but it is their reality. Still, we have little time. I do not wish for our presence to be reported before our arrival. Brandt, give him a few minutes and then encourage his return."

Brandt nodded and jogged into the grass, followed by Farson.

A short time later, they were all in the saddle heading toward the blockade. Unlike other travelers, they did not dismount upon arrival. They held back until the travelers in front of them had been processed, and no one behind attempted to pass. The travelers, mercenaries, and soldiers watched with interest, and eventually, whispers of *Dark Tidings* encouraged others from the camps to crowd the road. The soldiers at the barricade looked on anxiously as the new arrivals plodded forward in the final approach. The officer in charge was easily identified. A silver chain stretched across his chest from one shoulder to the other. From the chain dangled the various emblems of rank and awards he had earned throughout his career. This man had many, which meant he had either found himself uncharacteristically in trouble, or, more likely, the kingdom considered the barricade position to be of great importance.

"We demand an audience with King Privoth," Dark Tidings said from behind the mask.

The officer glanced between the mounted warriors. Each was wearing a black tabard bearing green lightning bolt and a hooded black cloak, beneath which were shadowed faces painted with thick black lines running vertically from the hair line, through the eyes, over the cheeks, and ending at the jawline. The only member of the party not dressed in such a way was the priest of the Maker who rode at the back.

"Who should I say is calling?" the officer asked, and the mutterings of *Dark Tidings* grew louder.

"Tell him the King of Cael, True King of Ashai, has arrived," said Dark Tidings.

The officer turned to the soldier at his side and said, "Get my horse and one for the fyer." To Dark Tidings, he said, "I am Myer Lour. I will deliver the message personally. This is Fyer Volt. He will take you to the overgress."

Dark Tidings tilted his head in acceptance. They followed the myer and fyer into the city, the blockade preventing anyone from following, at least to the first gate. Within the gates, the road split into two parallel paths—one for use by riders, wagons, and official business, and the other open to pedestrians. While people began crowding the footpath to watch their procession, none crossed the boundary to interfere with their passage. Rezkin appreciated the order of it, having been uncomfortable with the crowded chaos of the cities he had visited thus far. He supposed the paths needed to be clear if one was to navigate the discordant honeycomb that was Drovsk.

The party was led through increasingly attractive sections of the city. Eventually, the myer left to report to the castle. The fyer led them to an empty plaza, in the center of which was a stone dais. Around the perimeter were rows of steps that rose to an upper walkway lined by a stone colonnade.

"This is the overgress," the fyer said.

As they entered, soldiers quietly slipped into the spaces between the columns. The fyer invited their party to dismount, but Rezkin remained in his saddle, a signal to his companions to do the same. People dressed in colorful court finery began to trickle into the plaza to take up seats on the steps. They muttered and pointed, and some laughed, but it was anxious laughter. As they waited, the assembly grew more uncomfortable with the mounted warriors in black who were obviously uninterested in socializing. Pride had been trained to keep his nickering and snorts to a minimum when commanded to do so, but the other horses were becoming restless.

Eventually, a trio of brown-robed men descended the steps. The soldiers between the columns spread apart, and seven more brown-robed men stepped into the spaces between them. Rezkin could feel the buzz of mage power, and it grew to a roar before the lead purifier came to a halt a few paces from him.

"Afflicted," the man hissed, and he lifted his hand to point a crooked finger at Wesson.

A wave of angry shouts and fear-filled shrieks passed through the crowd, and the soldiers raised their bows in answer.

"Surrender him to us!" the purifier said.

"No, but you are welcome to try to take him. You will not survive the encounter."

"He cannot unleash his foul scourge in this sacred place. The runes—"

Wesson produced a ball of swirling fire over his open palm.

"Are ineffectual," Dark Tidings said.

"Seize him," the purifier shrieked.

The purifiers raised their arms, and Wesson's fireball fizzled in a thin puff. Wesson was overwhelmed with alarm as the power of ten mages wrapped around him. He felt imprisoned, trapped. His outward calm was in complete contrast to the internal battle he was waging against the confines of power. He knew Rezkin could probably feel the purifiers' attack, but if so, he gave no indication. After the initial panic began to subside, Wesson realized the restraints felt wobbly and frayed. Part of him was still wondering how he was able to fight them at all. He had seen the numerous runes carved into the columns, roof, and floor, and he should not have been able to light a candle, much less create a fireball. Even now, he could feel his strength mounting, and he knew that if he kept pressing, he could overcome the assault. Whether he could do it in time to save himself was another matter.

"I invoke the rule of the Interkingdom Accords," said Dark Tidings. "The mage cannot be touched. As you have seen, he is not as limited as you hoped."

"The Interkingdom Accords apply only to monarchs and diplomats," the purifier replied. "You are neither."

"Stand down, Mage," Dark Tidings said, eliciting a deep scowl from the purifier, and a flurry of angry grumbles from the crowd. "That is not *your* decision to make." He nodded toward another man descending the steps.

The purifiers turned and bowed toward the new arrival. King Privoth paused at the base of the steps, and Dark Tidings finally dismounted. His warriors followed in unison, maintaining positions beside their mounts. It was a display they had practiced to proficiency.

"You are audacious," said Privoth, "to come here to *my* kingdom, to demand an audience with the king, to bring with you but a handful of warriors, and to deliver unto us this scourge-infested demonkind. If you think to intimidate me, as you did Ionius, you will be disappointed."

Privoth was a young king of merely thirty years. His brown hair was cropped short in the Gendishen military style, as was his short, pointy beard. He wore the uniform of a soldier but with a ruby encrusted gold crown atop his head and five embellished gold chains stretching across his chest. He carried himself with the assurance of a general, but unlike most of the monarchs about the Souelian, Privoth had *earned* an officer's rank before taking the throne.

Dark Tidings said, "I do not come to press or beg"—he grasped the black mask and pulled it from his face—"but to bargain." He met Privoth's hard stare and was pleased to see the dutifully concealed surprise in the king's dark eyes. Unlike his warriors, Rezkin had not painted his face. The strikers and the baron had said they saw in him a resemblance to the Ashaiian royal family, and he wanted Privoth to see it, too.

"Your Majesty," the lead purifier said, "the afflicted …"

"Yes," Privoth said, diverting his attention, "read him."

Rezkin felt a rise in the buzz of mage power directed at Wesson. The purifier's face contorted in anger—an anger that gradually morphed from righteous indignation to fear.

"He is strong. No, *too* strong. He wields inconceivable destructive power. Your Majesty, we cannot hold him. He will break free. I implore you to seek safety. We must kill him now before his power is released."

King Privoth was unmoved. He stood, stoic, as he examined the black-clad warriors who remained as still and unperturbed as their leader.

The purifier stepped closer to his king and hissed too low for any but Rezkin to hear. "Your Majesty, we cannot wait. Why do you delay?"

"I wait for *him*," said Privoth with a nod toward Rezkin.

The purifier stared at his king. "Have they used their demon-gotten power to corrupt your mind?"

Privoth sounded as if he were schooling a child as he spoke. "Look at them. They do not appear concerned. Why are they not concerned?" He turned hard eyes on his zealous servant. "Read *him*."

The purifier looked doubtfully at Rezkin but did as his king bade him. The tingle of power slipped over Rezkin, and he could feel it trying to grasp something within, but nothing answered. The purifier shook violently and stepped back.

"He is … *cold*. It is a deep, bitter cold, and disturbing, but he is not one of them."

"What does it mean?" Privoth said.

The purifier lifted his nose and said, "I am sure it is nothing. He has probably spent too much time in the presence of the scourge afflicted."

Privoth appeared unsatisfied with the answer. He raised his voice and said, "Bring the old woman."

A runner dashed away beyond the colonnade. Rezkin spent the next few minutes studying the spectators and guards while Privoth studied him and his companions. He nodded in appreciation of Minder Finwy's presence, and then the man's gaze lingered on Yserria, which was not surprising. Women were not permitted the same freedoms in Gendishen as they were in Ashai. Aside from that, even Rezkin had noticed that the woman looked particularly stunning in her present attire. Her pale, freckled skin glowed beneath the black cloak and tabard, her green eyes were like fire blazing through the darkness of the black paint, and a few stray red curls danced around her face in the shadow of her hood. With her determined gaze and the array of exposed weapons, she was a beautiful but deadly viper. Rezkin thought her well suited to play the role of enchantress.

His attention flicked to the top of the stairs. An old woman in a worn frock made of layers of colorful fabric was shuffling down the steps with the aid of the young runner. Long, silver hair, streaked white with a few remaining black strands, was tied back in a tail that hung past her waist. Her skin was pale, wrinkled, and marked with many years of age spots. When she reached the base of the steps, she paused and looked up at their party. Her aged grey eyes flashed with intrigue when her gaze landed upon Wesson.

"Greetings, young one. It has been many years," the old woman said. "You are underdressed."

Rezkin glanced back at his mage. Wesson appeared startled and uncertain if he should speak. "You are acquainted?" Rezkin asked.

"Yes," Wesson replied. He turned to the old woman and performed a shallow bow. "Greetings, Master Reader Kessa. It is an honor to be in your company."

Rezkin looked back at the old woman. Her eyes flashed with mirth as she said, "King Privoth is wise to treat you all well."

Privoth said, "What is this? What do you know?"

She looked at Wesson with a pleased smile. "I am certain your purifiers have already told you what you need to know."

"I will be the judge of that. You were invited here to teach and to serve me. Do as I say and answer the question."

Kessa pursed her lips and frowned at the young king. "King Privoth, you do not understand how an *invitation* is supposed to work." She glanced from Wesson to Rezkin. "With an invitation, the recipient has the option to refuse."

"Answer the question, old woman," Privoth said.

Kessa pointed at Wesson. "I know that no one can force that one to do anything he does not wish to do. You would be wise not to press him." Her grey gaze turned to Rezkin. "I know that if this one has managed to garner the loyalty of the mage, then he is most dangerous."

Privoth growled in frustration. "Do you know him as well?"

"No, I do not, but the likeness is enough, do you not agree? In which case, you should be very concerned."

"Read him," Privoth demanded.

Kessa gazed, unfocused, at Rezkin for a long time. She became unnaturally still, and her lips began to turn blue. Her focus returned, and she shivered violently. "Co-o-o-ld," she said through chattering teeth, and a puff of frosty air escaped her lips. She pulled her shawl tighter around her and studied Rezkin's face anew.

Privoth prompted, "What does it mean?"

"He is not a mage," Kessa said. "I can say this with certainty."

"Then what is he?"

The old woman shrugged. "A man?" At Privoth's dissatisfied look, she said, "He is probably under the influence of a spell, one that I cannot see." She nodded toward Wesson, "He may be capable of such a thing."

Privoth looked pointedly at the woman and said, "If he is not afflicted, then he cannot be of the Ashaiian royal line."

Kessa looked at Rezkin skeptically. "*That* I do not believe."

The purifier stepped forward with a gleeful grin. "Your Majesty, perhaps he has been cured. What if the power of the fiery Hells has been ripped from him, leaving behind a frozen, purified vessel?"

Rezkin did not like the idea that a piece of his innate being had been stolen. He said to the purifier, "You bear the *talent*, same as the mage. It is the source of your power."

"We bear the curse of demon power so that we may identify and bind those afflicted with the scourge. It cannot be used any other way. The Maker deemed it so and blessed us with these runes"—he waved a finger around the adorned structure—"to assist in our crusade."

Rezkin glanced at the runes. "These were created by mages like you and him. How you choose to use your power is your prerogative, but we both know you are capable of much more."

Kessa grinned and King Privoth glanced at the fuming purifier. He lifted his hand to forestall the imminent, vicious tirade. To Rezkin, he said, "You are clever. I recognize your attempt to divide us, and it will not work."

"I seek only to expose the truth of your hypocrisy," Rezkin said.

"Like my fathers before me, it is my prerogative to use whatever resources are available to maintain the balance of this kingdom."

"By balance, you mean the existing power structure."

"Indeed, for it is by the blessing of the Maker that my family has ruled this kingdom for twelve generations. You said you came here to bargain. You call yourself the King of Cael, True King of Ashai. By your looks alone, I *might* be inclined to believe the latter has some substance. Cael, however, belongs to *me*."

"Ionius said the same."

"Channería has only ever claimed that worthless rock to vex us. Now, it seems, they have given it to *you*—but with a few stipulations." Privoth chuckled. "I hear he gave to you his daughter. You must have been very convincing in your methods. In the matter of Cael, though, I believe Ionius said that *I* must recognize your claim. It is interesting that he should do so. Our people have never agreed on anything regarding Cael, and now we should consent to give it to *you*. What incentive do I have?"

"I have more resources than either you or Ionius realize."

"Oh?" Privoth smirked. "I heard you went to Ionius practically begging for favor."

Rezkin grinned devilishly. "Men hear what they wish, men of power especially."

Privoth's expression soured. "I can only assume your candidness is designed to convince me of my own desire to give to you my land."

"On the contrary, I have no need of your gift. As I said, I came to bargain."

"Very well, what is it you have that I should want?"

"You and your predecessors have been seeking an alliance with the tribes of the Eastern Mountains for more than a hundred years. A trade relay would be of great value, particularly one bearing a strong force in the mountains that could assist with that nasty drauglic problem."

Once again, Privoth hid his surprise well. "That would be a valuable deal, indeed—one that I do not believe you are capable of delivering."

"For Cael, it will be so," Rezkin said.

"Why do you want it?" Privoth snapped.

Rezkin smiled. "We are refugees. It is our *home*. What would one *not* do for one's home?"

Privoth scoffed. He glanced at the assembly, pausing on the rows of councilors and military officers and then on his four daughters who were present out of the eight. When he turned back, Rezkin could see that he had not been swayed.

"What you offer is a worthy price, but I do not accept. There is something else of greater value, and I will accept nothing in its stead."

Rezkin had anticipated a counter offer but not complete rejection. As such, he was left in wonder as to what Privoth would demand. He did not like entering negotiations lacking such knowledge. Regardless, he gave the king a knowing look and said, "What is your price?"

"The Sword of Eyre."

Rezkin waited, but nothing more was forthcoming. It was not at all what he had expected. He schooled his features to appear unfazed; but, truly, he was at a loss.

"You desire the Sword of Eyre? The sword that is said to rest beside your very own throne?"

King Privoth frowned but glanced back at the councilors. He balled his fist and looked back to Rezkin. "The sword beside the throne is a fraud—a blight on my house. The real Sword of Eyre was stolen on the day of my father's death. I *will* have that sword returned, even if I must bargain with you to get it!"

"You would trade Cael for a single sword?"

"It is not just any sword," Privoth shouted. "It is the Sword of Eyre!"

Where previously stood a sensible military commander, now brooded a fanatic. The man's behavior was in contradiction to all the reports Rezkin had received.

He cautiously said, "I understand the sword has mythical significance—"

"It is not a myth!" Privoth said. "The sword is bound in prophecy. As such, this kingdom is bound to it as well. The prophecy is as old as the kingdom."

"Gendishen is eleven hundred years old. The Sword of Eyre was forged only two hundred years ago," Rezkin said.

"*Of course,* the sword did not exist when the prophecy was spoken," Privoth said, as if it were obvious. "And still the sword exists, and every king since its creation has ruled with it at his side, knowing that he could be the king of prophecy—every king but me!"

"But the prophecy states that the sword will burst aflame," Rezkin said, "and the kings of Gendishen do not bear the *talent.*"

"It is not the demon-cursed scourge that impels the prophecy, but the might of the Maker's cleansing power. Oh, I have spoken with the purifiers. I know that the scourge fire cannot be embedded in a blade, and the afflicted cannot brace the fire to the blade long enough to satisfy the remainder of the prophecy. It is proof that the Maker's grace and the blood of a mighty ruler of Gendishen is that which will bring forth the glory foretold in the prophecy."

"What is the remainder of the prophecy?" Rezkin asked. Although the beginning was common knowledge, a story told in legends, the final passages of the prophecy had been kept secret for so long, most believed them forever lost.

The king's gaze cleared as if night had abruptly turned to day. "It is none of your concern." He shook a finger at Rezkin and said, "Do not think I am unaware of what happened to my men. You came up from the coast where three purifiers and a double patrol disappeared, ten of them turned to stone! As soon as I was told of your arrival, I knew it was you! You and that demon cursed!"

Rezkin shrugged with nonchalance and said, "We were on a peaceful, diplomatic mission, during which we were unjustly detained and assaulted on our way to meet with you, the king. We had every right to defend ourselves."

"I do not need your excuses. It is because of this that I think you might have a chance at succeeding. If you fail, a thorn will have been plucked from my side, and I will have lost nothing. Bring to me the Sword of Eyre, and Cael is yours. I think you will not be so eager once you learn of its taker."

Indeed, the news was grim. Rezkin had no desire to contend with Privoth's problem, but it was the price he had to pay to acquire Cael and maintain peaceful relations with both Gendishen and Channería. Privoth dismissed the court; and, at Kessa's assurance that the guards and purifiers would be ineffective, he begrudgingly instructed them to go as well. Only the king's personal guard and the old woman remained for the revelation. Rezkin later regretted that he could not have dismissed his own entourage for this particular news.

Once Privoth revealed who had stolen the sword, he turned away to instruct his guards to gather an escort. Kessa stepped closer and brushed her frail fingers across Rezkin's hand. She held his gaze, her focus so intent he thought she might have been trying to communicate with him through her mind, and he was disappointed that he could not hear her. She said, "I wish for your success and hope that you return safely with the prize so that you may help your people—*all* of your people."

The king called the old reader away, and she departed without another glance. The armed escort led Rezkin and his party to a guesthouse where they were to stay the night. The place was barely a step above servants' quarters with only two small rooms besides the common room and a single hearth to heat the entire structure. The furnishings were functional, and by the layer of dust that had accumulated, it appeared the place had not seen company in quite some time. It also had no cistern or running water, so Farson stepped out to search for the well. Since Wesson's status had been exposed, he was free to ward the residence against eavesdroppers and uninvited guests.

"This is an insult!" Malcius grumbled.

"It is meant to be," Kai said as he piled a few logs onto the hearth.

Malcius slapped dust from the seat of a chair with an equally dusty rag he had found in a cupboard. "You are a king, Rez. You should not put up with this."

"To react would be to let him win," Rezkin said. "He is a military man. To complain about these lodgings, which are luxurious compared to an army camp, would be to admit weakness."

"How did they get so many *readers*?" Wesson said to no one in particular. "They are so rare!

Rezkin found a cauldron in a cabinet beside the hearth and began wiping it clean.

"What are you doing?" said Malcius.

"Is it not obvious? I am cleaning the pot so that we can make dinner."

Sergeant Millins gingerly walked over, offering to perform the task, and Rezkin acquiesced only because he had other concerns.

Wesson mumbled, "Perhaps it is unlike other *talents* and breeds more strongly in the blood."

"Why would you need to make dinner?" Malcius said. "We are on palace grounds. We are guests, even if they do not care to have us here. I am sure they will prepare a meal for us."

"We will not be eating anything they serve," Rezkin said. "You should know better."

"So, lame travelers' stew again?"

Rezkin glanced up from inspecting the underside of the table. "Lame? I thought you liked my stew."

Yserria sat down in the chair Malcius had just finished dusting, much to his chagrin, and said, "Ignore him. He is a spoiled noble who doesn't appreciate what others do for him."

Malcius's eyes widened in fury. "I could lash you for such insolence!"

Yserria laughed. "You think you could? I'd like to see you try."

"So would I," said Brandt with a snicker.

Malcius blurted, "Rez, this woman is insufferable."

Yserria batted her lashes and said, "Oh, *Lord* Malcius, do you always go running to *daddy* for help?"

Malcius spun around and growled in frustration. When he turned back, he waved a hand at the woman and said, "You look stupid made up like that, by the way."

Yserria stood and narrowed her eyes at Malcius, a retort hanging on her lips.

Rezkin could not see what Malcius found offensive in her attire. He went back to examining the contents of the trunk beside the divan and said, "I think she looks powerful and sensuous—a goddess of war."

His senses went on alert as the room suddenly became still and silent. He glanced up to see everyone staring at him. Yserria's face flamed nearly as red as her hair. Malcius gave her an uncomfortable glance and then stomped into the adjacent room, slamming the door behind him.

"What?" Rezkin said.

No one said anything, but Farson stood in the doorway with a smirk, shaking his head.

He thought for a moment and then looked at Wesson. "I think they are stealing them."

Wesson blinked several times as his brain worked to catch up. "Um, what?"

"The readers. You said they are extremely rare in all the other kingdoms. Master Reader Kessa did not join Privoth willingly. I think they may be hunting and kidnapping them."

Wesson nodded. "Yes, that would make sense. It would be even easier considering readers are apparently born with ability to see the *talent*. It does not activate in them later in life, like other mages, although their other powers will if they have any. Not all readers can perform spells. When I first met Master Reader Kessa, she explained that the more powerful the reader, the smaller the chance of his or her having any other affinities. It also would make them easier to capture and control. Plus, if they take them very young, they can raise them to believe in their twisted doctrine."

Brandt said, "If they hate magic so much, why do they want the sword? What good is it if they do not believe in the prophecy?"

Kai sat in the chair Yserria had vacated and said, "Oh, they *believe* in magic. They believe in the prophecy, *strongly*, I might add. They just hate power they cannot control, and the prophecy is a favorable one for the king."

"I thought prophecies were myth," Brandt said. "I have never heard of any prophets. Not real ones, anyway."

Rezkin said, "According to ancient Adianaik texts, prophecy is reserved for the Blessed of Mikayal, the God of the soul and knowledge—also sometimes referred to as the God of war. Mages are the Blessed of Rheina, the Goddess of the firmament and the Realm of the Living, and thus they do not possess the power of prophecy. I have not heard or read of any Blessed of Mikayal since the prophecy of the sword was foretold. That prophecy was recorded twelve hundred years ago by a Knight of Mikayal, although he noted that he was not the prophet. He was merely one of the Graced."

"Graced? Blessed? What does that all mean?" Brandt said.

Rezkin noted the brown and black feline that abruptly jumped from outside to sit on the window sill beside where Minder Finwy was standing. The others stared at the cat as well. He knew that everyone was unnerved by the furry little creature that tended to appear and disappear at will and seemed to follow him everywhere without trouble, but it was a conversation he was not ready to broach.

"It is a long story," Rezkin said. "It is a tale of the beginning of time and of the land and of the sky—of different realms and of all the peoples who have dwelled within them. In this realm, the Realm of the Living, the story does not begin with humans. There were ancient beings and peoples long before us. That is the tale of the Ahn'an, Daem'Ahn, and Ahn'tep. Unfortunately, the few remaining records of such things were poorly preserved, and most of the knowledge has been lost with time. What I have been able to put together would not do the story justice." He glanced at the cat that watched him with interest and said, "I hope to be able to fill in the blanks someday." The cat blinked lazily, and he might have imagined that it grinned.

Rezkin surveyed the room. Wesson and Brandt were fixated on his telling, Millins was filling the cauldron with the water Farson had collected, Jimson had gone out to retrieve more, and the minder, Farson, and Kai were watching the cat, which was just being a cat. Yserria sat at the table with a small bowl of water rubbing furiously at the paint on her face. It was now smeared in a grey mess, as if she had stuck her wet face in a pile of ash. She would not meet his gaze, and he thought it had nothing to do with the paint.

4

Hilith Gadderand dropped her bag as she stepped down from the gangplank onto the blessed ground. She stumbled as the solid stone of the dock seemed to sway beneath her feet. Smoothing her skirt in vain, she surveyed her surroundings. The grandest doors she had ever seen stood open to reveal a chamber large enough to fit her entire estate—well, what used to be her estate. Now, it belonged to the Raven, like everything else in the Ashaiian underworld, including *her*.

Small white specks were shuffling about the chamber, moving crates and bags, sweeping, and cleaning. She narrowed her eyes for a better look, and then one of the white specks turned toward her. As it got closer, she could see its pasty white skin, long claws, and sharp teeth more clearly, and she began to backpedal. Just before it reached her, she bumped into something that stopped her retreat, and she yelped. She looked up to see a handsome blonde looking down at her.

He said, "Careful, my lady. You would not wish to fall into the water."

"Oh, that thing!" she said pointing to the creature that seemed to be grinning up at her with pleading, pale blue eyes.

The man took her elbow and moved her aside as he bent to retrieve her bag. He handed it to the little white creature who grasped it with care as it waited. "He will not harm you," said the big blonde. He tilted his head as he looked at her again. "Have we met? You look familiar."

She blinked at him and realized he was wearing the uniform of a soldier but with an unfamiliar tabard. She hated when she ran into people she was supposed to know but could not remember. Who was she supposed to be? "Um, I-uh—"

The man smiled as his gaze lit with knowledge. "Lady Gadderand. I remember you, now, from Port Manai."

"Oh?" she said, still not making the connection.

He smiled and said, "I would not expect you to remember me, my lady. You were rather preoccupied with Lord Rezkin at the time."

Hilith flushed, a rare reaction for her, but she could not deny her attraction to the mysterious young lord. She said, "He is a most distracting individual."

"Many concur," said the guard.

After an uncertain glance at the little white creature, Hilith turned to the man and gave him her full attention. Her appreciative gaze blatantly roved over his form, and she said, "*You* are an impressive specimen, as well. Your name, sir?"

The man gave her a polite bow and said, "I am Second Lieutenant Drascon of the king's army. It is a pleasure to make your acquaintance, Lady Gadderand."

"Yes, of course it is," she said playfully. "But, the King's Army—here?"

He motioned toward the massive opening in the mountain and said, "Welcome to Caellurum. I serve the King of Cael, True King of Ashai."

"It is true, then? I was there when the mysterious Dark Tidings announced his claim to the Ashaiian throne, and I heard rumors of the new kingdom." Hilith placed the back of her hand to her forehead and swooned. "It was a dreadful voyage. We had not even been allowed to disembark in Serret before more refugees were shoved onto the ship. We were held there for weeks before we were finally sent to Uthrel. We had no guarantee a ship would collect us once we were there. They said that if none arrived, we would be sold to the slavers. I have been terrified for months."

"I am sorry for your troubles, my lady, but at least you managed to escape Skutton. Many were not so fortunate."

She laid a hand on his arm and said, "Thank you, Lieutenant, your concern is heartening. Such sentiments are rarities these days." With a fearful edge that was only partially feigned, she said, "But, what of this new king—Dark Tidings? Is he severe? Will he be gracious? What will become of me—of all of us?"

The lieutenant said, "He is certainly severe with his foes but seems gracious enough with those in his charge. I am sure you have little reason to worry since you are already acquainted."

"I know the king?" she said, genuinely surprised.

"Yes, the Lord Rezkin is now our king."

"Lord Rezkin?" she mumbled in shock. "But he is so—um …"

"Young? He may be young, but he is more knowledgeable than anyone I have ever met. Please, Lady Gadderand, follow me. I will personally see that you are assigned decent quarters."

"Thank you," she said absently as she followed the lieutenant. The little white creature scurried after them, lugging her bag, and he seemed overjoyed to be doing it.

Hilith had no such feelings. She was supposed to stay close to Lord Rezkin, to keep an eye on him. How was she going to get near the *king*? Prior to this assignment, she had never even heard of Lord Rezkin. He was no one—insignificant. She had chased the mysterious man the length of the Tremadel, through battle and misery, and across the Souelian Sea, only to find that he was completely out of her grasp.

She had thought the Raven's assignment was meant to punish her—to get her out of the way; but now it seemed a pivotal role. The Raven had to have known. It could not be coincidence that the Raven had proclaimed his support for the True King and that the True King was the very man to whom she was supposed to ingratiate herself. She was now certain that the Raven would reappear; and, when he did, he would expect her to deliver.

Hilith was shaken from her thoughts by the mesmerizing display of glowing crystal mosaics, and she nearly bumped into the lieutenant when he stopped to allow a couple of women pass in front of them. Something tickled her memory, and then a flutter of hope snaked through her.

"Lady Frisha!" Hilith said as she rushed forward.

The young woman paused and looked at her with surprise. "Uh, L-lady Gadderand?"

Hilith took Frisha's hands in an overly familiar grip and said, "It is good to see you well. I was so very concerned for you—for you and all your companions. Please tell me you all made it to this wondrous refuge safely."

Frisha's confusion was instantly replaced with melancholy. "Thank you for your concern, Lady Gadderand, but no. My cousin, Palis, did not make it. He was"—her eyes welled with tears—"he was killed in the escape."

Although unexpected, Hilith was glad for the boon. "Oh, you poor dear," she said as she stroked Frisha's hair. "I know what it means to lose someone you love dearly. If you ever need to talk—or just sit in silence—with an empathetic friend, I would be honored to be of service." Frisha shied away, and Hilith pulled her hands back with a gasp. "Oh, I am so sorry, Lady Frisha. I only just found out that you are to be queen!"

Frisha shook her head. "Oh, I—"

Hilith fluttered her hands as if flustered. "I have acted inappropriately. Please forgive my lack of formality. It has been an arduous journey, and I am out of sorts."

"Of course, Lady Gadderand. You are most welcome here. It is good to see that you are well, but I am sure you must be terribly exhausted." Frisha waved to a man who had several pouches tied to his waist, each overstuffed with scrolls. "We should see that you are assigned quarters immediately."

Drascon said, "I was just escorting Lady Gadderand to the quartermaster."

"There is no need. I will make the assignment," said Lady Frisha. She looked at Hilith. "We all share quarters here—at least for now. We had a bit of trouble some weeks ago, but it seems to be over, so we shall not worry you over it now. Still, it is better if someone knows where you are at all times. You may share quarters with Lady Evena in the ladies' wing of the palace." She smiled and said, "You will only be a few doors away from mine."

Hilith's grin was genuine. Things were going better than she had hoped.

Rezkin sat at the table in his suite poring over the map. Like all maps, it was slightly different from those he had previously studied. Some cartographers were better than others, and maps that had been reproduced were not always as accurate as the originals. This one had been provided by Privoth, and it was a far more recent and detailed accounting of eastern Ferélle than he had expected. It seemed Privoth had been planning this for some time.

He glanced out the window as something bright captured his attention. A woman in a long, flowing red skirt ambled from stall to stall examining the wares. The vibrant red fabric rustled in the breeze, and it reminded him of the ten statues standing in a ring in a plantation courtyard beneath a flowering vine. He did not know why his thoughts should go to those men now. They were no longer of consequence. A loud clap sounded in the distance from the direction of the docks, breaking him from his reverie, and he went back to examining the map and making notes. Several minutes later, he heard a *rat—tat, tat—tat, tat, thump*. He rounded the table to admit his companions.

Kai entered first, lugging one end of a squirming, overlarge burlap sack. He was followed by Farson, who maintained a tight grip on the other flailing end. They tossed the lump onto the settee, and Kai laughed as the subject struggled to free himself. Farson leaned against the wall with a bemused smirk. His face straightened as soon as he met Rezkin's hard gaze. Rezkin had not yet figured out the striker's intentions, but he would be prepared upon revelation.

A head of shaggy brown hair emerged, and Tam shouted, "Hey now, what was that all about?" His gaze landed on Rezkin, and his face brightened. "Rez! You're here!"

Before Rezkin could reply, Tam began a rambling monologue of his experiences in Uthrel over the past few weeks. "And then he just threw his ale, and what was I supposed to do?" He blinked at Rezkin, but the question seemed to be rhetorical because he did not wait for a response. "Now, I know I was supposed to keep a low profile, but come on! I was drenched, and the Golden Dripper's ale smells like piss. So, I—"

"Tam—"

"—told him I'd meet him out in the alley and we could settle it like men, and then—"

"Tam—"

"—well, you know, he got all huffy saying he wasn't gonna wallop some desperate refugee kid—"

"Tam—"

"You know that's what they call us, now, right? Every Ashaiian outside of Ashai is called a refugee. It doesn't matter if they're here on legit business—"

Rezkin raised his voice, "Tamarin Blackwater!"

Tam's rambling abruptly stopped as he stared at Rezkin. "There's no need to shout, Rez, I'm like four feet from you."

At that, Farson burst into laughter.

Rezkin stared at him in wonder. "You find this humorous?"

"Yes, yes, I do," the striker said. "That young man has no idea who you are, and to hear him scold you in such a way, and you just stand there … I am almost inclined to believe he is actually your friend."

Tam huffed and squared off with the striker. "I *am* his friend. Who are you to talk? You trained him. You're like the only family he's got, and all you ever do is talk about him like he's some evil menace. I may not know everything about him, but I know he's a good person and a good friend."

Farson looked back at Rezkin. "You have done well, even managing to incite true loyalty. I wonder how long it will last."

Rezkin gripped Tam's shoulder halting his response. "Pay him no heed. We have more important things to discuss."

Tam threw the striker a vicious glare. "I don't know why you let him stick around."

Rezkin returned to his place behind the desk and leaned over the map. He met Farson's gaze over Tam's shoulder and said, "Better to keep your enemies close." Farson clenched his jaw and then looked away. Rezkin said, "Let us move on."

Tam said, "Why did you kidnap me?"

"You are not supposed to be associated with us. You are here to spy. We did not want anyone seeing you enter the building." Rezkin glanced at the strikers. "Your abduction was probably overkill. I might have erred in allowing Kai to choose the method."

Tam scowled at the grinning man and then turned back to Rezkin. "Don't you think dragging an unwilling person through alleys in broad daylight is kind of obvious?"

Rezkin shrugged. "Gendishen takes a hands-off approach to slavery. They do not engage in it but do not interfere, either."

"So, they just let people be kidnapped?"

"No, I am sure these two"—he motioned to the strikers—"were surreptitious, but the few people who might have seen would probably rather not get involved. Now listen."

Rezkin briefly explained the nature of his mission, and Tam was almost bursting with excitement.

"A mythical sword? A *real* mythical sword. From prophecy. I can't wait! When do we leave?"

Rezkin shook his head. "You are not going."

He watched as Tam's entire world collapsed with those four words. "What do you mean, I'm not going?"

Rezkin sighed. "It is a ridiculous task. The sword cannot be *magical* in the way described in the prophecy."

"What do you mean?" Tam said, refusing to be deterred. "There are plenty of enchanted swords. *You* have enchanted swords."

Rezkin glanced at Wesson, who had been practically hiding in the corner while maintaining the sound ward. The mage looked up, startled by the sudden attention. "Oh!" he said and leapt from his chair.

Wesson cleared his throat. "Ah, where to start. Well, you see, certain enchantments like preventing rust, maintaining a sharp edge, or strengthening against breakage are intended to preserve the material already present. They do not change the nature of the substance itself. Other enchantments, like the bond, those used for tracking items, or those that prevent people from using the weapons are personal enchantments. They are designed to draw power from whoever is handling the weapon. They can store a certain amount of power, but eventually, the spells will fade.

"The Prophecy of Eyre states that all of the Souelian will be swallowed by darkness, an invader will sweep across the lands; and, if left unchecked, it will consume the world—or something like that. I was never very good with poetry, and of course, prophecies are always told by poets. Or maybe we only remember the prophecies that rhyme. Anyway, it goes on to say that a great king of Gendishen will lead an empire in the fight against the evil. We will know him because he will bear a magical sword, the flaming Sword of Eyre, that will burn with the cleansing power of the Maker. Again, I am paraphrasing. There is supposedly more to the prophecy, but it has either been lost or the Gendishen have been spectacular at keeping the secret.

"The problem is we cannot enchant blades to bear fire. The elemental powers are earth, fire, water, and air. A fifth power is life, but we do not generally refer to it as an element. I do not know why. Ah, that is not important right now. The point is we cannot force one element to power another element. Earth and fire are often in confluence, but they both exist separately in their interactions or combine to form something new. If we add fire to metal, it gets hot, becomes soft, and then melts. The metal's form is not sustained. To preserve the blade, we would have to add a protective shield, which would keep the metal and fire separate."

Tam nodded vigorously. "The blade would be surrounded by fire, but the fire would not be *in* the blade. Wouldn't that satisfy the prophecy?"

Wesson shook his head. "No, because the metal cannot power the fire. They are two different elements, and they would be separated by the shield anyway. So what would power the fire?"

"The wielder?" Tam said.

Wesson nodded. "It would have to be, but there are a few problems with that. First, it would mean the sword itself is not enchanted; second, none of the kings of Gendishen are mages; and third, the wielder would have to be a mage with a significant affinity for fire. I am such a mage, so I know how difficult it would be. Creating fire can be sloppy—a quick light of a candle flame is easy, but you could just as easily burn down a forest. Igniting a sword, maintaining the shape, controlling the size and extent of the flame, fueling the flame—would all require extreme focus. Plus, you must avoid setting yourself on fire. Just because we generate the fire does not mean we are immune to it. We must integrate wards into the fire spells to shield ourselves. Plus, to generate fire, you are using a lot of vimara, and the well is not infinite. *I* am an extremely powerful fire mage, and even I would only be able to maintain all those spells for a brief time. It would last a few minutes at most."

"Is that not long enough?" said Tam.

"No, it is clear from the prophecy that the sword will burn for the duration of the war. I am telling you, it is not possible to enchant a fire sword. If it were, every swordsman would have one. They would burn down the kingdom."

"But, it is a prophecy! It must come true."

Rezkin handed Tam a cup of water. He said, "You are getting worked up over nothing, Tam. I have read many so-called prophecies, and I have yet to find one that came true. They are spoken by charlatans to earn fame or reward."

Tam was crestfallen. "Then why look for the sword?"

Rezkin shook his head. "It is what Privoth wants. The Gendishen are fanatical about the prophecy. I am sure you can understand why. Somehow Gendishen gains an empire and saves the world. It is a fantasy tale."

"Then, at least let me go with you," Tam pleaded. "So what if the sword is a fraud. It will be an adventure, nonetheless."

"This task is too dangerous, and you already have the attention of too many who might wish you harm. Besides, I need you here."

Tam's face screwed up in anger, he balled his fists, and then he lurched to his feet before proceeding to pace rapidly in front of the table. "No. No! *You* were undefeated in the King's Tournament. *You* have met with *two* foreign kings. *You* saved a princess. *You* claimed an ancient palace of legend. *You* have dead elven wraiths bowing to you. Now, *you* are being sent on a quest to retrieve a magical sword of prophecy." He spread his hands and stared at Rezkin. "Where was *I*? You said I could join you in your adventures, but you leave me out every time!"

Rezkin frowned. "I had no intention of leaving you out of anything. You have been at my side for most of those events."

"No, I wasn't *at your side*. I was *being safe* on the ship or *being safe* in the stands or *being safe* in the warehouse."

Rezkin shook his head. "Perhaps you misunderstand my motives. I have not set out to have adventures. I am only carrying out tasks needed to fight a war against tyranny to make sure you all are safe."

"Exactly!" Tam said. "You are out saving people and fighting wars while I am stuck drowning in piss ale in musty taverns."

"Tam, your role here is not insignificant. Uthrel is a major shipping port, and with the current political climate, it is probably the most significant on the Souelian. How is your Gendishen?"

Tam paused with the abrupt change in subject. "It's fine. I mean, I'm doing okay. I don't sound like a native, and I can understand a lot more than I can speak, but I do okay. The mages sped up my learning, but it left me with a terrible, persistent headache. They said it'll go away, *eventually*. You had this planned since Skutton, didn't you? Everyone else was mourning Palis's death or gossiping about their troubles, but I was learning Gendishen."

Tam glanced down as drops of blood dripped onto his pants. He pulled a blood-stained kerchief from his pocket and held it to his nose. "I think I need to see a healer. These nosebleeds are coming more frequently."

Rezkin glanced at Wesson. The mage said, "How often?"

"Oh, about every other day. What do you think it is? Is something wrong with me?"

"It is probably just the weather," Rezkin said, and Wesson slid him a dissatisfied glance. "How about—"

"No, wait," Tam said. "You're keeping something from me. What is it? Does this have to do with the headaches?"

"You will be fine," Rezkin said.

"*Rezkin*," Tam snapped.

Rezkin sighed and leaned against the desk. "What the mages did to help you learn more quickly is not exactly … healthy."

Wesson frowned at Rezkin. "What he means is that it is dangerous and banned by the mage academy."

"What? You mean you're damaging my mind?"

Rezkin said, "Well, yes, but only a little. If it was safe, everyone would do it, and everyone would be experts in everything. The mages had to open a path into your mind, to your memory, which allows information to flow in unfiltered and become trapped there. The mind is not meant to work like that. In a few weeks, Healer Jespia and Mage Ondrus will visit to close the window and repair most of the damage."

"*Most* of the damage?"

"The body is resilient," said Rezkin.

"So, I have a magical hole in my head, *and* I was stuck in Uthrel while you were off fighting monsters and meeting with the king. I thought that if you did anything important in Gendishen, I would get to go with you, but *no*. Now you're off to … where are you going? Let me guess. You are going to fight a dragon or make a deal with the Fae Queen."

"The fae do not have a queen. They are led by the Ancients."

Tam scowled at him. "That wasn't the point. Where are you going?"

"Ferélle."

"What's in Ferélle?

Rezkin glanced at the strikers and said, "The Adana'Ro."

"Alright," Tam said with a huff as he plopped into a chair. "What's that?"

"It is *they*, and *they* are why you cannot go with me. The Adana'Ro are a guild of assassins."

"*Another* assassin's guild?"

Their attention piqued, Kai and Farson both looked at Rezkin quizzically. He ignored them.

"They are not strictly assassins," Rezkin said. "More like a political movement. In Ferélli, *adana* means *warrior*, and *ro* roughly translates to *the innocent*. They have an unusual definition of innocent, however. To them, there are people who understand the world, how it really works, people who have encountered death and murder and corruption. They are called the *ruk*. They are people who know how to swindle, lie, and cheat—the kind of people who know about assassins' guilds. People who know the darkness."

With less confidence, Tam said, "People like you."

Rezkin tilted his head. "Yes, people like me. People like *them*," he said with a nod toward the strikers. "But the Adana'Ro recognize a different kind of people—the *ro*, the people of light. People like you and Frisha, the Jebais, and Tieran."

Tam scrunched his face. "How can you call me innocent, Rez? I've killed before."

"That is how their definition differs from yours. The *ro* live in the same world as the rest of us but see it differently. Many of you know the darkness exists, but it is apart from you. Every once in a while, you are forced to interact with it. Maybe you are robbed or must kill in defense of a friend, but those times are exceptional to you. People like you see beauty and goodness in others, you seek adventure for the sake of adventure, and you believe that good will prevail. You walk in the light."

Rezkin glanced at Farson. "I was taught that the *ro* were inconsequential. In the real world, the light gets little done. To make a difference, one must travel in darkness. The Adana'Ro recognize this as well, but they believe the darkness should remain within the darkness. They believe it is their duty to protect the *ro* and not just in a physical sense. They protect the *ro* from becoming a part of the darkness, to preserve their innocence."

"But you said they are assassins. Isn't that hypocritical?"

"They walk in the darkness so you do not have to. *You* are *ro*, Tam, but I have been training you to be a warrior. I believe it is in your best interest to know about the world, about the darkness, so that you can protect yourself from it. I have introduced you to parts of the darkness you would never have known as a carpenter's apprentice. I have been actively drawing *ro* into the darkness, and not just you. In the eyes of the Adana'Ro, this is the most wicked of crimes."

"How would they know what you've been doing? Why would they care? Men are trained for the military or join up with thieves and bandits all the time. I don't hear about an army of assassins swooping in to save their innocence."

Rezkin sighed. "I attracted their attention a while back, and they have been trying to find and follow me ever since." He noted the shared look between Farson and Kai, and he knew they would have questions. "By the time I find them, they will have already figured out what I have been doing."

"So what? You're a king. You are supposed to create an army. That's what kings do."

Rezkin said, "They have other reasons to be interested in me."

. . .

While Tam might not follow through on that line of thought, Rezkin knew that, with the seed planted, the strikers would not stop until they knew his secrets. It was inevitable that they would figure it out, eventually.

"This is one of those things you're not going to tell me, isn't it?"

Rezkin tilted his head. "If *I* do not go to them, they will continue to seek me, and there is a greater chance one of you will get hurt."

"But you said they protect the innocent!"

"They seek to protect you from becoming one of us. Some of them would rather see *ro* dead than tarnished."

"So, you're saying that you're going into a den of assassins who hate you and would kill me so that I don't end up like them."

"Now, do you see why you cannot go with me?"

"How is the garden?" said Frisha.

Apprentice Mage Aplin Guel stood from where he had been planting new seedlings in the freshly tilled soil. He wiped his hands on his robes and tossed chocolate locks from his eyes.

"Greetings, Lady Frisha and Lord Tieran. The plants are doing well out here. We are still having trouble getting anything to grow in the city, though. I think maybe it has to do with the soil."

"What do you mean?"

"Well, soil needs decaying plant material, insects, worms and the like if new plants are to survive. Otherwise, well, it is just sediment. Nothing was living within the city for the longest time. Mage Morgessa is considering replacing what is there with fresh soil from beyond the corveua."

"That sounds like a lot of work."

Tieran said, "Show her your project."

Frisha forgave him the interruption upon hearing the excitement in his voice.

Aplin chuckled and said, "Ah, Lord Tieran, I do not think Lady Frisha would be interested—"

"Nonsense, it is fantastic. Show her."

Frisha smiled at the mage's endearing embarrassment. Aplin was a handsome young man a few years her senior. According to his masters, he already had several accomplishments to his name, not that he ever spoke of them,. Aplin was not the sort to brag.

"Yes, my lord, if you insist." He glanced at Frisha and said, "Please, come this way, Lady Frisha."

Little white creatures scurried between them, lugging pots and gardening tools to various parts of the garden. The mage led Frisha and Tieran around a path and through another garden to a newly constructed building that lay just outside the corveua. It had a stone frame and was open on the sides and top. She could not see them, but Aplin explained that the open spaces were covered by wards.

"We can change the wards to permit different amounts of light, water, and air."

"I suppose that sounds important," Frisha said. "I have heard that some plants prefer more light than others."

Aplin smiled. He smiled often, Frisha had noticed, and his smile was easy, genuine. "Yes, and this structure allows us to control many factors that are important for experimentation. I have never seen one so simple to maintain. Journeyman Battle Mage Wesson made the wards. I am ashamed to admit that, like the other mages, I was skeptical that someone with a natural destructive affinity could create anything this efficient and stable. These wards are much simpler in design than what I am used to seeing, and they require less frequent charging. I would love to be able to create something this refined."

"Have you considered working with him?" Frisha said.

"Me? Oh, no. I have not worked up the nerve to approach him."

"You are afraid to speak to Wesson? I'm sure he would be happy to meet you. He is knowledgeable and kind, very much like you."

"Th-thank you, Lady Frisha," he said.

His gaze dropped to the ground, and Frisha realized how her words had sounded even though she had spoken only truth.

Tieran cleared his throat. "Shall we see your work?"

"Oh, yes! Here," Aplin said as he skirted a massive table in the center of the structure, leading them toward the rear. On either side were long tables covered with potted plants, sacks of soil, pitchers, and gardening tools. At the end of the room was a small tree. Its trunk was bent, and its gangly limbs were twisted to fit within the confines of the building. The bark was nearly black, and the leaves were small, crimson things with many points. Amongst the leaves were orange and purple orbs of varying sizes.

"This is what I made," Aplin said, and Tieran grinned in appreciation.

"You made a tree?" said Frisha.

Aplin looked at the plant again. "Ah, I guess it does look like a tree now that it has grown. It is actually a mass of vines. They are so tightly entwined that it looks like a single, large trunk. I did not *make* it exactly. I mean, we cannot create life, but we do breed different plants together to develop new ones."

"Don't farmers do that kind of thing?"

"Yes, but *we* tweak them with vimara. Sometimes we are able to combine plants in ways that would not be possible under mundane conditions. It is like making a mage material, only with something living. We call them vimaral plants. Some mages do it with animals, but the practice is highly regulated by the Mage Academy, and it is almost impossible to obtain the necessary permits. There are fewer restrictions on creating vimaral plants. This one is a combination of the beans we brought on the ship and a plant one of the mountain men collected somewhere across the bowl." He frowned. "I think we are all tired of beans. We have not identified many edible native plants on the island, at least not any that taste good. Lord Tieran has been encouraging us to make something more appetizing."

Tieran grinned and rocked on his feet. "It is a serious priority."

Aplin reached up and plucked an orb the size of his fist. "They start out orange. As they ripen, they darken to purple. This one looks perfect." He handed the fruit to Frisha. "Go on. Try it."

Frisha bit into the orb and was pleasantly surprised by the sweet, tart burst of flavor. "Oh! This is amazing."

Aplin shook his head. "Yes, but you should probably not eat too much. They are quite intoxicating."

Frisha glanced down at the purple and orange delight as it dribbled succulent juice onto the dirt floor. "The *fruit* is intoxicating?"

Tieran grinned and plucked one for himself. He took a large bite and said, "Yes, the juice is like sweet wine. We do not even have to wait for them to ferment."

Frisha rolled her eyes and handed the fruit to the mage. "I should have known."

Tieran slapped Aplin on the shoulder and said, "He is a genius."

Aplin diverted his gaze. "I am only an apprentice."

"Well, you are far more knowledgeable and skilled than I," Tieran said.

"Oh, I doubt that, Lord Tieran. You have a significant *talent*."

"Technically, I am only an apprentice as well."

"Still, you are to be duke."

Tieran frowned. "A title I was not required to earn, and I have done nothing to deserve it." He shook his head and lightened his tone. "I give credit where it is due."

Frisha gave him an incredulous look and said, "No, you usually don't."

Tieran appeared surprised she would say such a thing, and Frisha was, too. He then turned to Aplin and said, "*You*—you have worked hard. My *talent* is raw, unrefined. This"—he gazed at the tree—"is a masterpiece."

Frisha glanced between the two men who were busy stroking each other's egos. She smiled and said, "This is all great, but weren't you trying to make *food*?"

"Come now, Frisha. Surely you can see the benefits. Cael needs exports. We will be the only kingdom to supply this wine, and we can do it faster and easier than anyone else."

Frisha pursed her lips. "Yes, but *they* don't know that."

Both men looked at her with uncertainty, not knowing if she was supporting or rejecting the idea.

She said, "Look, if only *we* are producing the wine, but everyone wants it, then it becomes a delicacy. Delicacies are expensive. Less is more."

"Ah," Tieran said. "I like the way you think. If we sell fewer bottles, the price grows higher."

"Exactly, but we have to be careful to maintain the proper balance. We sell only so much that people are willing to pay more to get their hands on them, but we must be careful not to drive the price so high that people lose interest. We will have to market it in such a way that the higher classes see it as a privilege to acquire but also so that their peers expect them to serve it at formal occasions."

Tieran chuckled. "I had no idea you were so adept at manipulating the nobility."

"Well, I am not an expert by any means, but I did listen to my father *sometimes*. He wanted to make sure I could run the businesses in case my future husband turned out to be inept. It's just that … well, I wasn't very interested, so I didn't pay enough attention."

Tieran rubbed the back of his neck. "I suppose I can understand that."

Frisha turned to Aplin. "Thank you for showing us your work. It sounds like what you've done is not easy. You should be proud of yourself."

"Thank you, Lady Frisha. You are most welcome to come back anytime."

As they strolled through the freshly cultivated gardens, Tieran said, "What do you really think?"

Frisha smiled ruefully. "I know little about plants. My home in Cheswick was in the city. We had a small herb garden, but mostly my mother and the maid took care of it. I think it did not require much maintenance."

A cool sea breeze, mixed with the scent of soil, fresh cut plants, and blooms, tugged at Tieran's tunic and ruffled the green scarf Frisha wore somewhere on her person nearly every day.

He said, "I try not to think of home often, but this place brings up old memories. We had many gardens on our estates. My mother enjoyed spending time in them, but she did not like getting her hands dirty. I had a private tutor in the *talent* for a while, but my father said it was beneath a duke to toil in the garden. *We have servants for that*, he would say."

"But, plants are your *thing*, aren't they?"

Tieran nodded. "Yes. My *talent* presented early. I was only twelve. I remember that, as a child, I always enjoyed spending time with my tutor in the garden. My father, however, spoke disparagingly of him. My father is so confident, so self-assured. He is the duke. People respect him. No one would dare contradict him." He sucked in a sharp breath and said, "The last time I saw my tutor, I was fifteen. I said to him, *If plants could grow coins, then your talent might be worth something*. It was what my father had said to me the night before at dinner. My tutor refused to work with me after that, and now that I look back on it, I cannot say I blame him."

Frisha had no idea how to respond, so she said nothing. They ambled along the path toward the palace in awkward silence. Eventually, her uncontrollable tongue got the better of her. "You surprised me back there."

"How so?"

"Well, you usually don't show much appreciation for those of lower station."

"He is a mage," said Tieran.

"Yes, not nearly a duke," she replied, "and he is only an apprentice."

"He has worked many more years on the *talent* than I. He has earned his place. What have I earned?"

"What have you *tried* to earn?" she said. Tieran again looked at her as if she had lost her mind for saying such a thing. She smiled playfully. "Oh, I don't really blame you. I can't say that I've done anything worth mentioning."

"I am the heir of a dukedom. You are much younger … and a woman. You are not expected to do anything."

Frisha nodded. "I know, but should I not *try* because it is not expected? To be honest, I never even thought about it. I knew I would marry and have children. All of my friends were the same, except Tam, of course. But, now I know women who are mages. Yserria is a swordmaster! Even Reaylin has worked hard to become a warrior. During all the time they were training and learning, what was I doing? Dreaming about my future husband is all. Worrying over how terrible he might be, hoping for the best."

"Perhaps you might have done more, but you still have time. And … there is one very big difference between you and me." He paused, and she with him. His gaze traced her face and then caught on the scarf. He started walking again and said, "You treat everyone well. You are always kind to them, and you are not afraid to speak on their behalf. Their stations in life do not seem to matter to you. You have done well with our task."

Frisha shook her head. "Rezkin put us *both* in charge, although I'm still not sure why he chose me."

"You are to be his queen," Tieran said, and she knew he had seen her wince. "People feel comfortable working with you. More come to you with their problems than to me. People like you."

"I am sure they like you, too. They are probably just intimidated by you," she said, her tone hopeful but not convincing.

Tieran turned his gaze to the road. "I think Aplin likes you." Frisha smiled, but he did not see since he was busy staring at the stones on the path, his brow furrowed in contemplation.

"I like him, too," she said. "He seems very nice."

Tieran shook his head. Without looking up, he said, "No, that is not what I meant."

Her cheeks heated, and Frisha suddenly found the path to be interesting as well. "Oh, I don't think he thinks of me like that."

"No? I doubt he would ever say it. No one wants to upset the king; and besides, I cannot imagine you would give up a chance to be queen for a mage."

"I don't want to be queen," Frisha blurted.

Tieran's head came up, and he stopped. "You do not wish to marry Rezkin?"

"No, that's not what I meant. I was only referring to the part about being queen; but, well, I'm not sure about the other either."

Tieran looked astonished, and he did not bother to hide it. "You cannot be serious. I know Rezkin would do pretty much anything to make you happy."

Frisha nodded slowly. "Yes, but I'm beginning to think he does it because he thinks he *has* to for some reason." She fingered her scarf and said, "He gave this to me when we first met. I thought it was a courting gift. Now that I know him better, I think he just didn't want me to get cold."

Tieran furrowed his brow. "That is the point of a scarf."

Frisha huffed. "I know, but I don't think he did it because he *cared*. I think it was just practical."

"I am not convinced, Frisha. He went to a lot of trouble to get the peerage—especially *me*—to accept you. You probably have no clue what he has done for you."

"No, I probably don't, but you said he wants me to be happy. What if I am not happy with him?"

Tieran was at a loss. "How can you not be happy with him? He is ... *everything*. He can *be* everything. Whatever you want him to do, he can do it."

"Can he love me?"

"What difference does it make? You were never guaranteed love. Nobles do not have the luxury of love. *I* will not have love."

She turned to stare across the bowl at the mountains beyond. "But we are no longer in Ashai. We are not bound by the rules of Ashaiian society. Rezkin makes the rules. Rezkin wants us to be happy."

Tieran spun, exasperated, and waved his arms as he spoke. His emotions began to erupt. "It is not so simple, Frisha. We are going back to Ashai. I have a responsibility to Wellinven. You will be married to Rezkin or whomever Marcum chooses. Rezkin will be king. Everything will return to normal."

"Do you really think that? We stand here, in a magical kingdom across the sea while war rages in Ashai. Do you really think anything will go back to normal?"

"Yes! —It will! —It must!"

His outburst was punctuated by a horn blast from the docks. Tieran took several deep breaths and then turned back toward the palace.

"Tieran—"

"*What*?"

Catching up to him, she said, "You won't tell him, will you?"

He met her gaze. His look carried as much turmoil as she felt. "No. Surely it is only cold feet. It is normal. You will come to your senses."

~

The chill slid over Rezkin's skin as soon as he had passed the corveua, and now that he was on the dock, he could feel it seeping deeper into his flesh and muscles. It was not the biting, frigid cold of winter, but rather the soothing, cool embrace of a pool on a warm summer day. He felt relaxed, like he had returned … home. He immediately checked the stone hanging from his neck, and it was still in place. After a quick test, he realized it was still protecting him from the worst of the calming effect.

His people had come to greet the ship, as usual. Many prepared to mount a defense in case the peaceful arrival was a ruse and the ship had truly been captured by insurgents. Rezkin realized that in the several weeks he had been absent, they had been afforded plenty of time to plot against him. He furtively scanned the faces around him, careful not to give away any clues that he might suspect betrayal. For each individual, he calculated the odds that he or she might want to do him harm, and two of the greatest threats approached him first.

Tieran bowed, and said, "King Rezkin, I am pleased that you have returned and appear to be well."

Rezkin studied Tieran. Did his cousin appear different from when he had left? He knew the display had been for the crowd's benefit, but were the words sincere? He doubted it could be so simple. At Tieran's side stood Frisha. She was wearing a dress, the loose skirt having enough fabric for her to easily hide a number of weapons. Was the green scarf over her head supposed to be a distraction? She smiled at him. Was it genuine? He thought he saw uncertainty in her gaze.

"King Rezkin, I, too, am glad to see you," she said as she performed a practiced curtsy.

Rezkin glanced at Tieran. He knew the other nobles had been working with her on her speech and language. The greeting was more formal than she would normally have given him, and it did not sound sincere. The stone on his chest heated, and his head began to clear of a fog he had not realized was present.

He blinked at the two, his cousin and his … betrothed? Again, he saw the uncertainty. He shook his head. It was apparent he was having another *episode*. He had nearly forgotten about them since he had not had one the entire time he had been gone from the island. It was a concerning revelation. His friends exchanged looks and shifted uncomfortably. He realized he had not yet greeted them, and everyone was waiting. He smiled.

"Greetings, Cousin," he said to Tieran. "Frisha, you look well. I trust all has been calm in my absence?"

"Oh, yes," Frisha said. "You will love the new programs we have implemented."

"You have implemented programs?" he said.

Tieran donned a cocky grin. "My hybridization project has produced promising results, and Frisha has negotiated a warrior training program."

Rezkin looked to Frisha. "*You* started a warrior training program?"

She lifted her chin and said, "What? You do not think I am capable? I recognize what you want for this kingdom, and I can help make it happen."

"Are you a part of this program?" he said.

"I am … sort of. I am trying, anyway. Actually, everyone is required to attend basic lessons. There are incentives for reaching advanced levels."

"And who is teaching these lessons?"

"That is being us," said a booming voice that echoed through the warehouse to the dock.

Just as the Eastern Mountains men approached, a black and brown fur ball shot past, scurrying between their legs.

Tieran said, "You took your cat with you?"

"No," said Frisha. "I have been feeding his cat. Where did that one come from?"

Gurrell and his men saluted Rezkin with a fist across the heart. "We teach the ways of the Eastern Mountains, a tribute from the Viergnacht Tribe to the people of our chieftain. Cael will be a great warrior kingdom!"

Rezkin's gazed passed over the two mountain men standing behind their leader and then came to rest on Gurrell. The man was a leader in his own right, and he had ample time while Rezkin was away to gain influence with the nobles and mages. He had obviously won over Frisha, somehow convincing her to allow him to train the people. What insidious betrayal was he planning?

Kai stalked by leading Pride from the ship as he grumbled about the ornery beast. The horse chomped its teeth and snorted at the striker as if it could understand. A flick of its tail lashed Rezkin's hand, jarring his thoughts from the murky fog that had silently invaded his mind. Inhaling sharply, he tilted his head to stretch the muscles tensing in his neck. He pushed the paranoid thoughts away, recognizing that Gurrell had never appeared to covet power.

"Excellent," he said. "The people of Cael are honored by your generous gift."

Gurrell and his men grunted in unison, a gruff, celebratory cheer. "If you are wanting to witness the training, we are meeting in the central square an hour after midday meal."

"Thank you for the invitation, but I have little time."

Frisha's eyes widened as the others disembarked, each leading a horse or two. "You brought horses?"

Brandt said, "Not just any horses. These are Gendishen reds. We stole them from the army."

"You did *what*?"

Brandt grinned. "Not to worry, Frisha. They no longer needed them since they were all dead."

Malcius punched him in the arm. "Shut up, Brandt. Why would you tell her that?"

Brandt looked at his friend. "You have completely lost the speck of humor you once had. Besides, she is going to hear the story. Not even *you* would keep it to yourself. We have war stories, Malcius. *Real* war stories."

Tieran said, "I thought you were going on a diplomatic mission to speak with the king."

Brandt grinned. "We did, but we had to destroy a double cavalry patrol and a horde of drauglics to get there."

"*Shut. Up.* Brandt," Malcius said. "If you want to tell war stories, you cannot tell the good parts first! You have ruined the story."

"You're both idiots," Yserria said as she passed.

Tieran sputtered. "You are going to let her speak to you like that?"

"You are welcome to try to make her stop," Malcius grumbled.

Tieran looked to his king. "Rezkin, are you going to do something about this? We have a hierarchy for a reason."

Rezkin watched the redheaded warrior trudge into the warehouse under the weight of her armor, weapons, and pack, while leading her newly acquired horse. She had not complained once during their excursion, and she had set aside her emotions to put up with undeserved criticism.

He looked back at Tieran and said, "Arrange a ceremony."

Rezkin dropped his belongings in his room and checked on Cat, who vibrated when he stroked her fur. After changing into a set of simple traveling clothes, he left the palace. Before anything else, Rezkin wanted to check the site of the battle against the demon. Although people kept constant watch on the area and were mapping the tunnels, he preferred to perform his own assessment. As he walked through the city, he had a sense of being watched. It was not an unusual sensation, considering the seventeen elven wraiths that inhabited the citadel, but this felt more substantial. He checked around every corner and in every shadow and still found nothing. Something about the island or the citadel made him suspicious, and the only way he had found to counteract it was the stone he wore around his neck. Even that was not completely effective.

He stepped beyond the corveua, taking the garden path around the city's perimeter toward the wooded area. The tenseness in his shoulders began to relax as he walked further from the citadel, and he realized that his concerns must have been in his mind. As he approached the drop-off that led to the pool where Yserria and the others had been held, he felt the thrill of battle energy burst through his veins. He felt a sense of motion in the air, a spurious whistle on the wind. He dodged then ducked behind a tree. He looked back the way he had come, searching for the source of the attack. Then, he surveyed the tree trunk to find a slim, silver throwing dagger lodged in its bark.

After calculating the direction of the projectile's source and maximum possible distance over which it could retain enough force to sink into the tree, with consideration of its size and probable weight, he realized the assailant had to have been within ten yards. Rezkin withdrew the small crossbow that was hidden beneath his cloak and made a circuit of the area. Despite his earlier sense of impending doom, he no longer felt the presence of another. As he returned to his original position, he spied Shezar and Millins walking toward him. When they reached him, Shezar's gaze flicked to the crossbow. Then, he examined Rezkin with a critical eye.

The striker said, "May we assist you, Your Majesty?"

"Yes," said Rezkin. "You can search for whoever just attacked me."

Shezar and Millins both tensed and glanced around them. Shezar said, "He got away?"

Rezkin surveyed the foliage as he spoke. "I never saw him. I sensed the attack and managed to avoid the knife he threw at me." He pointed to the tree, but the knife was gone.

Shezar and Millins both looked at the tree and then back to him. Shezar said, "We have seen no one out here besides you. Where is your escort?"

"I need no escort."

"My pardon, Your Majesty, but if you are being attacked—out in the open, no less—you should be accompanied by guards and at least one mage."

Rezkin considered the details of the attack. "I do not believe it was his intent to kill me. It was an excellent throw, well-practiced. Perhaps it was a warning or an announcement of his presence."

Shezar glanced back at the tree and then returned his gaze to Rezkin. "Are you sure it was an attack? Perhaps a branch broke—"

"I know an attack," said Rezkin. "It was a small, silver throwing knife, only slightly different from my own."

"Are you missing any?"

"No, and I own none like it." He eyed Shezar suspiciously and then dismissed the idea. The attack would have come from the wrong direction, and Shezar had been with Millins.

Rezkin stepped up to the tree. He could see a divot that *might* have been caused by the tip of a blade. With another glance backward, he ordered Shezar to lead the rest of the way to the demon attack site. Millins took the rear. Rezkin was uncomfortable with the man at his back, but Millins was slow. He was sure he would be able to fend off an attack from the sergeant.

In the receiving chamber of the makeshift throne room, Frisha looked at herself in the strange mirror. In the dark, the mirror was clearer than glass and she could see right through it, but the light of the lamp caused it to become reflective. The image was of her wearing one of the few gowns she had kept for herself. For this particular occasion, she felt a more somber appearance would be appropriate. It was not *her* ceremony, after all. *Her* appearance was not all that important. She had donned the black skirt with the fitted tunic bearing Rezkin's crest or, rather, the crest of Cael.

"Are you jealous?"

Frisha glanced at Reaylin. "No, of course not. Why would I be jealous?"

Reaylin shrugged. "It's *Yserria.* Tall, beautiful, exotic Yserria. *I'm* jealous."

"Well, I don't see any reason to be jealous," Frisha said. "I never really thought it through before. I mean, it was new and different and seemed exciting, but"—she glanced at the warrior chieftain standing across the hall—"since Rezkin has been gone, I have concluded that this is definitely something I don't want."

"I guess you know yourself best, but I think it's just an excuse. I didn't realize Rez was paying that much attention to Yserria—you know, after the thing with Palis."

"She deserves this. She is a strong warrior, and that is important in this new kingdom."

Reaylin said, "I still think it's weird that *you're* involved in the ceremony."

As Frisha turned toward the entrance to the largest chamber where a dais had been built, she said, "So do I." She then entered and stood upon the raised platform between Tieran and Ilanet.

Rezkin appeared at the entrance to the hall, and her thoughts of not wanting him fled. Even when he had been dressed in filthy traveling clothes and worn armor, he had been strikingly handsome, but the dark warrior king who looked at her now with ice in his eyes was something otherworldly. His confidence flowed with every graceful motion, a certainty of his being endowed each movement with intent. His fluid approach was on silent feet, and she briefly wondered if this ethereal man was, in fact, another specter forged of the mystical citadel.

He stopped in front of her, a few steps short of the dais. He gave her a slight bow and said, "I am pleased that you agreed to be a part of this. A public show of your support will be significant in the future."

Frisha caught herself staring at his lips and then reminded herself to speak aloud. "Of course, I am honored you would ask me, but I do not see how my involvement is important."

His topaz gaze was enchanting, and she could barely follow his words as he said, "Everyone knows of our betrothal. The people were already inclined to look to you for guidance." He glanced at Tieran and back. "It has been brought to my attention that you have gained the favor of many. Yserria is about to receive an official position of power. She, being a woman, will need your support."

"I understand," she said, "but I still feel uncomfortable with this."

"I know," he said, "but you will get used to it."

He then turned to greet Ilanet who stood, as both a visiting royal and Rezkin's ward, to Frisha's left.

Ilanet smiled and said, "Master Tamarin will be upset that he missed this."

"I have no doubt," Rezkin said. "He is already frustrated with me about not taking him on my next mission."

"Well, I am glad of it," she said. "I do not know where you are going, but it sounds like it will be dangerous. You will not leave Tam in Uthrel for long, will you?"

"He is performing an important task, but he will return once my business with Gendishen is concluded. Are you so eager for his return?"

She blushed. "He is my friend, the first I have had, I think. But, well, he has barely spoken to me since discovering who I am. I wish to make amends."

Rezkin said, "I will do my best to conclude the matter quickly." She smiled, and then he stepped onto the dais to take his position.

A few minutes later, the doors opened again, this time to permit the long train of guests. Rezkin's subjects approached first in pairs and were introduced formally by name and title as they bowed to their king. The visitors came next, seemingly appreciative of the spectacle. Once the audience was gathered on either side of the hall, two lines of the king's guard entered to take up positions along the path to the dais. Wesson strode up the aisle next, wearing a black fitted robe overlaid with black panels trimmed in red. Unlike the other mages, Wesson did not wear the sigil of Cael since he had never sworn fealty to Rezkin. Despite this, he took his position on the dais to the king's right, the position that was, by tradition, filled by the King's Mage or First Counsel, depending on the kingdom. While there had been many whispers about the journeyman being the king's choice for the position, and many more rejecting the ridiculous notion, this was the first time Rezkin had made his decision clear.

Since they did not have the luxury of a carpet, Life Mage Ondrus Hammel came next, dispensing fresh flower petals over the polished stone. As he passed, each one sprouted a tiny fragrant blossom of its own. Yserria entered next, followed by the three strikers, lined up as if to prevent her from turning for escape.

. . .

Yserria stepped into the hall, her bare feet cushioned from the cold stone by plush flowers. She had been shocked, anxious, and uncertain when Rezkin informed her of his decision. It was not an offer she would have considered rejecting, however. Her black dress dragged the floor as she strode up the aisle purposefully, with grace, the grace of a warrior. When she reached the dais, she saluted her king, as would any member of the royal guard, and lifted her chin in defiance, a silent protest against any who might reject Rezkin's decision. One such person was the man who spoke next.

Tieran looked at Rezkin sideways, as if making sure he still intended to go through with the *absurdity*, as he openly referred to the event. Rezkin's hard glare was confirmation enough. Tieran stepped forward and intoned, "Yserria Rey of the King's Royal Guard of the Kingdoms of Cael and Ashai, you have been summoned to appear today, in this hall, before the king and his subjects. Do you know why you are here?"

"Yes," Yserria said, glad to hear strength in her voice, rather than the fear that was quaking in her core.

"And do you accept this honor?"

"I do," she said, and again her words did not waver.

"Then kneel before your king," Tieran said.

Kai and Shezar approached on either side of her, placing over her head a black and green tabard, now with additional silver embellishment. A wreath of twisted black vines and crimson leaves was placed on her crown, and she looked up just as the black sword came to rest on her shoulder. Crystal blue eyes stared down at her like stars from above.

"For acts of bravery in multiple battles, for achieving mastery of the sword, for performance in your oath-bound duty and selfless defense of your king, and for saving the life of Malcius, heir to the Great House Jebai, I hereby raise thee to Knight of the Realm." Yserria blinked up at him, holding back her tears by force. He said, "You have already sworn the oath, so I will not require you to repeat it. You may rise."

She rose and turned toward the audience. Farson stepped forward to strap her sword about her waist. The handle had been rewrapped, and the scabbard adorned to represent her new station.

Rezkin said, "All see and know Lady Yserria Rey, Knight of the Realm."

The audience applauded—*most* of them—but before Yserria could take a step, the two priests of the Maker stepped into her path. The strikers immediately bristled but held their ground.

The minders bowed and then Elder Minder Thoran said, "This young and inexperienced king sees in you something that others would not. You are the first woman to be granted official knighthood in all the kingdoms of the Souelian, and he has done so without seeking the blessing of the Temple."

The elder minder scowled as Minder Finwy stepped in front of him. Finwy smiled and bowed again. "Lady Yserria, I have personally witnessed many of the accounts for which you have received this honor, and on behalf of the Temple of the Maker, I would like to bestow upon you our blessing. Would you accept?"

Yserria felt a flutter of joy for something she did not realize she had been missing. She said, "It would be a great honor to have the Temple's blessing."

As Minder Finwy raised his hand toward Yserria's head, an elven wraith appeared between them. Several people shouted, and Minder Finwy jumped back in fright. Although most had seen the wraiths from time to time from a distance, few had ever been confronted by one.

"This knight cannot accept the blessing of the tri-god," said the wraith.

Rezkin stepped down from the dais to confront the wraith, but Yserria was first to voice her discontent.

"What do you mean? Of course, I can. It is none of your business."

The wraith turned to her in the most disturbing way, its front becoming its back in a vaporous wisp. "To accept the Blessing of the tri-god, a knight of Caellurum must first prove worthy of the Blessing of the three Gods. This human"—it said with a stretch of its long, wispy finger toward Minder Finwy—"does not possess the power to bestow such a blessing."

Rezkin said, "Shielreyah Manaua, the blessing offered by the priest of the Maker is not one of power. It is a kind of metaphorical blessing. He offers the support and acceptance of their Temple. That is all."

The shielreyah turned to stare at Minder Finwy.

Finwy's jaw wagged several times before he finally said, "Only the Maker can bestow power."

Wispy tendrils shot out from the vapor and then wrapped back inward as Manaua communicated with the other shielreyah. Finally, he said, "This *metaphorical* blessing is acceptable."

With a puff, the shielreyah disappeared. The onlookers chattered and grumbled, and after a few minutes, Minder Finwy performed the blessing without interruption.

5

Rezkin slipped around the corner of the yard ahead of her. Frisha hurried to catch up, knowing how difficult it would be to find him again. The previous night's celebration had lasted nearly until dawn, and people were slow to rise that morning, thanks to Apprentice Aplin's wine. Frisha had not indulged, having spent the evening fretting over her own worries. She noticed that Rezkin had also abstained, which concerned her. If Rezkin chose not to do something, there was usually a good reason for it. He had risen early for training, as she knew he would, and now she was chasing him through the streets hoping to catch him alone for a private word. It was growing nearly impossible. She rounded the corner to find herself alone in a courtyard.

"Rezkin!" she called. "Rez?" She huffed in disappointment, knowing she would never find him. A part of her was relieved. She really did not wish to have this conversation, but at the same time, she really did. She turned to leave and nearly bumped into a wall of muscle. "Oh!" she sputtered with grace. "There you are. I—didn't hear you."

He raised his brow. "Did you need something?"

"Yes, um …"

Heat rose to her cheeks as she was suddenly at a loss for words. Broaching the subject was more difficult than she had thought it would be. Finally, she mumbled, "I was hoping to talk to you about … something. We haven't spoken in a while."

"We spoke yesterday," he said. "Several times."

She rolled her eyes. "Yes, but, I mean we haven't *really* spoken. You know, between you and me." He furrowed his brow in confusion. She said, "I guess I have some concerns."

His gaze shifted to scan the tops of the courtyard walls, and then his shoulders relaxed ever so slightly. "Very well, Frisha. What is it that concerns you?"

She dropped her gaze to his chest and immediately regretted it. He wore a thin linen undershirt that was unlaced down to his navel and soaked in sweat to translucence. She jerked her eyes upward, cleared her throat, and said, "Striker Farson says you know how to sing, that you can *serenade your love with the best of them*. He says you know poetry. Why don't you ever recite any to *me*? Why don't you sing for me, Rezkin?"

He tilted his head curiously. "Why would I?"

Flustered, she said, "Because I'm your girlfriend, of course!"

He nodded. "Exactly. Ballads and poetry are meant to coerce, to *entice* a lady into feeling a sentimental attachment. Why would I do that to you, Frisha? You are already my Girl Friend."

She thrust her hands onto her hips and scowled furiously. "So you think I don't deserve to be enticed?"

Rezkin looked at Frisha uncertainly. He had thought it strange when she followed him from the palace, but since Farson's name had graced the conversation, he knew this was more than the typical social call. With her hostile stance and angry gaze, this felt like a trick question. Slowly, he drawled, "No?"

"Oh! I can't believe you," she screamed before storming out of the courtyard.

A hearty laugh, followed by slow applause, erupted behind him from across the yard. Recognizing the voice, Rezkin inwardly groaned. He turned. "What do you want, Farson? Why do I feel like this was *your* doing?"

Farson strolled forward. As usual of late, he took no precautions, and Rezkin wondered if the man had already accepted his fate. Farson said, "You have no clue what just happened, do you?"

Rezkin furrowed his brow and glanced in the direction Frisha had fled. He considered bluffing, but he doubted the striker would buy it at this point, and he needed information. "No, it makes no sense."

Farson looked at him with a familiar expression, the one he had worn when Rezkin was young and unable to grasp a concept that should have been obvious. "She wants you to sing and spout poetry to her, Rez."

"Why would she want that?"

Farson chuckled. "You are asking *me* to explain women?"

Rezkin said, "You are a trainer. It is your job to explain."

Meeting his gaze, Farson said, "I *was* a trainer." He paused then seemed to think better of his next words. Looking away, he finally said, "I suppose it is for the thrill of it. People want to be drawn by another's desires."

"You are saying she *wants* me to manipulate her?"

The striker sighed heavily. "No, she wants it to be real, for you to express your *genuine* feelings."

"But I have none."

Farson's gaze hardened and his hidden contempt reemerged. "Therein lies the problem." The striker backed toward the gate and disappeared around the corner.

Rezkin stood in the courtyard alone for several minutes. He was not supposed to develop feelings for anyone, yet his former trainer seemed to disapprove, and Frisha was angry and hurt. He decided to focus on more immediate tasks. He finished collecting his personal supplies and then headed toward the docks to survey the progress on the ships.

Two ships now belonged to their armada, *Stargazer* and *Marabelle*. *Marabelle* had been a passenger vessel independently owned and operated by its captain. The collectiare in Channería had selected it for refugee transport because it was not associated with any of the great merchant companies and had no political affiliations. Rezkin had been told that one of the priests knew the captain personally and felt it unlikely the passengers would end up at the slave market. The *Marabelle*'s Captain Geneve had been determined to retain ownership, but Rezkin's offer was more than she could refuse, especially since she would maintain possession of the vessel. The *Marabelle*'s purpose was to shuttle passengers and supplies; while *Stargazer* was, at that very moment, being outfitted as a military vessel and its crew trained accordingly.

Carpenters, metal workers, soldiers, and mages worked with enthusiasm to complete the tasks assigned to them. Rezkin had thought most of the outworlders on the mainland lacked resolve, but this group seemed driven.

"Why do they work so hard?" he said as he watched the laborers.

Captain Geneve, a fiery Sandean woman nearing thirty, turned to look as well. She said, "They need something to keep their minds off their troubles."

Captain Estadd said, "Some of them seem to think that if they work hard, they'll get to go home."

"You do not believe it?" said Rezkin.

Estadd's shoulders tensed, and his expression was troubled. "I think too much has changed. It has *been* changing over the past couple of years, slowly at first. Maybe some of them will return home, but I believe they will not like what they find."

Rezkin narrowed his eyes as his gaze landed on a man who stood wrestling with a thin rope between two posts from which hung a half-made fishing net. He nodded in the man's direction. "Who is he?"

Geneve hummed under her breath as she thought. "I believe his name is Connovan. He came here with a woman on the last ship. He's a Channerían fisherman."

"What else?" said Rezkin.

Tiny, silver charms twinkled in her short, onyx hair as she shook her head. "He's good with rope. He's been making nets and lines for the ships. That's all I know of him."

After dismissing the captains, Rezkin watched the man work his way down the row of his net, his movements sure and practiced. After a few minutes, Rezkin stepped into the shade of the warehouse and headed toward the palace. He still needed to choose his companions for the next trip, and it would require careful consideration. If the Adana'Ro truly wanted him dead, he would not prevail against them alone. After witnessing the events at the Black Hall, they were unlikely to offer him the same courtesy.

He entered the palace through the kitchen, sending the staff into a tizzy. They provided him a meal, which he scarfed down quickly. He was still uncomfortable with eating food that he had not prepared; and, in that moment, his concerns were validated. His face heated like the midday sun and the roof of his mouth itched as though swarming with ants. He used his knife to shuffle through the items on his plate—a pile of beans, sliced potatoes, a few chunks of gamey meat, and a green vegetable he did not recognize. He waved to the cook. Before his throat swelled completely shut, he said, "Who prepared this meal?"

The head cook appeared a bit concerned, but he smiled. "It has been my pleasure to prepare your meal, Your Majesty." He nodded toward the other occupants of the kitchen, a young woman and man, each barely old enough to be considered grown. "My assistants helped." They both grinned and nodded enthusiastically.

Rezkin fished in one of the small pouches on his belt. He drew out a small packet and dumped its contents into a fresh goblet of water. Then, he opened a small vial and heated it over the candle the cook insisted he have for ambiance. He poured the warm liquid into the goblet, stirred it with the tip of his knife, and then forced the entire contents down his swollen throat. Meanwhile, the cook watched with worry.

Once his breathing eased, Rezkin rose from his seat and strode over to the pots that held the meal. He examined each one and then turned to the cook. "Who placed the beans on my plate from this pot?"

The cook said, "I did, Your Majesty. Is there a problem with them?"

"No," said Rezkin. "These are fine. Who entered the kitchen between the time you served the beans and I received my plate?"

"Ah, no one, as far as I'm aware. It's just us three right now. More are scheduled to arrive soon. If there is a problem with the food, it will be my pleasure to prepare you another."

Rezkin glanced between the three. One of them could be a Master of Deception, perhaps Adana'Ro or a member of the Order, but it was more likely they were innocent. He pointed to his plate and said, "Burn this." The man's face fell. Rezkin did not want to cause a panic, so he said, "This food has been tainted. Do not allow anyone to eat the scraps. The rest should be fine."

He requested an extra plate of scrambled eggs and then headed toward his chamber, only to be intercepted by another woman. Mage Threll stepped into his path with her arms crossed and chin held high.

"I heard you are leaving tomorrow." Her body language spoke of determination, but he had no idea what she wanted.

"Yes," he said.

"I"—she glanced at the plate in his hand—"Am I interrupting your breakfast?"

"No," he said as he lifted the plate of eggs. "This is not for me."

"Ah." She flushed and then cleared her throat as she said, "Do you plan to take my uncle?"

Rezkin had no desire to spend more time with the surly striker, but desire was rarely accommodated by necessity. "I have not decided."

"I am going," she said.

He tilted his head. "Why should I take you?"

She inhaled deeply and fisted her hands at her sides then said, "I came with you to Cael because I wanted to be a part of your cause. I believe you are trying to help Ashai, and I think you can pull it off. You need help from others, though. You have only just returned, and you are already leaving tomorrow. Since you are in a hurry, I can be of use. As you know, my affinities are for water and fire. I can fight in battle *and* make the ship travel faster."

Rezkin tilted his head. "You are trained to use your powers in battle?"

"Well … no, but fire burns. You do not need much battle training to do damage."

"What does your uncle have to say about this?"

She pursed her lips. "I am an independent woman. I do not need his approval."

Rezkin glanced at the plate of scrambled eggs and said, "See Journeyman Wesson. He is overseeing the mage force for the journey."

Mage Threll's eyes lit with excitement. "Thank you, Your Majesty. Um, would you like me to reheat those?"

He shook his head. "No, that is not necessary."

She grimaced, glancing again at the cold eggs, then looked back at him. "About Journeyman Wesson. If you do not mind me asking, why do you not raise him to Mage?"

"It is not my place to do so."

"You are the king."

"I am not a mage." He stepped around her but turned back just as she started down the corridor. "Mage Threll."

She turned. "Yes?"

"Do you love your uncle?"

She appeared surprised but smiled fondly. "Yes, he is the last of my family."

Rezkin paused and then said, "You are your uncle's weakness. If you fall, he will break."

Nanessy nodded slowly. "I know that you are right. I am *one* of his weaknesses; but, I believe that *you* are his other."

"He knows that I can defeat him."

She shook her head. "No, that is not what I meant." She started to say more and then seemed to think better of it. "I had best find Journeyman Wesson."

Rezkin continued down the corridor and finally made it to his quarters where he bathed and dressed. The cat stared at him as he went about his business, although he was not entirely sure it was just a cat.

He settled on the colorful rug someone had woven from scraps of fabric, crossed his legs, and sank into a meditative trance. He was deep in his memories, searching for information, when he was abruptly assaulted by a furry tail in his face. Cat had crawled onto his lap. It mewed and purred as it rubbed against him. He decided this creature was, in fact, the cat and that it desired to have its fur stroked. He picked it up and held it in front of him so that he could stare into its yellow eyes. It blinked lazily as it continued to purr. He had been told that felines could sense danger, and he wondered why it sensed none in him. Setting the cat down, he returned to his meditation. The little beast curled up between his crossed legs as Rezkin shuffled through the scenes of his past. Something—or *someone*—was out of place.

When he was satisfied with his conclusion, he donned his armor, secured the Sheyalins at his hips, and strapped the black blade across his back. He collected the plate that been licked clean and returned it to the kitchen. His vassals would have been frustrated with his insistence on performing the mundane tasks of feeding and cleaning up after the cat, but he figured it was his duty, since he had stolen the thing from its home. Even the shielreyah seemed to think it humorous when he had asked them to keep the furry beast out of trouble as it explored the palace. He supposed it did seem like a rather inconsequential task for thousand-year-old dead elves, but it was hardly a burden on them. On the other hand, they seemed incapable of finding the katerghen.

Rezkin turned down a corridor toward the room that had become his office but took only a few steps before he encountered Ilanet, who was accompanied by Xa. He glanced at the assassin suspiciously and then turned to the smallwoman.

"Greetings, Princess. Has your escort been with you all morning?"

Ilanet glanced at Xa and said, "Yes, we were visiting the new southern garden. It is beautiful in the early morning light. The ictali are so helpful, now that they are not trying to kill us. They are sweet and kind. I like them very much." She pulled a letter from her pocket. "I was coming to give you this. It was left by the table in the room I share with Frisha. It has your name on it."

Rezkin took the missive and examined the outside before opening it. It was a letter from Frisha. He had seen her writing before, and this matched precisely. Still, it was odd that she would send a letter to ask him to meet with her in the garden. He nodded at Xa as he spoke to the princess. "Was he with you when you found this?"

Xa looked at him quizzically and then glanced at the letter with a bit more interest.

"No, he had not come to my room yet," she said. "We could not find you, so we went to the garden for a while."

"You are sure he has been with you since then?" This time Xa scowled at him, as if he realized he was being accused of something.

"Yes," said Ilanet, "since we left my quarters just after dawn."

Rezkin looked at Xa and said, "Stay with her."

He turned from his intended destination and headed toward the garden. He had the sense that he was being drawn somewhere, but he could not discount the possibility of paranoia. He had always been sure of himself, but since arriving on Cael, he had begun to see enemies everywhere. He wondered why that would bother him so much. Prior to leaving the fortress, he had assumed that everyone was a potential enemy. What had changed?

There was a chance that Frisha was truly waiting for him. She did not possess the *Skills* to elude him, so it was unlikely she was the assailant. Shezar seemed to think he had imagined the attack in the woods, and the cook had been equally confused about the poisoning. No one had witnessed those events, and he was lacking evidence. This time, he had the note to prove his sanity.

The moment Rezkin stepped beyond the corveua, he was forced to swipe an arrow from the air. Two more followed. As he spun to avoid them, one cut through the ribbon at his nape, causing his hair to spill over his shoulders. He searched in the direction from which the arrow had come and caught only a glimpse of a fleeing figure. He was careful to remain cognizant of his surroundings as he ran after the assailant. He had no idea how many lay in wait. The cloaked figure scaled a garden wall with ease, glancing back, as if in challenge. Rezkin caught a glimpse of white teeth beneath the hood. The attacker had smiled at him. He followed the intruder over the wall and down the hill into a gully at the edge of the valley. The maze of steep embankments cut back and forth across a swath of dry streambeds. As he tracked the attacker, he caught sight of the figure in a channel adjacent to him. He knew it was only a matter of time before he lost track of the perpetrator.

At the next intersection, Rezkin ran up the face of the embankment, grasping roots, and digging his fingers into the loamy clay. He scrambled atop the broken earth, leaping over the crevices between the grassy blocks of the broken surface. A *scuff* to his right caught his attention. He leapt to the next block but heard the whistle too late. He was midair when the arrow caught him in the thigh. It was a glancing blow, a flesh wound, but he realized the assailant had somehow gotten behind him.

As Rezkin landed, he flung a throwing star toward his attacker. A hand whipped out from behind a block to catch the star and lob it back at him. Rezkin now knew for certain that the assailant had intentionally missed in the original attacks against him. The open attack, the poisoning, the letter—they were all intended to lure him beyond the corveua, to this place. He hugged the ground as he scanned and listened. Was it to be an ambush? Was it a test? How many intruders had invaded his island, and how had the shielreyah not known of it? He already had suspicions as to who his attacker might be. The method and motive were what eluded him.

The attacker obviously desired pursuit. Rezkin had a choice. He could continue to play the game, or he could wait for the attacker to come to him. If he chose the latter, he risked the intruder disappearing and bringing harm his people. Hugging the ground, he backed to the other side of the block and then slipped over the edge. His feet settled in the loose dirt of the streambed. He focused, casting his senses about his surroundings. His breaths were deep and long as he listened. The musky smell of earth hung strongly in the air. A slight breeze rustled the grass above, and somewhere in the distance, seagulls squawked. Then, he felt it—the slightest tingle. It was barely discernable from the natural buzz of the life that surrounded him. He padded toward the sensation on silent feet, slipping Kingslayer from its fur-lined sheath. The prickle that danced across his skin grew stronger, and its source shifted closer to him.

Rezkin raised his sword and struck as he rounded the block. His blade met steel as he came face to face with his attacker. The man ducked when Rezkin threw a punch. The man rolled to the side, out of Rezkin's reach and then attacked in an overhanded strike. Rezkin dodged as he brought his sword up under the man's extended arm toward his exposed side. Rather than twisting away from the strike, as would most, the man twisted into it, smacking Rezkin's blade away using a previously concealed dirk.

After the failed attack, the man whipped his dirk back, scoring the armor covering Rezkin's abdomen. Rezkin blocked a low attack, shifted feet, and kicked his leg up, arcing around to hook the man's neck. He locked the assailant's head behind his knee and blocked a strike from the dirk with his vambrace. He released Kingslayer and grabbed each of the man's arms, wrenching them so that they could no longer grip. He and the assailant fell to the ground with Rezkin wrapped tightly around the man.

To Rezkin's surprise, his attacker squirmed and shifted until he managed to free himself from Rezkin's grip. The man rolled to his feet, drew another hidden dagger, and stabbed at him several times as Rezkin ducked and dodged. Rezkin grabbed for the man's arm, but the man was fast. The battle energy simmered just below the surface in his chest. The stone that rested there warmed as he released the energy in a quick succession of hand strikes. Then, he spun low to the ground, sweeping the man's legs from beneath him. The man recovered quickly and issued his own attack. Rezkin noticed that the man's speed was dependent on Rezkin maintaining his distance. As he worked his way into the man's guard, he withdrew two knives. In a flurry of slashes, most of which the assailant managed to block, Rezkin began to overwhelm him. He ducked a punch, and in return, offered a sharp blow to the man's jaw. With another to the torso, the man went down. He quickly rolled away from Rezkin but remained on his knees looking up at him.

Rezkin was about to launch another attack when the man said, "If you kill me, you will never have your answers." Rezkin stepped forward, and the man backed away. The man said, "When you did not know who I was, I could excuse the exchange. Now that you do, I shall be forced to fight you to the death if you persist." Rezkin swept forward with unmatched speed, grabbing the man by the collar and placing a knife to his throat. The man said, "You should not close the distance unless you know I am unarmed."

"I am aware that you still possess multiple weapons. I am also aware that divesting you of those weapons would not make you less dangerous. You did not bring me here for a duel to the death. What do you want?"

The man smiled. "I want to give you answers—in exchange for a price."

"You are willing to share information?"

"On a few conditions," said the man. "Let me go."

"You went to a lot of effort to make me catch you."

"Yes, I have my reasons, but we should not have this conversation here. Release me, and I will come to your office with my companion in one hour."

Rezkin narrowed his eyes. "You are more likely to disappear."

The man shrugged. "If I do, you will catch me again."

"I do not have time for games," said Rezkin.

"Nor do I. It is imperative that you and I come to an agreement—for both our sakes."

Rezkin thought about the man's proposal for only a breath. While it was dangerous to allow him to live, he might be the only one in any of the kingdoms who could give him answers. He also knew that the man would not, *could* not, be taken into custody.

Rezkin released him and stepped back. "Very well. One hour."

An hour later, Rezkin stepped into his office. It was now furnished with a desk made of wood from the forest on the southern half of the bowl. Tam had constructed it for him and had even carved Rezkin's sigil into the front panel. An inscription of loyalty and friendship adorned the underside. It was truly a beautiful piece, and Rezkin thought that Tam would have had a successful future as a carpenter. Tam had said that he found woodworking to be boring, but Rezkin thought that if Tam had put as much care into his other projects as he had the desk, he would have been lauded a true craftsman.

The other furnishings were modest by comparison since few luxuries existed on the island. Rezkin was averse to having an office bedecked in fineries when there were so many residents in need of basic items, but his people seemed to find pride in the contribution. The chairs and sofa were hastily made, but he had been told they would be replaced when finer items had been crafted. The black and green swirled glass goblets had been created by the earth and fire mage Morgessa Freil, with the assistance of her apprentice Calen Loom, whose affinities were for earth and water. The vases on the stone pedestals were projects made by a few of the other apprentices and were filled with plants grown in the new gardens and greenhouses. The wall hangings and rug had been embroidered or woven in the sewing circle led by Lady Shiela, who had mostly avoided Rezkin since Palis's death. She preferred, instead, to focus on what she called the *feminine traditions* of the nobility. The decorative touches about the room were proof of her success.

Shezar was already present when Rezkin entered the office, as was Wesson. A moment later, Kai entered bedecked in weapons and looking ready for war.

"Is he on his way?" said Rezkin.

"Yes, Farson is escorting them."

"Farson?"

"Yes, is that a problem?"

Rezkin pondered for a moment. "It is … interesting. Did he request the duty?"

Kai frowned. "No, I was busy when the order came. I asked Farson to bring him."

Rezkin surveyed the room's current occupants and said, "Retrieve Yserria and Frisha. I suppose Malcius should attend as well."

As Kai left to gather the others, Rezkin turned to study a painting he had not seen the previous day.

Shezar said, "Viscount Abertine, it turns out, has a talent with the brush. This was his gift to you."

"What do you think he is trying to say?" Rezkin mused.

Shezar studied the image. "I would say he fears you."

The painting was of Dark Tidings standing in the portal to a crystal-studded hall with an army of elven wraiths at his back. In the foreground was a dim courtyard piled high with bloodied swords and broken shields, the cobbles awash in crimson. Reflected in the blades was the overcast sky filled with ravens, some gripping entrails in their talons.

Rezkin turned as his assailant, a man probably in his early forties, and a veiled woman were escorted into the room. The man stooped timidly and appeared shaken as his gaze darted about the room. The woman held the man's arm, her unadorned frock rocking gracefully with each step.

"Please, have a seat," Rezkin said, motioning to a couple of upholstered armchairs. He poured two goblets of wine and then strolled over to the pair. As the man took the goblet, he muttered a thank you. He met Rezkin's gaze for the briefest moment before his soft blue eyes turned toward the floor. The woman did not raise the lacey black veil but whispered her gratitude.

Tieran stumbled into the room looking as though he had not slept the previous night and was probably still under the influence of the wine. "Rez, I have asked you how many times not to send those phantoms after me? Would it kill you to use a traditional messenger?" He held a hand out to Kai who was leading the others into the room. "You sent the striker for *them*. Can you not offer me the same courtesy?"

Rezkin said, "The shielreyah are faster, and you can be almost certain the message came from me."

Tieran slumped onto the sofa. "Says *you*. You know how I feel about them." He spied the odd couple sitting in the chairs and said, "How about you pour me some of that wine?"

Kai growled, "You do not ask the king to pour you wine."

"I was not asking the *king*," muttered Tieran. "I was asking my cousin, who thinks the world of me."

Frisha and Malcius both bore looks of confusion as they entered the room. They took their seats on the sofa with Tieran so that Frisha sat between the two men. Yserria followed, taking up position by the door after closing it upon Rezkin's request.

Rezkin handed Tieran a goblet of wine, primarily because it was a good excuse to place himself between his cousin and the assailant. He said, "I have gathered you all here for an introduction. This is Master Connovan and …" He glanced at the woman expectantly.

"Mistress Levelle," said Connovan. The man's voice was gruff and held a hint of Channerían accent.

"Greetings, Mistress Levelle," Rezkin said with a bow, causing a few discomfited shuffles from those who no doubt felt the king should not bow to a commoner. "Master Connovan, I am told, is a fisherman. He aided Mistress Levelle in her escape from hostile forces in Channería. They were on the ship of refugees that arrived while I was away."

Connovan glanced at Rezkin with shifty eyes and said, "Y-yes, that's right."

Rezkin looked around the room. "Have any of you met Master Connovan?"

A few shook their heads, but most simply stared at the man. Rezkin did not take his eyes off the assailant as he said, "Striker Farson, surely *you* remember Master Connovan?"

Farson immediately tensed, his stance becoming defensive, his gaze predatory.

Almost faster than anyone could see, Connovan snapped a dagger toward Tieran. Rezkin snatched it from the air and had already launched it back by the time his cousin reacted. Tieran tossed wine all over Frisha as he scrambled into the seat of the sofa and then fell over the back with a thump and shout. Frisha practically jumped into Malcius's lap. Connovan had caught the dagger and slipped it up his sleeve by the time the strikers and Yserria had drawn their weapons.

Rezkin ordered his guards to halt before they could rush the assailant.

Then, he casually said, "Master Connovan tried to kill me on three separate occasions today."

Connovan's demeanor changed. He sat straighter and affected a semi-cultured air. In perfect Ashaiian, he said, "You can hardly call it an attempt on your life when I fully expected you to survive." His gaze roved over the strikers, Yserria, and Wesson. "It is interesting that you would choose to bring *all* of your best fighters into the room with me. Even more so that you would bring these three." He nodded toward the sofa. "Why would you intentionally place them in this position of danger?"

Rezkin said, "They are in no more danger in here with you than they were out *there* with you. Tieran, as heir, has a stake in this." He called over his shoulder to his cousin, "You may resume your seat, Tieran."

From where he crouched behind the sofa, Tieran said, "That man threw a knife at me! He is insane."

"He was only testing me," Rezkin said. "Not even that. More like toying."

Tieran's head barely topped the back of the seat as he said, "This is a *game* to you? It is *my* life! What if you had missed?"

Rezkin turned and frowned at Tieran. "I would not have missed." He said it just as another dagger flew at him from behind. Without looking, he slapped it from the air, *and* the one that followed, and then turned back to the smiling Connovan. The veiled woman placed a hand encased in a black lace glove on Connovan's arm, and he seemed to deflate.

To the woman, Connovan muttered, "I was just checking."

Rezkin went on as if they had not been interrupted. "To answer your question, each one has a purpose here. You brought a lady into the king's office, and I do not believe her to be your wife. It would be improper for her to be alone with so many men. Ladies Frisha and Yserria are here for her benefit. Lord Malcius is Lady Frisha's familial escort. Lady Yserria is a Knight of the Realm and is also my ward."

"Yes, interesting that," Connovan said with a wink for Yserria. The woman scowled and flicked the pommel of her sword in warning. Connovan chuckled and turned his gaze on Frisha. "Marcum's niece. I hear you sought a betrothal, although I cannot imagine how it fits into your plan. Did you intend, from the beginning, for it to fail. I think you will find that the lady is no longer certain of her desires."

Rezkin glanced at Frisha, his curiosity piqued. She flushed and looked away.

Connovan twirled a finger, indicating the room in general. "This is a bit ostentatious for you, is it not?"

"This?" Rezkin said, perusing the hard-gotten luxuries. "This is not for me. It is for *them*. It is a gallery to display the accomplishments of the people of Cael, and what better way of honoring the people than to display their works in the king's office?"

"Right, the *king*," Connovan said mockingly. "I have tried to piece together the events, but it seems you have been all over the place. I think, by now, your influence has spread farther than *you* know. Where are your ghosts, by the way? I have heard they rise to your defense. Perhaps they are not as attentive as you thought."

"No doubt why you directly attacked me only outside the corveua." Connovan tipped his head, and Rezkin said, "They have specific instructions."

Connovan nodded. "Interesting. You recognized me on the dock."

"I remember your many disguises—a delivery man, a horse trainer, a mercenary, a messenger. You remained afar, but when you came, you were always watching."

"I told Bordran it was a mistake for you to see me, but he wanted updates."

"Who are you?"

"You already know."

"Rez."

Connovan grinned.

Malcius sat up straighter, pushing Frisha off of him. "Wait, you are *the Rez*?"

The man tilted his head. "No more. My duty was to serve Bordran." He looked at Rezkin and said, "Why do you continue to call yourself Rezkin?"

"It is my name."

The man rolled his eyes. "Really?" He glanced at Farson, who shrugged and then locked his gaze on the far wall. Connovan said, "That is not your name. It is a title—one you should not be wielding in public." He sat forward, as if to give a lesson. "While you were in training, you were Rez *kin*, the kin of the Rez. Once you completed your training, *you* became the Rez."

Rezkin frowned and dove into his memories. He looked at Farson. "That is why you started calling me Rez. I thought you were shortening my name like the others, but you *knew*."

Farson turned to him. "I thought *you* knew. I believed your apparent lack of knowledge to be an act."

Rezkin looked back at Connovan. "What is my name?"

"You do not have one, just like *I* do not have one, and every Rez before us did not have one."

"Everyone has a name," said Malcius. "Even a deceased infant is given a name."

Connovan leaned back. "To receive a name, you must have first taken a breath. Your mother was told you were stillborn, so you were never given one."

Frisha gasped. "He was *stolen* from his mother?"

"At birth."

Uninterested in the useless details, Rezkin said, "Why have you come to this island?"

Connovan sat back and swirled the wine in his goblet, but he did not drink. "Before Bordran's death, there were only three people who knew of my existence: Bordran, Marcum, and Queen Lecillia. It was *my* duty to serve Bordran. It was *your* duty to serve his successor. Bordran died early, and you were not scheduled to finish training for close to ten years. I was forced to serve Caydean until you could take your place as Rez."

"If I am now the Rez, then what are you?"

Connovan chuckled. "*I* am no one. I am no longer supposed to exist. The first duty of the Rez, as you should know, is to seek out and kill his predecessor." He tilted his head in a manner strangely familiar. "Shall we go into the yard and have that duel to the death? I am certain you will win. You probably desire answers first, though."

"You are willing to talk?" Rezkin said, knowing that a Rez who offered information could not be trusted.

"I am obliged to share," said the man. "After all, I have nothing to lose. Besides, I am hoping you will return the favor. I have many questions."

Tieran still clung to the back of the sofa as he scowled at Connovan. "Rezkin, before you kill him, I have a question. Caydean is a monster. If he did not know of you, why did you serve him at all? I do not think Aunt Lecillia or Marcum would have been displeased had you disappeared."

"He is the king," Connovan said, as if it were obvious. "It was my duty to serve him." He looked at Rezkin. "It is *Rule 1*."

Frisha glanced at Rezkin. Her voice shook as she said, "I thought *Rule 1* was to protect and honor your friends."

Connovan frowned at her and then turned to Rezkin. "*That* is the directive you have been following? You did not make it to Caydean then?"

Rezkin shook his head.

"The scene at the fortress was confusing," Connovan said, "particularly since I arrived at least a month after your departure, and you disturbed it when you collected all the weapons. Tell me, how did you kill all the strikers *and* both the masters, and more importantly, *why*?"

Frisha gasped, and the air seemed to heat as several of his companions directed their horrified gazes at him.

"I was given the order to kill the strikers, but the masters killed each other. And, I did not kill *all* of the strikers. One stands there," he said with a nod toward Farson.

Connovan glanced at Farson. "I noticed one was missing at the scene. I figured you killed him elsewhere. Why have you allowed him to live?"

"Because I am no longer beholden to any master, and I will decide if he needs killing."

Connovan paused, as if frozen in place. He said, "You are free?"

"I am to honor and protect my friends," Rezkin said, "and I have sworn fealty to no one."

The woman beside Connovan raised a hand to hold back a sob that escaped as a whimper.

Connovan said, "You came up with this True King business to wrest the crown from Caydean?"

"Not I," said Rezkin. He nodded to the room's other occupants. "*Them.* It was their interpretation of Bordran's designs, and their implementation. They are my friends, and Ashai is no longer safe for them. To make it safe for them to return home, I must unseat Caydean and put things back to rights."

Connovan's narrow-eyed gaze was calculating. "You expect me to believe that these strikers and nobles got together, without your influence, and decided to tell everyone you are the rightful king? And Lord Tieran went along with this?"

Tieran finally popped up from behind the sofa and said, "I am not an idiot. I know my duty to Ashai. I recognize Rez as the True King because he *is* Bordran's rightful heir, and he has the document to prove it."

The woman gripped Connovan's arm tightly. He said, "You have proof of this claim?"

Rezkin withdrew the tube containing the parchment and tossed it to the man. Connovan unrolled it carefully, showing it to the woman as he read. The woman choked back another sob as she reached for it. He allowed her to take the parchment as he looked back to Rezkin. He said, "The majority of the document was written in Bordran's hand. The second belongs to Jaiardun."

He tapped the arm of the chair and then got up to stand behind the woman, gripping her shoulders. "I can see how this could be interpreted in such a way. More telling, though, is the sword. I have seen the official list of Sheyalins. I have had to … *reacquire* … a few in my time. None are named *Kingslayer*. Bordran changed the name of that one." He said the last with a nod toward the longsword at Rezkin's hip. "I think his intentions are clear enough." The woman gripped his arm again, and he patted her hand as if truly concerned.

While the others appeared pleased with further proof of their suspicions, Rezkin followed a different line of thought. "You did not answer my question. If you serve Caydean, and you know I am to kill you, why have you come here?"

"I no longer serve Caydean," said Connovan. "You freed me."

"How?"

"As soon as you completed your training, I was released from my oath. Ironically, it is a built-in protection for the new king's honor. It would not be honorable for the new Rez to kill the old one if the old one is forbidden from fighting back."

"So every Rez has killed his predecessor? What guarantees that new one will succeed?"

With a shrug, Connovan said, "Sometimes they do not, but usually the old one is slower than his younger counterpart. If you had failed, I would still be bound to serve the new king until the next Rez was trained. You have not killed me, and you have not technically failed because you have not attempted it; therefore, I remain unbound. Do you know the *purpose* of the Rez?"

Most of Rezkin's information regarding the Rez had come from Tam's book and hearsay. Rezkin glanced at Farson as he said, "To protect the king and serve as his assassin—or in whatever capacity he requires?"

"Oh, *he* would not know," Connovan said with a glance at Farson. "What you have said is the *public's* belief—the one told in stories. The truth is a secret held only between the reigning king, the Rez, and the *secret* archive. Bordran broke the rule by telling Lecillia and Marcum. The secret archive is enchanted to remain a part of the kingdom's charter. The position of the Rez can never be changed, no matter who sits upon the throne, so long as Ashai exists." He waved a hand around the room. "Shall we discuss it here, amongst *all* these people?"

"Just get on with it," said Rezkin.

The man smirked. "Very well. I suppose we can kill them later. The Rez, as I said earlier, is known only to a few. His *purpose* is a secret for the king alone. Not even Marcum or Lecillia know this. A king is always encouraged to have at least three sons—an heir, a spare heir, and a third to become the Rez. I know of only once that a daughter was taken because there were no extra male royal offspring. The reason the third son is trained as the Rez—always in secret, mind you—is because the Rez must have a legitimate claim to the throne. Bordran rejected the order, though. He said he would not give up his son—Lecillia's son—to become what I am. Although Bordran did not know me as a child, I think he loved me—and he hated me."

Rezkin said, "You are also of the royal family."

"I am Bordran and Deysius's younger brother—the third son." He paused, then said, "It was the third king of Ashai, King Fehrwin, who created the Rez. His own father, Coroleus's son Urhyus, had lived too long, some stories claiming nearly two hundred years. In his old age, the king became melancholy. He made poor decisions that damaged the kingdom, but he refused to abdicate. When Fehrwin finally received the crown, the kingdom was a terrible mess. He decided the king was too powerful, that the kingdom needed a safeguard. Thus, he wove the Rez into the charter in a way that would forever be sustained. If a ruler becomes a threat to the kingdom, it is the Rez's primary responsibility, his duty above all others, as dictated by the laws of this kingdom, to kill the king."

After a prolonged silence, Malcius exclaimed, "If that is all true, then why would you continue to uphold an oath to a madman?"

"It is a mage oath," said Wesson.

"Indeed," said Connovan with a tilt of his head. "I knew Caydean was mad, but he had not yet done anything to warrant his execution—at least, nothing I could prove."

Malcius was undeterred. "But, if Rezkin was meant to kill you, and you and Bordran both knew this, why would he send *you* to watch Rezkin when he was young?"

With a frown, Connovan said, "I was the Rez. It was my duty to serve Bordran, as it was my duty to battle the new Rez when he came for me. It is all in the *Rules*." He lifted a hand toward Rezkin and said, "*This* Rez, however, far surpasses any Rez that has come before him. He has managed to master *all* the *Skills* and then some."

"You did not?" said Rezkin.

Connovan laughed. "In all my years, I have barely mastered a quarter of them." At Rezkin's dubious look, he said, "You do not believe me? I suppose you should not. I am *the Rez*, after all. Perhaps you will believe them," he said with a nod toward Rezkin's friends on the sofa—and Tieran who had not regained the courage to come out from behind it. "You have not figured it out because you had no one to whom you could compare yourself. The masters and strikers were to act as though your ability to absorb knowledge was normal, unexceptional. Perhaps Journeyman Mage Wesson would do us the honor of selecting a book from the shelf?"

Wesson glanced at Rezkin for approval and then said, "Which book?"

"Any will do," said Connovan.

Behind Rezkin's desk were a few shelves containing whatever books had made it to the island.

Wesson chose one at random and then looked to the former Rez. "How about *The Design of Character: The Disposition of Jerean Architecture*?"

"Are the pages numbered?" said Connovan.

"Yes."

"Turn to page … hmm … forty-seven. *King* Rezkin, would you tell us the third word in the second paragraph?"

"Utility," Rezkin said immediately.

"That is correct," said Wesson.

Connovan said, "Please begin recitation of the first line in the third paragraph on page seventeen."

Wesson flipped through the pages, and Rezkin began. "*The dynamics between service and the formalized cultural traditions and practices of the era are unique to the provinces …*"

"Thank you, I think that is enough of that book," Connovan said.

Wesson glanced up. "He is correct. Every word."

Malcius said, "For the Maker's sake, Rezkin, how many times have you read that book? I could not force myself past the first two pages."

"Why would I need to read it more than once?" said Rezkin. "It is not enchanted. The words do not change with each reading."

Wesson blurted, "You are a *scrivener*!"

Rezkin looked at him with confusion. "I am capable of writing, but I did not write that book."

"No, not a *mundane* scrivener," said Wesson. "A *scrivener* is a very special type of mage."

Farson suddenly broke his silence. "That information was kept from him. We were *very* careful to make sure he never knew of scriveners. Actually, we kept much about mages from him. It seemed odd since we were assured he was not a mage; but, we had orders, and we followed them."

"What is a scrivener?" said Malcius.

Wesson frowned at the striker and then turned to Malcius. "Scriveners have perfect memory and recall. They can memorize anything they hear or see the first time; and, more importantly, they can recall it flawlessly. It explains so much. That is how you were able to master so many skills in such a short time."

Farson said, "It does not explain his physical prowess."

"No, but I am sure it helps," Wesson said then turned to back the others. "Imagine that you can learn any knowledge by listening to someone or by reading a book *one* time and never forget *anything*. No studying required."

Tieran said, "If knowledge is power, then it is a very powerful talent. It is also exceedingly rare, more so than readers and illusionists. In fact, I know of only *one*." He turned toward the woman in black and said, "Queen Lecillia."

The woman dabbed at her eyes with a kerchief beneath her veil and then lifted the black lace over her head. She looked up at Rezkin and said, "It is true. I am Lecillia, and you are my son."

"How can this be?" Tieran said. "We determined that we were related, but we thought he was Bordran or Deysius's bastard."

Lecillia's expression became furious. "You, Tieran Nirius, will *not* call *my* son a bastard! He is a true and legitimate prince of Ashai."

"Prince?" Frisha said and quickly covered her mouth as her face grew pale.

Tieran held up his hands. "My apologies, Aunt Lecillia. I meant no disrespect. I already recognize Rezkin as my king, so you will get no argument from me."

Lecillia was somewhat appeased, and she turned back to Rezkin. "I am so sorry. I was told you were stillborn. I never knew. I cannot believe Bordran did this to me. I did not believe Connovan when he told me. I had to see you for myself. I almost died when you stepped off that ship. Part of me wished you *had* been a bastard. It would have been easier to accept that Bordran had strayed than that he stole my baby boy straight from my womb and told me he was dead!" She looked back at Rezkin and said, "No, I am sorry, my love. I did not mean it. I am glad that you are alive and that I will have the chance to know you, even if I missed your childhood."

Rezkin did not reply but instead looked back to Connovan. "You said Bordran refused to send his son to be trained as the Rez."

"His own oaths would have forced him to uphold the charter; but, in the end, it was Caydean that decided it for him." He squeezed Lecillia's shoulders again and said, "Caydean was merely seven when you were born, but his cruelty was evident even then. He had already killed three puppies, beaten one of the servant's children nearly to death, and tried to kill his own brother twice. He claimed they were all accidents, but Bordran knew. He hoped he and others could teach Caydean—that, somehow, he would grow out of it. After Caydean nearly drowned Thresson without remorse, Bordran knew he had to prepare for the worst.

"Bordran later told me that the night you were born was the worst of his life, as were all the days after. I was ordered to kill the healer who had helped birth you, and the queen was told that you were dead. Bordran spent a few hours with you, and then you disappeared. I think he did not trust me with the babe. Of course, I knew where you had been taken, but I was ordered to stay away unless he requested an update."

Rezkin looked to Wesson. "Perform the test."

Lecillia's face fell.

Frisha said, "Rezkin, can't you see she's hurting. Don't be so cold. She is your mother."

"So *he* says."

Tieran said, "Rezkin, this *is* Aunt Lecillia. I have known her my entire life."

"But you do not *know* that she is my mother. *She* does not *know*. She knows only what he has told her."

"Why would the queen lie about your legitimacy? Why would *he*?" said Tieran.

Rezkin looked to Wesson. "The test."

6

Wesson hurried to collect a vessel for the blood and then paused upon approaching the queen mother. Lecillia gave hers willingly, with tears in her eyes. Then, he took a sample from Rezkin. Although Rezkin always seemed alert, he appeared particularly aware at that moment, as though he were surrounded by drauglics ready to rip him to shreds. The spell finished with a resonant pop, and Wesson announced that Lecillia was definitely Rezkin's mother.

Rezkin turned to Connovan. "Very well, I accept that Queen Lecillia is my mother, but there are several holes in your story. For one, you claim that I am a scrivener, and even though I am a direct descendant of the royal line, I am not a mage."

Rezkin felt the tingle of mage energy emanate from Connovan and prepared for an attack. The man smiled and said, "You will have to try much harder to influence *me*, although I believe Striker Farson is now convinced."

"What are you talking about?" said Rezkin.

"*I* am a *reflector*. It is a power that has served me well in my duties. I am able to reflect spells cast at me and direct them onto others of my choosing." He looked up thoughtfully. "I suppose *refractor* might be more accurate, but that does not have the same ring. *Your* spell just struck Striker Farson."

Rezkin shook his head. "It is not *my* spell."

Wesson said, "I could never sense the *talent* in him, so I decided a spell must have been cast onto him that allows him to influence others."

Rezkin said, "I do not realize I am using it most of the time."

"I also have never sensed the *talent* in you," replied Connovan. "The truth is, I do not know what you are. Your masters seemed to have an idea, but they would not share their knowledge with me. What I do know is that, aside from healing, we have never been able to make *any* spell stick to you. Any power that comes from you is your own."

Rezkin pondered the Rez's words. He did not know how much of the information he could trust, but so long as the man was being candid, he would collect as much information as he could. "And the masters? Who were they?"

"That, I also do not know, not specifically anyway. I think you know *what* they were, though."

"Goka?" suggested Rezkin.

Connovan tilted his head. "More importantly, they were SenGoka."

"Why does that sound familiar?" said Tieran.

Malcius's eyes widened. "Necromancers," he shouted. He looked to Rezkin. "You told us of them—the necromancers of the Jahartan Empire. You were trained by *necromancers*?"

Connovan said, "Elite warrior necromancers, to be precise. It was a good thing, too. No one could live through *his* training." He perused their horrified faces. "What? You did not think you actually *survived* all of that."

Rezkin turned his accusatory gaze on Farson. "You *killed* me?"

Farson would not meet his glower at first but finally acquiesced. "I did not know. There were times when we were certain you were dead. Peider was known to be a healer, though—and Jaiardun, to some extent. They assured us every time that you were alive and could be saved. We strikers argued often over it. We thought they must have been the most magnificent healers that ever lived." With a glare toward Connovan, he said, "*Sen* did not cross our minds. I did not believe they existed." He looked back to Rezkin. "A person simply cannot engage in battle for two days straight without a break, without sustenance. I do not know how you managed to last that long, but when you finally fell, you were surely dead."

Rezkin glanced between the two of them. "How many times have I *died*?"

Both men shrugged.

"I have no reason to believe either of you," he said.

Connovan shook his head. "The proof is in your skin."

Rezkin glanced at his hand and then frowned at the man. "What are you saying?"

"You know about the Sen?" said Connovan. "You know they make marks on the skin, tattoos—a record of how each death occurs, the length of time spent in death, and the identity of the Sen who retrieves your soul. You have such marks."

"Uh, *no*, he doesn't," said Frisha. "He doesn't have a mark on him." Everyone turned to her, and she froze as her cheeks turned pink. She buried her gaze in the far wall as Malcius glared at her and then Rezkin.

Rezkin looked back to Connovan. "I do not have any marks."

Farson said, "I have never seen any marks either."

Connovan tilted his head. "I believe the masters taught you to hide them. When you were too young to receive intense combat training, they started with your mind. Much time was spent on making others see what you want them to see. You had less control when you were young, and I was occasionally able to reflect your influence to see the marks."

Yserria said, "Wait, you are saying he died as a *child*?"

Connovan ignored the interruption. "For you, the habit is dictated by the *Rules*. *Rule 3—reveal nothing, Rule 10—do not leave evidence,* and *Rule 237—bear no identifying marks*." He glanced at Kai and Shezar. "The strikers break that one with their tattoos. *They* must have them removed before going on assignment. *You* learned to hide yours. I do not know how, but I believe it has become so engrained in your mental process that you no longer think of it."

Rezkin knew instinctively that what Connovan said was true. The longer he thought of it, the more he could feel the marks, as if they were crawling under his skin, marks he had not recognized were there. Then, he wondered if they were truly there at all. Perhaps Connovan was an illusionist or had another *talent* that made Rezkin question himself. He chose to change the subject.

"Peider and Jaiardun were not old enough to have trained you."

"No," said Connovan, "I was trained by strikers."

"How did a couple of SenGoka become my masters?"

"Jaiardun, I believe, was from Jaharta. Peider was from Galathia. There was a third named Berringish, also from Jaharta. They arrived before the queen even knew she was pregnant. They said they had been sent by a Knight of Mikayal to train you."

"Me, specifically, or the next Rez?"

"It had to be *you*," said Connovan. He glanced at Tieran and grimaced. "There was a time when Bordran considered sending that one. He would have broken before touching a weapon."

"Hey, now!" said Tieran. "I am not weak just because I am not a heartless killer." He glanced at Rezkin. "Ah, neither are you, of course."

Rezkin considered correcting him, but Tieran seemed happy in his belief. He turned to Connovan. "Why were they sent to train me?"

"I do not know. I am not sure *they* knew. They would have traveled for months to reach Ashai. The fact that the Sen knew of your existence before you were conceived was proof enough for Bordran. You know that the Goka are renowned warriors, nearly the equals of the Soka. He was not about to turn them away. Their assertion about the knight gave Bordran hope that Mikayal favored you. Who wouldn't want a god on his side?

"Still, Bordran was not yet willing to give up on Caydean. He insisted that if they were to train you, at least one would stay behind to teach Caydean and Thresson. They did not care for the bargain; but, ultimately, they left Berringish to the task. He was furious all the years that I watched him. Eventually, he disappeared. I questioned Peider and Jaiardun, but they insisted he had only joined them *after* they had received the message from the knight, and they did not know what had happened to him. They were not the easiest men to question, though. They wielded great power, and men who do not fear death tend to fear little."

Rezkin stared at the king's assassin of legend. He said, "You still have not said why you came *here*."

Connovan sighed. "Caydean sent me away several months ago. It was a pointless mission. I knew even then that he was getting me out of the way for something. I did not know he intended to move against you, though. He must have given the order before you completed your training. He had known about you for maybe a month before the attack. Technically, I was supposed to inform him of your existence upon Bordran's death, but he never asked about the next Rez in training, so I neglected to mention it. When I was forced to tell, I may have informed him of your *planned* completion date and omitted the fact that you were years ahead of schedule and far beyond my own training. He sent me away shortly after learning of your existence.

Malcius said, "I still do not understand why you did nothing about Caydean. You said killing the mad king was your job."

Connovan glanced at Lecillia. He said, "I could not move against Caydean for two reasons. One, I was not his Rez. In order for me to act, he would have to do something blatant, requiring immediate removal from the throne. It is the nature of my oath. Two, he had not done anything overtly damaging to the kingdom. While there were plenty of rumors that he had killed Bordran and is responsible for Thresson's disappearance, I was not present for those events and have not found evidence to prove it." He paused and looked at Rezkin. "I may have taken longer to return from my last mission than was strictly necessary. I believe he did kill Bordran, and I did not wish to serve him. By the time I returned, you had completed your training, and Caydean had already tried to have you killed. It was he, I am sure of it; but, again, I have no proof."

"So he planned to kill *me* before starting his war, but he only sent *you* away. How did he intend to prevent you from dethroning him?"

"He found a loophole. You were supposed to be his Rez. By mage oath, he would not be able to kill you—except that you were not fully trained yet, so his oath recognized *me* as the Rez. That left him free to order your death. If you were dead, I would continue to be the Rez, and I would be oathbound to return to him once I completed my mission. He would be prepared for my arrival. Because of the kingdom's code of honor, if I decide to dethrone Caydean, he has the right to defend himself. We are no longer protected from each other. I believe he thought he could defeat me. His plan was spoiled, though, when you finished your training early. As soon as you passed the final test, I was released from my oath until you sought me out. I did not return to Caydean, and he failed to kill you. I do not believe he knows that he failed."

"How so?" Rezkin said.

"You killed everyone. No spy was left to report back to him." Both of their gazes slid to Farson, who scowled in return. Connovan continued. "Caydean did not know where the fortress was located. The only people remaining who know are in this room. I doubt he will find it. The fortress is not so easy to find for those who do not know where to look."

"It is enchanted?" Rezkin said.

Connovan shrugged. "It is unclear. As far as I know, no one has discovered any wards, but it is possible they were constructed by the more powerful mages of ancient times. The fortress is old."

"So you returned from your journey and did not report to Caydean. What then?"

"After discovering what had happened at the fortress, I eventually went to check on Lecillia. He could not override *Rule 1*, of course, but Bordran's standing orders with me were to always protect Lecillia and Thresson before any other duty. That was how I found out you had left the fortress. Marcum went to Lecillia because she was the only one who knew how to contact me. He rightfully feared that you were the next Rez, but Marcum knows only the stories that everyone else knows—that the Rez is the king's assassin. He does not know the Rez's true purpose or that you and I are members of the royal family.

"Wait," said Frisha. "Uncle Marcum knew, not only that were you a sword bearer, but also that you were the *Rez*?" She swallowed, and her gaze became distant. "I need to apologize to him."

Connovan looked at her with disinterest and then turned back to Rezkin. "I heard of Caydean's attempt to have Marcum killed and then caught wind of a plan to move against the houses. I helped Marcum and Adelina escape and then spirited Lecillia away. I sent Marcum to the fortress, by the way. Your wards are allowing him and his loyal soldiers to pass. I have no idea how you are doing that."

Rezkin scowled at the man. Even if he had the power to make wards, he certainly could not make something that extensive and complex, nor could he maintain it from so far.

Connovan said, "Since I am presently free of my oath, I was able to tell Lecillia about you. She wanted to find you, so here we are." He narrowed his eyes at Farson and said, "We should kill that one. He is the only one to escape the fortress. It is possible he was a spy."

Rezkin said, "I have considered that and am still debating his fate."

"He is an unnecessary threat."

Farson said to Connovan, "*You* are an unnecessary threat."

Connovan nodded. "That is true." He turned to Rezkin. "You should kill me as well." Waving a hand around the room, he added, "I will kill all of them first, if you want. They know too much and should be eliminated."

"That would be counterproductive," said Rezkin. "They are the support force."

"We will see how loyal they remain now that they know who you really are."

Rezkin glanced at the frightened and disturbed faces of his friends. "They wish to go home. They know that I am their best chance of achieving that goal.

Until their desires change, or they believe they have found another solution, they will remain loyal."

Malcius leapt to his feet. "How can you say that? You know we are your friends, and we have all sworn fealty. Our loyalty should not so easily be dismissed."

Rezkin was genuinely surprised. "You say this after what you have just heard?"

Tieran said, "What I heard is that you are a legitimate prince of Ashai with a responsibility to kill the mad king. Ah, sorry, Aunt Lecillia. I know this must be difficult for you."

Rezkin turned back to Connovan and Lecillia. "Tieran is right. You two are the greatest threat."

Tieran grew defensive. "What? I said no such thing."

Rezkin turned to his cousin. "Connovan may be using Lecillia's familial relation and his long-winded story to get close to me. Lecillia, let us not forget, is also Caydean's mother. She does not know me, yet she has been present for Caydean's entire life. She may wish to kill me to prevent me from killing him. This entire scenario is a clever ploy. They entice me with what I desire most —information."

Lecillia grabbed Connovan's arm and said, "Why is he saying this?"

Frisha abruptly stood to join Malcius. "Rezkin, that is your *mother*. Do you not care for her at all?"

Rezkin did not take his eyes off Connovan and Lecillia as he said, "I do not know this woman from any other. There are plenty of stories in the histories of mothers killing their offspring, especially in defense of another who is more favored. This man is an admitted assassin, and she is the mother of a madman who likely killed her husband and younger son. Where was she? She was living in the palace the entire time, dining with their killer. I have no reason to trust either of them."

Connovan leaned toward Lecillia and said, "I told you what he is. Do not take it personally. He is not capable of feeling. His humanity was driven out of him when he was but a small child."

Lecillia stood, her chin held high as she held her hands in front of her. Despite the tears in her eyes, she had the bearing of a queen. "It is true. I stayed in the palace but not because I wanted it. I could not leave. Where was I to go? Who would help me? Caydean would have killed anyone I told. He tried to have Marcum killed several times because he *thought* I had said something. Connovan could not assist because he was bound to Caydean. It was only after he was released from his oath that he was able to help me escape, and the fact that he remained free told us that you were still alive. Neither of us wish you harm. If you cannot believe we care, then think logically. If you die, Connovan must return to Caydean's service, and he will likely kill me. It is in our own, selfish interests that you live."

Lecillia lurched back as a phantom wraith suddenly appeared. Rezkin said, "These two are to be a watched carefully. They are possible enemies. They are not to leave the corveua."

Shielreyah Elry bowed. "Yes, Spirétua Syek-lyé."

Connovan said, "So you *can* summon them with your mind. That is fascinating. Can anyone do it?"

Elry turned his vaporous orbs on the man. "It is an honor to serve the Syek-Lyé, and we respect the Spirétua. *You* are neither."

Rezkin said, "You two may remain on the island under supervision. They do not need eyes with which to see or ears with which to hear, and your weapons and *talents* will be useless against them. If you challenge them, they will kill you. Do you understand?"

"Yes," Lecillia said as she blinked tears from her eyes.

Connovan nodded as he studied the phantom.

Rezkin said, "You have been assigned quarters?"

"Yes, in the city," said Connovan.

"You will be moved to the palace," Rezkin replied. "Frisha and Yserria will escort the queen mother to appropriate quarters. Wesson and Shezar will escort Connovan."

"Are you taking me to the dungeon?" said the man. "You know I cannot be captured alive. It is against the *Rules*."

"You have not been captured," said Rezkin. "You are to wash for the midday meal."

Connovan smiled and picked up his goblet. Sniffing it suspiciously, he met Rezkin's gaze, then drank to the last drop.

Frisha walked down the corridor beside the queen mother, with Yserria guarding the rear. After a few minutes of uncomfortable silence, Lecillia said, "He is my son, and I love him. I want him to be happy, but why would you consider marrying such a man? He is so cold, so empty."

Frisha glanced back the way they had come. "He did not seem that way when I met him. He smiled and laughed, and he was the perfect gentleman. I had no idea he was the …" She stopped and placed her hands on her knees as she took several deep breaths. She fanned her face and said, "Oh, I cannot believe I was scolding *the Rez* for being rude to his mother."

Yserria looked down at her with a frown. "You have spent months with that man. You have mooned over him and screamed at him and kissed him. He was no less the Rez then than he is now."

"That makes it even worse," Frisha said with a groan.

"You had no idea?" said Lecillia.

"No, how could I know? It was not like he went around killing people all the time. I mean, he was great when we were attacked by bandits, but that was different. I have been listening to Tam go on about the Rez all our lives. The Rez is an *assassin*. The Rez is cunning and cold and merciless." She pointed back the way they had come. "The Rez is that man back there."

Lecillia stared down the strange, twisting corridor with its crystals and mystical mosaics. "But you loved him when you did not know?"

"I thought I did," Frisha said as she straightened. "At least, for a while. Now, I think I was in love with a fantasy."

Lecillia placed her hand on Frisha's shoulder. She said, "I have spent much time dealing with the squabbles and backstabbing at court, with kings and generals—with the Rez, and I have some understanding of how these people think. There was no reason for you to be in that room."

"Because a lady cannot be alone …"

"No, I am fairly certain your Rezkin knew who I was before calling us there. He at least had an idea, and he knew your presence was not necessary. Hers would have been enough," she said with a nod toward Yserria. "He asked you there because he wanted you to bear witness, to hear it from the source. He wanted you to know who he is. I promise you, the Rez does not part with that information lightly. The people who know him die—usually before they realize what they know. It is part of their rules. Anyone who was in that room is someone he trusts, someone for whom he cares." She paused and then added, "*Or*, he is trying to root out a spy."

Smiling sadly, she said, "I cannot say that I know my son—*any* of them, truly. I was closest with Thresson. He was a sweet child, sensitive. When he was young, I tried to protect him, but it often made things worse. I hated the idea of being parted from him, but I asked Bordran to send him away where he would not be bullied by his older brother. Bordran said he could not trust the dukes. We might have gone with Wellinven, but my husband said it would show favor. Caydean was *our* problem, and I am afraid Thresson paid the price." With a despondent sigh, she said, "Now Caydean is *everyone's* problem. Perhaps *Rezkin* is right to mistrust me."

Rezkin had put his faith in the shielreyah that they would keep the Rez from harming his people. He did not know why he had done that. He figured it had to have something to do with the mystical power of the citadel making him feel comfortable, complacent. If he had not been responsible for the safety of the hundreds of people he had brought there, he would have left long ago. He was surrounded by strange powers he did not understand and could not control. The katerghen had disappeared each time they disembarked, and he did not trust *it* either. The most confounding was the mystery of the power he supposedly wielded without conscious thought. The revelation of his parentage should have solved the mystery, but it had only left more questions. Why was he so different?

After living his life without knowledge of, or even interest in, his lineage, he had discovered a cousin, an uncle, *and* a mother. He had a *family*. What was he to do with a family, especially a family he could not trust? This meant the enemy he was supposed to kill was his brother. The missing prince was also his brother. Supposedly, family members had a duty to each other. Was he supposed to find the missing prince—to rescue him, if necessary? The histories were filled with tales of brothers who coveted each other's wealth or titles or lovers. Brothers fought over their father's favor or the family inheritance. Yet, he had read of brotherly love and loyalty as if they, themselves, were rules.

Rezkin felt none of this for Caydean nor Thresson. He felt nothing for his mother or uncle. To remain separate from his emotions was an important *Rule*, as were they all, and to fail to comply with it could lead to failure and death. His uncle knew this. The Rez would not expect sentiment and would probably exploit the pointless weakness if discovered. His mother, however, seemed hopeful. He wondered if he could pass the responsibility to someone else. Who among his friends was in need? Reaylin and Yserria had both mentioned losing their mothers when they were young. Perhaps one of them would care to have one. They were women, though, and Lecillia expected a son. Tam seemed like a good son. He spoke highly of his parents, but he had a mother. Could a man have more than one mother? Then again, was it *his* responsibility? He had not asked for a mother. Since his birth, he had not required one. He knew, however, that problems rarely went away when ignored. He had no more time to consider it, though. He had a sword of prophecy to acquire.

The docks were busy with personnel performing maintenance and resupplying both ships. Rezkin could hear his prey the moment he set foot outside the warehouse.

"If you don't hold still, I'm not going to heal you, and you can stack crates with a broken hand!" said a female voice.

A gruff voice replied, "Ya know, most healers are nicer to their patients."

The woman's frustration escaped in a growl. "Look, I don't want to be here. I don't want to help you. I'm only doing this because they say I have to. Now sit still and shut up."

Rezkin rounded a stack of crates to witness the petite blonde healer shove the sailor onto one of them. "Apprentice Reaylin, a good bedside manner is a requirement of passing your skills exam. It is a known fact that it is less draining on both the healer and the patient if the patient feels comfortable with the person helping him. Perhaps we should confiscate your bed until you are capable of performing at an acceptable level."

Reaylin fumed as she stalked up to Rezkin and raised a finger. "What does my bed have to do with this?"

"Nothing, but it would incentivize you to learn a good bedside manner."

"I didn't ask for this—"

"You swore fealty."

"You said I could still be a warrior."

"And you may. Heal him, and then we will discuss your assignment. Do it *nicely*."

Reaylin exhaled heavily, blowing the blonde locks out of her face. She spun around and smiled sweetly. "*Please* allow me to assist you. *Please* give me your hand, and *please* be still. This will only take a few moments."

The sailor glanced at Rezkin. He had stood and bowed upon seeing the king, and the man's face still bore the shock of seeing Reaylin berate him. Rezkin nodded, and the man straightened uncertainly before sitting back on the crate.

Once Reaylin was finished healing the broken hand, she spoke in the same syrupy voice. "*Thank you* for your patience. You may return to work now."

The sailor bowed to the king and then skittered away as if running from a fire. Reaylin crossed her arms and tapped her foot. “Well?”

Rezkin started to speak and then paused. He instead said, “Do you desire a mother?”

Reaylin’s retort died on her lips. “Um … *what*?”

“You do not have a mother. Do you want one?”

“Rez, what does this have to do with my assignment?”

Rezkin shook his head. “Nothing. It was an errant thought. You will be going on the next mission. We leave tomorrow. See Journeyman Wesson for details.” At that, Rezkin turned and left the dock.

7

Hilith stood in the shade of the building as she watched another wagon head toward the service tunnel that led to the warehouse. King Rezkin had only just returned, and he was already about to leave on another mission. She needed to get close to him, but she could not be too obvious about it. Luckily, she had come up with a brilliant plan to get into *Lady* Frisha's good graces. She stepped back through the entrance to the palace and made her way to the third floor despite the fact that the strange palace had no stairs. Pausing a few doors down from her own, she straightened her skirt and knocked.

The door opened, and she found a pensive Frisha staring at her. Hilith smiled. If Frisha was upset, her job would be that much easier.

"Greetings, Lady Frisha. I did not mean to disturb you. I only wished to see how you fare."

"Oh? Why is that?" Frisha said.

"I heard that Lord—I mean, *King* Rezkin is leaving on the morrow. It is a shame that you will not get to spend time with him. I thought you might need a friend."

Frisha's shoulders dropped. "Honestly, I don't know what to think. There are too many things swirling around in my mind right now."

Hilith donned a concerned expression. "Would you like me to sit with you? You know I have had to deal with so much, perhaps my meager advice could be of comfort."

Frisha seemed hesitant, but said, “Um, yes, thank you for the offer. That is kind of you, Lady Gadderand. Please come in.”

The sitting room was sparsely furnished but better than most on the island. They sat on short, wooden benches that were not particularly comfortable but had cushions, at least.

“I am afraid I don’t have any refreshments to offer right now.”

Hilith patted Frisha’s hand. “It is no bother, my dear. We are all experiencing the same—except for King Rezkin, of course, but it is only fitting that the king should have what luxuries are available.”

“Oh, no. Rezkin isn’t like that,” Frisha said. “I mean, he doesn’t care about luxuries—more like he puts up with them because it makes the people happy to dote on him.”

“I did not realize he was so humble.”

Frisha furrowed her brow. “I don’t think it has anything to do with being humble. He just doesn’t think they’re necessary. He seems to be more comfortable camping on the road in his armor.”

“A military man, then? That surprises me,” said Hilith, and she meant it. “He seemed quite the courtier when we met.”

“Yes, he’s very … um … versatile,” said Frisha.

“Well, that is too bad. It does explain his constant outings and choice of company. I thought it strange that he would knight a woman, but now it makes sense. Oh, pardon me, I should not say such things. Sometimes my tongue runs away with me, especially when someone I care about is concerned.”

Frisha straightened, her shoulders tensing. “What do you mean?”

“Oh, it is nothing, I am sure. But … well … it is not something that is done, you know—a female knight. It does provide him with an excuse to take her with him. Men of power do not like to do without, if you know what I mean.”

“He wouldn’t—”

“No, of course not. I have heard great things about King Rezkin—that he is honorable and *honest*.” Hilith saw a flash of doubt in the young woman’s eyes. She leaned forward and patted Frisha's knee. "You need not worry. He will not be like most men in his position. I have heard that he keeps you in close confidence. He probably tells you *everything*.” Frisha pursed her lips, and Hilith knew it to be denial. She said, “I admire you, you know.”

“*Me*? Why would you admire *me*?”

"Well, I could never be so trusting. My curiosity would get the better of me. After I caught my dear departed husband with the maid—"

Frisha gasped. "He *didn't*."

"Oh, I am afraid he did. I forget, sometimes, that you were not raised in high society. When it comes to these things, discretion is the only bound."

"You mean, you were okay with … it?"

"No, of course not. It tore my heart open, but there is nothing to be done for it. Out of sight, out of mind, so they say."

"What did you do?"

"Well, some women choose to remain ignorant, but my mind would never let it go. I recruited people—the staff, mostly—and some of our friends to keep an eye on him. They let me know when things were not as they should be, and I made sure that *he* knew that *I* knew."

"But, what good would it do to know if you can do nothing about it?"

Hilith shrugged. "Maybe no good, except that I felt better when he knew he could not get away with hiding these things from me. But, perhaps, it may be of use in the future. You never know. For a woman in our position, *yours* especially, it is important to build strength. Knowledge is power, you know."

"So I have heard," she said.

"Still, King Rezkin's *ward* is a strong, female swordmaster that he just knighted. I hear she is on the list to leave with him on the morrow."

"Well, she *is* a royal guard …"

"Yes, convenient that." Hilith paused to let the message sink in and then cautiously said, "You know, I see a bit of myself in you—when I was younger, of course. I am a well-traveled woman, and I care about you. I would be willing to keep an eye on him for you."

"You would do that for me?"

"Of course. But, well, I would need to be near him. If only there were a way for me to be included in his traveling party. I am not without skills. I could be useful. With a good word from someone he trusts, he might consider adding me to the list."

"Oh, I,"—Frisha smiled hesitantly—"perhaps, but it won't be necessary. You shouldn't be placed in such a position, and I don't feel comfortable with others spying on Rezkin."

Hilith swallowed her anger and frustration. She had overplayed her hand. Frisha did not yet trust her. She smiled placatingly and said, "I only want to help, but I understand. If you change your mind, I am at your disposal."

"Thank you, Lady Gadderand. If you don't mind, though, I think I'd like to rest a bit."

"Most certainly. I will see you at dinner, then."

Hilith left Frisha's quarters deflated. There was no way she would be able to convince anyone else to help her get on that list. She would have to find another way. As she turned the corner, she passed Princess Ilanet. She watched as the princess entered the quarters she shared with Frisha and then turned her gaze on the princess's guard.

"Excuse me," she said in the sweetest tone she could muster. "You are Lus, correct? I have seen you around. I hope you do not think this too forward, but I was wondering if you might like to take a turn about the garden with me."

~

The sky was grey the next day as the ship passed beyond the corveua. Within hours, the wind began to whip across the deck in great gusts, and the clouds had grown ominous, darkening to nearly black. The waves rose higher, and some of the sailors began to mutter that sea demons were awake and angry. Reaylin had her work cut out for her as the only healer on the ship. By midmorning, the sky began to fall in torrential rain, and any unnecessary personnel were ordered to remain in their quarters. Wesson and Mage Threll did their best to guard the ship from the worst of the waves and wind, but neither could keep it up for long.

"Why did you bring her?" Farson spat. The ship lurched, and he grabbed hold of a thick rope that had been used to secure a stack of crates to the inner hull.

"She has useful skills," Rezkin replied. He began replacing the items in the trunk he had been inspecting before they rolled away.

An overhead lamp swung wildly, nearly struck the beam, and caused shadows to dance eerily around the hold. Farson narrowed his eyes. "You did this to vex me. Is this my punishment for keeping information from you?"

Rezkin said, "*Rule 19—plan with logic and without vengeance or favor*."

Farson hissed, "These people are ruthless."

"Should I treat Mage Threll with favor because she is your kin? She is here because she has useful skills, and she requested the assignment."

"You did not bring any of *your* kin."

"None of them have useful *talents* or *skills* for this matter, except for my uncle, and he is as likely to aid the Adana'Ro as he is me. I already have to keep an eye on *you*, and I also must determine why Lus slipped aboard without permission. He is supposed to be watching Ilanet."

"I have better things to do with my time than watch a spoiled princess," said the assassin as he stepped out of a shadow.

Rezkin said, "If you are here to join the Adana'Ro against me, I will destroy you before you cast your first dagger."

Lus held up his hands. "I am not your enemy. I did not know that we go to the Adana'Ro until now."

"You boarded a ship without knowing its destination?"

"I knew you were headed to Ferélle. I wanted to find out why. Everyone who knows has been tight-lipped about it."

"I am not buying your story," Rezkin said, bracing himself against a mound of sacks as the ship lurched.

Farson's sharp gaze probed Lus. "Who are you, *really*?"

Lus grinned and leaned back against the wall as the ship rocked in the other direction.

Rezkin said, "We go to the Adana'Ro, and he must know who you are before we enter their domain. You tell him, or I will."

"Very well." With a nod toward Farson, Lus said, "He and I have already come to an understanding."

"Yes," said Rezkin, "I am sure it has something to do with which of you will kill me first."

Lus's smile fell. He said, "Has anyone ever told you that you have trust issues?"

With a scathing look at Farson, Rezkin said, "Apparently, I have died more times than they cared to count, and I do not desire to do it again soon. I think more than once is enough for a lifetime."

Farson huffed. "How was I supposed to know? You went in for healing. You came out alive and well. That you had survived was a more likely scenario than that you had somehow returned from the dead!"

Lus's gaze was suffused with fervent awe. "It is true, then? You cannot die?"

Rezkin frowned. "I just told you. I have died many times."

"But you do not *stay* dead." He turned to Farson and said, "My name is Ikaxayim. You may call me Xa. I am Jeng'ri of the Order, and I am a loyal servant of the Riel'gesh." He bowed toward Rezkin with the reverence due a god.

Farson rolled his eyes and sighed. He turned to Rezkin with a worn visage and said, "*You. You* are the Riel'gesh? *You* are the Raven? In all the time I was avoiding you and worrying over Nanessy, I was not thinking about the Raven. I should have known." He shook his head. "I *did* know, when I first heard of him, but I dismissed the notion. It was too public, and it made no sense." Pointing a finger at Rezkin, he said, "I knew you would hunt me. Why would you begin a mass appropriation of the criminal underworld? Even knowing you as I do, I would not have thought you could do it so quickly while simultaneously tracking me to Skutton. You collected the heirs of great houses *and* the general *and* soldiers *and* strikers *and* a battle mage *and* a healer—and the Black Hall! Why would you take over the Black Hall? You are a fiend!"

Rezkin frowned. "The strikers were dead. I needed a spy network to find you."

With a blank expression, Farson said, "You took over every criminal organization in Ashai to find *me*? You broke into the Golden Trust Bank! You killed hundreds of people. You killed a marquis—a *marquis*!"

"He was in my way," Rezkin said defensively. "And he threatened my friends."

"Rezkin, you have destroyed an entire kingdom just to find *me*!"

"I have not destroyed Ashai. Caydean is destroying Ashai. I am the sole unifying force against the tyrant."

Farson stared at Rezkin. After skipping a few breaths, he finally said, "You are right. As frightening as it is, you are right. But I know that was not your intention at the time, *and* you have unified the worst of the kingdom. You threaten to overrun all that is good with your terror pitted against the king's forces—which, if you intend to actually be king of Ashai, are your *own* people."

"I realize that, and I have been taking steps to avoid killing as many as possible. You should know better than anyone that I am not a bloodthirsty monster. *Rule 2* is to *kill with conscience*. I have decided that it means preserving the lives of those with the most potential and destroying those who threaten my plans."

Farson growled his frustration. "First of all, *conscience* is *not* a logical expression of useful supplies and personnel. Second, that is not *Rule 2*. The rule is supposed to be *kill with*out *conscience*. You were meant to be an assassin, Rez."

Rezkin turned to the Jeng'ri. "Do you have a conscience?"

Xa grinned. "I think that I do; however, I tend to ignore it. It is a poor guide in my profession—and *yours*."

Rezkin considered the new information. *Rule 2* did make more sense Farson's way. He wondered why Kai had not corrected him when they had discussed the rules. Kai wanted Rezkin to be a king, not an assassin. Perhaps it made more sense for a king to kill *with* conscience.

He met Farson's gaze and said, "I am no longer the king's assassin. For as long as this war lasts, I must be king. I prefer my version of *Rule 2*. A king is supposed to lead and protect his people. It is better for him to have a conscience. Do you not agree?"

"You do not even understand what that means."

"I have inquired on the subject. Journeyman Wesson has provided the most useful assistance. He recited a poem given to him by his master. It said:

My conscience is my guiding light,
And knowledge of my dark within,
To know my place from wrong or right,
And struggle in the places dim.
When questions knock and chances stalk,
My mind is made and spare routes fade,
So thee and I and they and them,
And most in all the world do win.

"I endeavor to understand the author's meaning. Journeyman Wesson told me that it has been essential to him in understanding the nature of his power."

"You speak of a battle mage who spurns his affinity," said Farson. "With all that you have done and intend to do, you expect me to believe that you desire to be a man of conscience?"

Xa studied Rezkin. "Perhaps the Riel'gesh can afford to have a conscience."

Rezkin looked back to Farson. "You should know me better than that. Desires are unaffordable weaknesses. I do not have to possess a conscience to abide by one. Ashai needs a new king, and a king needs a conscience." His gaze snapped to the Jeng'ri. "When not acting as king, I do not require one.

Now, tell me what is in that trunk," he said, pointing toward a large, green trunk with brass hasps and clamps.

Xa glanced toward the trunk—one Rezkin had not yet opened. "How should I know?"

"It was warded by *you*."

"What makes you think that? Several are aboard who are capable of creating that ward."

"I can feel that it is your ward," Rezkin said. "Now, tell me what is in the trunk before I search it."

Xa glanced at the trunk again and then returned his gaze to Rezkin. "You can break the ward?"

Rezkin advanced on the trunk, knowing the Jeng'ri would not answer. People insisted on following him, yet they continued to defy his orders. Some were too useful to dispose of for minor offenses, but he would make them understand that their disobedience had consequences. Having already checked for traps on the trunk's exterior, he prepared for whatever lurked within. It was an average trunk, with a good lock, but unadorned. He reached through Xa's ward, maintaining his focus and forcing it to bend around him.

Xa glanced at Farson. "How does he do that? I sense no interference."

Farson said, "I do not bear the *talent*, but his ability to negate others' has always been disturbing to those who are blessed."

"He does not negate it. He is capable of touching it, of grappling and using it for his own purposes."

"You should keep that in mind and consider it a warning," said Farson.

Rezkin touched the box and was suddenly filled with both foreboding and urgency. He picked the lock and then looked back at Xa. The assassin was attempting to ease his way around Farson to reach the door, and from the striker's lack of interest and the mage power Rezkin felt slip over his skin, he figured the Jeng'ri had cast a spell to prevent them from noticing his movements.

Rezkin returned his gaze to the trunk as he said, "Xa, you had best stay where you are. Farson—to your left."

The striker snapped his arm out and smacked the Jeng'ri back a few paces. Xa stared at Farson with genuine surprise as he recovered.

"You are faster than I expected."

Farson grunted. With a nod toward Rezkin, he said, "I have had years of conditioning to catch *him*."

Rezkin stood to one side of the trunk and glanced at Xa, hoping for some sign of what it might contain. With his heart pumping and the battle energy surging through him, he threw the lid open. He was immediately struck with … confusion. He looked at the Jeng'ri.

"Fish?"

Xa and Farson both watched him in puzzlement.

"What?" said Xa.

"You brought aboard a warded trunk filled with fish?"

Xa appeared truly perplexed for the briefest moment, and then he smiled. "Of course. I get hungry."

Rezkin returned his gaze to the trunk's fishy contents. The slippery, silver mackerel were flopping in a mound, with wide, beady eyes, and mouths gulping frantically. They were the noisiest fish he had ever heard. The trunk, however, contained no water in which to keep them alive.

Farson closed the distance so that he could peer into the trunk. He screwed up his face in frustration and looked at Rezkin. "You said they were fish. For what purpose would you attempt to deceive me? Is this a setup?"

Rezkin met the striker's angry glare. "What are you talking about? They *are* fish."

Farson narrowed his eyes and then turned his dubious gaze on Xa. He said, "I see a trunk full of birds. The small yellow ones that sing."

Rezkin also looked at Xa. "An illusion, then. What is it hiding?"

Xa spread his hands and shrugged. "I cannot make illusions."

Farson grabbed a dangling rope for support and drew his sword. The song of steel rang through the air over the flopping of fish.

"What are you doing?" Rezkin said.

"The illusion may be hiding a trap. You stand back, and I will see if I can spring it."

"By stabbing it?"

They both took a step back as the sounds from the trunk intensified.

"I have never heard birds make so much noise," Farson hollered over the din.

"And only after you threatened to stab into it," Rezkin said. He looked back to Xa. "Tell me now!"

Xa said, "I cannot. I am under oath. But, I would not suggest stabbing it."

The roar grew again, and Rezkin decided that either the illusion or whatever it concealed did not like being threatened. To Farson, he said, "Retrieve Journeyman Wesson."

Farson said, "Can you not break through it as you do the wards?"

"Perhaps, but I have never had the opportunity to break an illusion. What if I destroy whatever it is hiding?"

The cacophony rose once more, and Farson glared at Xa before departing the room. A few minutes later, he returned with the battle mage in tow.

Rezkin motioned to the trunk and said, "Journeyman, please do something about this."

Wesson's eyes widened as he peered into the trunk. "Puppies? Where did you get wolf pups, and what have you done to make them so upset?"

"I see fish. Farson sees birds. It is an illusion."

Wesson knelt in front of the trunk to examine the spell and had to grab onto the handle for support as the ship suddenly slammed into the trough of a wave.

"Be careful, Journeyman. It was warded by an assassin. It may contain a trap."

Wesson glanced at Xa and then back to the trunk. "I see the ward. Did you bend it like this? How did you get it to stay?"

"I am holding it," Rezkin said.

"You are able to hold it? Like a curtain?"

"Yes, I suppose."

"That is so very strange," Wesson mused as he plucked at the illusion to see the underlying spell. He continued muttering as he worked. "A ward is a spell, not an object to be handled. To modify or manipulate one, you must change the spell itself."

"What do you mean?"

Wesson fell onto his rear as the ship swayed, and Rezkin braced him before he tumbled over backward. Regaining his feet, Wesson said, "Imagine that a ward is like a painting of an apple on a table. The apple is not real. It is composed of lines painted in the shape of an apple as seen from one point of view. If you want the apple in a different location, you must paint over the lines and paint them again somewhere else. *You* somehow reach into the painting, grab the apple off the table, and move it to another spot."

Having no patience for a discussion of his supposed powers, Rezkin said, "The illusion?"

"It is crude and unstable, a beginner's attempt. That would account for the fact that we all see something different. It is well considered, though, since the sounds made by the respective animals are covering the sounds of the creature inside."

Rezkin said, "It is alive, then? Whatever is inside?"

"Yes, that is why all the images we see are animals. It is more difficult to mask living things as non-living and vice versa. I would say, with something this crude, the spell is dependent on your unconscious mind for the image. Whatever you are seeing is a rough representation of how you would see the creature if it were another animal—like a metaphor."

"You can break the illusion?"

Wesson nodded. "Oh, yes, easily. I wanted to make a thorough examination of the spell before I destroy it. Give me one second, and I will be able to see through … oh dear."

The illusion snapped away, and Rezkin's racing heart nearly stalled. He knew, in that instant, that he would have to kill Xa.

Rezkin reached a hand toward the quivering, petrified woman, and she squealed in terror. Tears streamed down her face as she tried to back further into the box. He stepped away and then rounded the trunk so that he stood out of her sight and between the Jeng'ri and the doorway. Before he killed the Jeng'ri, he needed questions answered, and his first was not the one Xa expected.

"To whom did you swear the mage oath?"

Xa looked over as the woman flung herself into Wesson's arms while crying hysterically. With a nod, he said, "To her."

"How did *she* convince *you* to swear a mage oath?"

"It was the only way she would get into the box."

Rezkin glanced over to catch a glimpse of dark brown, watery eyes before they were once again hidden in Wesson's robes. He felt a rising heat in his chest as he turned back to Xa. "So, you kidnapped Frisha by promising to keep her presence a secret from me?"

"That would be a strange kidnapping," Xa mused. "I did not ask her to come. I merely assisted."

"What was in it for you?"

Xa smiled graciously. "It was a request from the future queen." Then, his smile turned to a smirk as he said, "I wanted to see what would happen."

Rezkin's chest burned hotter, and the stone hidden beneath his shirt began to heat as well. "The experience seems inadequate to have cost you your life."

Rezkin drew Bladesunder and advanced on the Jeng'ri just as the ship rocked, throwing both of them to the side. The assassin backpedaled over a pile of sacks and lashed out with a whip-like tendril of power. Rezkin grabbed the streaming tendril and yanked, causing Xa to stumble toward him, narrowly deflecting Rezkin's slash with a dirk. The ship rocked in the other direction just as the steel clashed, and a screech broke through the heat that had filled Rezkin's body and mind.

"Wait, Rezkin! Please! Don't kill him. It was my fault! I asked him to help me."

Unleashing a torrent of speed, he kicked the Jeng'ri hard enough to send him flying into the wall.

"Stay down," he said, and then he rounded on Frisha.

Farson had moved to block the woman from flying weapons, and Wesson had raised a ward. Rezkin walked through the ward and then barked at Farson to keep an eye on the downed assassin. He towered over Frisha as she looked up at him with a fear-filled gaze. He huffed and then backed away a pace. He sheathed his sword and stood tense as he kept an eye on Farson and Xa in his peripheral vision.

"You permitted an assassin to lock you in a warded trunk hidden by an illusion. How could you possibly think it was a good idea to make yourself so vulnerable?"

"Well, I didn't know he was an assassin—"

"No, you did *not* know. You did not know who he is, and you let him put you in a locked box!"

"I thought he was a royal guard—Princess Ilanet's trusted, honorable guard! *You* told us so!"

"I never said he was honorable, and I certainly never said he was to be trusted."

"No," she screamed. "What would *you* know about trust and honor? You—you killed all those people. *You* put their bodies along the riverbanks." Her chest rose and fell with every heaving gasp. "*You* are the monster Uncle Marcum was trying to keep away from us! All that time, we were *with* you! While we were sleeping and shopping and spending time together, you were out slaughtering dozens, maybe *hundreds* of people. And then—*what*?—you just return like nothing happened? Now that I know, will you kill me? By the Maker, you're going to kill me!"

She pushed away from Wesson and continued until she hit the wall. The ship lurched, and she was tossed back into the mage. "Oh, did Wesson know? Wait, he didn't know, did he? Now he's going to die, too, and it's my fault. No! It's *your* fault. You're the murderer! And him"—she motioned to Xa and then Farson—"and *him*! You're all murderers, and now we're going to die."

Wesson glanced from Frisha to Rezkin. He scratched his head and said, "What exactly am I to die for knowing?"

Rezkin shook his head and held his hands in front of him in a manner he thought might be placating to the panicky woman. "I have no intention of killing either of you. *He*, however"—Rezkin nodded toward Xa—"is about to die."

Frisha balled her fists and stepped forward. "Why? Because he exposed your secret?"

Rezkin was fascinated with her strange behavior. She clung crying to the mage or cowered in the corner when faced with her own death, but she stood strong whenever he threatened the assassin.

"Why do you stand for him?" he said. "You obviously heard our conversation. He is the Jeng'ri, the second highest assassin in the Order. It is the equivalent of Ashai's Black Hall."

"Which *you* took over!" The light of knowledge glinted in her eyes as new truths dawned. "You were taking over the Black Hall while I was begging my uncle to let me marry you! And Tam! Tam told me you killed a lot of people. Tam knows, too?"

"No," Rezkin said firmly. "Tam does not know about this. You will not tell him. You will not tell *anyone*." He paused to make sure the message had been received and then said, "You did not explain why you stand for Xa."

"Because it wasn't his fault."

Rezkin was dumbfounded by her sincerity. The stone beneath his tunic warmed uncomfortably, and he realized the heat in his chest had dissipated. As he stared at Frisha, he felt a tug at the corner of his lips. Then, he chuckled, and the chuckle turned to laughter. Frisha and Wesson jumped, and Xa looked at him like he had lost his mind. Rezkin turned to Farson, who wore an inscrutable expression.

"She says the Jeng'ri is not responsible for his actions. The Jeng'ri, one of the most feared killers in Channería, is not to blame for locking her in a trunk or for putting her life in danger. He is not to blame for exposing the secret he was sworn to keep upon promise of pain and death. He is not responsible for his decision to defy me in undertaking actions he knew I would oppose. The

Jeng'ri of the Order is not to blame for delivering the innocent woman widely rumored to be my future queen to the *Adana'Ro*." His expression cooled to the icy gaze of the Raven, and he met Frisha's startled stare. "This man knows exactly what he does, and I am sure it goes far beyond your innocent desires."

Frisha glanced at Xa, who wore the same dark expression. He did look quite the assassin in that moment, and Frisha suddenly recalled the uncomfortable looks Ilanet had given him. The girl had been upset that Frisha had asked for his help, but she had thought Ilanet only concerned about going behind Rezkin's back. She realized that Ilanet had known about Xa. Did she know about Rezkin, too?

Rezkin strode over to Xa. "Your life is forfeit."

Xa said, again, "I did not know we were going to the Adana'Ro."

"Ignorance is no excuse, especially in your case where it is unbelievable."

"Then, let me help you. I will protect her."

"You were supposed to be *protecting* Ilanet. Where is she? Do you have her secreted in another trunk?"

"No, she is in Cael. She does not need my protection. This one does."

The heat began to return, and Rezkin growled, "Only because you put her in danger!"

Xa said, "I am too useful for you to kill over this."

"No one is too useful for me to kill."

"I serve the Riel'gesh," Xa said as Rezkin raised a dagger to his throat.

"You defy me," said Rezkin.

"I declare *do'riel'und*!" Xa lifted his chin toward Frisha. "For her."

Rezkin paused as a trickle of blood seeped down Xa's neck. "*You* would declare *do'riel'und* for someone? You claim to serve the Riel'gesh, yet you do not declare it for me."

Xa met his gaze and swallowed against the blade. "You would not accept it for yourself."

"Swear it," Rezkin said.

The Jeng'ri reached up to grasp the blade tight enough to draw blood. The buzz of vimara filled the air, and Xa said, "I declare *do'riel'und* Frisha Souvain-Marcum."

Rezkin spun the bloodied dagger around so that Xa could grasp the handle, then straightened and backed away. He glanced toward Frisha and said, "Your belongings have been delivered to the women's quarters."

Her mouth hung open. "You knew I was here?"

His gaze danced across the ceiling as the ship creaked. The rocking had slowed, and he hoped that meant the storm had passed. "I knew you were somewhere aboard. I admit that I did not anticipate *this* scenario."

"But, you were upset with him for bringing me because it wasn't safe. Why didn't you stop me if you knew?"

"I discovered that you were aboard a few hours after we embarked. You are *ro*—innocent, unknowledgeable of the night that opposes your day. So long as you were oblivious to my darker endeavors, you were safe from the Adana'Ro, protected even. By exposing you to my secret, he has put your life in danger. How they judge *ro* is difficult to predict."

Frisha looked up at him through puffy eyes and damp lashes. "So you were not upset by my coming? Only that I know who you are?"

Rezkin's expression cooled, and she thought that on anyone else, it would have indicated sadness. She was no longer sure he was capable of feeling anything—besides anger.

He said, "You will never know me, Frisha. I am not something you can understand."

He glanced at Farson, and it seemed some message had been exchanged. He turned back to her. "I am not your keeper. If you had told me you wanted to come, I would have explained to you why you should not, just as I did with Tam. You are intelligent. I think you would have made the right decision. If, however, you insisted, then I would have brought you. While you have never expressed your feelings of mistrust toward me"—he motioned to the trunk—"your actions show that I had already lost that trust. I have always been honest with you. I told you that I was keeping secrets."

Frisha fumed. "Dark Tidings, the True King, the Raven, the Riel'gesh—these are not secrets, Rezkin. These are completely different lives. Multiple lives!"

"Oh! You are the Raven?" Wesson said, finally grasping that last clue to the conversation. He nodded slowly, "Yes, that makes sense now."

Frisha looked at him aghast. "This doesn't bother you?"

Wesson shook his head. "No, not really."

She crossed her arms. "Please, explain why this does not upset you."

Wesson glanced at the others. They were all staring at Frisha. It seemed they were more concerned about her reaction than his, so he obliged. "Rezkin has always been more *and* less than he says he is. He is a master of half-truths. We all think we know him, and yet none of us know all of him. Some, like you, might say that we do not know his true self." He nodded toward Farson. "I believe the striker would say that he does not have one—that he is empty. The Jeng'ri believes him to be a demigod, a being incomprehensible to us. You are disappointed because he is not the person you thought he was. I cannot be disappointed because I never presumed to know him."

"*You* weren't supposed to marry him," Frisha huffed.

Wesson said, "Neither were *you*. Your guardian rejected him, and Rezkin did not press the issue. Now, perhaps you know why."

Rezkin interrupted the pointless exchange. "That is no longer a concern. Speak of this to no one. Assume anyone not in this room does not know."

He captured Frisha's gaze and nodded toward the Jeng'ri. "He is Xa. His life was forfeit and was spared only because he has sworn *do'riel'und* for you by mage oath. This means that his life is your life. If you die, he must kill himself—with that dagger, if possible. He has an interest in keeping you alive, so he is now your protector for the rest of your life. You do not have a choice in this unless you want him dead. Keep in mind that he is the Jeng'ri; and, therefore, difficult to kill. Like all good things, this comes with a drawback. If anyone finds out about his oath, they will know that to kill *him*, they must only kill *you*."

Frisha's face was pale as she stared at the Channerían assassin. Rezkin glanced at Xa and said, "He has also sworn to serve the Riel'gesh, which he recognizes as *me*. This means the only person from whom he will not protect you is me. I am bound by the *Rules*, which mean I am to honor and protect you as my *friend*, so do not make of me an enemy. Do you understand?"

Frisha gaped at him, glanced at Xa, and then back to Rezkin. "I think—"

"Good," he said. "Journeyman, please come with me." He ducked through the doorway, and Wesson followed with an apologetic glance.

Farson turned to the Jeng'ri. "You know he played you."

"How so?"

"If he had wanted you dead, he would not have stopped to chat. He was giving you an opportunity to make amends."

"Yes," said Xa, "but he would have killed me had I not."

Farson nodded and then looked at Frisha who was wide-eyed and shaking. He said, "I have never seen him angry. At least, not since he was a child and learned better. Was it fear for your safety? Anger that you had placed yourself in danger? Feelings of betrayal that you trusted Xa over him?"

Frisha winced.

He smirked. "I might think him sincere," he said as his gaze slid to Xa, "but it is more likely he wants us to *believe* he cares."

Frisha flushed in anger and embarrassment. "So, does this mean that he and I …"

Farson gave her a dubious look. "You would still marry him?" Her gaze quaked with fear, and he shook his head. "I thought not."

"You were trying to protect me. Before … in the courtyard … what you told me."

"I said as much."

She blinked away tears. "I didn't believe you."

"I know."

Rezkin motioned for Wesson to construct a ward around them as they strode onto the deck. Although the rain was heavy, the ocean had relaxed to an easy roll. The water slid off Wesson's shield in every direction, creating a glistening curtain between them and the outside world. Rezkin stopped when they were out of the way of the crew. He almost felt the need to brace himself. He felt drained of energy and famished. He put aside his discomfort to confront the battle mage.

"You do not have a problem with what you have learned?"

Wesson shook his head slowly. "No, I have many problems with it."

"And?"

"It is as I told Frisha. I do not presume to know you. The fact remains that King Bordran, *your father*, had you trained to be this way for a reason."

Wesson paused, resting his eyes on the cascading water. His gaze was distant as he continued. "My father worked at the palace before I was born. He was a minor noble—not important—at least, not in a political sense. He was an earth mage and an artist. I have seen some of his work. It is unusual for an earth mage to possess a delicate touch, but he created beautiful works of art.

He was responsible for maintaining the carvings and sculptures on the palace grounds and for creating new ones. Sometimes he did work for the cities or nobles like Lord Tieran's father. He died when I was eight, but before that, we spoke often about all nature of things—about serious matters people do not usually discuss with children. When I look back now, it seems as if he knew he would not live to see me grown."

He met Rezkin's intent gaze. "My father said that King Bordran was a stern man, not kind, but a good king who deserved our respect. I have watched you, and I think perhaps you are the same. My father believed in Bordran, and I believe in you."

Rezkin did not thank Wesson for his faith. To do so would have been petty and self-aggrandizing. The mage's faith, like that of his followers, was not a gift to be appreciated, but an assignment of duty to be fulfilled. Instead he said, "How did your father die?"

"When my mother was pregnant, he resigned from his job at the palace. He purchased a small estate in a rural village of western Ashai and took over as master of the local quarry. He later died in an accident, crushed under a pile of rock."

Rezkin tilted his head. "An experienced earth mage was crushed in an accident at a quarry."

Wesson looked at him with haunted eyes. "Yes."

8

The remainder of the trip to the Ferélli port city of Esk consisted of days upon days of rain, wind, and choppy seas. Frisha was frustrated with Xa's insistence on following her around the entire time. After nearly getting washed overboard *once*, he restricted her to the cabin. His protectiveness was worse than Rezkin's, and although Xa smiled more often, his humor was dark and his manners lacking. She missed the pleasant days when Rezkin strolled along the road beside her discussing the plants and animals. Then she remembered that those had been the quiet moments between storms. He had been out killing people and tasking thieves and assassins when she was not looking. Every once in a while, when she felt his gaze on her, she would glance up just as he looked away and wonder which of those people he was in that moment. Was he missing her, too, or was he thinking of ways to kill her? She then wondered what, exactly, she would have to do to lose his *friendship*.

"So, *I'm* a warrior and a healer," Reaylin said smugly. She nodded toward Yserria and Nanessy Threll and said, "She's a knight, and she's a mage. What is *your* function on this trip, Frisha?"

"Reaylin, you shouldn't be unkind," said Yserria. "Frisha has not yet found her purpose. That does not mean she has less value. Rezkin says potential is the greatest asset, and I think Frisha has much potential."

"Potential for what?" said Reaylin.

Yserria glanced at Frisha. "Well, I don't know, but potential without direction is still potential."

"It's alright," said Frisha. "I know I'm useless—useless and stupid." Frisha did not look up as she pushed her potatoes around her plate.

Reaylin and Yserria exchanged glances. Yserria said, "Why do you say that?"

"I just … I make stupid decisions. I'm not even supposed to be here. I stowed away."

Reaylin released a long whistle. "Oh, I bet Rezkin was livid."

"You have no idea."

Yserria nodded toward Xa who was seated at another table but still within arm's reach. "I guess that explains your new shadow. I can't imagine what Rezkin would do if something happened to his betrothed."

Frisha flushed. She had avoided talking about what had happened, mostly because the more she talked, the harder it would be to avoid their questions. Rezkin had not bothered to correct anyone when they made such comments, so she had not either. Why had he not said anything? Did he still think they would marry, or was he protecting her from the embarrassment? Perhaps it was part of some insidious plan. She did not want to be a part of the Raven's plans.

Frisha abruptly stood. "I need to speak with Rezkin."

It was only after she said it that she realized she had interrupted Mage Threll. The other women had moved on to a different discussion while she had been lost in thought. She apologized for the interruption and then staggered out of the mess. Although walking on the ship had gotten easier with time, the vessel occasionally plunged unexpectedly.

Rezkin was in his quarters deep in discussion with Strikers Shezar and Farson when Frisha stumbled into the berth.

"Oh, I'm sorry to interrupt," she said. She turned to leave but ran into Xa.

"No, stay," Rezkin said. To the strikers, he said, "Go eat. We will resume this discussion afterward." When they had gone, he told Xa that he, too, could take a break. When the assassin looked uncertain, Rezkin smirked. "I will not kill her while you are gone."

Xa glanced at Frisha in warning, as if telling her to behave.

After the door closed, Rezkin sat back in the chair behind his desk. "What do you need, Frisha?"

She bit her lip with uncertainty, then lost her footing. Rezkin waved toward the bed, and she hesitantly perched on the edge.

She said, "I've been thinking about, um, about you, I guess, and I'm terribly conflicted. When I see you, I see the Rezkin I've known, the one I thought to marry. Now, I don't know if any of that was real because there are these other things—terrible things—that have happened. I didn't see them happen, but I know they did, and you say you are responsible for them." Her eyes were large and pleading as she looked up at him. "How can you be someone I know and a complete stranger at the same time?" He had no answer for her, but she did not seem to expect one. She said, "Are you still angry?"

He watched her in silence for a while. Finally, he said, "I admit that I was *frustrated* with your lack of regard for your own life. I have dealt with those feelings and will endeavor to remain emotionally withdrawn, as I should have been all along. I apologize for my failure. I also recognize that your decisions were based on a false sense of security that I inadvertently instilled in you. The event has reaffirmed my belief that it is better for the *ro* to know the dangers they face. Still, I need people to continue functioning properly, so I cannot tell everyone the whole truth. It is apparent from your behavior that I may lose their trust and loyalty."

Frisha dropped her gaze to the floor. "I know I have made some stupid mistakes. I act on my feelings and don't always think things through."

"Perhaps knowing someone else's survival is dependent on yours will encourage you to be more responsible."

She glanced up at him. "I hadn't thought of it that way." Shaking her head, she said, "I can't do this. I can't be responsible for someone else's life."

"His life was over when he defied me for the last time. Attaching himself to you was merely an extension, and it gives him something to do besides vex *me*."

"How can you speak so casually of life and death?"

"I carry the responsibility of life and death for thousands, at the least. I cannot carry everyone. A drowning man is dangerous. He will drag you down with him if he can. You have to know when to let someone go."

"You remind me of Uncle Marcum. He says things like that." She paused and then took a deep breath. "Um … what of our betrothal?"

"That is entirely up to you, Frisha." Seeing her shock, he said, "You are surprised?"

"I didn't think you would still be interested," she said. "Everyone else thinks you should marry Ilanet. You are a king. She is a princess, and she was supposed to marry a prince of Ashai."

Rezkin shook his head. "I have no intention of marrying anytime soon. I will likely die before that day. The only reason I had considered it was to keep you with me. If you do not marry me, then there is no point in marrying at all."

Frisha's eyes welled with tears. "When you say things like that, my heart listens. It is terribly romantic, but now I wonder if you mean it at all."

Rezkin frowned. "I assure you that I have met no other woman I would consider marrying. It is not a priority. I will be satisfied to go through life without a spouse, if it would not be you."

"Do you love me?"

Rezkin stood from his seat and came around to kneel before her. He took her hands and met her gaze. "I have spoken with Farson. I know what you want to hear, but I must honor you with the truth. I will do everything in my power to make you safe and happy. I will give you a kingdom—I will give you *every* kingdom, if it is your wish. But, if love is what you desire, then it cannot be me."

Frisha looked longingly into his crystal gaze and then shook her head, her expression pained. "I'm sorry, Rez. I know you're doing what's necessary for the kingdom. I can't understand it all, and I really don't want to, but"—she took a deep breath—"I support you. You will always have my loyalty."

"But not your hand?"

She stared at their entwined fingers. It was rare that he touched her so intimately. "Tam says I'm a hopeless romantic, but I had resolved myself to the fact that I would never have true love. I thought I would marry a stranger who would only want me for my uncle's fortune. Then, I met you, and I had hope. I thought you really cared. A girl dreams of being swept away by a knight in shining armor, not a shadow knight of death. More importantly, she dreams that her knight loves her. I trust that you won't allow me to marry someone I don't want. If I am to be given a choice, I want to marry someone who loves me."

Rezkin lifted her chin and caught her gaze. "Is marriage your dream, Frisha?"

"I—I don't know. I didn't think I had a choice."

"You will not marry until you are ready. I will make sure of it. If becoming a wife and mother is your dream, there is nothing wrong with that. It is a position deserving of respect, equal to any warrior, healer, or mage; but, perhaps you should spend less time thinking of husbands and more time thinking of who you want to be."

An abrupt pounding on the door woke them from the depth of conversation, and Malcius strode into the room unbidden. "I heard you two were in here *alone*. Look, Rez, I know you are as good as betrothed, but I am *supposed* to be her escort. I am responsible for making sure she retains her virtue."

Rezkin rose to his feet and went back to the seat at his desk. "You are correct, Malcius, and it is especially important now that we have agreed to call off the betrothal."

"What?" Malcius said in alarm. "No! I mean, you two are supposed to get married. Frisha, tell me he is joking."

Frisha shook her head and chuckled as she wiped watery eyes. "I don't think Rez makes jokes."

Malcius's face reddened, and he turned on Rezkin. "Did you reject her? Suddenly you have other prospects, and she is not good enough?"

"No, Malcius!" said Frisha. "It was my decision."

Malcius turned his ire on *her*. "What is wrong with you? Are you mad? He is king! He is a *legitimate* prince of Ashai."

Rezkin clenched his teeth through the tightness in his chest. It was threatening to restrict his breathing, and he would have thought something seriously wrong if he had not already felt similar pain in the past. He now knew it was the pain of loss. It was stronger this time, and he wondered if it was due to the amount of time he had spent in the outworld. Perhaps he was losing his ability to distance himself from his feelings. He needed time to meditate. The stone on his chest heated as his pain grew, and Rezkin focused on the burning discomfort to take his mind from it.

"Malcius, calm yourself," Rezkin said. "It has been agreed that I cannot give Frisha what she desires most, what she deserves. You are aware, at least in part, of my upbringing. I am not fit to be her husband. As with all of you, I will ensure that she has all that she needs until my support is no longer necessary."

Malcius shook his head and looked at Frisha. "Who do you intend to marry, then?"

Frisha balled her fists and pushed to her feet, her show of strength slightly marred as she stumbled with the roll of the ship. She righted herself and lifted her chin. "I am not going to marry anyone."

"But your father and Uncle Marcum—"

"Are not here," she said, crossing her arms.

"Then, what are you going to do?" Malcius said with genuine concern.

"Well, I'm … I'm going to do … something." With feigned confidence she said, "I haven't decided yet, but it will be great."

Xa entered the room just then and smirked at Frisha's attempt to stand up for herself.

Malcius nodded toward the Jeng'ri and asked Rezkin, "Why do you keep assigning him to watch the ladies? Is he a eunuch?"

The assassin's grin fell, and he drew a blade.

Rezkin sighed. "No, he is not a eunuch. At least, not as far as I know. He will protect Frisha, though. Now, all of you out. We will soon arrive, and I do not wish to be disturbed until we do."

Rezkin barred the door and placed several traps around the room. He ate the food he had prepared earlier to fill his grumbling stomach, yet he was still unsatisfied. He then lay back on his bed to meditate and promptly fell asleep. For the first time in a long while, he dreamt.

The light of the day waned, and he stared into the darkness between the trees. The fire's heat seeped into his skin, driving out the chill. An owl hooted, and branches creaked as the wind swept through the pass. He heard a woman's voice, a whisper in the otherwise unbroken melody of the natural world, but he could not understand her words. He turned. He saw her clearly. He knew he had, but a glimpse was all he could remember. A glimpse of silver eyes and hair as white as snow.

Rezkin awoke to shouts announcing their arrival at port, and he realized he must have been asleep for several hours. He rubbed the sleep from his eyes and shook his head to chase away the grogginess. Alarmed that he had been so vulnerable in his unexpectedly deep sleep, he surveyed the room from his bed but found no evidence of an intruder. He sat up, and when he lifted his eyes, his heart immediately burst into a gallop as he saw two orange orbs staring at him from across the room. The wood-like creature had taken on the rough form of a table, a table with a face looking out from its columnar pedestal.

He exhaled in a rush. "Bilior, what do you want?"

The table twisted and snapped as the katerghen took its usual form. It stood awkwardly with one arm out to the side and its head tilted at an angle. Its leaves rattled, and the sound of rain, for once, was not coming from outside.

"Power dances on the wind," the katerghen said. "They come."

The katerghen popped and crackled then bounded through the porthole, stretching and twisting to effortlessly fit. Rezkin watched after him, noting that they were already tied to the floating dock, and the fae creature disappeared. Once he had finally cleared his mind of his muddled thoughts, Rezkin left his cabin. He had no idea what the katerghen was trying to tell him, but it sounded ominous. Without more information, it was pointless to speculate. He put the matter aside.

The ride to the sanctorum of the Adana'Ro should not have been a long one. The process of arriving, however, had become daunting. Since they needed to acquire more horses anyway, Rezkin had planned on purchasing some in Esk. It was unexpected that none of the horse traders were willing to sell. No matter their method of approach, somehow the traders always saw through their subterfuge. The road was fairly well traveled, and no word of trouble had reached their ears before the onset of their journey. After being attacked by bandits twice in the first hour of their jaunt, however, it became obvious they were being targeted. What would have been a few hours' ride by road turned into nearly a day's hike across wild terrain.

"I do not like this," said Farson.

"Nor do I," replied Rezkin, "but it was unavoidable that they would know we were coming."

"They have not attacked," Shezar observed.

"They have been slowing us down," Farson said. "Do you think they planned this from the beginning?"

"They stole the sword long before I had designs for Cael or dealings with Gendishen. It may be that someone whispered in Privoth's ear the suggestion to have me retrieve it, though."

"Privoth is shrewd enough to invest in that idea on his own," said Farson.

Malcius sidled up beside them. "I still do not understand why the Adana'Ro would be interested in *you*."

"The Adana'Ro are mysterious," Rezkin said.

Malcius huffed. "That is not an answer."

Yserria wedged herself between Malcius and Rezkin and said, "The king does not answer to you, Malcius Jebai."

Malcius said, "You may be a knight now, but I still outrank you. You will treat me with respect."

Yserria grinned sweetly and said, "When you say something worthy of respect, I shall oblige."

Malcius looked to Rezkin. "Why do you put up with her?"

"If you find her remarks offensive, Malcius, perhaps you should do something about it."

"But … she is a swordmaster!"

"Yes, and you are not. Her strength is earned, while yours is dependent on the diluted power of your forefathers. Knight Yserria is not a conniving woman. I would not have granted her the title if she were. Find a way to earn her respect."

Yserria grinned as Malcius fumed and then dropped back to walk beside Reaylin and Nanessy.

"You always take her side," Malcius muttered.

"We are all on the same side," Rezkin said as he studied the cliff face looming in the distance.

The sanctorum was located high upon a cliff that overlooked the River Rhen. The river's banks were dotted with scraggly bushes and the occasional twisted, scruffy tree. Patches of greenery grew where the water splashed off rocks, but the landscape was otherwise speckled with rocks and a variety of cactuses. The river flowed between high cliffs that appeared painted in varying shades of gold and red, and the road they had intended to take ran across the high ground. It would have taken a phenomenal archer and a generous amount of luck to target them so far below; but, from that vantage, it would be easy to track their progress and signal ahead for an ambush. Therefore, it was not surprising when they were suddenly surrounded by masked assailants.

Wesson and Nanessy immediately encapsulated the travelers in a glowing ward of their combined powers, intentionally rendering visible to all. It crackled with warnings in livid red runes scored across the swirling blue surface. An attempt to breach the ward would mean a messy death.

The assailants were mostly women, each dressed in black and covered from head to foot. All that showed from beneath their skin-tight coverings were their eyes, but the weapons they carried were obvious. Swords, knives, and bows abounded, while mage power buzzed in strength from a few. Thirteen were visible, which meant there were probably at least three more unseen. One stood out among them. She wore a head scarf of scarlet red, and her eyes danced with mirth as she met Rezkin's gaze.

"We meet again," said the secrelé in heavily accented Ashaiian.

Rezkin recognized her as the woman who had led the *cueret* at the Black Hall. "Do'grelah, Secrelé," he said in formal greeting. He switched to Ferélli, having already confirmed that none of his companions spoke the language. "*My companions are* ro. *You will not harm them.*"

After a quick perusal of the others, the secrelé said, "*Perhaps some of them are ro, but they dance along the fire line.*"

"*Only because they are in my company.*"

"*Then it is you who are responsible for their fall.*"

"*Only if you push them,*" he countered.

Her eyes narrowed as if she smirked beneath the mask. "*Why did you bring them?*"

"*To them I am king. They believe I need them.*"

"*Do you?*"

Rezkin shrugged. "*A king without vassals is a king in name only, and I have no need of titles.*"

At this, she chuckled. "*And yet you have acquired many.*"

Rezkin grinned in return. "*The first act of defense is to put a name to that which you fear. Without a name, I am only fear itself.*"

Her almond eyes became crescents again, and she said, "*Do you think we fear you?*"

He said, "*I think it is your wish.*"

"*Why would we wish for that?*"

"*Because you hope. You hope for the Riel'gesh.*"

She glanced at the others, who stood in tense anticipation. Another of the Adana'Ro, a woman with amber-colored eyes who buzzed with the *talent*, approached.

"*I have completed the study. They must drop the ward if they are to leave or strike outside of it,*" she said.

The secrelé looked back to Rezkin and spoke in Ashaiian. "You will come alone." Again, she grinned beneath her mask. "And, you will bare yourself."

Rezkin said, "I do not believe that is customary."

Her eyes glinted with silent laughter, and she replied, "We do not trust you."

He glanced back to the strikers.

Shezar said, "It is not worth the risk. With the mages, we can defeat these and leave this place. Once they have lost so many, they will reconsider their methods of negotiation."

When prompted, Farson shrugged. "You are the weapon. If you should need any others, you can take theirs. You will be at a disadvantage without the armor, though." He met the secrelé's gaze as he continued speaking to Rezkin. "If you die, it will not be the first time. They should worry about what you will do when you return."

The two women glanced at each other and then watched as Rezkin began to disrobe.

"Wait," Malcius exclaimed. "You are not seriously going in the nude."

Rezkin removed his armor and then his shirt. He then began unstrapping all the previously hidden sheathes and harnesses, tossing his knives, stars, needles, and other sharp objects into a pile on the ground. "They have something we need, and this is what I must to do get it."

Malcius watched as the pile of armaments grew. "I had no idea you carried so many weapons. Actually, I did not know it was possible."

"I do not always carry this many."

Malcius muttered, "A lot of good it does you if you just throw them away because they tell you to."

"That is precisely the good of it," he said as he pulled off his boots. "They know that, although we are surrounded, we are not incapable of defending ourselves. I voluntarily disarm and disrobe as a gesture of good faith."

"Good faith to a sect of assassins," Malcius muttered.

"Yes," Rezkin said as he dropped his pants and set to unstrapping additional weapons.

Malcius huffed and scowled at his female companions who showed no shame in watching the show. He turned back to Rezkin. "What if they try to kill you?"

Rezkin ran his hands through his loose, inky locks to show that he had no hidden weapons. "They likely will. I must survive."

"But they are fully armed!" said Malcius.

Rezkin grinned and flexed his biceps. "So am I," he said with a wink for the secrelé.

The woman's laughter was cut short as he strode effortlessly through the explosive mage ward. When the vimara slid like illuminated water over his skin, for the briefest moment, strange, archaic black, blue, and red lines and runes could be seen scrawled across nearly every inch of his flesh below the neck. In that moment, he truly looked the demonic lord many a rumor claimed him to be. The marks were gone in a flash, and onlookers would have been left to wonder if they had been there at all, had the others not also witnessed them.

Rezkin stopped less than a pace from the secrelé and caught her in his icy gaze. "Shall we go?"

"That?" she said, nodding to the stone that hung from the lace around his neck.

Although he was no longer in the citadel, he was anxious about parting with the stone. He would need it upon his return, and he did not want to lose the one object he knew could help keep his mind sharp.

"It is only a stone," he said. "A token from home. I prefer to carry it with me as a reminder of those who await my return."

She glanced at the stone and nodded solemnly. "It could easily be used as a weapon, but I will permit it. As you said to your friend, it is a gesture of good faith." She motioned for him to walk ahead. The other Adana'Ro surrounded him as they departed, and Rezkin's companions were left alone.

Malcius rounded on Farson. "What was *that*?" he said, motioning to his arms.

Farson said, "I have never seen them before. I assume they are the marks Connovan mentioned."

"So it is true, then?" Malcius said. "About him dying?"

Farson shrugged. "It seems the presence of the marks is true. As to their cause, we cannot say for certain."

Mage Threll said, "What is this about him dying, and what does it have to do with those marks?"

Ignoring the question, Malcius said, "So we are going to let him walk away with those people? What if they kill him? What if he does not return?"

"They enticed him here for a reason," said Farson. "I doubt they want him dead. Even if that is their purpose, he will not make it easy. They know this. They will have to decide if the survival of their sect is more important than killing him."

Malcius shook his head and huffed. "Why I am asking you? You are probably hoping they kill him. It is no secret that you have wanted him dead since you arrived."

Shezar said, "Your tongue has become loose, Lord Malcius. You speak to a striker with the same disrespect Knight Yserria showed you."

Malcius did not back down. He met Shezar's stare. "A striker receives respect because he dedicates himself to the service of the kingdom. I have accepted Rezkin as my king. This man has not. He serves no one. Until he does, he is no striker."

Farson straightened to his full height, his strength of presence making it appear as if he towered over Malcius, even though he was only a few inches taller. "I serve the Kingdom of Ashai. Right now, how best to do that is in question." He poked Malcius in the chest. "You accepted *Rez* as your king without knowing him. It is not supposed to be the duty of a striker to determine who is the rightful king. I am heartened to think there is an alternative to Caydean, but I am not certain the world can survive Rez. You should be concerned as well."

"Sometimes you must choose a side and hope for the best," Malcius said. He stalked away and practically ran into Yserria. "Did you get a good show?" he snapped.

Yserria's concern became a smirk. "I have never seen that much of a man before, but the others tell me he is a perfect specimen." She tilted her head and said, "Tell me, *Lord* Malcius, how do you compare?"

Malcius's face heated in anger. "You were never so forward with Palis. You will never know what it means to be a true lady."

Her smile fell, and she scowled at him. "Palis was a gentleman who respected me, and *you* will never know what it is to have a true *woman*." She spun on her heel and rejoined the other women who were seated on the talus slope.

Unable to leave the bubble in which they were trapped, Malcius plopped down on a boulder between Wesson and Brandt.

"She is infuriating!" he said.

Wesson shifted uncomfortably as he glanced at Yserria, who scowled in their direction while she and Reaylin conversed too quietly for them to hear.

"You antagonize her," said Brandt.

Malcius continued muttering. "I will never understand what my brother saw in her."

Wesson kicked a cobble and scratched runes in the dirt with his boot.

"Why any noble would marry a commoner …"

"I hope to," said Wesson as he tucked a curl that had grown too long behind his ear.

"What? To marry a commoner? *Why*?" Malcius said, aghast.

"Not just any commoner. There is someone specific," Wesson said.

"I did not know you had a woman," said Brandt

Glancing back at the dirt, Wesson said, "Well, I do not have a woman. Not really. I mean, I have not seen her since we were children. She was always special to me. Even then we assumed we would marry. But … she is probably already wed, now. Her father—he was not a patient man."

"You do not know?" said Malcius.

Wesson shook his head. "No, I used to write letters to her often. I never received a single reply. I—well, I did not leave home under the best of circumstances. She probably hates me. I have apologized so many times in my letters."

"You have not been home since you were a child?" Malcius said, truly surprised.

Wesson shook his head. "No, my master did not feel it was safe to let me leave until I was thoroughly trained to control my powers. There were … *other* … issues, as well. It was best I stayed away. I was hoping that, after I finished my apprenticeship, I could earn enough money to return my house to good standing and show her that I am not the person she thinks I am."

Malcius looked at him in horror. "What exactly did you do?"

Wesson pulled his gaze from the ground. "I am a battle mage, Lord Malcius. Consider uncontrolled destructive power in the hands of a child."

Malcius was quiet for a while, although he glanced at Wesson warily several times. Finally, Brandt said, "I thought most mages came into their power close to adulthood."

With a nod, Wesson said, "That is true for most."

"Was it because you are so powerful?" said Malcius.

"Usually, the amount of power has no bearing on when the *talent* will present itself. My master did wonder, however, if mine was just too much to contain."

The sun set early beyond the canyon wall, and Rezkin had nothing to protect him from the chill. He focused on warming his muscles as he jogged across the rocks at a steady pace. Although the sharp edges did not often break through his thick calluses, one would occasionally bite at the softer tissue between his toes. He kept on as if unperturbed. It was hardly the worst pain he had suffered. Once they left the flatter terrain by the river, he was forced to navigate, in the waning light, up the talus slope and between cacti, thistles, and sagebrush.

At the base of the cliff, he paused and looked back to the secrelé for guidance. She motioned up the wall of rock.

"You do not intend to guide the ascent?" he said.

"If you are the Riel'gesh, perhaps you can fly."

"If I am not?"

"Then we have no need of you."

The Adana'Ro had employed an ancient and effective method of security to prevent unwanted guests from reaching their cliff-side home. Foot and handholds had been carved into the face. There were many paths, but only one led to the sanctorium. If one took the wrong path, it was nearly impossible to backtrack. Once started, the only way to finish alive was to reach the top. Those who were poor in luck or memory met with the ground much more quickly than how they had left it. Rezkin managed to find the first foothold, but if he started with the wrong foot, his climb would be doomed from the start. With a fifty-fifty chance, he began with the left. Since the cliff was now in total darkness, he was glad for the fact that he had no boots and could feel for the cracks and divots.

The Adana'Ro had not followed him up the cliff, and as far as he could tell, only one or two now remained at the base. Once he was too high to turn back, several ropes had been lowered out of his reach, and the black-clad warriors had climbed the wall quickly.

The night climb would have been impossible under normal circumstances, but Rezkin intended to cheat. He felt around for the next handhold, but he could not find it, if it were there at all. Running his hand over the surface, he found a small crack. As he clung to the wall, he focused intently. The image of the potential ward popped into his mind, and with its function defined by his will, the imaginary construct solidified inside the tiny crevice. With a second thought, the potential ward expanded in a pulse. With a *pop*, fragments of rock rained down the cliff face. Rezkin dug his fingers into the newly made handhold and pulled himself higher.

He continued in this manner to the top, knowing it would be easy for the assassins to force him from the wall. From that height, a fall would guarantee death. He wondered if he could produce a potential ward large enough to cushion his fall or deflect an attack. Having never created one larger than his thumb, he had no idea if it was possible. Of course, now he wondered about the truth of his potential wards. Had he been misinformed as to the nature of what he was producing? Farson would not be able to answer the question since he was neither aware of Rezkin's potential wards nor a mage. Rezkin hesitated to discuss it with Wesson since he did not know what the future held. It was always a good idea to have a secret weapon, especially one that could not be found when searched.

When he was within thirty feet of the top, the warriors began tossing pebbles and cobbles down on him. None were large enough to knock him free of the cliff, but they were a sufficient distraction. After being pelted for several minutes to no effect, a bucket of water was dumped over him. The reason for this became apparent as the wind abruptly began swirling around him. The tingle of power in the air confirmed that a mage was involved. The cold night air whipped over his wet skin and prickled his flesh. It was not the first time he had endured such petty trials, and by the laughter he heard above, he knew their efforts were intended as taunts.

As soon as his fingers curled over the ledge, someone attempted to stomp them. He grabbed the woman's ankle and yanked her over the side. She smacked into the cliff face, her hands scrambling for purchase as she dangled upside down. A rope was tossed over the side, and Rezkin held her just long enough for her to grab hold. Then, he pulled himself onto the platform.

A young man, clad in black, leapt from the ground where he had knelt to check on the woman. He raised his fists and hissed, "That was foolish!"

"Yes, it probably was. I should have let her fall." Rezkin held up a knife. "I can still remedy the situation."

The man rocked back in surprise as Rezkin flicked the dagger toward the rope, missing it by a hair as the point dug into the dirt to the side. He said, "She may want that back when she reaches the top."

After rubbing the loose sediment from his hands, arms, and chest he stalked forward, unperturbed by the stares and remarks over his nudity. The entrance to the sanctorium was narrow and appeared to be a natural opening to a cave. Once inside, though, it became obvious that the structure had been in use for many generations. The walls had been carved to depict what was presumably the history of the sect, and additional rooms had been opened or widened along the sides. He had no idea how large the sanctorium truly was, but the grand hall was impressive. It was a dry cave, and the places not modified by human hands were characterized by smooth, swirling eddies of colorful banded rock shaped by the natural elements over time. Torches and mage lamps hung from the walls and ceiling, and sections of the floor bearing furnished seating areas were covered in thick carpets. Walkways and overhead balconies indicated at least three levels, and most of these were occupied by spectators covered in black with the occasional splash of red.

A woman in red sat on a golden throne at the head of the hall. The back of the throne bore two crossed bronze-gold short swords of the Jahartan style. Rezkin wondered if the weapons were functional or purely aesthetic. Behind the throne was a statue three times the size of a normal man. It was a representation of Meros, the ancient Verrilian god of joy, standing tall, his head held high, a broad smile gracing his strong jaw, his hands fisted at the waist. On either side of the throne were two women dressed in blue, each with weapons drawn. The entire scene was vaguely reminiscent of the descriptions of the Soka, the great warrior women of the Jahartan Empire.

The secrelé placed her fists together in front of her and bowed over them toward the seated woman. "Great Mother, we have brought to you the one called the Raven."

"And my children?" the woman said.

The secrelé glanced behind to where they had entered then turned back. "All are well, Great Mother."

The secrelé and the rest of Rezkin's escort then moved to the sides of the chamber so that he was left standing alone in the center before the dais. The great mother studied him with golden eyes rimmed in green. She pulled the covering from her face, allowing it to hang beneath her chin. She was an older woman, perhaps in her sixties, and her skin was darker than the typical Ferélli.

"Why have you come here?" she said.

"You know why."

With slender fingers, she gracefully motioned to a woman standing at one side holding a slate with a parchment and quill. "For the record, please."

"I seek the Sword of Eyre," he said.

She nodded. "For what use do you desire it?"

Rezkin glanced at the scribe as she scribbled on her parchment. He replied, "I have no use for it. It is King Privoth who desires the sword."

"Yet it is *you* who have come seeking it," she mused. She perused his form and then said, "You make yourself vulnerable on his behalf."

Rezkin shook his head with a grin. "Perhaps it is natural for people who cover themselves so completely to mistakenly think me vulnerable because I wear no clothes."

"At the least, it is a distraction," she said.

He squared his feet, planted his fists on his hips, and stood in a parody of the statue of Meros that towered over the throne.

"Are you distracted, Great Mother? Perhaps you are the one made vulnerable by my nudity."

The woman laughed and said, "You may be right."

She unwound the red scarf from her head. It fluttered on a delicate breeze between them before she released it into his hands. The tingle in the air died with the wind, and he wrapped the scarf about his hips.

She smiled and said, "A minor improvement, but I am satisfied that you bear no weapons."

Rezkin cocked his head. "*I* am the weapon. Anything else is merely a tool, and I count at least thirty-seven I could reach before your people posed a reliable threat."

The woman laughed again, perhaps not taking him seriously, since he stood at least five paces from any people or furniture. Then again, she was the Great Mother of the Adana'Ro, so she may have found joy in the belief.

She said, "Then, I am glad we had the foresight to ensure your cooperation."

The great mother raised a hand, and Xa appeared on one of the balconies to Rezkin's left. He was surrounded by two women in red scarves and one in blue, all with their swords drawn. Rezkin knew what would come next. The jeng'ri would not be parted from his charge. On a balcony to his right was Frisha. A single black-clad warrior stood behind her. Her face was pale, but her gaze remained strong. Rezkin looked back to the great mother, careful to school his expression to one of indifference.

"You should not blame him," she said. "The jeng'ri is good, but he is not better than a dozen Adana'Ro. He killed four of ours before we incapacitated him. He serves you well. I do believe he would have died to protect your woman."

"You needlessly sacrificed four of your people. I did not come here to kill you."

She said, "We will never know. After your show at the Black Hall, we had to be sure."

"I told you why I came. You have not yet said what it is you want."

"You have been avoiding us," she said.

"On the contrary, I have engaged your people every time they chose to interact. They lost."

"So I have heard," she replied. "I still find that difficult to believe. It is more likely you used some trick to enchant them. What is your *talent*?"

"I am not a mage," he said.

"You lie," she snapped.

He shook his head. "You bear the *talent*. Do you feel any of the power in me?"

With determination, the woman stood and stepped down from the dais. Unlike her warriors, she wore a long, airy, diaphanous robe that danced on a non-existent wind. She circled him several times, her spiral tightening until she came to a stop so close her breasts nearly grazed his chest. She looked up to search his icy gaze. Her callused fingers caressed the bare skin of his arm and then trailed across his shoulder to rest on his chest.

"No, I feel no power from you. It is impossible. You could not have scaled the cliff without it. And … you are warm. You should be wet and frozen."

Rezkin grasped her hand and held it tightly as he generated a small potential ward. He allowed the tiny ward to dance along her skin, spreading in a prickly wisp up her forearm. Her green-gold eyes widened as she tried to pull back her hand. She was strong, but he was stronger, and he did not release her.

He said, "I am not a mage." The great mother's wind and tendrils of power lashed at him, but he held firm as he leaned in and said, "I am something *more*."

His potential ward silently crackled and snapped, releasing energy along the fringes of its form. The woman yelped as it burned into her skin. The smell of scorched flesh reached his nostrils as she squirmed and yanked her arm, but she did not call for assistance from her people. When the marks blackened and began to bubble at the edges, he finally released her. It was the first time he had used a potential ward in such a way, and he was surprised that it had worked as he had intended.

The great mother beckoned a young man who rounded the statue, presumably from a hidden corridor. He hurried to her side, and Rezkin felt the trill of power as the healer prodded at the wound. The blisters healed quickly, but the blackened lines remained.

"What have you done to me?" she hissed.

"A reminder of your duty," Rezkin said. He pointed to the archaic script on the ceiling above the throne, an exact match to the scorch marks on her flesh. "Do you know what those symbols mean?"

She glanced up and then looked at him. With confidence, she said, "It is Jahartan for *Riel'sheng dak ro*, meaning *grantor of death to save the innocent*."

He hummed under his breath. "Actually, it is Adianaik, and it means *in service to the Gods*. It was universally understood, at the time, that the will of the gods was to protect the innocent. The inscription is a reminder to all that it was the responsibility of the knights who served their respective gods to eliminate those who threatened them."

"It is the same thing, then."

"An interpretation rarely holds the full meaning of the intent," Rezkin said. "Either way, it is something you have forgotten."

He nodded to where Frisha stood on the balcony at the mercy of her captors. The great mother scoffed and returned to her seat in a huff.

"I have difficulty believing she is *ro,* considering that she is betrothed to the Raven and protected by the jeng'ri. Regardless, I have no intention of harming the girl."

"So long as I cooperate," said Rezkin.

"Your cooperation was guaranteed. We can tell you where to find what you want in exchange for a price. *Her* presence was merely an assurance that you would not attempt to kill us before we made a deal." Her lips turned upward into a playful smile. "And we were curious. What kind of woman does the supposed Riel'gesh desire?"

Rezkin sighed in boredom. "I never said I desired her. She was a means to an end—one that is no longer relevant. The betrothal was called off before you took her."

The woman's smile fell, and she glanced at Frisha, who was looking at Rezkin in shock.

"Is that so?" the great mother said. She drew her fingers along the glyphs burned into her arm. "You seem very protective of one who means so little."

He tilted his head. "I was not protecting *her.* I was protecting *you.*"

"How so?"

"You are sworn to the code of the Adana'Ro, who follow the path of the

Riel'sheng. I take oaths quite seriously. If you break your oath, I will kill you. Shall we move on to negotiations?"

"Very well, but there is nothing to negotiate. We want one thing. If you want the sword, you will bring her to us."

"Her?"

"Oledia."

"You wish for me to kidnap Queen Erisial's daughter?"

The great mother waved her hand, and a black-clad small-woman bearing a tray laden with a pitcher and two goblets came to her side. "Oledia will come willingly. She has written to us several times requesting entrance to the sect. She wishes to learn the skills and develop the strength necessary to claim her mother's throne, presumably upon Erisial's death, although I would not put it past her to make the attempt sooner."

"So, I am to help her escape her mother's grasp?"

The woman shook her head as she poured liquid into two goblets and took one of them. "No, of course not. That would be too simple, and you know we are perfectly capable. You must bring Oledia to us with her mother's blessing."

"Erisial would never grant her daughter to the Adana'Ro."

"No, she would not, which is why you must convince her. It is the only way she will be permitted to join us and still return to Kielen to claim the throne."

Rezkin said, "The Riel'sheng do not seek crowns. You are meant to serve, not dominate."

The woman narrowed her eyes at him. "You are said to be the Riel'gesh, yet you have laid claim to *two* thrones." The small-woman with the tray stopped at his side, and the great mother nodded for him to take the goblet. She said, "We do not seek the crown of Lon Lerésh, only to gain influence with its next bearer. Oledia will be released from her duty to us if she is successful."

The great mother raised her goblet and stared at him expectantly. He peered into the metal cup. The golden-pink liquid was slightly syrupy and smelled of nectar. With a sigh, he raised the goblet, as she did hers, and together they drank.

Rezkin remained alert on the walk back to his comrades in the dark. His focus was split between the potential dangers of the desert wilderness, their proximity to the sanctorium, the jeng'ri who followed only a few paces behind, and his contemplations over how he might convince the queen of Lon Lerésh to part with her daughter so that he could deliver her to a sect of assassins.

"You didn't mean it, did you?"

His attention fractured once more to include a new line of focus. Frisha had finally broken her silent protest.

"Which part?" he said.

"You know which part," she snapped from beside him.

"I assure you that what I meant for the Adana'Ro I also mean for the jeng'ri who is walking behind you."

Frisha glanced back and seemed to understand his meaning.

Xa said, "You know I can hear you."

"Yes, and now neither of you know to whom I am being most sincere."

A silhouette, a large, imposing figure, stepped into their path. Farson's voice carried in the darkness. "I am no longer the only one who understands what it means to never trust anything this man says."

Rezkin said, "According to the *Rules*, Striker, you should never trust what *anyone* says."

Farson grumbled, "That may be true for you, but the rest of us have to function in a society where a certain level of trust must be granted."

Frisha said, "Well, I choose to trust you, Rezkin. I do not believe you were using me."

Xa stepped up beside her and said, "I trust that the Riel'gesh would not weaken himself with useless sentiment."

"Yet, you both cannot be right," said Farson.

"But they could both be wrong," Rezkin added.

The others fell silent as they walked, presumably to contemplate his statement. Finally, Frisha said, "You are intentionally confusing us."

"Yes," he replied. Changing the subject, he asked Farson, "Why are you here? You should be in the ward with the others."

"The mages could not keep that type of ward active for so long. It fell a while ago, replaced with something less threatening. We have been taking turns scouting in case we needed to prepare for another ambush or you required assistance. The camp has been moved to a better location. It is just around this bend."

Farson snuck back into the darkness, and Rezkin strode into what appeared, from outside the ward, to be a dark camp. Once he crossed the threshold, however, he was surrounded by ethereal light emitted by blue fluorescent swirls dancing across the interior surface of the ward. He was followed by Frisha and Xa, whom most of the others still knew as Lus.

"Frisha?" Malcius exclaimed. "What are you doing here? You were supposed to be waiting on the ship."

Frisha huffed. "I *was*—until a group of assassins swarmed the ship and kidnapped us."

"See?" Malcius snapped. "This is why you should not have come."

"You're going to blame this on *me*?" Frisha said. She balled her fists. "You know what your problem is, Malcius? You always blame the people you're *supposed* to care about for everything bad that happens."

Malcius stomped toward her. "That is because the people I care about keep getting themselves into trouble!"

Frisha's retort died on her lips as Rezkin whipped the veil from his hips and began dressing.

Malcius said, "Rezkin, must you do that *here*? There are women."

"Oh, no, he's fine," Reaylin said. "We don't mind."

Rezkin looked at Malcius as he strapped a few previously hidden knives to his legs, knowing he would have to adjust them later so his opponents would not know their exact locations. He said, "You would prefer I go *outside* the protective ward to dress?"

"No, I guess not, but they—"

"Have already seen. If they do not wish to see more, they may look away."

Malcius stormed over to Yserria, who was seated beside Reaylin, and said, "You are a knight. Have you no decorum?"

Yserria bounded to her feet to meet Malcius's hostile stance. "Firstly, Malcius Jebai, my oaths said nothing about not watching a man dress; and secondly, it is none of your business where I look!"

Malcius fumed as he stormed to the edge of the ward and sat with his back to the group behind the rock on which Brandt was sitting.

Shezar stepped closer to Rezkin and said, "That one is always angry."

"Yes," Rezkin said as he pulled on his pants.

The striker said, "It will get him killed."

"Probably," Rezkin replied.

"We should counsel him."

"You may try, but I believe this is something he must work through for himself. Then again, I have difficulty understanding these outworlders at times. I could be wrong."

"I have not yet known you to be wrong," Shezar said with a smirk.

Rezkin strapped on his sword belt and replied, "I am often wrong. I simply choose not to speak of it to others." With an edge of frustration in his tone, he said, "I was wrong about what Privoth would want, and now we are stuck going to Lon Lerésh."

"The sword is in Lon Lerésh?

"No, it is not. We are set to yet another task. They want Oledia."

"Who is Oledia?" Reaylin asked, obviously having been paying as much attention to their conversation as she was Rezkin's body.

"Queen Erisial's daughter."

"*Another* princess?" she exclaimed.

"She is not a princess," Rezkin said. "In Lon Lerésh, the crown is not passed down the family line, and the offspring of the rulers bear no more power or respect than any other member of a powerful house. Lon Lerésh is ruled by women. The women are the heads of the houses, and they maintain and control all matters of politics, business, and the personal lives of the members of their houses. For a woman to climb the social ladder, she must defeat someone higher than her, either through financial, political, or physical means. Accepted methods of defeat in specific matters are strictly governed by cultural tradition. To become queen, a woman must kill the sitting ruler."

Reaylin said, "So any woman can assassinate the queen and claim the throne?"

"Technically, yes, but she would not remain queen for long. If she does not have the support and strength of the highest houses behind her, she will be killed by a rival. You have played Queen's Gambit?"

"Yes, my father taught me when I was a child," Reaylin said. "I hate it."

"It came from Lon Lerésh. It is a game of strategy best won when your opponent cannot make any moves against you without destroying him or herself. When played with multiple players, one must manipulate the board so that any move by any player will be harmful to the other players. The player in the lead takes the Crest, and the other players are relegated to fighting each other to remain in the game."

"I know," Reaylin huffed. "I never win. Either a player has to sacrifice herself for someone else to have a chance, or the other players gang up on someone, which was always *me*, by the way."

"I wonder why," Frisha muttered.

Rezkin said, "The crown of Lon Lerésh is won in much the same way as the game. It might be easily gained through murder, but it is not easily kept. Queen Erisial has worn the crown for six years, which is a long time by Leréshi standards."

Malcius glared at Yserria as he stood to rejoin them and said, "What you are saying is that the Leréshi are a bunch of conniving, backstabbing women who are not to be trusted." He looked at Rezkin. "Great. When do we go?"

"You will stay with the other men on the ship. I will go alone with Yserria, Reaylin, and Mage Threll."

"That is absurd," Malcius exclaimed.

"Yes, it is," Farson said as he stomped through the ward. "She is not going in there alone."

Shezar also spoke up. "I am prepared to stand at your side."

Rezkin looked between the two strikers skeptically. "You two desire to go into Lon Lerésh?"

Both shifted uncomfortably, and Shezar said, "I do not *desire* to go there, but I will suffer the consequences to serve my king."

"And I will not let my niece go alone," Farson said.

"She will not be alone. Knight Yserria and Reaylin will be with her, and she is a capable mage in her own right. *You*, however, will be a liability."

"I will go," Wesson said.

Rezkin looked at him in surprise. "You understand the danger?"

Wesson scratched his head and shrugged. "So long as they do not know the strength of my power, I think I will be okay. I am not exactly their type."

Malcius exclaimed, "What are you all talking about? Why would you take them and leave us behind?"

Rezkin said, "I told you, Malcius. Women rule in Lon Lerésh. Any woman may claim any man as her consort."

"You mean as her husband?"

"No, it is extremely rare for a woman to declare a man to be her husband. To do so would mean that she recognizes him as her equal, and he would have the right to claim half her property and engage in business on behalf of the house. A consort has none of those rights. He is her companion, lover, and sometimes champion, but he is not her equal."

"So, he is her slave?" Malcius said with disgust.

Yserria said, "No, men hold the same position in Lon Lerésh that women do in Gendishen and most of the other kingdoms, including Ashai."

"It sounds like slavery to me," he said.

"It does, doesn't it," she snapped.

"It is the accepted culture in Lon Lerésh," Rezkin said. "Men vie for positions as consort to powerful women, conduct most of the activities requiring physical labor, and serve in the military. Men unsuited to physical labor raise the male offspring and perform domestic chores."

"So, any woman can claim a man. What if he is already taken or does not wish to be claimed?"

"The woman to whom the consort belongs is called his matria. If he has not been claimed, he belongs to his head of house, or *matrianera*, which would be his highest-ranking female relative. If a woman attempts to claim a Leréshi man, his matria has the right to challenge the claim. The matria may make a financial deal if the exchange is accepted, or she may name terms for a duel. The matria will name a champion, which may be the man in question if he does not accept the claim, and the challenger will also name a champion, usually a male from her household or another of her consorts. The terms of the duel are determined by the matria being challenged. If the challenger does not agree to the terms, she may withdraw her claim."

"Wait," Reaylin said. "You said *another consort*."

"Yes, it is not uncommon for a woman to claim more than one consort, but more than three is frowned upon, and they are usually of varying stations. A woman attempting to claim too many high-ranking men would be considered greedy. She would lose the support of her peers, which, as we have said, is vital to her staying in power."

"What if a man wants to claim a woman?" Malcius said.

"It is not permitted. If he has a good relationship with his matrianera, he can request that she approach a woman to determine her interest, and they may negotiate a contract in much the same way as is done for betrothals in Ashai. A dowry may be offered on his behalf. You must keep in mind, though, that if a woman does not desire a man who belongs to her, she may sell or trade him to someone else. The women in lower society often claim many men to use as workers. A woman is expected to provide for her men, though, and his quality of life should be at least equal to his station."

"But we are not Leréshi," Malcius protested.

"Foreigners are not exempt from their laws, Malcius, just as they are not exempt from those in Ashai. There are certain agreements, though, to keep the peace. Foreigners can be claimed, but they cannot be forced to stay in Lon Lerésh. Men who are already married in another kingdom are exempt, since their wives are not present to accept the challenge. Also, sailors and travelers cannot be claimed so long as they stay within the designated dock area. It does not matter your station, if you do not satisfy those conditions, you may be claimed. The only exception is royalty. A member of a foreign royal family may not be claimed."

"So that is why you can go," said Malcius.

Rezkin glanced at Shezar and Farson. "Perhaps."

Malcius said, "What do you mean? What is the problem?"

Shezar said, "Lon Lerésh has not recognized his claim to Ashai or Cael. They may not grant him the royal privilege."

Frisha said, "But he is the son of—"

"That is not common knowledge," Farson said with a pointed look.

Frisha crossed her arms and said, "Well, why is Wesson unconcerned? Are mages exempt?"

"Um, no," Wesson said. "It is just that, from what I have heard, I am not their type. They prefer men like the strikers or Rezkin. You see, the women are concerned with status, and the strength and masculinity of their men is most important. I do not exactly fit the profile."

"Men like Rezkin?" Frisha said. She crossed her arms and lifted her chin. "Fine. If the other women are going, then I am too."

"You cannot go," Malcius snapped. "I am your escort, and I am not going to be claimed by anyone! You are staying on the ship with me."

Yserria looked at Malcius and said, "I am sure you have little to worry about. You heard the mage. You are not their type."

As the conversation devolved, a thought occurred to Rezkin. He turned to Farson and said, "Why did you return from scouting so quickly?"

Farson watched the heated exchange between Malcius and Yserria, which was shortly joined by Frisha and Reaylin who tried to drag Mage Threll into the fray. He shook his head and said, "Because we are surrounded."

Rezkin nodded. "Surrounded by what?"

Wesson had taken refuge from the argument by moving to join them.

"Vuroles," said Farson.

"Lord Malcius is either brave or stupid," Shezar muttered as he watched the drama unfold. He turned to Farson and asked, "How many?"

"Perhaps fifty. They are difficult to see in the dark. It could be a hundred."

"Do you think we can wait them out?" Wesson said. "Perhaps they will lose interest."

"I doubt it," Farson replied. "They look hungry. Also, something is strange with their eyes."

"Are they black?" Rezkin said.

"Yes, how did you know?"

"In Gendishen, the ukwa driving the drauglics had black eyes. It seemed unnatural, and the way he threw them against us made no sense."

"Why did you not say anything?"

"*Rule 3*."

Farson sighed. "That does not apply when the information may be important to the group."

Rezkin shook his head. "It was not important until now, and *now* it has been revealed."

Shezar surveyed the darkness outside of the glowing ward, but the light made it difficult. "You think they are being driven? They are enchanted?"

"The Adana'Ro?" said Wesson.

Rezkin said, "I do not believe it is the Adana'Ro, but I do think they are under someone's influence."

"What makes you think that?" said Wesson.

"The cat at my feet."

The others looked down to see Rezkin's cat sitting patiently as it watched the women berate Malcius. The young lord was not backing down.

"What is your cat doing here?" Wesson said in alarm.

Rezkin looked at him and said, "It is not my cat."

All of them eyed the creature warily.

"That is the same cat that appeared when the drauglics attacked," Farson said.

"And I saw it at the plantation, too," said Wesson.

The cat flicked its tail and blinked up at them without concern.

"Is it a familiar?" Shezar said. "Have you bonded with it?"

"Not as such," Rezkin said, "but I do believe it is warning us of the impending danger."

The cat looked up at him, licked its lips, and then ran through the ward into the darkness.

"We should engage them now while we are awake," Shezar said. "The mages may drop the ward if they become too tired or run low on vimara. If we fight the vuroles now, we will be able to recover while we sleep."

Rezkin motioned to the group that looked to be ready to draw swords and said, "Very well. It is your plan. You get to break that up and prepare them."

The attack came swiftly after Wesson and Nanessy dropped the ward. Dozens of dark shadows shifted in the moonlight, their claws and fangs glinting brightly as they attacked. Wesson released a stream of flame at the front line, and then Nanessy followed it with a trail of water she had wrestled from the stream. When the water met the fire, it turned to boiling steam that cooked and blinded their attackers. The two mages tossed fireballs and caused rocks to explode in the densest gatherings, but the vuroles were fast and agile. They appeared as a mix between a wolf and a large cat with black and grey fur and sharp fangs that extended below their lower jaws. Moving with feline agility, they blended with the dark rocks around the party until ready to pounce. They attacked in numbers with several creatures jumping on a single person.

Malcius crashed into Frisha as a vurole jumped at him. He was trapped beneath the beast, and Frisha beneath him. Suddenly, Lus appeared above the creature. He drove his sword down through the back of the creature's skull. Frisha screamed as the combined weight of Malcius and the massive creature threatened to crush her. Lus shoved the monster off them and then leapt over their heads to fend off another. Yserria reached down and grabbed Malcius, helping him to his feet.

She said, "Stop lying around, you lazy oaf." She raised her sword to slash the abdomen of a leaping vurole, and Malcius ducked beneath her to score a second across its face. Then, Brandt charged in from the other side to stab it through the ribs.

"If I were lying around, it would not be with one of these things," said Malcius.

"I have seen you lay with worse," said Brandt.

"I told you to stop fantasizing about me," said Malcius.

"Look!" said Yserria, pointing to a shelf where several vuroles were gathered, ready to pounce en masse.

Wesson shoved his way between them and thrust his hands forward as he released a spell that streaked through the air like lightning. It struck the base of the shelf, sending vibrations through the rocks, causing them to fracture. The shelf broke away from the cliff, the back side dropping first so that the front collapsed on top of the creatures.

Malcius said, "I am glad you have a steady countenance, Journeyman,"

Wesson did not reply but rushed away to lob fireballs at several more creatures.

Shezar leaned over Malcius as he stabbed a vurole through the eye. "You should take a lesson from him and learn some control."

Malcius leapt forward when he saw Brandt go down. One of the vuroles raked its massive claws across Brandt's torso. His screams seemed to excite the beast to a frenzy. Malcius lopped off its tail and then its jaw when it turned on him. By the time the battle was over, everyone had suffered deep punctures and lacerations from teeth and claws—everyone except Frisha, who was curled beneath a small, personal ward that Wesson somehow maintained while also engaging the beasts. While Reaylin did not overtly complain about performing her duties as healer, her voice still held an edge as she *politely* asked people to hold still. Brandt's injuries were by far the worst, and Reaylin was fairly drained by the time she had finished with everyone.

"Why were there so many?" Malcius said as he attempted to tie the tattered pieces of his tunic to cover himself.

Wesson took a long gulp from his water skin and said, "They are believed to be vimaral creatures—a hybrid species created by mages long ago. Vuroles live in small packs in the desert. They will attack a lone man but usually avoid groups. Vimaral creatures are often attracted to vimara, though, so they were probably drawn here in number by the ward we were using to protect ourselves from the Adana'Ro."

A heavy rumbling reached their ears, echoing through the canyon from an unknown distance. Rezkin turned his gaze to the stars. Those directly overhead were now obscured by a filmy haze, the more distant lights having disappeared. In that empty darkness, the black silhouette of clouds appeared and disappeared as light crackled within them. He sighed and turned to his companions.

"No sleep is to be had tonight. We must vacate this canyon before we are washed away."

Despite the protests of his companions, he grabbed his pack and began the hazardous walk in the dark. Nanessy set tiny, floating sparks like fireflies hovering over the trail to light their way while Wesson set a weak ward to trail them, claiming it would at least prevent a stray vurole from pouncing on his back.

"But it isn't raining yet," Reaylin said as she crunched and stumbled over the scree.

"Not here," Shezar said, "but it is out there on the higher ground. The rain will fall afar and flood through the canyon in a torrent."

Reaylin said, "I hate Ferélle."

Malcius snagged his pant leg on a horrid, spindly plant with thorns longer than his thumbnail. He hissed as one of the spikes dug into his calf. "For once, you and I are in agreement."

9

The trip to Kielen, the capital of Lon Lerésh, was not much better than their previous voyage. The autumn storms were terrible, and the Bay of Bourdony was particularly choppy as it was stirred by inundations from its multiple tributaries. The rain had waned for a short time as the ship approached port, and the travelers could see, even in the gloom of the overcast sky, that Kielen was a rich city, awash in vibrant colors. Unusually tall buildings sometimes reached five or six stories, as if they were competing to touch the stars. They were painted in brilliant crimson, indigo, and purple, and every sill, frame, and ledge of even the smallest hovel appeared gilded. Most of the windows had no glass, and the shutters were left open to the cool sea breeze. In these open portals, colorful, sheer curtains pranced on drafts over streets and alleys, and beside them, vines clung to the façade from rooftop gardens overgrown with flowering plants and trees.

The Gendishen often claimed that Lon Lerésh had intentionally appropriated everything garish to spite their neighbors, but the Leréshi philosophy was to express passion in every aspect of life, from art and décor to business and war. The docks were no different. Every worker wore a uniform to indicate his or her position, and the ground was marked in colored paint to indicate the appropriate paths for the movement of people, goods, and animals. While most ports tended toward organized chaos, the Leréshi ports had a militaristic order that Rezkin could appreciate.

He turned from the view and entered the cabin where Yserria, Reaylin, Mage Threll, and Wesson were waiting. Malcius stood by the door watching for the signals. Rezkin collected a small box from one of his trunks, removed its contents, and then stopped in front of Yserria. He held the item up for her inspection. "You will wear this," he said.

The sunlight streaming through the porthole glinted off a gold and silver torque. Yserria's eyes widened as her gaze traced the brilliant gold setting that wrapped around a massive tourmaline. On either side of the central stone were smaller sapphires and amethysts. "It-it's beautiful," she said.

As he fastened it around her neck, Rezkin said, "It once belonged to Matrianera Gereldina. It is considered to be a famous work of art, both for its beauty and the story it holds. I stole it from the Adana'Ro. It is now yours."

"*What*?" Yserria blurted. "Why would you give me something stolen from the Adana'Ro?"

"Yes, Rezkin," Malcius said angrily. "Why are you giving Yserria expensive jewelry?"

Rezkin close the box, returned it to the trunk, and then turned to Yserria to explain. "Matrianera Gereldina was the head of a powerful house during the last reign. The torque was stolen by her consort, who used it to pay the Adana'Ro to kill her, but Gereldina found out about the plan and killed him and his male children, both her own and those from a previous matria. The Adana'Ro killed Gereldina anyway and kept the torque as payment. You will let it be known that the torque was a gift from me, which serves two purposes. Bestowing knighthood on you demonstrated that I value your skill and accomplishments, but gifting you this torque shows that I value you as a woman. Appearances are important to the Leréshi. A worthy male will make his appreciation known by gifting luxuries to his woman."

"But she is not your woman," Malcius exclaimed rather too quickly. He appeared discomfited when everyone turned to stare at him. He shook his head and added, "I mean Frisha …"

"Is not my woman either, Malcius, nor will she ever be. The betrothal was canceled. You need to accept that."

"What?" Reaylin, Nanessy, and Yserria all cried at once.

Rezkin was surprised by the group outburst. He said, "I thought someone would have mentioned it, since everyone is so eager to discuss my marital status."

Yserria cleared her throat. "Y-You said there were two reasons for the torque?"

"Yes, the second being that the Leréshi will know I acquired it from the Adana'Ro. Queen Erisial is aware that her daughter desires to join them, and she will likely make the connection. It gives my cause legitimacy."

"What if the Adana'Ro take exception to your stealing it?" said Wesson.

Rezkin shrugged. "If they did not wish for me to take the torque, they would have done a better job of holding on to it."

Wesson said, "You were not there for long, and I do not imagine they allowed you to roam around looking for things to steal. How did you find this treasure?"

Rezkin shook his head as he went to his desk. "It was not difficult. The great mother was wearing it."

"The great mother?" said Wesson.

Rezkin looked up at him. "Their leader."

Yserria tugged at the torque. "You stole this from the neck of the *leader* of the Adana'Ro?" She tugged at it again, but it would not budge.

Rezkin told her, "Stop pulling at it, or you will hurt yourself. It is enchanted not to come off unless removed by the person who clasped it shut."

"But you removed it from the great mother," Wesson observed as he stood to examine the torque. "And you would have to have done it quickly, or she would have noticed."

"She was rather distracted," Rezkin replied.

Malcius seemed even more frustrated when he said, "I recall that you were nude. Why were you so close to the woman, and how was she distracted?"

"Lord Malcius!" Mage Threll exclaimed. He appeared slightly abashed, until she looked at Rezkin and said, "Where did you hide it?"

A whistle, followed by shouts from on deck, signaled that the ship was about to be boarded. A smaller vessel had been escorting theirs since entering Leréshi waters. As soon as both were docked, a woman and two men boarded *Stargazer* without invitation, a privilege that was apparently reserved for female captains. The men were slight of build and wore loose, beige pants that tied at the ankles beneath matching smocks that fell to their knees. Their hair was shorn close to the scalp, and each held stacks of papers and a writing tablet.

The woman was a minister of the docks, tasked with inspecting foreign vessels and their cargo. She appeared to be in her late twenties and had straight, brown hair tied back into a tail that hung past her waist. Her eyes and lips were enhanced with powders and paint, and she had multiple rings piercing each ear. She wore a dark brown sleeveless overcoat that was fitted to her curves and crossed her chest to tie at one muscular shoulder. Her voluminous black pants gathered at the knee, leaving her lower legs bare down to her hard-soled slippers. The silky red sash that encircled her hips was tied at the side with the loose end hanging halfway down her thigh. At that moment, she also wore a scowl for the captain.

"I am telling you, it is a passenger vessel," said Captain Estadd.

The woman glanced around the deck at the recently added weapons and modified rails and said, "It looks like a military vessel to me."

Shezar approached, dressed in his formal black and green regalia. He smiled and genuflected as was appropriate for a man when addressing a woman of station. "Minister, may I have the privilege of introducing myself and this vessel's occupants?"

The woman looked him up and down and smiled appreciatively. "You appear to be a worthy male. You may speak."

Retaining his smile, he bowed again. "This is *Stargazer*, flagship of the Royal Navy of the Kingdom of Cael. I am Striker Shezar in service to the King of Cael, True King of Ashai. My liege desires a meeting with Queen Erisial."

The woman scanned the deck again. "I have never heard of the Kingdom of Cael. Your king does not seem to travel with the usual flair. Has he no women to speak for him?"

Shezar continued to smile. "He has many women, Minister. They tend to him now. I will inform Royal Knight Yserria that you wish to speak with her."

She looked at him skeptically. "Your king has knighted a woman?"

"Yes," Shezar said. "She is worthy."

Yserria stalked out of the cabin on cue, also wearing her formal uniform, with the addition of the priceless torque. She stopped in front of Shezar and the minister and looked down her nose at the shorter woman.

"Of course, I am worthy," she said. "Was there any doubt?"

"No, Knight Yserria," the woman said, shaking her head vigorously. "I was just surprised. I had not heard of a woman being knighted in any of the kingdoms."

Yserria turned and saluted Shezar with a fist over her heart and said, "Thank you, Striker Shezar, for allowing me the privilege of this duty."

Shezar tilted his head and departed without a backward glance.

The minister glanced between Yserria and the striker's retreating form. "He is your superior?"

"Yes," said Yserria.

The woman's face soured, and she huffed. "Why has he delegated this task to one of lower station?"

Yserria switched to Leréshi and replied, "*Because you desired to speak with a woman.*"

The minister blinked. "*You are Leréshi*?"

Yserria slapped a fist over the emblem embroidered onto her tabard and said, "*I am* Caelian."

The woman glance around skeptically and said, "*Alright, I will send a message to see if the queen desires a meeting with your king.*"

Striker Shezar stalked out of the cabin flanked by Mage Threll and Reaylin on either side. Reaylin carried her weapons and was dressed in armor, but her tabard looked like modified healers robes. The center was grey with silver lining, while the sides were black with a green lightning bolt stitched onto the breast.

Looking back at Yserria, the minister said, "*The women in your kingdom are encouraged to learn the sword? Even the healers*?"

Yserria grinned. "*Cael is a warrior kingdom.*"

"I see," the other woman said. Her gaze flicked to the striker, and she called, "Striker Shezar, you should dine with me. You may visit my home." She smiled devilishly and added, "It is located only a few streets from the docks."

Shezar turned and bowed. "I am honored by the invitation, Minister, but I cannot accept. I am assigned to the security of the ship."

She sauntered over to him and ran a finger along his jaw. "If we were not bound by the rules of the dock, I would not give you the choice. I will make it worth your while."

Shezar clasped her hand as he removed it from his face and said, "Tempting, but I am bound by duty."

"Pity," she said. Then, her demeanor changed, and she waved as if tossing the invitation away. "It is no matter. There are plenty of men to be had." She turned back to Yserria and said, "I will need to inspect the ship."

"Our king demands diplomatic immunity for his quarters and those of the strikers and myself, but you may examine the rest."

The woman tapped her lip thoughtfully and then spoke to her assistants.

"Send a missive to the dock mistress for permission to grant diplomatic immunity." To Yserria, she said, "I doubt you will receive it."

One of the men scribbled a message on his tablet, bowed, and then handed the quill to the minister. After signing the document, the man departed, and she said, "Let us get on with this. Guide the way."

Yserria showed the woman around the deck and then took her below to examine the other rooms and cargo. By the time they were finished, the dock mistress had arrived to personally assess the situation. She was an older woman with greying hair tied in an intricate braid atop her head. She wore a stern countenance. Her figure was fit, although her skin was darkened and leathery from too many years spent in the sun.

"*I hear we have an errant king aboard,*" said the dock mistress as Yserria and the minister approached. "*It seems this one has been making waves across the Souelian. I have heard of this new king, but I will see him before I make my decision.*"

The minister's eyes widened as Dark Tidings appeared behind the dock mistress. The older woman turned and jumped as he looked down at her. She was petite beside the towering wraith, and she was wary despite her sour visage.

"*I am the one you seek,*" said the unsettling voice.

The woman lifted her chin and said, "*Is that so?*"

Yserria moved to Rezkin's side. Her voice was sharp as she addressed the dock mistress. "*This is the King of Cael, True King of Ashai. You will show him proper respect.*"

The woman appeared uncertain but ultimately decided to adhere to diplomatic formalities. She crossed her arms in front of her, palms facing outward, and then touched her forehead to her wrists. The minister followed the dock mistress's example.

"*I do not wish to be kept waiting,*" said Dark Tidings.

The woman pursed her lips. "*Word has been sent to the palace of your arrival. You are not in your* kingdom," she said. "*You will be apprised of the pertinent laws and customs while we wait.*"

"*That is not necessary,*" Dark Tidings said. "*I am familiar with your laws. My entourage is entirely female, except for the journeyman mage and the priest of the Maker.*"

He nodded toward Minder Finwy and Wesson, who was doing his best to appear puny and insignificant. The woman scowled and sniffed disdainfully.

"*Are you sure he is not a girl?*" she said.

Dark Tidings tilted his head as he made a show of examining the mage. He replied, "*No, I am not.*"

The dock mistress dismissed Wesson and said, "*If you are granted a visit with the queen, I will approve your diplomatic immunity. If not, you will be subject to the same search as every other vessel, or you will leave port.*"

"*Dock Mistress, how long have you held your position?*" said Dark Tidings.

"*I acquired my position after my predecessor's downfall five years ago.*"

He said, "*How many foreign rulers have called to this port in that time?*"

"*Well, none that I recall.*"

"*No, and I am certain you would remember such an encounter. You need to revisit your lessons in etiquette lest you meet your predecessor's fate.*"

The minister who stood a step behind the dock mistress eyed her superior hungrily, as if considering how she might make that happen.

The dock mistress granted him an insincere smile and said, "*I will take your suggestion under advisement. You should expect to receive word within the hour. I will return if you are approved.*"

The woman bowed slightly and then strode from the deck down the gang-plank, followed by her remaining assistant and the minister. The minister marched imperiously past Shezar, not even glancing his way.

Once they were gone, Shezar turned to Rezkin and said, "The Leréshi do not take rejection kindly."

Rezkin nodded. "It is something to keep in mind."

They finished gathering their belongings while they waited. Frisha approached Rezkin when he was finally alone in his cabin, although she had to enlist Xa's assistance in circumventing Malcius to get to him.

"What are you looking at?" she asked. "Surely you have read all of your papers a million times by now."

"I took these off the dock mistress," he said absently as he read.

"But I never saw you get close to her, and I was watching from the doorway the entire time."

"You were supposed to be in your cabin."

Frisha cleared her throat to get his attention and said, "I think I should go."

Without the slightest hesitation, he said, "No."

"But Reaylin is going—"

With the look he gave her, she did not bother to finish the thought. She bit her bottom lip and then started, "The Adana'Ro …"

He glanced up, his gaze sharpening as he waited for her to finish.

"They … um … they offered to teach me. They said I could join them."

"No," he said again.

With an embittered expression, she crossed her arms and huffed. "Why not? You said I can choose what I want to be. You don't even discuss it. You just say *No*."

"You are not a warrior, Frisha. You have said as much."

"I could be. I am not weak, you know." She lifted her chin. "I can be just as strong as Yserria."

Rezkin rounded the desk and leaned against it as he gave her his full attention. "No one said you are not strong. You do not have to be a warrior to be strong."

"If I were a warrior, I would be someone you could … respect."

"I do respect you," he said.

Frisha huffed again. "The Adana'Ro protect the innocent. It seems like a worthy cause."

Rezkin rose quickly and was in front of her before she could blink. He captivated her with his crystal blue gaze. "Do not deceive yourself. The Adana'Ro live in darkness. They do dark things to protect the light. You may choose your path, Frisha. If it is what you wish, I will not stop you." He traced a finger over her cheek. "I did not understand why outworlders would choose to remain oblivious, vulnerable, but you have shown me something I had never seen—something of value. If you choose this path, the world will be a darker place."

Frisha blinked away tears and murmured, "You say such things …"

Rezkin dropped his hand and went back to his papers. "You should go. It is not appropriate for you to be in here alone with me." She turned to leave, and he said, "Frisha."

"Yes?"

"Please remain on the ship. We were lucky no one died when the Adana'Ro took you."

Frisha inhaled and straightened her spine. She looked him in the eyes and said, "I'm going with you."

When he answered, his voice held a hard edge she was not used to hearing directed at her. "If you are taken again, I *will* slaughter all in my path to retrieve you."

The dark certainty in his gaze sent a chill up Frisha's spine as she was once again reminded that he was Dark Tidings, the Rez, *and* the Raven. Her mind, fears, and moral fortitude were at war with her heart, but when she remembered him saying that he could never love her, her heart lost.

Frisha left the cabin and was immediately reprimanded by Malcius who had managed to work his way past Xa without getting stabbed.

"Every time you speak to him, you end up crying," Malcius said. "Why do you not tell him you have changed your mind?"

Frisha stared past the still, grey water near the dock to the darker blue of the ocean afar.

"Because I have not," she said. "It cannot be, Malcius. I am sorry." As she pushed past him, she added, "Perhaps you would be better to push Shiela on him after all. She would not care if he has no feelings."

The dock mistress did not return alone. An entire army platoon flanked by royal guards lined the docks, followed by the Ashaiian and Channerían ambassadors and four presumably high-ranking women dressed in palace livery, each sitting atop a glamorous white horse. Horns blared as the women rode side-by-side between the ranks of saluting soldiers. Rezkin turned from his porthole view of the ostentatious fanfare and donned his equally theatrical mask. He then joined his party on the deck. Yserria and Mage Threll led the way down the gangplank as Reaylin, Frisha, the minder, and Wesson followed behind Rezkin.

The ambassadors, both men, stood back as the four women greeted Rezkin. They remained on their horses as they introduced themselves as members of the queen's court, Erisial's most ardent supporters and advisors.

"We are to escort you to the palace," the middle-aged blonde on the right said. "You should expect to spend several days in our company.

"Under which diplomatic status am I to be received?" said Dark Tidings.

The woman's painted lips lifted at the corners. "That is to be decided by Queen Erisial."

Dark Tidings tilted his head. "Then warn her that it is in her best interest not to test me."

The red-head beside her said, "Bold words for a man displaced from his kingdom."

"I am often accused of boldness. The claim is not unwarranted. None who have chosen to test me have been disappointed."

The two who had spoken glanced toward the woman on the left, who had more grey than brown in her hair. She nodded, and the women drew their mounts to the side so that a carriage could be brought forward.

Rezkin had no desire to be trapped in an enclosed carriage. "I will ride," he said.

The younger women looked to the older woman again, and at her direction, a horse was brought to him. Knowing the Leréshi were fervent for formality, he had already planned accordingly, and their trunks were ready for loading. Rezkin's companions piled into the carriage, which traveled behind him as he followed the women toward the palace. They rode slowly with the royal guard running beside them as they moved through the city. Each of the guards carried a tall pole topped by a massive, colored flag slapping in the wind. While the flags were part of the fanfare, Rezkin knew they also served another purpose. Since the buildings were so tall and the matrianeras vulnerable in the open, the flags were used to obscure them from onlookers and deflect or entangle projectiles.

As they neared the palace, the buildings became spaced farther apart and had fewer levels, but they were just as colorful. The more opulent estates were surrounded by walls or gardens filled with statues and carved fountains, most of which depicted men serving or prostrating themselves before their matria. Some were of men in battle or women teaching other women, and it was not uncommon to see images of men and women engaging in acts of lovemaking.

Women walked freely and confidently along the walkways, trailed by male and female retainers or family members. The men wore their hair at various lengths, but all had one long braided strand that hung from the temple.

From her seat inside the carriage, Reaylin leaned over Wesson to watch a group of men walk by unaccompanied by a woman. She said, "Why do they wear their hair like that?"

Yserria said, "It indicates their status. A blue ribbon means a man belongs to the house of a matrianera but that he is not related to her or claimed as consort. A green ribbon means he is of relation to the matrianera but not a consort. A red one means he has been claimed by a matria as consort. He will combine it with a blue or green one if his matria is not the matrianera. My father's was silver. You will not see many of those. After he escaped to Ashai with my mother, she claimed him as her husband, which meant she recognized him as her equal in the relationship.

"The women's ribbons having similar meanings. If a woman does not wear one, it means she is a matrianera, or the head of her own house. Blue means she belongs to another's house but is of no relation, and green means she is of relation to her matrianera. Since my mother belonged to her older sister's house, she wore a green one. After she claimed my father as her husband, she added a silver, and when she established her own house in Ashai, she removed the green."

Nanessy said, "If a woman can establish her own house, why would she continue to belong to someone else's?"

"So long as a woman belongs to another's house, she is entitled to physical and political protection and basic financial support from that house. If she declares her own house, she is giving up all the privileges of the other house."

Frisha said, "Then it is the same as staying in your family home in Ashai."

"Yes," Yserria said hesitantly. "In Ashai, it is the man who establishes his own house, whereas here, it is the woman. A woman is required to serve her matrianera, though, so many choose to leave if they do not want to serve another. Also, a woman cannot claim a man without her matrianera's permission, so if she wants to claim someone otherwise, she must leave her matrianera's house."

"It sounds very complicated," Nanessy said.

Yserria shook her head. "Not really. A woman trades power and wealth for independence. If she is strong, her house will also become successful."

Nanessy watched as a young woman who looked like a maid scurried after her matrianera. She said, "Not everyone can be a success, though. I imagine there are many who fail."

Yserria pulled her gaze from the same scene and said, "They return to their former matrianera's house in disgrace. It is up to the matrianera whether she will accept her back and what position the woman will hold. If the matrianera does not accept, she may petition to join another's house, but she will probably become no more than a servant."

"What about mages? Are there different rules?" Nanessy said.

Yserria shrugged. "I believe it is the same, but someone who has enough *talent* to become a mage will usually have the wealth and abilities necessary to have her own house."

"I do not understand why the men put up with it," Wesson grumbled.

Yserria blinked at him in surprise. "This is the culture. The men have helped to define it as much as the women. My father was very dedicated to my mother. He would have served her for the rest of his life, whether she had claimed him as husband or not. It is a matter of personal honor for the men to belong to houses run by strong women, and they are devoted to ensuring their matrianeras and matrias achieve the greatest respect and recognition. The consort of a strong matria may be of higher status than a woman of a much lower house."

"So, the men are not just slaves?" Wesson said.

"No, of course not. Women and men both engage in research, music, and the arts, and they may dedicate themselves to a craft. While the women run the government, houses, and businesses, the men are free to pursue other interests for which they are better suited like hunting, construction, or combat training. Leréshi men are great warriors. Champions are prized among the houses, so a man with strength and skill will be sought by many women."

"Your father taught you the sword even though you are a woman," said Frisha.

"Yes, women may pursue these interests as well, but most choose not to because they are preoccupied with generating political support and wealth to become independent. In Ashai, everything was backward, and I would have had no chance to create a house of my own. My father had hoped that he could acquire enough wealth working for the duke to see me through, at least until I married or returned to my family's house in Lon Lerésh, but Ytrevius was not a generous employer. My father taught me the sword to protect myself and because it was the one skill he knew best. If nothing else, I could join the army or work as a guard, assuming I found an employer to accept a woman."

"Which you did," Nanessy said with an encouraging smile.

Sadness filled Yserria's green eyes. "Yes, but at great cost."

"Palis wasn't your fault," Reaylin said.

Yserria turned her gaze toward the colorful flags and buildings. "Not everyone agrees."

Rezkin rode ahead of the carriage, his vigilance intensified by the fact that he had already acquired two new daggers that had been generously tossed his way. It seemed not everyone was excited for his presence in the city. He did not believe the weapons to be a true attempt on his life since anyone good enough to throw one with accuracy would know the amount of armor he wore would make it nearly impossible to land a fatal strike. The weapons were meant to serve as warnings or tests of his skill. In a land where people acquired their positions through challenge or assassination of their betters, such things were apparently commonplace.

The palace was not located within the city proper. It sat atop a knoll surrounded at its base by densely packed briars and soggy, brine marshland that had been created artificially by a manmade canal that led from the sea. The canal was a deep, dry chasm at that time, though, the gates opening to fill it only when the marsh began to dry. The bridge that passed over the empty canal and marsh transitioned to a steep road with several switchbacks to make it possible for the carriage to travel safely. A stone stairway led straight up the side of the hill to the palace for those who desired a more direct foot route.

The wall surrounding the grounds was not as tall as the walls of some cities, but due to the steep slope upon which it was built, it was still formidable. The elaborately decorated palace had three tall spires surrounding a central domed complex. The walls were made of white stone, and the wooden beams and balustrades were bleached white or blonde like driftwood. From every window fluttered curtains, banners, or flags, a bright contrast to the overcast sky.

The four matrianeras who had escorted them from the docks guided the party from the courtyard entrance through several passages and stairwells within the main hold. The corridors were lined with guards, and curious onlookers gawked and giggled from farther down the blocked side passages. The corridors were painted different colors and bore tapestries, paintings, and sculptures to match a theme. A corridor painted the same yellow-gold as the soldier's tabards contained militaristic artwork with scenes of battles, presumably famous leaders, or weapons and armor; while a green corridor had portraits of men, women, and children whom their guides identified as members of the queen's family. It was in this passage that their third-floor suite was located, and it consisted of a sitting room and three bed chambers that they were apparently expected to share.

Rezkin surveyed each of the rooms and then returned to their escorts. The matrianeras had removed the overgowns of livery, and each was now displaying far more of herself than was appropriate in any of the kingdoms he had visited.

He said, "Why are we assigned to this wing?"

The blonde smirked. "The queen does not trust us, of course. No one is permitted in this corridor except for her consort and family."

"Yet you are here," he observed.

"We made a deal for the honor of escorting you," she said as she ran manicured fingers over her exposed midriff.

Her pale blue silk skirt hung low on her hips, and the matching corset she wore, sans blouse, barely reached her lower ribs.

"What was the deal?" he asked.

"It is not important for you," she said. "You will not see us here again, but be assured that you *will* see us." She strode closer and toyed with a loose lock of her wavy, golden curls. "Will you not remove your mask so that we may know you?"

"You should not be so eager to know me, Matrianera …"

"Telía." She smiled coyly and said, "Why is that?"

"People who know me often do not survive."

Telía's expression faltered, and the brown-haired woman who had been silently observing finally spoke. "We should go, Telía. Erisial will not be pleased that we have lingered in her wing."

"But he has not yet given us his name," Telía said as she looked back at him expectantly.

Rezkin felt the buzz of mage power alight, but it did not come from Telía. It was the older grey-haired woman from whom the vimara emanated.

He said, "I do not have a name."

The older woman inhaled sharply. "He speaks truth."

Telía's smile quivered again. "A nameless one? How fascinating."

Dark Tidings turned his black gaze to the older woman. "You are a truthseeker?"

"I would not say that I seek the truth, only that I hear it," the woman said. "I am Matrianera Vielda. "What kind of man does not have a name? Everyone in every kingdom is given a name at birth."

Dark Tidings cocked his head eerily and said, "What gave you the impression that I am a man *or* that I was born?"

"Let us go," said the brown-haired woman as she tugged at the red-head's arm.

Matrianera Vielda said, "Yes, Telía, come. We will let Erisial know that he is here." To Rezkin, she said, "A feast is being prepared in honor of your arrival. You and your"—her eyes flicked to his companions—"*guests* will join us at seven bells."

The women departed, and Rezkin gave the sign for Wesson to ward the room against eavesdropping. His survey also revealed three objects enchanted for that purpose, which Wesson quickly dismantled.

"What was that about not being born?" Frisha said with a huff as Rezkin removed his mask.

"Theatrics, Frisha. I do not want these women to become *personally* interested. It is better they fear me."

"Yes, Telía seemed *very* interested," she snapped.

"Matrianera Telía. Formalities are important here. You cannot drop her title unless you have one of equal or greater status."

"Fine," she said, "but I cannot believe they would walk around like that. They were practically spilling out of their clothes."

"Their sense of propriety is different here. In Lon Lerésh, a woman's body belongs only to her. She is not required to submit to anyone else's ideals of what is appropriate to do with it."

Reaylin said, "So a woman could strut naked down the corridor, and no one could say anything?"

"Exactly," Rezkin said. "But they also use their feminine attributes to get what they want, so they do not tend to give away for free what they feel should be earned."

Frisha said, "What if a man tries to *take* something that she's not offering?"

"You will not find a place with harsher punishments for such a crime. For a man to attack a woman is torture and death."

"What if the man is innocent?" Frisha said in horror.

Rezkin said, "The truthseekers ensure the woman is not lying."

Nanessy added, "The Leréshi have the greatest number of truthseekers in any of the kingdoms. I do not know of *any* in Ashai, but I hear there are dozens in Lon Lerésh."

"What are truthseekers?" said Reaylin.

"Their vimara allows them to sense what is true. Some can see truth through enchantments, illusions, and disguises. Others can hear when someone speaks truth or lies as Matrianera Vielda demonstrated. This one is tricky, though, because it is dependent on whether the person speaking the lie *believes* it to be true."

Frisha shivered. "So Matrianera Vielda will know if we are lying?"

Reaylin said, "Then, why did she believe you when you said you don't have a name?"

Nanessy seemed just as perplexed.

"Because I do not," he said.

"But your name is Rezkin," Reaylin said.

"Rezkin is not my name. It is what some people call me."

Minder Finwy said, "How is it that you do not have a name?"

"I was not given one at birth," Rezkin said. He pointed to a stained-glass door through which they could see a deep pit set in the floor surrounded by colorful bottles and stacks of drying cloths. He said, "There is a bathing chamber. We have been traveling a long while. You all should take advantage of the luxury before the feast."

"But anyone can see in," Frisha exclaimed.

"Journeyman Wesson, Minder Finwy, and I will remain in my bed chamber until you are finished. They will share the room with me, and the four of you can divvy up the other two."

"I will stay in the temple," Finwy said. "I have never visited a Temple of the Maker in Lon Lerésh, and many Leréshi are said to be highly devout." He bowed, collected his single traveling pack, and departed.

"I can sleep in the sitting room," Wesson said. "Actually, I would prefer it."

Rezkin gave him a quizzical look but shrugged with indifference. "Very well, but you will come to my room while the women bathe."

"Of course," Wesson said as his cheeks flushed.

A few hours later, a knock sounded at the door. Doing his best to appear meek and inconsequential, Wesson answered wearing plain grey mage robes. A young woman was bent with her rump in the air picking up items that had spilled from a basket that looked rather too large for her to carry. He cleared his throat, and the woman squeaked in surprise as she jumped and spun to face him.

"*Eskyeshele tua*," she babbled in a rush.

Wesson scratched his temple and looked at her curiously. She was close to his age with large, brown, doe eyes and mousy brown hair pulled back into a long braid that hung past her waist. A thinner braid, intertwined with a green ribbon, hung from her temple. Her pink silk bodice barely covered her breasts, and her filmy skirt was split up one side to her hip. Her eyes were shadowed, her lashes darkened, and her full lips painted to glossy, pink perfection.

He clasped his hands behind his back to keep from fidgeting and said, "I am afraid I do not speak Leréshi."

"Oh!" the young woman said as she blinked back at him. Slowly, with her brow furrowed in concentration, she said, "Sorry to you. My words of Ashai are not good."

He nodded but remembered not to smile since he did not want to encourage unwanted attention.

"I … bring …dress," she said and then frowned. "Dress-s-es. For dinner."

"Ah," Wesson said and then stood aside to let her enter.

As she moved to pick up the basket, he stepped forward to assist. Each of them took a handle, and they bumped and stumbled through the doorway, nearly spilling the basket's contents again. The woman smiled and thanked him and then stared at him expectantly.

He scratched his head again. "I … ah … guess I will get the women?"

The woman smiled and nodded, so Wesson knocked on Frisha's door. She and Mage Threll answered together, and Wesson motioned over his shoulder.

"The lady has brought you some dinner clothes."

Both women came forward slowly, eyeing the basket as if it were a poisonous snake. Wesson next alerted Yserria and Reaylin, who looked equally skeptical of the basket's contents. The young woman introduced herself as Celise and then began enthusiastically holding up strips of silky fabric, none of which looked large enough to cover any intimate details.

Frisha said, "Um … don't you have anything that covers, you know, *more*?"

Celise looked at her in confusion and then Yserria rattled off some words in Leréshi. Celise smiled and dug through the basket to pull out a long, violet frock that would fit snuggly but would cover from the neck to the toes. Unfortunately, it was completely sheer. Frisha looked at it in horror.

Nanessy said, "Perhaps if we layer them?"

"No," Frisha said. "Absolutely not. I will wear my own clothes."

Celise eyed Frisha's burgundy gown dubiously. While it would not have been appropriate court dress in Ashai, it was certainly an acceptable dinner dress.

Reaylin reached into the basket and pulled out a long, chocolate brown drape that seemed to have no shape, ties, or straps. "What do you do with this?" she asked.

Celise took the fabric and began wrapping it around Reaylin over her tunic and pants. It wrapped over one shoulder, cut across the breasts, twisted around the hips, and then tucked into itself at the hip. Wesson thought that one firm tug would pull the entire garment off. His face heated at the thought.

"I, ah, I will be in R—ah, the king's room," he stuttered.

When he turned to leave, he nearly ran into the man himself. Dressed as Dark Tidings, Rezkin hovered behind the Leréshi woman. She jumped back as he came around to peer into the basket. He plucked a dark green bustier from the pile and held it up to Frisha. She recoiled from the contraption, mortified. He tilted his head, and she shied away further, so he handed it to Yserria. He turned to Celise and said something in Leréshi. Celise appeared thoughtful and then bowed before running out of the room.

"What did you say to her?" Frisha said.

"I told her that you get easily chilled and asked that she bring winter gowns for you to examine. I doubt they will cover much more, but you might find something."

Yserria held up the bustier. "You want me to wear this?"

He said, "We are in Lon Lerésh. A woman wears what she wants to wear."

Reaylin eyed the brown wrap. She smirked and then looked at Frisha. "Come on. Don't you want to try it? When will you ever be able to wear something like this in public again?"

"Why would I want to?" Frisha said.

Reaylin shrugged and glanced at the bustier in Yserria's hands. "I don't know. Rezkin seems to like it."

Frisha and Yserria both blushed furiously and then Frisha turned on *him*. "What about you? You can't wear that to dinner. Would you wear something like this?"

"Those are women's clothes," he said.

She rolled her eyes. "You know what I mean."

"Uh, don't forget he went to the Adana'Ro naked," said Reaylin.

Wesson responded to the tapping at the door and again assisted Celise in dragging a heavy basket of clothing into the suite. The young woman held up a garment that crossed over the bosom and then draped over the hips in filmy layers of pastel petals all the way to the floor. The back was open, but it had several lacey ties to keep the dress in place. Frisha still appeared uncertain until Celise pulled out a matching shoulder wrap. She finally acquiesced, gingerly grasping the layers of fabric in shaky hands.

Celise turned to Dark Tidings and said, "*Your Majesty, would you like for me to send a male with clothing for you and your son*?" With this last, she nodded toward Wesson.

"*That will not be necessary,*" Rezkin said, "*and he is not my son. This is Journeyman Mage Wesson, in service to the crown.*"

Celise looked at Wesson in surprise and then back at Dark Tidings. "*I apologize for the misunderstanding. He is small for a man.*"

She turned back to the basket and tugged a small trunk from beneath the clothing. She set the trunk on a table beside a cushioned bench and snapped the lid open. Inside were numerous brushes of varying sizes and bottles, vials, and packets filled with colorful powders and creams. Celise waved Frisha toward the bench and said, "I do *perliana* for you."

"*Perliana*?" Frisha said, eyeing the assortment that looked like a portable alchemy shop.

"The face paints and powders," Yserria supplied.

"Oh, I don't need—"

"Yes, you do," Reaylin said as she shoved Frisha toward the bench. "We are doing this, Frisha. Stop being so boring. Remember, you insisted on coming."

Tam's boots were waterlogged as he slogged through the muddy street from a dilapidated tavern toward the room he was renting above another dilapidated tavern. The storm had moved up from the south quickly, and now he was stuck in the downpour. He was suddenly struck from the side so that he tumbled into a pile of crates beside an abandoned market stall. He glanced up just in time to avoid the club that was descending toward his head. He kicked his assailant in the kneecap, using the force to push himself from the pile of broken slats. His feet slipped in the mud as he took to the alley, realizing the mistake too late. Men grabbed him from either side, but he took the first by surprise with a head-butt. The grip on his arm loosened, and Tam smashed his elbow into the man's jaw. He spun into the other man's grip and then used his body weight to push him off balance into the first. Tam was nearly pulled into the tangle when the man's foot slipped so that he smashed into the ground.

Tam took off running in the other direction, but his assailants turned out to be many. Three more followed him through the vacant street. With the rain obscuring his vision, he missed the two that were coming at him from the opposite direction. He drew his sword and met the first with a slash to the abdomen. The man's entrails spilled onto the ground between Tam and the next assailant who stood in shock over what had just happened to his comrade. Tam's blade slipped through the hesitant man's throat before he could recover, then continued down the street with three in pursuit.

From behind him he heard a short burst of whistles, and he knew that somewhere more were waiting for him. He was breathing so heavily, he felt like he was drowning in the rain. He ducked around a corner and covered his face for just a moment to catch his breath and then began running down another alley. His stomach dropped when he realized the rain had obscured the form pacing him atop the roof. Two men stepped into the alley in front of him. He glanced back to see his three pursuers closing in on him. Suddenly, he tumbled to the ground in a tangle of netting. He was struggling to cut himself free with the sword when he was struck from behind, and all went black.

10

Yserria stood gawking at the entrance to the dining hall with Frisha, Reaylin, and Nanessy. It was opulent and bright with warm yellow light radiating from mage-lit chandeliers. Round tables occupied the center of the room, draped in crimson table linens, with crystal goblets and filigreed porcelain place settings. No one was seated at the tables, though. All the women and their consorts stood in groups or gathered on the plush sofas and benches that were clumped around the room's perimeter. The women were dressed in whatever they desired, from ballgowns to sheer strips of fabric. Every man in the room was massive and built like a warrior.

"I do not understand," Nanessy whispered to Yserria. "Are there no *normal* men in Lon Lerésh?"

Yserria said, "I believe it is the same as anywhere, but these are some of the most powerful women in Kielen. They choose the most impressive champions to accompany them to palace functions."

"Not every woman wants a warrior," said Nanessy.

Yserria looked at her knowingly. "I have seen the way you look at our king. Can you say you would not choose him?"

Nanessy glanced around, obviously concerned that someone might overhear. "He is different. He is more than a warrior. I would not be interested if he were nothing more than a bunch of muscles and a handsome face."

"I see," Yserria said. "So, you are judging them for their looks. You do not know these men. How do you know they are not *more*?"

Nanessy flushed and tugged at her layers of fabric, wishing they were not so snug. She had decided to wear the sheer gown over a calf-length skirt and blouse that looked to be made from woven ribbons. She said, "That is not what I meant. You said that is the reason they are chosen. It does not seem like they are valued for anything else."

A sultry voice crawled up Nanessy's neck.

"Believe me," a woman said as she moved to join them, beckoning to her consort. "We appreciate them for their *many* talents." She purred in the man's ear as he grinned appreciatively. The man had dark hair and hazel eyes, and his sun-darkened skin was stretched tight over thick muscles displayed openly beneath a loose, green, embroidered vest. The woman ran manicured nails over his exposed pectorals and said, "Banen, here, has amazing hands." She met Nanessy's discomfited gaze. "He is one of the court musicians who will be entertaining us tonight, and he is also one of the palace's top archers, a member of the royal guard."

Banen seemed to have eyes only for the woman. He stroked her jaw and pressed his lips to her neck before mumbling in her ear, "There is no need to brag, my dear."

"Of course, there is!" she said, fluttering her darkened lashes. "You are amazing, and I am proud to call you mine."

"As it should be," he replied. He held her in a tight embrace, pressed a lingering kiss to her lips, and said, "I must take my place, my love. Please be sure to enjoy yourself." He held up a finger and added, "But not *too* much."

She giggled and swatted his rear as he strutted toward the musicians. As she turned to them, small jewels sparkled in the light where they dangled from her auburn hair. "You look surprised," she said.

"No," Nanessy said quickly and then stuttered, "Well, yes. I mean, I have never seen people so … affectionate … in public."

The woman nodded knowingly. "I spent a short time in Ashai. This is where you are from, yes? You are all very cold."

"Cold?" Nanessy said.

"Yes," said the woman. "You do not share yourselves—your true selves. You are distant. *Reserved*, I believe, is how you say it. The women *and* the men. You try to act like you are not human—as if you have no feelings and desires. We

Leréshi are a passionate people. We express ourselves openly in our dress, our art, our *love*"—she smiled fiendishly—"and in *war*. You do not want to cross a powerful Leréshi woman." She eyed each of them as they remained huddled near the entrance. "I am Nayala, Matrianera of House Tekahl. Banen is my first consort. My second consort, Heylin, remains in the home to care for the male children."

Reaylin pushed to the front of the group. "You have *two* consorts?"

Nayala looked her up and down and then nodded approvingly. She said, "Yes, Heylin is a good father. Several have tried to claim him from me, but Banen is a great champion and has always won him back. Together, they help to make my house strong. The strongest houses are those with the best balance."

"Nayala," said a vaguely familiar voice. It was the blonde, and rather forward, Matrianera Telía. She sidled up to them and said, "Do you intend to keep our guests to yourself?"

Nayala's smile did not reach her eyes as she replied, "I was only introducing myself. They are curious about our ways."

Telía looked over at Yserria. "I heard a rumor that you are Leréshi."

Yserria glanced at the others and said, "My parents were Leréshi. I was born in Ashai."

As Yserria spoke, Telía's judgmental gaze roved her form. Yserria had wrapped a shawl around her torso, and her slinky skirt reached all the way to the floor. The woman pursed her lips at Yserria's modesty.

"You do not carry yourself like a Leréshi," Telía said.

"Telía, it is not for you to judge her dress," Nayala hissed.

Telía ignored her as she ran a finger down Yserria's neck to tug at the shawl. "You do not *own* your body."

Yserria pushed the shawl away from her midsection, baring her abdomen—and the sword hilt at her waist. "If you touch me again, I will show you how well I own my body."

Telía pulled her hand back, doing her best to hide her surprise. "I had forgotten that you carry a sword. Someone mentioned that you are a knight. Do you know how to use it or is it a ceremonial position?"

An eerie, deep voice rumbled through the doorway. "I would wager she can wield it better than your champion," Dark Tidings said as he came to stand among the women.

He towered over them, his shadowy presence in contrast to the colorful array of silks and jewels. The empty black gaze turned toward Telía, and he added, "Should she challenge you for your champion?"

A man in a palace guard's formal uniform, presumably Telía's consort by the concern on his face, cautiously approached but did not interrupt.

Telía's voice wavered as she said, "No, of course not. What would I gain should he win?"

Rezkin stepped behind Yserria and tugged the shawl from her shoulders to expose the green, lacy bustier hidden beneath. He reached around and ran a finger over her bare skin just below the torque. "This," he said.

Nayala and Telía's eyes widened, and Yserria's skin reddened as everyone's attention followed a tide of whispers straight to her bosom.

"Adana'Ro," Nayala whispered.

"It was a gift," Yserria said quickly. "A gift from my king." She turned and executed a formal curtsy toward Dark Tidings. It was awkward for her, but she would have felt ridiculous saluting in her state of dress.

"Do you accept the challenge?" Dark Tidings said, his attention on Telía.

Telía drew her gaze away from the torque, glanced at the sword, and then stared into Yserria's green eyes. "No, I do not desire the challenge."

Dark Tidings said, "Although the ladies with whom I travel are all attractive, I did not choose them for their beauty. They are all capable, so you should not press them."

They now had the attention of everyone in the large room. Telía shrugged as if suddenly unconcerned. "I was only curious. Leréshi women do not usually carry swords. We have champions to do that sort of thing for us."

Yserria's painted lips pulled into a tight grin. "Then it is a good thing your champions are always near when you need them."

Telía's spine straightened, and she smiled in return. "Quite," she said and then walked away, her consort trailing behind her.

Nayala's grin was genuine as she watched Telía's departure. "That was beautiful," she murmured. Turning back to them, she said. "Telía almost never backs down from a challenge. Dayleen"—she nodded toward a laughing brunette surrounded by several friends—"will have drawn ahead now that Telía has lost significant ground. Be wary. She will seek to gain it back."

Yserria said, "I was not trying to become involved in your politics."

Nayala shrugged one shoulder. "She was rude, and her plan—whatever it was—backfired. She should have known better, but she is becoming desperate, I think."

"Desperate for what?" Reaylin said as she peered around Nayala.

"The throne, of course."

Reaylin looked back to her with wide eyes. She appeared thoroughly engrossed in the political drama. "What do you mean?"

Nayala pursed her lips and then sighed. "I suppose there is no harm in explaining it to you. Before Queen Erisial took the throne, Telía's family was expected to produce the next monarch. They had the greatest political support in the court, seconded only by Erisial; and Telía's mother, Paksis, had made some profitable deals that had gained her favor with several prominent echelons."

"Echelons?" Reaylin said.

"The governors of the provinces," said Dark Tidings.

Nayala blinked up at him as though she had somehow forgotten his presence.

"Yes," she drawled, looking at him suspiciously. "Erisial knew that if she waited much longer, Paksis would take the throne, so she claimed it first and sent Paksis on a diplomatic mission to Gendishen. She did not return. Since then, Telía's house has been in decline. There are now three others of nearly equal influence. You have already met them. They escorted you from the docks."

Reaylin said, "You're saying that the four women who are most likely to *claim* the throne from Queen Erisial are her closest advisors?"

Nayala smiled again. "Oh, I doubt they do much advising or that the queen has any interest in what they have to say. I believe your kingdom has the phrase as well—*keep your enemies close*. Erisial has always been daring. She keeps one guessing. She has plans within plans. Even the slightest move against her could have disastrous consequences. She has been very generous with her *advisors*. To have *four* high houses of nearly equal strength is unheard of and a sure way for her to keep her head."

"So none of them are strong enough to challenge her," Reaylin said with a giddy grin.

Dark Tidings said, "*You* do not seek the throne, Matrianera Nayala?"

Nayala again appeared startled, as if noticing him for the first time. She laughed and said, "No, the path to the throne leads to an early death. I would prefer to see my daughters grown. Still, I have been named a contender for the Sixth Echelon. It is a nice province, distant but peaceful."

Reaylin bounced on her toes. "Congratulations." She looked at Yserria and

Nanessy who were standing to either side of her and said, "This is so exciting."

Frisha, who hovered beside Rezkin behind them, mumbled, "I don't see what's so exciting about killing each other for positions of power."

Reaylin rounded on her. "They're *women*, Frisha. *Women* with power, and not all of us are handed the chance to become queen."

"Well, not all of us *want* it!" Frisha snapped.

A haunting melody echoed through the hall as the musicians began to play, and Nayala smiled happily as she turned to watch her consort. She called over her shoulder, "The queen has arrived."

On cue, several royal guardsmen entered the hall from the end opposite them. A woman in her midthirties followed, wearing a gown made entirely of cream colored feathers tied loosely with silk cord. The feathers swayed and floated as she walked, allowing glimpses of the tanned skin underneath. Her golden-blonde hair was pulled back so that thick waves of curls flowed behind her. Atop her head was a glittering crown of yellow gold and diamonds, and a long strand of saltwater pearls rested between her barely concealed breasts. She stepped onto a short pedestal at the front of the hall, turned, and waited.

The attention turned toward the visitors. Nayala quickly stepped out of the way, retreating with a Leréshi bow. Rezkin whispered a reminder to the women to present themselves. Yserria led the procession, crossing the hall with as much confidence as she could muster, her shawl hanging loosely behind her.

She curtsied before the queen and spoke in Ashaiian for the sake of her companions. "I am Yserria Rey, Knight of the Realm, Royal Guard of Cael."

Erisial's honey colored gaze lingered on Yserria's features. Finally, she said, "Yserria, daughter of Ienia and niece of Yenis of House Rey."

A wave of whispers passed through the onlookers.

"That is correct," Yserria said with a quick glance around her.

Erisial's gaze traversed the crowd and came to rest on an older woman who bore a pensive expression. "Yenis, your sister's daughter has returned, yet she serves another ruler, a *man*. She wears the Torque of Gereldina." She turned back to Yserria. "I am told you were given this as a gift by your king."

"Yes," Yserria replied, her voice heavy with caution.

Erisial's voice was firm but casual. "Give it to me."

"I cannot," Yserria said. "It is enchanted."

"If you *could*?" Erisial said.

"I still would not give it to you. It belongs to me."

Erisial said, "And if I challenged you for it, would your king serve as your champion?" Her gaze was no longer on Yserria. Her attention rested on Dark Tidings, who remained at the other end of the hall.

"I have no need of a champion," Yserria replied, "but if you want the torque, you will either have to remove my head or convince my king to unclasp it."

Erisial looked down to Yserria. "A man has placed a collar on your neck, and you not only accept it, but fight for it. Dear girl, do you know *why* he did this to you—with *this* necklace? Because he wants me to know he *can*. He takes a strong woman, a knight, a future matrianera of House Rey, and chains her."

"With all due respect, Queen Erisial, you misunderstand. I placed the collar on my own neck when I chose to swear fealty to him. It is his prerogative."

Erisial's expression changed, and she smiled with pleasure. "No, I understand." She waved a hand around the crowd. "Almost any of these women would wear that torque if he presented it to them. *That* torque, that comes either with the blessing of the Adana'Ro or the strength of one who took it from them, also bears the weight of the untouchable King's Tournament Champion, the rebel King of Ashai, he who claims the princess of Channería, a warrior who defeats a Gendishen army and is brazen enough to demand payment from its king. *That* torque on *your* neck in *this* hall means *he* is at your call. You may not need a champion, Daughter of Rey, but he is yours nonetheless." Her gaze roved the faces again. "Every woman in here knows this. *He* knows this. It was well played."

She captured Yserria's gaze and said, "If you intended to stay in Lon Lerésh, I would kill you now lest you steal my throne." To Yenis, she said, "Do you accept Yserria back into your house?"

Yenis, who had earlier appeared so uncertain of the queen's reaction, practically leapt forward. Excitedly, she said, "Yes, Queen Erisial, my sister's daughter is most welcome in the House of Rey."

Erisial nodded, obviously having expected it, and said to Yenis, "You may join my council."

Yenis grinned broadly and practically ran to join the sour-faced advisors.

Yserria glanced back at her companions and then past them to Rezkin. He had told her the torque had meaning, but she had not imagined the gift might make her a contender for the throne. She looked down at Frisha, who would not meet her gaze and then turned back to the queen.

Erisial was watching her carefully, and Yserria had no idea what the woman saw in her. She had the same sharp, endless gaze that Rezkin often wore, the one that seemed to see through everything and everyone at once.

The woman said, "You may introduce your companions, Yserria of House Rey."

Yserria stepped aside and said, "This is Mage Nanessy Threll, Swordswoman and Apprentice Healer Reaylin de Voss, and Lady Frisha Marcum."

The woman's senses zeroed in on Frisha. "Marcum … as in relation to the Ashaiian General Marcum?"

Frisha gripped her filmy shawl tight to her shoulders and said, "Yes, I am his heir."

"With what interesting company your king travels," the woman mused. "Who is the boy?" she said with a nod.

Nanessy quickly said, "That is Journeyman Mage Wesson."

"You are his tutor?" Erisial said.

"Um, sometimes, I suppose," Nanessy said uncertainly. They had been instructed not to lie, since there were truthseekers present, but to downplay Wesson's role where they could.

"Explain," said the queen.

Nanessy said, "He did not attend the mage academy, so there are some formalities with which he is unfamiliar. I am also assisting him in his pursuits since he is young and has not yet reached the rank of full mage. He has not been able to achieve his goal of becoming a life mage."

Seemingly satisfied, the queen's attention lifted to the dark wraith at the opposite end of the hall. The others moved out of the way as he strode forward on silent feet. His forward motion ceased at the foot of the pedestal, upon which the queen stood nearly at his eye level. He performed the slightest bow in greeting but not one that could be mistaken for submission.

"Am I to treat with a mask?" she said.

Rezkin removed the mask and met her amber stare. Her attempt to conceal her surprise was not lost on him.

"So young," she murmured. "Your name?"

"As I told your council, I have none."

"Impossible," she said.

"You should know. Your power has saturated the room since you entered. You are a truthseeker, are you not?"

"Yes, yet I sense no power from you."

Her power surrounded him as he met her dispassionate stare. "I am not a mage."

"What are you?"

"I am the King of Cael, True King of Ashai."

A spark lit in her honey-colored eyes, and she gazed around the room. Her voice echoed off the walls as she said, "Lon Lerésh does not recognize your claim to Cael until it is recognized by Gendishen, and we do not recognize your claim to Ashai until you wear the crown. *You* are not granted the immunity due one of royal blood—*unless* you would like to submit proof of such a claim?"

Rezkin said, "Any woman who attempts to claim me will end up disappointed and without a champion."

Erisial grinned. "We shall see. For now, you will be my personal guest at the table, and we shall dine."

She waved a man forward. He had the bearing of a soldier, but the clean-cut impassivity of a politician. "This is my consort, Serunius. He will serve you."

Rezkin's icy gaze flicked to Serunius. The man did not look pleased. Erisial observed Serunius's expression and said, "Is there a problem, my love?"

The man turned to her with dark eyes, and some unspoken message passed between them. He appeared resigned as he said, "No, My Queen. I understand."

Rezkin understood, too. The fact that the queen would have her consort serve him made her intention clear.

He said, "You will not get what you want."

She smiled knowingly and said, "You will change your mind."

They spoke no more of it during dinner. Instead, they discussed numerous other subjects from history to politics to art and culture. At first, Rezkin felt like he was being quizzed by his masters, but he knew what the woman was doing. It was for the same reason that she had listed his accomplishments and emphasized the power behind the gift of the torque. She wanted to impress. She wanted everyone else to know of his superiority. Like the woman, Nayala, with her consort, the queen was bragging.

When Rezkin and his companions finally returned to their suite, he was disconcerted.

"What is wrong, Rezkin?" said Frisha.

He glanced at her and then went back to checking for traps and poisons. "The queen intends to claim me."

"What? No!" she blurted. "I mean, she can't do that, can she? You are a king. She can't claim a king."

"She does not recognize me as an independent monarch. We are in her country, and she may do as she pleases."

Frisha said, "But, you don't have to *accept* her. It's not like she can force you."

"She can. She has the entire army of Lon Lerésh at her disposal, and I cannot possibly escape with all of you in tow. Plus, we would leave without Oledia."

Frisha's anger and frustration seemed to get the better of her as she said, "You don't need her daughter. You don't need King Privoth's recognition. You said before that we can just keep Cael. It's enchanted. No one can force us from it."

Rezkin said, "No, they likely cannot make us leave, but they *can* besiege us. You all are expecting me to take back Ashai, and darker forces are in play. I cannot prevail without allies and trading partners. Still, you are correct. I do not have to accept her claim if I beat her champion. Only a woman can challenge her claim, though."

"Well, I can—"

"No."

"Why not?" Frisha said.

"You are not Leréshi. The only way she would recognize your claim is if you were my wife, which means you would have to marry me."

Frisha seemed at a loss for words, and he shook his head. "We are not doing that, Frisha. You made your decision after much deliberation. You will not change your mind in a moment of perceived duress."

Reaylin, who had been watching the interplay with rapt attention, said, "Yserria is Leréshi, so she wouldn't have to marry you, right?"

Rezkin glanced at Yserria who flushed deep red. "Yserria is my ward," he said as he crossed the room to inspect the fireplace.

"Yeah, but it wouldn't have to be a big deal," said Reaylin. "She claims you as her consort, but it's not like anything has to come of it."

"It doesn't work that way," Yserria mumbled. "If it were so easy to claim a consort who can serve as your champion, don't you think all women would go around claiming everyone?"

"What do you mean?" said Reaylin.

Rezkin pulled his head from the chimney and said, "For Yserria's claim to counter the queen's, I would have to accept it. If I accept the claim, the union must be consummated—in front of witnesses."

"That's barbaric," exclaimed Frisha.

Rezkin said, "The Leréshi are much freer with their lovemaking." He then crawled onto the floor and slid halfway under a sofa to examine the underside.

Nanessy bent over to look at him as she said, "You think the queen intends to force a claim on you?"

"No," he replied, sliding from beneath the furniture. He stood and frowned when he looked down at himself. "She is confident that I will change my mind. In fact, she is so confident that she is giving her opponents time to scheme and present their own challenges. She believes I will accept her claim and choose to fight as her champion against any challengers. I have no idea what she intends to hold over me."

"Us, maybe?" Frisha said, worrying at her lip. "Do you think she would hurt us or hold us hostage?"

"It is possible, but she is conniving. Threatening you would serve no purpose besides changing my mind, and that would alienate me in the process. I would guess she has bigger plans."

Now covered in soot and dust, and frustrated with his lack of insight, Rezkin no longer wished to continue the conversation. He excused himself to bathe with instructions that none of them were to leave the suite.

Just as Rezkin closed himself into the bathing chamber, a timid knock sounded at the door. Wesson opened it to admit Celise and then took a seat on a chair in the corner, hoping to go unnoticed.

"Lady Yserria," Celise said. "I am in the middle."

They all looked at the woman, waiting for her to say more.

Celise looked at the curious faces and said, "I am in the middle?" When they did not respond, she said, "There is a man. I speak with you, and I am in the middle." Still, they were puzzled, so she tried, "The man … um … wishes to be with you, and I am in the middle."

After not receiving the response she had expected, she sighed and switched to Leréshi.

Yserria said, "Ooh, she is acting as an intermediary."

Celise nodded and said, "Your matrianera would to be *intermediary*, but he asks me. I know the man."

Yserria nervously fingered the hilt of her sword. "You are saying that a man wants me to claim him?"

"Yes, Lady Yserria. This man wants to be claim of you."

"No—" Yserria started.

"Wait, Yserria," Nanessy said. "You should at least hear about this man. He might be the love of your life. Can you imagine having a man totally devoted to you?"

"Yes," Yserria hissed. "I almost had one."

Nanessy said, "I am truly sorry about that, but you should at least hear her out."

Yserria said, "Fine, what about this man?" She had attempted to soothe the acid from her tone, but she was not sure she had succeeded.

Celise smiled. "His name is Coledon. He is handsome. He is good sword man. Very large man and strong. He is royal guard. He is good choice for consort. My mother … she want for me claim him."

"But you haven't," Reaylin said suspiciously.

Celise looked embarrassed. "No. I have not claim."

"Why not?" Frisha said.

"My mother. She want warrior man for me. Big man. Guard to be champion for me to be higher. But … big mans are … um … I am afraid."

Frisha said, "I thought Leréshi men are good to their women."

"Yes, yes, are good, but warriors are dangerous. Um, they have a look. They *want*. Um … *desire*. Some say they can be rough. Some matria like this. I do not like this." She looked quickly to Yserria. "But this man is good, and you are strong. You are warrior. You are not afraid, and he is desired by many."

Reaylin said, "If he is so desired, why hasn't he been claimed?"

"His matrianera, his sister, will not let him go. He is great champion. She does not want to lose." She turned to Yserria and nodded toward the bathing chamber where Rezkin could be seen soaking in the bath through the stained-glass windows. "If *you* claim Coledon, she will not risk her consort to challenge claim."

Yserria crossed her arms. "So, this Coledon does not have any interest in *me*. He just wants to get away from his sister."

Celise shook her head. "No, you are beautiful and strong. You not give to queen as she wants. Coledon likes this."

"I have no interest in claiming anyone," Yserria said. "Besides, I have accepted my king as my guardian. That means he must approve of anyone I marry."

"You give him this power?" Celise said, obviously bewildered. "Your king does wish to *marry* you?"

"No!" she said, shaking her head emphatically. She glanced at Frisha's bitter expression and, less certainly, said, "I don't think so. I-I don't know."

Celise stared at the torque around Yserria's neck and gave her a doubtful look.

Yserria balled her fists and tried to keep her voice low as she pointed at Frisha and exclaimed, "He was supposed to marry *her*!"

Celise glanced between them and then finally turned to Yserria. "You will speak with Coledon?"

"No," Yserria said. "I am not claiming anyone."

Celise appeared crestfallen. She nodded and turned toward the door, thanking Wesson as he hopped up to open it for her.

When he turned back around, he paused and said, "Where is Rezkin?"

The ladies turned to peer through the stained glass, but Rezkin was gone.

Rezkin clung to the stones on the parapet as the wind whipped around him. Most of the shutters were locked tight against the approaching storm, and the wall patrol was having a difficult time keeping the torches lit. He climbed over the barrier of the walkway just as the first drops threatened to make the walls too slippery to climb. The door stood open, and Rezkin wrapped his cloak around him tightly as he stomped into the guardhouse, turning and shaking as he went, sure to keep his face hidden as he made his presence obvious. The guards paid him no attention as they waxed and oiled their supplies, continuing with their banter and complaints about the turning weather.

"*It's starting already, is it*?" the one with a long mustache muttered. "*Can't get a dry night, can we?*"

"*The foreigners brought it with 'em*," said a younger man.

"*Bah, that's a load, and you know it. It's been rainin' for more than a week, and they just got here*."

"*Don't mean they didn't bring it. It's an omen*," said the younger.

"It's not an omen, you idiot. It's called the changing of the seasons. Happens every year or are you too green to remember. Mayhap you were still suckling your mother's teat last year, eh?"

"I'm just saying, there's a king in the palace. You know that's an ill portent."

"Queen says he's not a king. It don't count."

"Yeah, well, I hear things go wrong everywhere this one goes. He took the Channerían princess, and now they're in a civil war. The latest is there's trouble in Jerea, too."

"He hasn't even been to Jerea," said the older man. *"At least, not that I've heard."*

The young man shrugged. *"They're sayin' it's his fault, anyway. And you heard about the torque. He's been to see the Adana'Ro, which means he's been to Ferélle."*

"I haven't heard of no trouble there."

"If he's in league with the Adana'Ro, there's trouble. Now Gendishen seems to think they're fulfilling that old prophecy, but the purifiers are saying he's not human, and he's got a mighty powerful mage with him."

"The woman? Mage Threll. She's a pretty one. I wouldn't mind being claimed by her," said the older man.

"No, I heard it was a man, a battle mage."

The older man chuckled, *"Must be one scary bastard to have the purifiers shaking in their boots."*

The men went on to discuss less interesting gossip, and Rezkin left the guardhouse, entering the palace wing typically reserved for visiting officials. After slipping from the bathhouse via a secret passage he had found behind the water fixtures, he had slinked through the palace to the barracks where he had hoped to procure a uniform. The building was crawling with people who obviously knew each other and would have noticed a newcomer. One particularly intoxicated guard, who had apparently thoroughly enjoyed the feast, had the misfortune to require the use of the outhouse. Rezkin shot him with a blow dart laced with a toxin that would induce sleep for several hours. He was taller than the other man, but most people were too preoccupied to notice an ill-fitting uniform.

He watched the maids carrying trays to and from the rooms to determine the location of his target and then rapped on the Channerían ambassador's door. The ambassador's aide answered and admitted him without question.

"He is not here," the aide said as Rezkin surveyed the suite. "He enjoys taking advantage of the benefits of Lon Lerésh. He rarely spends time here."

"It was my understanding that ambassadors to Lon Lerésh must be married to prevent a conflict of interest," Rezkin said.

The man said, "They are. Most of the Leréshi do not care, though, so neither does he." After latching the door, the aide warded the room to prevent eavesdropping. He approached Rezkin, saluted, and bowed. "Your Majesty, it is my honor to serve you. Please tell me I am to be recalled."

"You do not care for your assignment, Striker Akris?"

"Your Majesty, I will serve in whatever way is required, but this assignment was supposed to last no more than eight months. Bordran sent me here nearly three years ago. I had begun to worry that I was forgotten."

Rezkin nodded. "It is possible. I cannot say." He made sure he had Akris's attention and said, "I am not Caydean."

Akris peered at him pensively. The man was on the leaner side, for a striker, making him *appear* less formidable. He had the dark, wavy hair and eyes more common to Channería. Even now, he spoke Ashaiian with a Channerían accent, probably out of habit.

Finally, the striker said, "I know you are not Caydean."

"And you know that I am his rival," Rezkin said. "If you serve him, then you are obligated to attempt to kill or capture me."

"I do not know Caydean well. Since I spent little time in the palace, I only met him briefly, on a few occasions when he was younger. Everyone who has ever spoken of him claims him to be insane. With each piece of news that reaches my ears, I am more convinced these are not rumors politically motivated by his opponents."

"And what have you heard of me?" Rezkin said.

"Some call you a rebel. Others say you are the rightful king. I heard that two strikers have sworn fealty to you already. Apparently, they did so after you took the entire tournament without so much as a scratch. Some say you killed Prince Thresson, while others say you kidnapped or rescued him. Most reports agree that you are holding the Wellinven heir hostage, along with a few others. From there, the rumors become increasingly unbelievable. I have heard that you are a powerful battle mage who fixed the tournament and then tried to destroy everyone when they would not give you the prize. They say you stole the bride of Prince Nyan of Jerea. I have even heard that you are a demon who wields a black blade forged in the Hells."

"Your rumors are surprisingly thorough yet only salted with truth," Rezkin said.

"As I thought." The man glanced down to the hilt at Rezkin's waist and said, "Is that it? Is that the so-called black blade?"

Rezkin frowned. "This? No, this is not mine. It belongs to the man from whom I borrowed this uniform. It will kill, should the need arise."

"Of course," Akris replied. "So, are you here to recruit me, kill me, or just seeking information?"

Rezkin said, "Do you want to be recruited?"

"I heard you carry proof of your claim. I am willing to see it, if you are willing to share."

Akris read the paper Rezkin proffered. Without looking up, he said, "I wish to go home to my wife."

Rezkin said, "No one in my company will soon be returning to Ashai. In addition, the families of those known to be in my company are slated for imprisonment or death. Caydean is not a friend to the strikers, though. If they do not slough their honorable ways to do his dirty work, he will treat them the same as any enemy. You are an absent striker, yet to make your loyalty known. When he hears of my visit, he may consider you to be an important player. He may have already contacted you."

The tingle of power filled the air, and Akris said, "I swear by mage oath that I have had no contact with Caydean, his agents, or any other strikers since I took this assignment."

"And yet you could be acting on your own accord, satisfying your duty to report to your king or carry out his decree regarding my capture. You are an unknown factor."

"But you made contact anyway," Akris said.

"I am not afraid of the unknown. I recognize that if you choose to serve me, it might end in betrayal. It will not stop me from using you in the meantime. Be assured that I make contingencies for such events, and your efforts will fail."

Akris appeared skeptical. "Even a failed betrayal can do much damage."

Rezkin shrugged without concern. "The final result is what matters."

"So you do not care who gets hurt in the process?"

"No one is indispensable," Rezkin said with a trifling discomfort in the back of his mind. Upon noticing Akris's displeasure, he felt it prudent to amend his statement. "My concern extends only insofar as my duty to those I must protect and honor. I have taken responsibility for many people, and I am seeking responsibility for more, including all of Ashai. I would prefer for few to suffer, but war is generally not accommodating."

Akris acknowledged Rezkin's statement with a solemn nod. "You assume the ideology of a striker, duty above sentiment. It is a paramount quality in a soldier, but I am not sure it is best in a king."

Rezkin said, "The qualities of a king are irrelevant so long as he is born first and to the right parents."

"Yes, I see your point, but I am still bound by oath to serve the King of Ashai."

"Then you should decide who you recognize as king. Your position here is valuable because you can spy on both Channería and Lon Lerésh; but, the truth is, I do not need you. My network spreads quickly, and I already have agents to feed me information."

Rezkin told the lie with confidence, but it was worth the surprise and suspicion in the striker's eyes. Whether he ended up serving Rezkin or Caydean, it was to Rezkin's advantage for the striker to believe he had more than he did.

Akris returned his gaze to the parchment, his expression one of intense contemplation. The man had made a mistake in revealing his weakness, his desire to return to a wife they both knew could already be dead. Rezkin thought it a sentiment unbecoming of a striker, though. It stunk of a desperation he doubted the man felt. He might truly be desperate for liberation but for some reason other than the one he stated—probably boredom. For a striker, three years of serving as an ambassador's aide in a nonhostile queendom would be akin to torture. *Or* he might be trying to gain his way into Rezkin's company by appealing to Rezkin's ability to empathize, in which case he had not only failed but revealed that he had no idea with whom he was dealing.

Rezkin interrupted the man's internal struggle. "You do not have to decide now. If you wish to serve me, report to the strikers on my ship before we leave."

"They are here? Shezar and Roark?"

"Shezar is here," Rezkin replied. Shezar and Roark had sworn fealty to him in front of everyone at the tournament, so it was not a surprise that their names were known. It was interesting that Akris had intercepted such detailed reports, however.

"Then you have more than two?" Akris said, failing to conceal his surprise.

Rezkin grinned but did not offer more. Instead he said, "The only information I desire from you at the moment is what you know about Erisial's plans regarding me."

Akris shook his head. "I am afraid I have nothing to offer on that front. The woman is fanatically independent. She tells no one of her plans, especially the important ones. I doubt she even confides in her consort."

"What of him?" Rezkin asked.

"Serunius has been with Erisial for many years. He is intelligent enough to challenge her but smart enough not to. He is fiercely loyal and protective, and he is the father of Oledia and their two sons. I think he is truly in love with Erisial, although I know not if she returns the sentiment. Her callousness has allowed her to hold the throne for this long, and he had no small part in helping her to gain it. He is a master of several weapons, including the sword, and a natural battle mage. In short, he is the most desired champion in the queendom, thus far capable of meeting any challenge. At least, until *you* arrived, and she has made her interest in you obvious. She has declared you fair game and given her opponents time to scheme. I expect blood to be spilled. If you are not careful, it will be yours."

"My blood does not run so freely," Rezkin said.

"Every man's blood runs like water when his guts are laid open, with or without a crown on his head."

"Then I had best keep my guts intact," Rezkin said as he held his hand out for his document. Once it was secured, he said, "I intend to liberate Ashai from Caydean and make it a peaceful, prosperous kingdom where my people will be safe. You may choose whichever side you prefer but know that the actions you take thereafter are by *your* choice and not the mere fulfilment of your oath."

Rezkin left the ambassador's suite, taking a different route on the return trip. It had started raining heavily, and he would not be able to scale the slippery walls. As he neared his next turn, he saw something curious. A young woman was scurrying down the opposite corridor when a masculine arm reached out from a doorway and yanked her into a room. Although she was out of sight, Rezkin heard a muffled squeal and the scuff of soft shoes across the floorboards. He might have stayed out of the mess if this did not happen to be the woman who had been assisting his companions. There was a good chance that Celise's abduction had something to do with him.

He slinked silently toward the room and hovered beside the doorway. A quick glance revealed the entrance to a supply room. A hulking man in a guard's uniform towered over the petite woman. He held Celise against the shelves with one hand pressing against her chest while his other clasped an illuminated mage stone.

"*You do not have permission to touch me*," Celise said. "*I will report you.*"

"*I think you won't*," the man said as he inhaled the scent at her neck, the blonde whiskers of his beard scraping across her skin. "*You like it.*"

Rezkin pulled back as she turned her head toward him, even though her eyes were shut, as if she did not wish to see her assailant up close.

Her voice wavered as she said, "*What do you want, Morlin*?"

"*I want you, Celise. Why will you not claim me*?"

"*You are a brute*," she snapped. "*You take liberties, and you smell horrible.*"

Morlin chuckled. "*If you truly don't want me, why have you not reported me*?"

"*You know why. Your matrianera has even less honor than you. If I report you, she will challenge me, and I will be forced to choose a champion.*"

"*And you have not, so I know you are not serious. You want me. Admit it already.*"

"*No, I do* not *want you. With my position, no one will act as my champion without a claim. I will not allow your disgusting ways to force me into making a claim I do not want.*"

Anger filled Morlin's tone as he said, "*There is a reason no one would be your champion without a claim. You selfishly hoard the power of your position when you should be sharing it with a consort.*"

"*And you want me to choose* you. *That will never happen, Morlin. When I do finally choose one, I will be sure to send him your way.*"

Morlin laughed. "*Then you will be sending him to his death, for I will not hold back, no matter the terms of the duel. In fact, I will take out anyone you claim. You will be mine, Celise.*"

Realizing the confrontation had nothing to do with him, Rezkin was once again faced with a conundrum. Logically, he should walk away. Getting involved would only cause him unnecessary problems, and he could not foresee any benefits. Celise was *ro*, though. He had told Frisha that he had found some value in the *ro*, and it was true. Without the *ro*, he had nothing to protect, which meant he had no purpose. But, unlike the Adana'Ro, he was not committed to protecting *all* the *ro*. He had only to protect his friends. Celise was not his friend.

He started to walk away when the man grunted in pain. Next, he heard a slap, and then Celise's pained cry, followed by a sob. Rezkin mentally groaned. Celise could not protect herself against the trained soldier who was twice her weight. Frisha would be angry with him if he did not help. If he wanted to honor Frisha, he had to help Celise.

Rezkin drew the soldier's sword at his hip, rounded the corner, and thrust the blade through the man's side. Morlin froze with his hands around Celise's neck. He looked down in shocked confusion and then turned his gaze on Rezkin. If Morlin had been breathing, he might have drawn in a few before he finally recognized the face behind the stolen uniform. Rezkin withdrew the sword slowly. Blood spilled from the wound as the man slumped to the ground with one final, wheezing breath. The mage stone winked out, leaving the cupboard in shadowed darkness. Rezkin picked up the stone and focused so that it glowed again.

Celise choked and coughed as she struggled for air. Her lashes batted frantically over her wide, frightened eyes. As she pulled in steadier breaths, she stared at the pooling blood and the dead man's stare. She had not yet looked his way, and Rezkin knew he could disappear before she recognized him. Still, he waited, uncertain as to why.

Blinking away tears, she stared only so far as his uniform at first.

"*You killed him*," she gasped.

He responded to her Leréshi. "*Yes, he was trying to kill you.*"

She shook her head. "*No, he would not have killed me.*" She finally looked up to his face and then rocked back in surprise.

Rezkin said, "*I cannot be seen in this uniform. You will wait a mark and then report the incident.*"

She shook her head emphatically. "*No! They will think I killed him. His matrianera will blame me!*"

"*You will tell them the truth. Tell them that I killed him. When they question me, I will confirm it.*"

"*You would do that for me*?"

Rezkin frowned. "*It is the truth. Just do not mention the uniform,*" he said, patting his chest.

She seemed momentarily relieved but then began crying. "*No, it will not matter. Matrianera Depheli will find a way to blame it on me. She will say that it was a scheme, that I encouraged and then betrayed him or some such. Can we not hide him? We can pretend this did not happen.*"

Rezkin raised a brow. "*I could dispose of the body, but the truthseekers will eventually figure out that you had something to do with it. By then, I will be gone, and there will be no one to corroborate your story.*"

The young woman sobbed, "*Oh, what am I to do? You should not have killed him!*"

"*You need not concern yourself. I will serve as your champion should someone challenge you over this.*"

"*You?*" she exclaimed, and then she narrowed her eyes at him. "*What do you ask in return?*"

Rezkin shook his head. "*Only that you not try to claim me.*"

Her eyes widened. "*Oh, no! I would never. No, no, no. I have no intention of angering Queen Erisial.*" Again, the suspicion entered her gaze, and she said, "*Are you doing this to gain her favor, because it will not work. She cares nothing for me.*"

Rezkin tilted his head. "*You are a member of Erisial's house?*"

Celise shrugged. "*It does not surprise me that you do not know. I am grateful that I am accepted as a member of her house, but she does not claim me otherwise. I am her eldest daughter. Her mother forced her to make a claim when she was only fifteen, and she hated the man. Serunius is not my father. That is why she does not like me. Queen Erisial says that Oledia is her only true daughter.*"

"*She makes you call her Queen?*"

"*I am just another servant in her house. She will not allow Serunius or any other member of the house to stand as champion for me if I am challenged —not unless the goal of the challenge is to damage the house standing. This*" —she waved at the body on the floor—"*she will blame on me. Even if she presented a champion on my behalf to preserve the house's honor, she would still expel me. But, if* you *stand for me—I do not know.*"

"*Do you know what her plans are for me?*"

"*It seems obvious that she intends to claim you, but the queen would never speak to me, much less confide in me.*"

"*Why did Morlin think you held a position of power?*" Rezkin said.

She looked at him pensively. "*Some people think Queen Erisial loves me and that she only pretends otherwise in public to protect me. Some think she is trying to distance me from the house so that if she is killed, I might be spared. Others believe that she wants her enemies to think I hate her so that they will try to gain my confidence and assistance in overthrowing her. None of it is true; but their beliefs, and the fact that I am still a member of her house, mean that I am in a higher position of power, even though I am only a servant.*"

"*Yes, people's perceptions are often more powerful than the truth,*" Rezkin mused. "*You could take advantage of those perceptions and declare your own house.*"

Her face scrunched with worry. "*Yes, but I would have to claim a consort for champion.*" She glanced down. "*Someone like him.*"

Rezkin shook his head, knowing the guard from whom he borrowed the uniform might wake before he was able to return it and avoid suspicion. "*I am out of time. Report this in a candle mark, and I will stand as champion.*"

"*Okay, but how do I know you will follow through*?" she said.

"*You will just have to trust me.*" Even as he said it, he knew it was much to ask of any Leréshi.

A heavy knock sounded at the door. Wesson approached with confusion. It was not the soft, hesitant knock of the servant woman, Celise. Queen's Consort Serunius and several guards stood beyond the portal, and he looked as if he would be all too pleased to dispense with them all. He did not even glance at Wesson as he pushed his way into the sitting room.

"We are here for your master," he said. "I believe some call him Rezkin."

Wesson shook his head slowly, glancing at Yserria and Nanessy who had come out of their rooms to investigate. Frisha and Reaylin followed, all looking equally concerned.

Wesson said, "Um, he, is not, exactly, here, I believe." He drew out the words, stalling for a few extra seconds to think.

Serunius rounded on him, and Wesson understood what the Queen of Lon Lerésh saw in the man. He was a lion prepared to rip into his enemies, and he held himself with the confidence of a man who could.

"The journeyman means that I was in my private bedchamber," Rezkin said from the doorway. "There is no need to intimidate the young man. He is only doing as I asked."

Serunius glanced at Wesson with a viper's gaze. "It is not difficult to intimidate a mouse. He had best hope he grows into some real power or he will never be claimed."

Yserria straightened her spine and sauntered over to stand between

Serunius and Wesson. "It is fortunate for the journeyman that our ways are different from yours."

Wesson knew that Yserria was trying to do him a favor by redirecting the man's attention, but the constant belittlement was causing his generally well-controlled anger to simmer hotter. He inhaled deeply to calm himself and then returned to the chair in the corner where he might go unnoticed.

The distraction worked. Serunius perused Yserria's figure and said, "*You*, my lady, could claim any man you want."

Yserria smiled sassily and placed her hand on her hip. "*Any* man?"

Wesson wanted to laugh. Reaylin had been working with Yserria on developing some skills in flirtation all afternoon, but it was comical since he knew how uncomfortable Yserria was with performing the act.

Serunius's expression became stormy, and he turned to Rezkin. "You are summoned to the court. There has been some trouble, and you have been named a … *person of interest*."

Rezkin smiled jovially and said, "Of course! I would be glad to assist with your investigation in any way I can."

Serunius appeared thrown by the change in Rezkin's demeanor. By the man's tense stance and the number of guards he had brought, Wesson thought he had expected trouble. Wesson had no doubt that, no matter what had happened, Rezkin was involved.

The Queen's Consort glanced at the others and said, "Your people will attend as well. We may have questions for them."

Rezkin clapped his hands and rubbed them together with enthusiasm. He strode over and threw his arms around Yserria and Frisha's shoulders. He said, "Excellent! Let us all go. It will be interesting to see your proceedings. None of us have been to a Leréshi court. Tell me, are they usually conducted at this late hour?"

Serunius gritted his teeth, apparently frustrated—whether at Rezkin's ostensible lack of concern or his ridiculous behavior, Wesson was not sure. Remembering his part, Wesson rose lazily and sighed loud enough to get their attention.

"Do I *have* to go?" he whined. "I have been practicing all evening, and I am tired."

Serunius frowned at him. "Pathetic. Everyone must go." The man turned and imperiously strode through the doorway to await them in the corridor.

As they passed through the corridors, surrounded by guards, Rezkin waved his arms with enthusiasm for the tiniest things.

"Look at these colors," he said. "We should get some of these colors for the citadel. Which do you prefer most, Yserria?"

Yserria blinked at him in surprise. "Me? Um, I don't know—"

"What about you, Frisha?"

"Well, I guess I like the blue—"

"Blue it is! Your wing will be blue." Rezkin laughed, ridiculously pleased with the pronouncement.

"*My* wing?" she said.

Rezkin laughed again. "Well, there so many, I have decided we must name them. I thought to name one after each of you."

"No, I don't think I like that idea," Frisha said.

Wesson glanced at Serunius. The man appeared to be further bristling with Rezkin's every word and chuckle. Although he did not understand the why of it, he realized what Rezkin was doing.

Wesson said, "I agree with Frisha. That could get a bit awkward. Hey Brandt, how about we go sleep in Frisha tonight, and then we can work out in Yserria?"

Rezkin giggled. It was not a manly laugh or even a chuckle. It was the kind of girly sound that should never be heard from a grown man, especially one of Rezkin's size and build.

Serunius abruptly stopped and spun on his heel to face them. "Will you please be quiet? People are sleeping in these rooms, and you are disrupting them."

Rezkin appeared momentarily chastised. Then, he smiled and made a booming announcement. "I apologize everyone! Sorry! It was my fault! Completely my fault!"

Through gritted teeth, Serunius said, "Lord Rezkin—"

"*King*," Rezkin said.

Serunius sighed loudly. "Yes, I am sorry for your people. *Our* people, however, do not recognize your claim to that title. You are lucky that I call you *Lord*."

Rezkin sniffed and said, "Well, there is no need to get testy. It is only a matter of semantics, after all."

"No, it is *not*," Serunius said. "We are talking about *kingdoms* and people. Real people."

With a growl, Serunius turned and began stalking down the corridor at twice his previous speed. The shorter members of their party were forced to jog, and Rezkin laughed and made jests about the artwork along the way. By the time they reached the throne room, Serunius was fuming, and the shorter ladies … and Wesson … were out of breath.

Wesson scurried beside Rezkin as he strode into the throne room dressed for his part. He was no longer Dark Tidings. He was King Rezkin. He wore a dark blue military style coat with silver buttons and two silver and blue embroidered baldrics crossing his chest to support his Sheyalins at either hip. His smooth, raven black hair was plaited and tied with a silver ribbon. The only indication of his station, though, was a silver brooch bearing his sigil pinned to his baldric over his left breast. The fact that he had dressed for the occasion only reaffirmed Wesson's belief that Rezkin had known it was coming.

They stopped in front of the throne. Queen Erisial was not seated. The dark wood, stained red and carved to appear like enticing tongues of flame, sat empty as she stood before it. The queen now wore a red silk robe that might have been a night-rail in any other kingdom but was apparently appropriate for court in Lon Lerésh. Her feet were bare, but she still wore the crown in addition to a necklace bearing more rubies than Wesson had ever seen in one place —with matching earrings.

The woman's brow was furrowed. She looked to Serunius and said, "Did you force them to run the entire way? That is not considerate of our guests."

"The man was being disruptive. I wanted to get him here as quickly as possible so that he would not upset the peace more than he already had."

Erisial looked around the room. It appeared that nearly everyone of any importance in the palace had shown up for the proceedings. She said, "Did he resist our summons?"

Serunius growled. "No. He was more than willing to come."

Rezkin smiled and said, "I was merely commenting on the splendid opulence of your palace. Your consort did not care for my observations."

The woman's eyes narrowed slightly as her attention shifted between the men. Finally, she said, "Well, you are here now, and it is late, so we should get on with this. A member of Council House Leyet, a palace guard named Morlin, has been killed. A member of *my* house"—she nodded toward Celise who stood to one side pensively chewing at her lip—"has accused you of killing him."

Rezkin continued to stare at the queen without comment while people in the crowd whispered.

"Well?" Erisial said. "How do you plead?"

"Plead?" said Rezkin. "Are you charging me with a crime?"

Erisial calmly explained, "There are no charges as of yet. I just want to know if you killed him."

Rezkin did not look at Celise, but Wesson could see in her gaze the fear that he might deny the claim. Wesson had no idea what had happened, but he was fairly certain that Rezkin had, in fact, killed the man.

Without the tiniest hint of remorse, Rezkin said, "Yes, I killed him."

A woman stepped forward from the excited crowd. She was the red-headed woman who had been one of the four to escort them from the docks. "He is lying. *She* killed Morlin, and she has convinced him to take the credit since he is a visiting diplomat."

Erisial looked to the woman. "Depheli, you forget that I can hear that he speaks the truth."

Depheli turned to Rezkin and said, "What gives you the right to come to *our* home and kill *our* people?"

Rezkin met her accusation with an icy stare. "I need not explain myself to *you, Advisor*."

Erisial cut the woman off before she could retort. "I would appreciate it if you would explain yourself to *me*."

Rezkin tilted his head and said, "He was attacking your servant girl over there. According to Leréshi law, it is legal to kill a man caught in the act of assaulting a woman."

Depheli gawped, her face turning red with indignation. "Morlin would never attack a woman! She instigated this!" Depheli shook a finger angrily at Celise. "She did something to make it appear that he was attacking her!"

Celise shook her head. "No, I did nothing! I was only performing my duties when he grabbed me."

Depheli said, "You are a liar and a tease. I challenge you for the honor of my fallen house member."

Erisial glanced between the older woman and Celise and then casually took a seat in her throne. Her robe fell open to expose nearly the entire length of her thighs, but she did not appear to notice, much less attempt an adjustment.

Erisial asked him, "What were you doing in that corridor without your escort?"

Rezkin raised his hands innocently and said, "I got lost?" She smirked but did not challenge him. He said, "Can you not hear that she is telling the truth?"

Erisial smiled indulgently and said, "Of course I can, but you seem to understand Leréshi law quiet well. You already know that the word of a truth-seeker cannot be used in court, and that includes my own. The challenge must stand. Celise, call your champion."

"You do not intend to provide her with a champion, knowing she is innocent?" Rezkin said.

"Another question to which you already know the answer. No, she is only a servant, and it is past time for her to choose a consort. She must provide her own champion."

He smirked as he said, "And you know already that I intend to serve as her champion."

"Of course," Erisial replied. "You and I know how this scene will play out. Depheli, however, had not considered that *you*, the self-proclaimed True King of Ashai, so-called King of Cael, might fight on behalf of a servant. If you had not, I am sure *Knight* Yserria would have." At Yserria's nod, Erisial said, "Either way, Depheli's champion, who is also her consort, will die. He is good, but I am confident that you are better, and I doubt you would allow Yserria to fight a battle you did not think she would win."

Depheli's worried gaze danced between them as she took a withering step backward.

Erisial did not give the woman a second look as she said, "Her inability to consider the possible outcomes of this challenge has proven her to be a weak head of house. In the past few minutes, she will have lost a significant following, and by the time we are done with this discussion, she will have lost her place among my advisors. It is just as well since I suddenly find myself with one more than I prefer. The only way for Depheli to retain her place would be to win the challenge. Now she must decide. Does she go through with the challenge in a desperate bid to save face and lose her consort in a pointless fight, or does she back out and accept her fate as the matrianera of a middling house?"

Depheli's consort stepped forward and took her hand. Quietly, he said, "I will fight for your honor if you wish it."

She shook as she replied, "No, I withdraw the challenge."

With tears in her eyes, she dragged her consort through the crowd and left the hall.

Erisial did not watch her go. She stared absently across the hall, as though unconcerned by the upset to her council. Once the commotion died, she said,

"You see, battles need not be fought when both sides are intelligent enough to perceive the outcomes before they begin. It is a pity. The battle would have been more exciting." She paused to make sure he was paying attention, then said, "*You,* Lord Rezkin, are playing a game with my Serunius. I do not know what it is or why, but I assure you it is unnecessary."

Serunius frowned and looked at her quizzically before turning his narrow-eyed gaze on Rezkin.

The queen chuckled and said, "Serunius is an intelligent man like you, and he would be able to see it if he were not so emotionally involved. He is … *possessive*." This last she said with a sultry smile and a wink for her consort. Her gaze roved over the crowd and then returned to Rezkin. "That said, tomorrow, after the midday meal, I intend to claim you, Lord Rezkin."

"You know I will not accept," Rezkin said.

She smiled. "You will dine with me. We will have a discussion, and then you will change your mind."

"Why are you telling me now?"

"You do play an odd game, Lord Rezkin. For a man with so many secrets, you like everything stated in the open. I am giving others the chance to plan their challenges, but you know that. Perhaps some of your own wish to lay claim to you?"

The queen's gaze landed on Frisha first, so he knew Celise had been reporting on them to someone, if not directly to the queen. Her attention shifted to Yserria next. Yserria did not squirm under the scrutiny this time. She held herself as a warrior although it might have been because she was once again wearing her own clothes. When Yserria did not give any indication that she planned to challenge the claim, Erisial's gaze slid swiftly over Reaylin and Nanessy.

To Rezkin, she said, "You will meet me in my quarters at midday. Court will commence afterward."

Erisial abruptly stood and left the hall without a backward glance. The guards began escorting the spectators from the room, and Celise scurried over to their group with a bright smile gracing her pixie face.

She said, "*Thank you. I was worried that you might not admit to what happened.*"

"*Why would I not?*"

"*For several reasons, I guess. You might not want to upset Queen Erisial, for one. I know why you are here. You want Oledia.*"

"I *do not want Oledia. I agreed to retrieve her as part of a deal,*" Rezkin said.

"*Oh, yes, I know. She wants to go with you. Queen Erisial has her locked in her chambers under guard in case you try to steal her away. I think she is more afraid Oledia will claim you so that you will act as her champion against any challengers. You know, because then she would be able to leave with you without Queen Erisial's permission.*"

"*I would not accept Oledia's claim, regardless, and I have no intention of absconding with her without Erisial's permission. If I intended to do so, I would already have her and be gone from here with all of you none the wiser.*"

"*She is quite secure—*"

"*Are you certain she is still in her rooms? It is possible that I am the unwitting distraction and the Adana'Ro have already secreted her away.*"

Celise blinked as concern crossed her face.

"*In fact, the Adana'Ro may have been responsible for the attack on you. Perhaps it was no coincidence that I happened to be in that corridor when you happened to be assaulted.*"

The young woman glanced at his companions as if to see whether he was speaking truth, but only Yserria could understand their words, and she did not appear optimistic.

"*But I do not believe that,*" he said. "*I believe another culprit was responsible for your attack. I believe it was Erisial who goaded Morlin into trying to force a claim, and I do not think she intended for me—or anyone else—to intervene.*"

"*But, why would she do that*?" Celise said.

"*I doubt it was personal. She needed to get rid of an advisor. Morlin's attack would have done enough damage to his house to see to that, especially if he had been able to finish what he started. In addition, she would have made Morlin's punishment and execution a public spectacle, a show of her strength and an ill-conceived attempt at intimidation aimed at me. It is convenient that the attack occurred on the eve of the arrival of her guests—one of whom she intends to claim.*"

Celise clenched her jaw, obviously trying to stymie the tears threatening to spill from her eyes. "*She is my mother. Of course, it is personal.*"

The hall had cleared so that only their group and Celise stood in its center. Serunius remained listening near the exit through which Erisial had departed. Rezkin glanced back at Frisha who was watching the exchange with concern.

Although the others did not know what was being said, they could easily see that Celise was upset. He met Yserria's hard stare. She looked angry, and her gaze seemed to be challenging him to do something. Apparently, he was going to have to remain involved in this little family feud.

He tilted his head toward Serunius and grinned wolfishly. Then, he unpinned the sigil brooch on his baldric and handed it to the young woman. For Frisha's benefit, he spoke in Ashaiian.

"If anyone else gives you trouble, I will act as your champion. If anyone causes you harm, I will avenge you, regardless of their station. You need not pay me for the service."

She held the brooch loosely, as if it might bite her. Since he had switched to Ashaiian, she attempted it as well. "Why you do this for me?"

He grinned again and stared at Serunius as he answered. "To frustrate your mother, of course."

When they returned to their quarters, Wesson said, "I do not understand. Why are you trying to upset the queen when we need her to give us her daughter?"

"She intends to claim me. I am making it clear that doing so will not be pleasant even *if* she somehow convinces me to change my mind. Also, Celise is the daughter she does not want, and I have offered myself as her champion; meanwhile, I have not even asked after the daughter for whom I came, the one she loves. She may begin to wonder if I will not take Celise instead. The Adana'Ro only want a daughter of Erisial. I doubt they truly care which one."

"Then you have made Celise a target," Wesson said.

"Celise was already a target. She was nearly killed tonight. I have placed her under my protection, which makes her very powerful. Few would dare challenge her for anything. She could even declare her own house without the need for a consort. So long as I am her champion, Erisial cannot afford for Celise to break from her house. If she does not convince Celise to remain, Erisial's rivals may gain the confidence to challenge her for the throne."

Nanessy said, "You are forcing Erisial to recognize Celise as her daughter?"

"I am not forcing Erisial to do anything."

Frisha crossed her arms and said, "There is more to it, isn't there? The queen said you were playing a game with her consort. What are you up to?"

Rezkin gave her a placating smile. "You are right, Frisha, but now is not the time for this discussion. It is late. Let us sleep."

"Do you plan to sleep?" Frisha said. "Or are you going to be scurrying about the palace again?"

"No, I intend to remain in that room over there for the remainder of the night."

Frisha pursed her lips and gave him a stern look. He smiled again, and her scowl deepened.

He said, "Good night, Frisha." He wished the others the same and then went to his room.

A field of white silk rustled in the breeze. The glistening strands separated and whipped about in a wild dance that was quickly shrouded by a midnight hood. The figure turned and called to someone. The hood floated free, snatched by the wind. A pale hand rose to shield a face from the angry gust. Between her slender fingers, white lashes blinked over silver irises that glittered brightly in the rising sun.

Rezkin awoke with a start. He could smell the earthy scent of evergreens and feel the sting of the wind across his exposed flesh. The stone against his chest burned nearly too hot for him to touch. Enough light stole through the gaps in the shutters for him to see that the heavy weight on his lap was a rope. When he reached to remove it, the rope suddenly squirmed. As it coiled around itself, Rezkin froze. It was a snake; and, in the dim light, he could not see which kind. It was not the first time he had awoken with snakes in his bed. The strikers at the fortress had used the training scenario several times and not just with snakes. He had several options but ultimately decided he had best capture the creature to study it in better lighting.

Very slowly, he reached up to grip the edge of the bedcovering. He whipped the blanket off while simultaneously leaping from the bed and twisting the material so that it spun around itself. The snake thrashed within the wrapped blanket before finally settling. A brief survey of the room revealed that no other creatures or people had invaded. After finding the head, he unwrapped the creature's body. It had the markings of a constrictor common to the region, nonvenomous and too small to have caused him serious harm. When he finally uncovered the head, he sighed and dropped the snake.

He looked into one yellow-orange eye and said, "What do you want, Bilior?"

The snake raised its head, which began to distort in grotesque bulges until it appeared vaguely humanoid, somewhat resembling a drauglic.

A black, forked tongue silently tasted the air, and then it hissed, "The *you* brings the army to the *we*."

"I am working on that," Rezkin said. "I have not yet secured our sanctuary that you promised."

The snake's body twisted back and forth in a mesmerizing display of patterned scales. "They come," it said, and then it burst into millions of beetles that swarmed up the wall and through the gaps in slats of the shutters.

Rezkin peered out the window to see that the sun had just barely left the horizon and was mostly obscured by a drizzling overcast sky. He armed himself and dressed for training. Stepping lightly, so as not to wake the others, he slipped into the main corridor. The guards did not notice him right away, and he was several steps ahead when they finally called out to him.

"Ah, my lord, where are you going?" the blonde guard said.

Without stopping, Rezkin replied, "It is *Your Majesty*, and I am going to the practice yard."

"But … you are not supposed to leave your room without an escort," said the second guard.

Rezkin continued walking as he said, "Then, you had best catch up."

The blonde remained at the door while the second, a bearded, brunette in his late twenties, jogged to join him. "Sir, ah, Your Majesty, the queen has authorized you to use the royal family's facilities, which are in the other direction."

"I prefer to visit the main practice yard."

"But, Your Majesty, it is raining."

"I am aware of that," Rezkin said.

"The royal practice yard is covered and raised so the ground will be dry."

Rezkin stopped and looked at the man who was several inches shorter than he was. "Guardsman, have you ever been in a battle?"

The man proudly said, "Yes, I have been in a number of confrontations between the echelons. I was also captain of the city guard before being given the honor of serving in the palace."

Rezkin said, "Did all of those confrontations occur on a dry day?"

"No, of course not."

"Then we should practice in the rain," Rezkin said as he continued in his brisk walk.

"*We*, Your Majesty?"

"You are to guard me, yes? In the event that I should decide to cause trouble, it is your duty to subdue me?"

"Well, yes, I suppose, but I am also assigned to protect you."

Rezkin said, "Then you and I had best see where we stand."

By the time Rezkin was finished with him, the guardsman could barely stand at all. They had entered the practice yard unnoticed at first. Rezkin had drawn a drab brown cloak over his head, as had most of the people scurrying around in the rain, and his plain brown traveling pants and beige tunic were unremarkable. One of the other guards recognized Rezkin's escort, though.

"*Hey, Mik, what are you doing here? Aren't you supposed to be on duty?*" said the guard. He looked to be a few years older than Rezkin's escort. The man stood from a bench at the side of the practice yard and slogged through the mud to join them. Two others who had been chatting beneath the awning of a supply room came to join them.

"*I* am *on duty*," Mik said, with a glance at Rezkin.

The first man nodded toward him. "*Who's this, then? One of the foreign king's guards? Don't remember him bringing a man. Too bad it ain't the woman, eh? She's a looker.*"

Rezkin kept his gaze on the men practicing in the yard as an excuse to hide his face. He said, "*She would destroy you.*"

All the men but Mik laughed. The older man said, "*I don't think I'd mind being destroyed by that one. I might even let her win if I thought she'd use me to celebrate.*"

"*She does often use her fallen opponents to celebrate,*" Rezkin said, and the men all nodded appreciatively. "*She places their heads on a pike and parades them through the streets like a victory banner.*"

The other men guffawed and slapped the first on the back. One of them said, "*Your head would look good on a pike, Ger.*"

Then another said, "*It would look better there than on your body.*"

Ger replied, "*I already got a head on a pike, and I'll be using it to do the stabbing.*" The men laughed again, and Ger said, "*What are you two doing down here, then?*

"*Mik is going to show me what he will do to me if I cause trouble,*" said Rezkin.

Mik shook his head. "*You know, I don't think that's such a good idea.*

Queen Erisial will be angry if you are injured."

Rezkin removed his cloak and said, "*If you manage to injure me, perhaps she will claim you instead.*"

The practice had been a weak warmup, and Rezkin was not satisfied. It was all he had time for, though, given that he was supposed to meet the queen for the midday meal. Several of the guards would be missing their shifts, and they all agreed to leave him alone if he caused trouble. The consensus was to let the mages handle it. Even so, he had restrained himself from seriously injuring anyone.

Yserria was standing at the edge of the practice yard when Rezkin finished. She smirked and said, "Did you leave any for me?"

"I warmed them up a bit. You can finish them off."

Both of their gazes slid to the men, who were unconvincingly trying to appear tough while hobbling around nursing their wounds.

"What are you doing here?" Rezkin said as he wiped his face with a drying cloth provided by one of the guards. Although the rain had stopped, he was soaked and covered in mud.

Yserria said, "I figured you would be stirring things up, so I listened for the loudest noise. It does not surprise me that you are also filthy, although I might have expected it to be blood and gore." She nodded toward the small crowd that was gathering in a courtyard beside the practice field. "What's happening over there?"

"Shall we see?" Rezkin replied.

Mik limped up to them as Rezkin dumped a pail of water over his head to wash away the mud. The guardsman was accompanied by Bruthes, the captain of the royal guard, who was also limping but on the other leg. Rezkin introduced Yserria and then inquired about the gathering.

Bruthes said, "It is a scheduled challenge between House Mierette and House Jesqueli. Mierette says that First Consort of Jesqueli tried to seduce one of their house members. Jesqueli denies the claim and challenged for the First Consort's honor. The champions are both first consorts and palace guards, so they decided to have the duel down here."

They all wandered over to watch the spectacle and chose a vantage point under the shade of a tree. Now that the sun was shining, the air was becoming humid and the insects were biting. Rezkin wrapped his soggy cloak around him and implored Yserria to do the same before anyone recognized her.

Bruthes pointed to a blonde man with short, wavy hair and said, "He is

Dorovick, champion for Jesqueli." He nodded to the other contender and said, "That is Hyenth."

Hyenth had a close-cropped beard and short brown hair; and, like Dorovick, he wore one long braid at the temple, woven with a red ribbon.

Dorovick abruptly ducked behind a group of friends and house members, glancing around to see if anyone was looking. He then walked to a tree with a subtle limp and rubbed his thigh.

Bruthes shook his head. "That is not good. His old injury is acting up again."

"He will win," Rezkin said. "And he is likely guilty."

The captain narrowed his eyes and looked at Dorovick again. "Why would you say that? On a good day, Dorovick will win against Hyenth maybe two or three times out of four, but Dorovick is injured."

Rezkin said, "He is feigning injury to gain the advantage. He limps only when he has made a show of looking around to check for observers, except that he never looks in Hyenth's direction, which means that he wants Hyenth to witness his actions. Considering that he is willing to use such an underhanded tactic in a duel against a fellow guardsman, it is likely he is also willing to cheat on his matria and seduce another woman."

Bruthes frowned but nodded as he witnessed the deception for himself. "I see what you are saying about the limp, but I do not think you can conclude that a poor sportsman is also a cheat."

"Dorovick's matria is not here," Rezkin said.

"No, she is visiting her mothers' estate."

Rezkin nodded to an eager young lady who was anxiously gripping and wringing her shawl while trying to blend with the crowd. He said, "I would guess that is the young lady from House Mierette. She looks terribly concerned for Dorovick's well-being."

"This is not justice," Yserria said. "Honor should not depend on the strength of a man's arm."

Bruthes sighed. "I had best warn Hyenth of the deception. This matter will not end here if Dorovick wins and continues his escapades with the young woman. Dorovick's matria may return and blame the Mierette girl for the affair. The last thing I need is a house feud among my guards."

"Yserria will fight as champion for House Mierette," said Rezkin.

"What?" she exclaimed.

He said, "You claim that honor should not depend on the strength of a man's arm. Let it depend on a woman's."

"That is not what I meant. Besides, we have not seen him fight. He could be better—"

"He is not," Rezkin said with confidence.

Bruthes glanced between them and then looked to Yserria for confirmation. Yserria watched the girl who was pining for another woman's consort and then looked at the man who rubbed his phantom wound.

She nodded to Bruthes and said, "I will fight as champion if Mierette accepts the offer."

Rezkin remained under the tree as Yserria and Bruthes walked over to speak with the Mierette matria and her champion. Rezkin was observing the exchange from afar when Serunius stepped up beside him.

"You never stop," Serunius said. "You are always moving the pieces, plotting, manipulating—even now, in an insignificant challenge between middling houses. What could you possibly gain from this? It will have no effect on Erisial's decision—or do you simply enjoy the blood?"

Rezkin did not take his eyes from the scene as he answered. "I have acquainted myself with Bruthes, your captain of the royal guard. He is a straightforward man. He is also strongly entrenched in Leréshi ideals of honoring women. By showing my support for Mierette and placing my undaunted faith in Knight Yserria, I have gained his respect beyond that due my position."

"Gaining Bruthes's respect will not prevent him from performing his duties."

"That was not my intent, but we shall come back to that." Rezkin nodded toward Hyenth. "He made it a point to speak several times with one of the court musicians who performed last night, First Consort of Matrianera Nayala Tekahl. They appeared to be friends. It is reasonable to assume House Mierette is a supporter of Tekahl. Nayala was ambitious enough to introduce herself to my companions, while most others remained cautiously aloof or blatantly forward. She takes calculated risks but is satisfied for her house to remain on lower, stable ground. She sought only to benefit from the association while making it apparent that she was open to more possibilities.

"Nayala is under consideration for the Sixth Echelon. The Sixth Echelon produces wool, several food crops, and marshglove clover, a rare plant whose extract is used in many mundane and alchemical tinctures—all of which are products useful to my people. A boost for House Mierette could make the difference in securing the Sixth Echelon for House Tekahl. House Jesqueli, however, combines its crest with that of House Goldren, Fourth Echelon, which has dealings with House Ichthris of Ferélle. House Ichthris has ardently advocated for a campaign to rid Ferélle of the Adana'Ro.

"Erisial has made clear her intention to claim me. The stated intent alone, regardless of the outcome, will have a severe impact on her support structure. This morning, I demonstrated my strength to the palace guards in the practice yard; and, in Bruthes's eyes, I have placed my champion, a woman, on the side of justice in this duel. Yserria bears power of her own in this court, and she and I have backed Mierette, thereby uplifting Tekahl, which is a strong supporter of Erisial. Yserria's victory will be a severe hit to House Jesqueli, which will upset Goldren. Goldren may break with Jesqueli for the embarrassment or continue the association. Either way, it may destabilize the house enough for Erisial to attain approval to replace Goldren as Fourth Echelon. This will take pressure off the Adana'Ro, which will please your daughter Oledia and make her transition easier."

The seemingly insignificant courtyard duel unfolded before their eyes as they spoke. Yserria advanced on Dorovick, who did not appear to take her seriously. The man's arrogance was punished by a score across his forearm.

Serunius said, "So, Bruthes respects Erisial for her decision to claim you, Yserria gains power, Tekahl is granted Sixth Echelon, you acquire favorable trade, Goldren loses Fourth Echelon, the Adana'Ro are momentarily secure, and Erisial is pleased—and you devised this plan within a few minutes of learning of the duel."

Rezkin did not reply as he watched Dorovick strike the dirt with his face and then quickly regain his feet as Yserria stood back and waited.

Serunius said, "Why are you interested in pleasing Erisial?"

Rezkin said, "Despite my aversion to her claim, I require Erisial's cooperation. She is the one with whom I am conducting negotiations, both for Oledia and my kingdom. What is good for Erisial is good for me."

"I am not convinced of your sincerity," said Serunius. "I know that I am missing something, but it will come to me. I am not ashamed to admit that Erisial is more intelligent than I am. She is quick, and she has been doing this much longer than you. She will succeed, and you will fail."

"You think too small, Serunius. I have more pressing matters than Erisial's claim. Your petty politics mean nothing to me beyond securing Oledia and advancing trade. I otherwise care nothing for Lon Leresh."

"Then, once you leave here, you do not intend to recognize the claim?"

"As far as I am concerned, there is no claim."

Both men watched as Yserria smacked Dorovick in the head with the side of her blade.

"You do not deserve her," Serunius said.

"Who?"

"Erisial," the man snapped. "She is cold and calculating but beautiful and passionate. Any man would thank the Maker for the blessing of her slightest attention. I think you protest too much. You resist only for the sake of negotiations."

Yserria stomped on Dorovick's hand and kicked his sword away, to the delight of the cheering crowd. The man clutched his injured fingers as he sat up and wiped blood from his chin. His anger was overshadowed by his embarrassment as he rolled to his feet, grabbed his sword, and pushed through the crowd.

Rezkin nodded toward the beaming, victorious red-head and said, "Why would I want Erisial, when I could have *her*?"

Serunius clenched his teeth as he stared at Yserria for a bit too long. As the invigorated swordswoman joined them, Rezkin clasped arms with her in congratulations and then turned to Serunius with a grin. He said, "What did you think of Lady Yserria's performance?"

Serunius crossed his arms in front of him and pressed his forehead to his wrists, a sign of the highest respect. Then, he said, "I think perhaps more of our women should take up the sword. We would be an unbeatable force."

Rezkin knew Serunius's compliment would have made the woman blush if her face had not already been flushed from the exertion of the duel. He said, "Yserria is an exceptional woman, even by Leréshi standards."

"Indeed," Serunius said, and then he glanced up to a balcony that overlooked the courtyard. She was no longer there, but Rezkin knew the queen had been watching the challenge. Serunius excused himself and reminded Rezkin that he was to report to the queen's chambers.

"As if you needed the reminder," Yserria muttered once the man had gone.

"It does not matter," Rezkin said. "I have ensured that we will have Oledia when we leave."

"Then, they have agreed?" Yserria said.

"They have, although they are not yet aware of it."

11

The guardsman rapped on the queen's chamber door, and another guard opened it from the other side. When Rezkin had returned to his chambers, he had found a set of clothes awaiting him. A soft, knee-length black tunic and trousers of brushed cotton had been lying on his bed, each embroidered along the edges with jagged, silver and blue scroll that looked like thorned roses entwined with lightning bolts. Beside them was a matching cape lined with royal blue silk.

"You're supposed to wear that to lunch?" Frisha said, obviously displeased with the queen's gift.

Rezkin had inspected the material carefully to make sure there were no hidden pins or poisons.

"It is ceremonial garb," said Yserria.

Frisha had crossed her arms and narrowed her eyes at the swordswoman. "For what kind of ceremony?"

With a roll of her eyes, Yserria replied, "You already know."

Frisha had looked to Rezkin, then, her eyes pleading. She said, "You shouldn't wear it. If you do, it'll seem like you're accepting her claim."

Fingering the silver and gold scroll and eyeing the blue silk, Rezkin said, "I am to meet the Queen of Lon Lerésh in her private quarters for a meal. It would be rude to reject the gift. Wearing it is not an acceptance of her claim. I am a visiting monarch. I must observe the traditions of acceptable court behavior."

"But she does not even recognize you as royalty."

"Which is all the more reason not to press my luck. I am a man in her queendom. In many ways, I bear fewer rights here than you."

"Are you sure you don't want me to—" Her words had withered with his icy stare.

"No, Frisha. I would not accept your claim if you tried. You have made your feelings clear."

Frisha had glanced away, fighting back tears. She said, "If I didn't know any better, I might think you sounded hurt." Then, she had escaped to her room, slamming the door behind her.

With echoes of the memory playing in his mind, Rezkin now stood to enter the queen's chambers. He was uncomfortable with the knowledge that a cunning woman thought she had something strong enough to convince him to accept her claim—and he did not know what it was. The woman was too intelligent to believe she might seduce him into it. She would have something more substantial.

The meal was set at a table on the balcony. Rezkin thought it a poor choice for a monarch who stood to lose her position through the cultural tradition of assassination. He felt the ward that surrounded the structure in a half dome. It had the signature of Serunius, and Rezkin wondered if the man had designed it to allow projectiles through that were targeting *him.*

Erisial smiled as he joined her at the table. "Those clothes suit you," she said.

"Yet, I sense that I am not the one you would prefer to see in them."

Her gaze slid to the side where Serunius stood beside the serving table. Rezkin did not know if the man was standing as guard, providing chaperone, or simply being intrusive.

"Serunius did look delicious on his claiming day," she mused.

"You have only one consort," he observed.

"I have never had need of another. Serunius provides for my every need."

"Until now," he said with a glance for the consort. The man clenched his jaw but did not express the anger that was simmering in his dark gaze.

The queen said nothing as they ate. Rezkin still preferred not to eat meals prepared by others, but it was the nature of his role that compelled him. Outworlders often formed bonds over food, whether those bonds were of a personal or business nature. He wondered if exposing the vulnerability of hunger was essential to forming trust or showing fearlessness. It seemed an unnecessary risk to him, but it was an unfortunate cultural requirement.

The servants removed the dishes and left the suite. Celise came to stand beside the queen with a tablet and quill. Erisial said, "You are a stunning young man, far too attractive and talented to be unclaimed; but, I am not easily swayed by a handsome face—or body, so do not delude yourself into thinking that is the reason for my claim. What is your age?"

Rezkin had not been prepared for the question. It seemed inconsequential, but then again, outworlders often focused on age as a measure of a man. He wondered if the truth would benefit or damage his cause.

Rezkin said, "My age is irrelevant."

"It is required for documentation of the claim," the queen said. "And remember, I can tell if you are lying."

"I have not agreed to the claim," he replied, "but my age is not a secret. I am nineteen."

Erisial looked stunned, and her disbelieving gaze immediately sought Serunius. The man stared at him as if just noticing a new species of mythical beast. Celise shifted uncomfortably and glanced several times at the queen for confirmation that he was lying.

Erisial said, "I would never have guessed. You are barely more than a child."

Rezkin captured her with an icy stare and said, "I was never a *child*."

Erisial shivered and abruptly rose. "The breeze is cool out here."

Rezkin might have believed she could be cold in the filmy garment except that there was no breeze and only stagnant heat and humidity had followed the rain. She entered her sitting room, apparently expecting him to follow, which he did. Serunius closed the doors behind them. Celise took a seat on a bench beside a table, preparing to take notes, and Erisial turned to stare at Rezkin for a long moment.

Finally, she said, "You are young—too young for my tastes, although you demonstrate a maturity not common to men your age. You say you have a legitimate claim to the Ashaiian throne. You are the right age, and you have the looks. Could it be that Lecillia's youngest secretly lived? Or are you bastard born? Why have you not claimed royal blood?"

"What I claim and do not claim is my business. We are here about *your* claim."

"This changes nothing," she said. "I will claim you, regardless."

"You have no ground on which to stand," Rezkin said. "You will hand over Oledia whether I agree to the claim or not."

Erisial chuckled. "Do not think that I have missed your play. I know of your efforts with my men, with the captain of my royal guard. I know what you have been doing to my Serunius." She gazed at her consort and said, "I have seen the way he looks at her. She is the physical embodiment of a powerful Leréshi woman, and she is beautiful. With your backing, she could take the throne. She could gain favor by claiming my Serunius. He may even accept her claim."

Serunius scowled at her, to which she shrugged one shoulder. She said, "There are few men I could choose as champion who might have a chance at defeating him. If he leaves me, it would be difficult, if not impossible, to retain the throne. This means that, if I am to remain queen, I must convince you to either accept my claim or leave and take your knight with you. This means giving you what you want. You have played an effective game. The only problem is that it was completely unnecessary. I have already decided to give you what you want and more."

"How so?"

Erisial strode over to a settee and took a seat, motioning for Rezkin to sit on the sofa across from her. Celise rose and poured each of them a cup of tea, then returned to her place on the bench by the writing table.

"I have been queen for over six years. It is an eternity as far as my opponents are concerned. They grow anxious. I have already uncovered several plots to assassinate me, and a few have used ridiculous promises in an attempt to seduce Serunius into assisting. Celise, of course, has been a target. Despite what many think, she has never been permitted to serve me directly until now. Technically, she is here to serve *you*. She is quite committed to you now. I know how she is, though. She would never consider trying to claim you, even if I had not already announced my plans. She is weak and timid, traits she surely inherited from her father's side."

Rezkin noticed that Celise kept her eyes on the tablet in front of her, her face heating in embarrassment. He said nothing, though, but waited for the queen to make her point.

"I am only now entering my prime, and I have no intention of letting those vultures get to me. I need security. That is where you come in."

"Claiming me will not stop others from plotting against you."

"No, indeed, it would only stop them from openly challenging me. The prospect of assassination becomes more appealing to them. No, I need more. I do not intend to claim you as consort. I am claiming you as my husband. You will be the first king of Lon Lerésh."

Rezkin stared at the woman, attempting to judge her sincerity as his mind ran away with all the possible reasons for her to do something so absurd. She smiled, apparently pleased to have left him speechless.

"You are surprised," she said.

"No queen of Lon Lerésh would ever consider taking a husband. It is antithetical to your entire power structure. It is a sure way to incite rebellion."

She set her teacup and saucer on the table between them and said, "I benefit little from claiming you as consort, especially since you will be leaving as soon as I release Oledia. Lon Lerésh is a matriarchy, a structure that has defined our culture since the founding of our queendom, and no one of any consequence wants that to change. If you are my husband, however, then you have equal right to the throne. If someone kills me, you become ruler. No one wants that to happen. Therefore, they must kill you *before* they kill me. You will not be here. You will be off fighting your war and claiming other kingdoms for your empire. It will be in everyone's best interest, including that of my enemies, for me to continue living."

"So long as I am alive," Rezkin said.

"Yes. Of course, it will mean additional people after your head, but I doubt a few more will make much of a difference. They will have difficulty contracting with the Adana'Ro since you have dealings with them, and I intend to make refusing contracts against you a stipulation of allowing my daughter to join them. If they do not wish to take the endeavor into their own hands, I suppose my enemies could contact the Order or the Black Hall. With your disruptions in Channería and Ashai, one of them may be willing to take a contract against you."

She tapped her bottom lip thoughtfully. "I have recently received an odd report that the Raven has endorsed your claim to the Ashaiian throne, so the Black Hall may not be an option either. Regardless, I am confident that you can handle whatever they throw at you."

"So, you wish to place a target on my back to save yourself."

"You want Oledia. I want to live."

"Besides your release of Oledia to the Adana'Ro, which I believe you intend to do regardless of my decision, what do I gain from this deal?"

"By our traditions, as husband and wife, we are to be equals. That means we must have equal power over the people. It does not mean we will share the *same* power. I will continue to rule where I know best. I will maintain the business and politics. *You* will get the army and navy. I believe you will find them useful when waging your war. You must remember, however, that as a ruler of Lon Lerésh, your first duty is to *our* people. You will use our military to the advancement and security of *our* people. You will not carelessly sacrifice them to win Ashai."

Rezkin placed his saucer and cup on the table and leaned forward. He said, "You overplayed your hand. Your disinterest in your eldest daughter has nothing to do with her or her father and everything to do with Serunius."

Erisial was thrown by the abrupt non sequitur. "You speak of things you do not understand."

"I understand that, in Lon Lerésh, daughters are prized above wealth and power, regardless of their sire. A daughter is a blessing of the Maker, and a fondness for one's daughter is expected. True love for one's consort, however, is cause for concern, a possible weakness."

Erisial laughed. "It is no secret that I care for Serunius. He has been invaluable in helping me achieve my goals. His mind intrigues me, and he is a superb champion and an attentive lover. He knows his place, though, and he expects no more."

"You love Serunius but cannot admit to it for fear of others discovering your weakness. In fact, I think you would do anything for him. You did not challenge Yserria for the torque because you would not risk losing him in a challenge against me."

"You think too highly of yourself," she snapped.

"Perhaps it is *you* who thinks too highly of me. The target you place on my back frees you and Serunius from plots against you, and you expect me to fend off all your enemies. You would never consider claiming Serunius as your husband because you would be immediately overthrown and killed—both of you. You want Serunius to know how you feel, though, so you have sacrificed your greatest love for him." He nodded toward a wide-eyed Celise. "She is not his daughter, so you have disowned her and treated her with disregard and antipathy, all in a bid to prove to him your love."

"That is absurd."

"It is no coincidence that on the very night you announce your intention to claim me, you arranged for her attack. She might have been raped, your personal sacrifice to appease your guilt over claiming another man."

"I did no such thing," she said with a quick glance at her consort.

"You do not have to deny it. Serunius already knows. In fact, it is his own guilt over your treatment of your daughter that has led him to be so protective of her. He has never been far when she has been in my presence, but I wager it was he who assigned her to serve my party. It was also his idea for her to serve us here today, was it not? He has been arranging for her to serve in positions of honor far above the station you assigned her, giving others the impression that you secretly care for her."

Erisial glanced at Serunius, who continued to stare at Rezkin blankly. "Why would he do that?"

"He shows his love for you by helping to raise the standing of your daughter while you work to tear it down. She has been the unwitting pawn in the struggle between your culture and your love for each other."

Erisial looked at Celise disdainfully and said, "That is an interesting fantasy, but Celise is the product of a union between myself and a man I hated, nothing more. I do not see what any of this has to do with the present situation."

"You have just proposed taking a man other than your consort—the man you love—as your husband and king. I interfered in the attack on Celise. How will you assuage your guilt now?"

"I have no guilt. It is a political maneuver, no more. Serunius understands the circumstances, and he will continue to perform his duties as Queen's Consort with honor." She stood and retrieved something from a drawer in a side table. She turned to him and held up a silver ribbon. "I am going to claim you either as consort or husband. The former will do us little good. You would not have to accept the claim, which means we would not be required to consummate it, but you would still be mine. The latter is dangerous and distasteful, but we both gain much. Which will it be?"

Wesson opened the door once again at the timid knock. He always felt uncomfortable when Celise, or any of the Leréshi women, came to their rooms. She never even glanced at him, like he was not a real man, and yet he was supposed to be grateful for it. This time, Celise seemed particularly anxious.

"You are all summoned to the throne room," she said. She paused as if to say more and then closed her mouth, apparently deciding against it.

Wesson's companions joined him in the sitting room. Knowing it was coming, they had all dressed in their uniforms to show unity and support for their king. They felt that this was a battle, whether it ended in a challenge or not. Frisha and Yserria had been blatantly irritable, Mage Threll and Reaylin unusually quiet. Wesson tried to stay out of the drama between the women, but he knew more than one of them were attracted to Rezkin. It was to be expected, though. Rezkin was everything a woman wanted in a man, in addition to being powerful and wealthy. The one thing he seemed to be lacking, though, was the most important. According to Frisha, Rezkin was incapable of feeling.

Wesson did not believe it. He had seen the effect Frisha had on Rezkin, and he did not think the man would go to so much effort to help people for whom he had no feelings. He wondered if it was not that Rezkin was incapable of love, but that he was incapable of loving Frisha.

They followed Celise down the many corridors and stairwells to the throne room that held at least three times more people than on the previous night. Looking around, he realized it truly was difficult to tell nightclothes from court dress in Lon Lerésh. Wesson had wondered, the night before, if it was appropriate to attend court in one's nightclothes, but now he considered that the Leréshi probably did not own nightclothes.

Rezkin was already standing before the dais in the gifted garb, and Queen Erisial lounged on the throne with her consort standing behind her. The woman did not look pleased, and Wesson was both relieved and concerned that Rezkin had probably not agreed to her terms. Knowing Rezkin, though, he had likely managed to manipulate the queen into adopting his own plans. He thought it an ill omen when the massive chamber doors were suddenly closed and barred behind them, with guards stationed at the exits. He turned back to see the queen staring at him with a smirk on her painted lips.

"This is a claiming," she said in explanation. "We always bar the doors. It is not uncommon for men to try to run from their destinies." The observers laughed and nodded appreciatively as if it was a common joke, and it probably was. Then, the queen pursed her lips and said, "You need not worry, Journeyman. You will probably never have that problem."

The crowd laughed again, some of them leaning to whisper to each other in jest, while others did not bother to conceal their crude remarks with lowered voices. Wesson felt a welling within him, the anger and drive for destruction that he so carefully kept bottled at his core. He muttered his mantra over and over in his mind and thought of hazel eyes framed by strawberry blonde locks.

Once he had reacquired his distance, he focused on the present. The queen was now standing and appeared as a goddess incarnate in the silky-blue strips of fabric she called a dress. They hung from her shoulders, stretching to the floor with gaps between them. The only thing holding them in place over her otherwise bared flesh was a silver sash at her waist and a few narrow horizontal strips designed to cover her intimate bits. Wesson wondered why she had bothered. He thought she might as well have been standing on the dais naked, and then he wondered if perhaps she sometimes did. He forced himself to stop wondering about that and looked to Rezkin for any indication of what might happen next. As usual, the man gave away nothing.

Erisial's voice rang clearly throughout the hall. For the benefit of her guests, she spoke in Ashaiian. "I claim this man, the man with no name, the one known to his people as Rezkin." She paused as the echo faded. Everyone watched in silence. "I claim him as my husband and name him King of Lon Lerésh."

The crowd burst into an uproar. Although Wesson could not understand what was being said, it was obvious the people were angry. Queen Erisial held up a hand, and Serunius came to stand beside her with his sword drawn. When the crowd had settled down enough for her to be heard, she said, "Of course, anyone is welcome to challenge the claim."

Matrianera Telía stepped forward. "I will challenge you. You have no right to claim a husband."

Erisial smiled viciously. "Of course, I do. Every woman has a right to claim a husband. Your disapproval does not give you the right to disparage or reject *my* rights. You will risk your consort Naltis in challenge?"

Telía said, "I am not afraid of Serunius. Coledon will fight as my champion." One of the royal guards stepped from around the dais and reluctantly took his place beside Telía. The man had broad shoulders, a chiseled jaw, and a hard stare. By the misery that suffused his stance and every mannerism, it was obvious he did not relish the fight.

Erisial said, "So you risk your brother but not your consort."

Telía raised her chin. "Naltis is not here. You know Coledon often serves as my champion."

"Too often, Telía," Erisial snapped. "You are selfish. He should have been granted to another long ago. Regardless, he will not be fighting Serunius. I name Rezkin as my champion."

Alarmed, Frisha leaned across Wesson to question Yserria, who stood to his other side. "She can't do that, right? Not unless he accepts her claim?"

Rezkin did not look back at them as he said, "I accept the challenge."

"Wait, no," Frisha hissed. In a forced whisper, she said, "Yserria, do something. Challenge her."

Yserria leaned across Wesson and replied, "If I challenge her, he could still fight as her champion. If he accepts, then I would be fighting *him*. If he doesn't, I would fight Serunius. If I win, I would have to claim him."

"Better you than *her*," Frisha said.

"I do not *want* to claim him, and he would not accept."

"Then be my champion, and I will claim him," Frisha said.

Yserria said, "He already told you he would not accept."

They glanced up to see that everyone was watching them. Rezkin turned and met Frisha's gaze. His eyes were cold and empty as he said, "I have accepted her claim. Now be silent."

Frisha gawped and then clamped her mouth shut. Her surprise was overtaken by expressions of anger and disgust, and Wesson could almost hear her thoughts as she seemed to remember Rezkin's alter egos.

"The challenge stands," Telía said.

Erisial's gaze hardened. She said, "The challenge is to the death."

Coledon glanced at Rezkin and then to his matrianera. "You have heard the reports of the tournament, and I saw him practicing this morning. *I cannot win*, Telía."

Telía scowled at him with cruel eyes. "The reports are exaggerated, and your humility is unnecessary, Coledon. You can and will win. *I* will be queen, and we will put an end to this madness."

"No, Telía, be reasonable—"

"I am your matrianera, Coledon. You do as I say. I have named you my champion. You fight or die."

Coledon unbuckled his belt and let it drop to the floor as he yanked angrily at his coat and shirt. Once his chest was bared of any hindrances, he bent to retrieve his sword from its sheath. He rounded on Telía. "Since this is the last time we speak, Sister, I am taking the opportunity to say that you are a heartless wretch, unworthy of your position, and it would have been a blessing to have been born to *any* other house."

The man turned to face Rezkin and waited expectantly.

Rezkin said, "You are prepared to fight a battle you know you cannot win?"

"She will never let me go," Coledon said, his pain and frustration obvious for all to see. "If I am to die, I would die fighting."

"Killing you serves no purpose," Rezkin said. "I have not seen you fight, but I have been told that you are an accomplished champion. I offer you an alternative."

Coledon glanced at an equally confused Erisial and back to Rezkin. "Your matria has set the terms of the challenge. It is not your right to change them." He raised his sword in preparation for the duel.

Rezkin said, "I do not offer as a Leréshi. I am the King of Cael. In exchange for your oath of fealty, I offer you sanctuary as a citizen of Cael."

"You cannot," shouted Telía. "He belongs to me!"

"You are welcome to present another champion in the matter of the claim, Matrianera Telía, but this," he said, motioning toward Coledon, "is no longer a personal challenge between claimants. I am the ruler of another kingdom offering sanctuary to a potential defector. Any challenge must be issued by the queen, and she must present a champion or prepare for war."

Erisial stared at him blankly as everyone turned to see what she would do. She descended the steps and stopped in front of him. Now that she stood on his level, he towered over her. She reached up to stroke his face as he looked back at her dispassionately.

She smiled and said, "He is magnificent, is he not? He stands before the queen, in the midst of the Leréshi court, and offers sanctuary to a defector, and everyone is too afraid to move against him. I have already stated my intent to claim him as husband, and we have negotiated the terms of our marriage. He has control of the military. If we go to war over this, we go to war against ourselves."

Telía said, "The claim is not yet binding!"

"The marriage contract has been signed," Erisial said, motioning to Celise who hurried forward with an apologetic glance for Frisha and Yserria.

"But … but there has been no ceremony," Telía said, "and it has not been consummated before witnesses."

Erisial waved away the concern. "Minor technicalities that will be remedied before the morrow. As for this matter"—she ran a hand over Coledon's bared chest as she passed him on her way back to the dais—"your king has given his guardsman permission to apply for citizenship in another kingdom. I do not intend to stand in his way." She stood upon the dais and gazed around the room at the stunned faces. "Besides, we had best put this matter to rest before he makes the same offer to other disgruntled champions."

Some of the women appeared worried as they shook their heads in agreement, and many of the men looked around as if to discourage anyone from getting ideas of defecting. Meanwhile, Coledon dropped to his knees, placed his sword on the ground and crossed his arms before him. He pressed his forehead to his wrists and muttered a string of words in Leréshi. Two of the few words Wesson understood were Rezkin and Cael, so he assumed it to be an oath of fealty.

When the man rose, Rezkin said, "You may join my royal guard."

"It is my honor, Your Majesty," Coledon said. He retrieved his shirt but left his Leréshi guardsman's coat lying on the ground. He then moved to stand behind Rezkin's entourage.

Rezkin glanced about and said, "Does anyone else wish to declare a challenge?"

Telía seethed at the queen. "You are weak, Erisial, and you know it. You hide behind this man just as you have hidden behind Serunius for so long."

Erisial laughed. "This is why you will never be queen, Telía. I have gained the advantage of the most exquisite weapon on the Souelian, one that none in this court is brave enough to face."

"You think you have conquered him?" Telía spat. "He is a rabid animal. You will see. He will betray you and destroy this kingdom. He has already wreaked havoc in Ashai and Channería, and he is not yet done with Gendishen." She looked around at the crowd that was stunned into silence by her outburst. "You will all regret not killing him where he stands!"

Erisial turned from the crazed woman, smiled to the crowd, and said, "Shall we get on with the ceremony?"

A servant hurried forward with a tray covered in black velvet, upon which lay two silver ribbons. Serunius stopped the servant in his tracks and took the tray. The queen's consort carried the tray to where Erisial and Rezkin stood upon the dais. Rezkin removed the black ribbon that held his hair in a queue, allowing it to fall loose. Erisial smiled tightly at her consort as she took a silver ribbon from the tray and muttered foreign words as she wound it into a smaller braid that hung from Rezkin's temple. The silver gleamed brightly in his raven black hair, and her hands began to shake as she tied off the end. Rezkin followed suit, twisting a silver ribbon into the queen's golden locks as he spoke the same words, but Erisial looked away as if she could no longer meet his icy stare.

Both of them turned to view the audience, and Minder Finwy and an older priest stepped up to the dais. Rezkin did not glance at the priests as his predatory gaze roved the crowd and caught on something at the rear of the hall beyond Wesson's view. Whatever he was seeing held his attention for a minute before he moved on to scan the rest of the far room. His gaze finally fell on the priests as they were finishing their benedictions in both Ashaiian and Leréshi, and Wesson wondered if Rezkin had heard any of it. When the priests stopped speaking, the crowd applauded, although the enthusiasm seemed to be lacking. As far as Wesson could tell, no one in the room was happy about the union, including the newlyweds.

Wesson felt the slight tingle of power and then beside him, Frisha yelped. From her other side, Nanessy whispered, "Just something to dry your tears before they fall."

Frisha nodded but appeared incapable of speech at that moment. Wesson was just as surprised as the rest of them. He had been expecting Rezkin to come up with some wild announcement or crazy plan to get out of the marriage. The noise of the crowd had risen steadily as people gossiped about the proceedings.

"Maybe he'll kill her," Frisha whispered. Her companions all looked at her aghast. "What?" she said with a shrug. "He does that—kills people, I mean. Maybe he'll kill her before they … you know … consummate it. Then he can take the throne and whatever he wants." They continued to stare at her in surprise, and she said, "I'm not saying he *should*."

Without even looking their way, Rezkin turned to leave with the queen. A small voice called out from somewhere near the dais.

"Queen Erisial!"

At first, the queen did not seem to hear, but the crown quieted as the voice called again. "Queen Erisial. I-I would like to make a claim!"

Erisial paused and turned back to see Celise standing at the foot of the dais. Everyone moved back to give her space, and she looked around anxiously.

"*You* wish to make a claim?" Erisial said. "*Finally*?"

"Yes, I do," Celise replied. "I want to claim a consort." Her Ashaiian sounded much better to Wesson's ears, as if she had practiced.

Erisial glanced at Coledon and then back to Celise. "Very well, Celise. Make your claim."

Celise looked at the crowd again and then turned back to her mother. "I claim Journeyman Wesson as my consort."

Wesson watched the queen's expression darken and then noticed that everyone was looking at him. Finally, Celise's words caught up with him. He felt a heavy thud as his heart began to race. He blinked a few times and then said, "*What*?"

A firm hand nudged him from behind, and Coledon whispered in his ear, "Best go up there, boy. You are not getting out of this one."

Wesson shuffled past his friends to stand beside Celise, just then noticing that they were about the same height. She did not look at him. In fact, he was not sure she had *ever* looked at him.

"I do not understand," he said.

For the first time, the young woman glanced his way. She gave him an apologetic smile and then returned her attention to her mother. Erisial appeared as if her head would burst into flame. Wesson briefly considered making that happen, and then he pushed that little destructive voice to the back of his mind.

Erisial said, "You finally claim a consort, and you choose this puny boy who has not even achieved mage status?"

Wesson shook his head vigorously. He did not want to be claimed. He had other plans.

Celise glanced at him and then said, "Yes. He is"—she paused to search for a word—"kind. The Ashaiian women"—she nodded toward Wesson's companions—"they like him. He is … um … respected. And, he is cute—like a puppy."

Erisial's gaze shot daggers at her daughter. "A puppy? I would buy you a litter of puppies. I would fill this room with puppies! But you do not claim a puppy for your consort!"

"He wishes to be a life mage. This is good person—not dangerous," Celise said.

Erisial stormed down the steps to the foot of the dais. She frowned as she noted with her judgmental gaze that Wesson was a hair shorter. She said, "Celise, you *need* someone dangerous for your consort. You *need* a champion who can protect you and your interests. There is an entire yard of palace guards who would fight to be your consort. Do not choose this boy who cannot even finish his spells."

Celise dropped her gaze to the floor, and Wesson felt a breath of relief that her mother had gotten through to her—even if it was at his expense.

"I choose Wesson," she muttered without looking at her mother.

Erisial fumed at her daughter and then turned her heated gaze on him. "Do you accept her claim?" she snapped.

"No!" Wesson said. "No, I do not want to be claimed. I already have someone."

"You are married?" Erisial said, apparently relieved.

Celise looked up at him in alarm.

"Well, no, but I want to marry her."

"Then you are betrothed?" Erisial said, and he wondered if she would accept it in lieu of marriage. Unfortunately, they would know if he was lying.

"Um, no."

Erisial sighed. "But you *will* be?"

"Probably not," he said with defeat. "She is most likely already married by now."

Erisial closed her eyes and then turned to glare at Rezkin, as if blaming him. Rezkin, however, was smiling for the first time since he had caused the disquiet the previous night. It was not the smirk he sometimes wore, but a broad grin, and laughter danced in his blue gaze.

Panic took over, and Wesson blurted, "You think this is *funny*?"

Rezkin laughed. He actually laughed, and Wesson nearly blasted him with a fireball.

"I am sorry, Journeyman, but, yes, this is funny. The woman wants a puppy, so she chooses *you*."

Wesson noticed that others were beginning to look at him suspiciously, and he wondered why Rezkin would make such a spectacle. Rezkin never did anything without a purpose.

Erisial was staring at Rezkin as if seeing him for the first time. She shook herself from the trance and gazed around the room. "Someone may choose to challenge the claim." Coming from her lips, it almost sounded like an order.

Wesson began to worry as people whispered and nudged each other.

Erisial looked down at him and said, "It is obvious he cannot win a challenge. It would be an easy win."

"No!" said Celise. "No one wants him like I do." She looked at the crowd in a panic. "Please do not take him from me."

Coledon stepped forward. He pointed at Wesson and said, "I will stand as champion against any challengers for Celise's claim on this man."

Those who looked as if they might challenge the claim stood back, and the whispers died. Celise beamed up at Coledon and then took Wesson's hand with girlish glee. Wesson stared at her in amazement.

Erisial tromped up the steps and hissed at Rezkin, "Come, *husband*, we must consummate our marriage. We will discuss this later."

Rezkin grinned at Wesson and then turned to follow Erisial without as much as a glance for Frisha. Wesson wanted to feel bad for her, but he had problems of his own. It seemed like Rezkin had thrown him to the wolves just to get under Erisial's skin. Well, not *wolves*. Just one wolf. Or maybe she was more like a fox. He looked into the large brown eyes that glowed with happiness. Definitely a fox. He wondered if Mage Threll might use her spell to prevent his tears.

Erisial stormed through the corridors, not even pretending to be a happily married woman. Rezkin figured her open display of disgust could be blamed on Celise's decision and not on the fact that she wanted nothing to do with him. He briefly wondered if he could make her angry enough to reject the consummation altogether. He chided himself for the wistful thought. He had decided the farce of a marriage was a small price for an army, and Bilior had been most adamant about reminding him of their deal. Armies were not easily gotten; and, according to the fae, demons were on the rise.

"You laughed," Erisial shouted as she stomped through her suite.

Serunius closed the doors and leaned back against them. The man's mood appeared to be somewhere between stormy and somber, but Erisial was all tempest.

"How could you laugh at that!" she said. "*My* daughter chose the weakest, puniest, *prettiest* little boy in the kingdom."

"He is not a little boy," Rezkin said blandly as he took a seat on the settee. "He is eighteen, same as Celise." He smirked and met her gaze. "He is less than a year younger than I, your *husband*."

Erisial's face heated as she looked to Serunius for support. None was forthcoming. She looked back at him. "You are more than a man. I do not know what you are, but none would mistake you for a boy. Everyone in this kingdom quakes at your feet. No one would think twice about running over the journeyman. Celise has enemies. *My* enemies."

"And a mother who would have her killed," Rezkin said.

"I was not *trying* to have her killed. She was collateral damage, and I do not believe he would have gone that far."

Rezkin hummed as he reclined on the plush seat. "I would think you a terror if I had not been trained by worse. The difference, however, is that I was taught to defend myself from my enemies, whereas Celise was left to survive on her own. She likely has more strength than you realize, and intuition as well. I have not sensed her use of *talent*. I wonder if she is a truthseeker."

"What makes you say that?" Erisial said.

"Sit down and relax, *wife*. Your daughter chose the most dangerous man in that room, perhaps in this kingdom—besides me, of course. Although, she may withdraw her claim once she learns of it."

Erisial abruptly sat on the sofa across from him and said, "What are you talking about? He is only a journeyman, a failed life mage."

Rezkin shook his head. "Do you really think I would come with so little strength behind me? It is true that Journeyman Wesson failed as a life mage. That is because he is a battle mage—one with a natural affinity for destructive magic, and he is three times more powerful than Serunius, perhaps more."

"You lie," Serunius said as he strode across the room to hover behind Erisial.

Rezkin looked to the queen and said, "Do I?"

She did not answer but reached up to clutch her consort's hand as she stared at him in disbelief.

He said, "It was Wesson who stood before King Privoth with me and fended off a dozen purifiers without so much as casting a spell. If you anger him, he could probably level this whole palace."

Rezkin did not actually know how much damage Wesson could do, so he was not lying. It could very well be that the journeyman was capable of such a thing, although it was unlikely.

Erisial suddenly laughed, and then she laughed some more. "I called him a puny puppy."

Rezkin donned a sober expression and nodded knowingly. "Yes, you are lucky he has an unflappable resolve. Someone less equable might have set your head on fire."

"How did you come across such a powerful mage," Serunius said with skepticism, "and how did you convince him to serve you?"

"I offered to kill his donkey," Rezkin said. At their blank expressions, he said, "That is another story. Let us be done with this. I do not wish to spend any more time in Lon Lerésh than is necessary."

Erisial smoothed the ribbon-like strips of her dress and said, "As much as I would like to make this quick, our laws do not make claiming a husband easy. We must remain intimate the entire night. You are not permitted to leave these quarters until dawn. The evening meal will be served here. It is against my wishes, but Serunius has insisted on serving as witness. Vielda will be the second. I do not care for her much, but she is a councilor and a truthseeker, so she can certify that we have met the requirements."

"Requirements?" Rezkin said. He had never heard that there were any requirements beyond consummation.

"Yes, it is not necessary when claiming a consort; but, for a marriage, both participants must achieve maximum pleasure. Without it, the bond cannot form, and the marriage will not be recognized."

"Bond? You said nothing of a bond."

She waved her hand in the air as if it was nothing and said, "I have always thought it a metaphorical bond. I have not met many who took a husband. Serunius is concerned that a bond forms, in truth, between mages who are married. He thinks the ceremony in which we participated was a kind of spell and that the consummation and subsequent climax activates it. You are not a mage, though, so perhaps it is not important."

"Yes, perhaps," he drawled. Enduring a marriage that would not be recognized outside of Lon Lerésh was one thing, but he was not prepared to be magically bonded to the woman in any way.

Erisial said, "Do you wish to have witnesses present?"

Rezkin had no desire to be present, much less have witnesses, but this was one situation in which he was sure to need backup. This kind of scenario had been a terrible lesson during his training, and now he was expected to revisit that lesson with possible hostiles in the room. He suddenly wished Kai were there—or any of the strikers. He might even accept Farson, only because he knew Farson had no love for the Leréshi. As a royal guard, Yserria would be his next choice, but he did not think she would appreciate being present for this. Besides that, the other occupants of the room were mages, Serunius a battle mage. Either through some nefarious plot or simply out of jealousy, he might attack while Rezkin was distracted by his duties. He needed Wesson. The journeyman was not going to like this assignment, but at least if a magical bond did form, Wesson could witness the event and perhaps design a spell to counteract it.

"Journeyman Wesson will stand as witness."

12

Wesson opened the door to the suite, and Rezkin followed him into the sitting room, heading straight for the bathing chamber. After wandering over to the sofa to lay down for a few minutes, Wesson noticed that it was already occupied. Celise's head popped up as he peered down at her.

"Oh, you are here!" she said. "This is so great honor. My consort taken to be witness of queen's marry night. I am sad you are not here, but is good for house."

Wesson squinted as he tried to figure out her words. He was too tired to interpret poorly spoken Ashaiian at that moment.

He rubbed his tired eyes and said, "Why are you here, Celise?"

She smiled. "You are my consort."

He sighed heavily. "I understand that you claimed me, but why are you *here*? Why did you not go back to wherever you live and sleep in your own bed?"

Her smile slipped as she worked through his words. Finally, she said, "You are not in my bed. I come here for you, but you are in queen's bed."

"No!" he blurted and then lowered his voice. "No, I mean. I was not in the queen's bed."

She thought about her words again and said, "You are in queen's bed*chamber*?"

He ran a hand over his tired face and said, "Yes, that is true."

He sunk into a high-backed chair and was just dozing off when one of the other doors swung open to emit Reaylin.

"You're back! How was it? What happened?" she said as she rushed over and knelt beside his chair.

Wesson groaned. "I do not want to talk about it. Ever. I want to leave Lon Lerésh and pretend none of this ever happened."

"No, Wess! You have to tell me something," she said as she tugged at his arm.

Just then, Rezkin strode out of the bathing chamber wearing nothing but a drying cloth wrapped about his waist. His chest and back bore scratch and bite marks that reminded Wesson of the horrors he had witnessed all, night, long.

Rezkin closed his door behind him, and Reaylin turned back to Wesson with a questioning gaze.

He waved a hand toward Rezkin's door in frustration and said, "Was that not enough? Please, Reaylin. I am tired. We are leaving in an hour. Let me rest."

Celise popped up from the couch and said, "I go put things in bags and trunk."

Wesson was suddenly more alert than he had been for the past six hours. "*What*? Why?"

Celise looked back at him as she opened the door. "We leave. I take the clothes."

"What, no! You are staying here. Leréshi claims are not recognized outside of Lon Lerésh. You can stay here and claim a dozen men, and I am leaving."

She shook her head and smiled. "My Wesson." She came over to kneel at his other side and said, "I have finish all training for lessons in love making. I am very good. You will like. I will teach you. You are my consort. I leave with you."

Then, she got up and left without a backward glance.

Once she was gone, Reaylin punched Wesson in the arm. "Hey, Wess, you got yourself a girlfriend."

"Do you think I can convince Rezkin to leave a bit early? Maybe before she comes back?"

Reaylin said, "Come on. She's cute, and it sounds like she really wants to make you happy." This last she said with a wink.

"I know. I am sure she is great, but I want someone else."

Reaylin nodded. "I heard, but you also said she is probably already married. Might as well move on."

Reaylin returned to her room, presumably to pack, and Wesson fell asleep even before her door shut.

The ride back to the ship was tense. With the addition of Celise and Oledia, they required two carriages. Queen Erisial and her consort did not make an appearance that morning, and everyone was glad of that. Oledia was quiet. She looked much like her mother, with darker hair but the same honey-colored eyes. She had dressed in a long frock that would be considered acceptable in most places outside of Lon Lerésh. Celise had not. She was wearing a green bustier, a short, black skirt that barely reached her knees, and gold sandals with straps that wrapped around her ankles. Since Wesson refused to wear the red ribbon she had presented, she wore it for him, together with the green one for her mother's house. She maintained that she was not yet ready to establish her own house.

It was obvious that Oledia and Celise had somehow developed a sisterly relationship, despite the difference in the way they were treated in their mother's house. They chatted amicably, although Wesson did not understand a word of it. From their frequent glances his way, he assumed much of it was about him. Oledia was otherwise quiet and preferred to stare out the window in deep contemplation over engaging in conversation. To Wesson, she seemed more like a librarian than an assassin for the Adana'Ro.

Rezkin dismounted and turned to assist his companions from the carriages. Frisha would not take his hand nor would she look at him, and the other women seemed distant as they, too, avoided his gaze. He and Wesson had an unspoken agreement to never acknowledge the previous night, but Celise wanted everyone to know that *her* consort had served as witness to the queen's matrimonial consummation.

Once everyone was free of the carriages and the ship's crewmen had collected their bags and trunks, Rezkin bade Wesson and Yserria to wait with him and Oledia on the docks. Shezar strode down the gangplank to join them, and Rezkin was grateful for the striker's professionalism. At least he would wait until information was offered, rather than pester him with needless questions. Reaylin convinced Celise to board the ship with them, and she seemed happy to have found acceptance with the other women. After the parade of soldiers and guards finally departed, those hidden in the shadows emerged into the light.

The blue-eyed secrelé smiled beneath her mask as she approached. Her comrades hurried forward to collect Oledia and her belongings, all of which were quickly ushered aboard a small cutter docked beside *Stargazer*. Despite the presence of the others, or perhaps because of it, the secrelé spoke in Ferélli. "*You went to great lengths to bring us the daughter of the queen, First King of* Lon Lerésh. *I am impressed. You spent an entire night with a Leréshi queen and survived.*"

Rezkin was having none of the woman's flirtations that morning. He said, "*You have the girl. Give me the sword as agreed.*"

The woman tisked. "*Testy this morning. Perhaps you are grumpy because you were forced to leave your matrimonial bed so soon.*" She lost her playful demeanor. "*We do not have the sword. The deal was for us to tell you where it is.*"

"*And*?" Rezkin snapped.

"*King Moldovan has it. It was he who paid us to take it in the first place.*"

Rezkin eyed her suspiciously. "*Moldovan hates you.*"

She shrugged. "*Yes, but it does not stop him from using our services when it suits him. If you want the sword, you will have to take it up with him.*"

Once the woman had departed, Yserria said, "What did she say? Where is the sword?"

"We go back to Ferélle. We must meet with another monarch."

13

"Please, do not be angry with me more."

Tieran was *trying* to pretend to read through the papers on the desk, but he had only managed to shuffle them into disarray. He finally gave up and looked at her.

"Ilanet, you effectively kidnapped our future queen."

She shook her head vigorously. "No, no! She is with the king. She went to him with will."

"Willingly," he said.

"Yes, willingly."

"Except that it does not *appear* that she went *willingly*. She did not *walk* aboard the ship and bed down in a cozy bunk. Where *is* she, Ilanet?"

"Um, she is surely with him *now*. They are weeks gone."

He slammed his fist onto the desk. "She was wrapped in an illusion that *you* made and locked in a *warded* trunk! If you had learned anything about your power, you would know that an illusion spell can have disastrous consequences on a person if not made correctly. But you, a novice just come into her powers, put an illusion on the *queen*! He might never be able to find her!"

"But Lus—"

"Let us both hope he is as trustworthy as you claim."

Her doubtful expression was not encouraging.

"Please, Lord Tieran, I do not wish to be placed in my room more."

"You are remanded to your room until Frisha has returned safely. This is the problem. We have all be treating you like a grown woman, but you are still only a child."

Having remained silent to this point, Brandt said, "Perhaps you should take that into consideration. She is still a child, and she is Frisha's friend. She thought she was helping. Frisha is the one to blame."

Tieran ground his teeth. "*Why* would she do it?"

Ilanet said, "Because she loves him?"

He glanced at her. Tieran knew that Frisha was a romantic, but she had been having doubts about the union with Rezkin. "That is difficult to accept. I think you know more than you are saying."

Ilanet bit her lip. "She-she says she does not think he is truth with her."

He wearily ran a hand down his face. "Truthful."

"Yes, I am saying truth."

"No, the word is—never mind. You are saying that she went to spy on him."

Brandt said, "That does sound like something she would do."

Tieran nodded and sighed heavily. After glancing at Brandt, he returned his gaze to the princess. "Very well. You may leave your quarters, but you are under strict orders *not* to use your powers except under the supervision and direction of a mage."

Ilanet beamed. "Thank you, Lord Tieran. I will be very good. I will make no trouble."

"You are an illusionist. Your purpose in life is to make trouble."

The heavy pounding on the door had the signature of Kai. The striker opened the door from the outside to permit Captain Jimson and Healer Jespia.

"You have returned. Please tell me you were successful."

Jimson saluted and said, "Lord Tieran, we were unable to find him."

Tieran's stomach dropped. "What do you mean, you were unable to find him?"

"We waited in his room for over a week. We surveyed all the local establishments and questioned the locals. He has disappeared. Millins and Mage Yerlin stayed behind in case he returns."

Ilanet said, "You are speaking of Tam? Tam is missing?"

Tieran waved to Brandt. "Take Ilanet—somewhere. Out of here."

"Wait, no! I wish to know of Tam. Please, what of Tam?"

Brandt pulled her by her elbow through the door, and Kai stepped in before shutting it.

"We will need to put together a real search party," said the striker.

Tieran looked at Jespia. "What is the prognosis?"

Jespia frowned. "This should never have been done in the first place. By the time we find him, it may already be too late. The human mind was not designed to receive information in this way."

Kai said, "We had no idea, at the time, that the healer who suggested it was a demon."

"You knew the dangers," she said.

"The king wanted Tam to be prepared. Tam wanted to be involved, but he did not have the skills necessary to carry out the tasks without getting himself killed."

"Well, that is exactly how he is going to end up now."

"We will find him," said Tieran. "We have to. Rezkin's number one priority is his friends, and two have gone missing on *my* watch."

"Bah, Frisha is with Rezkin," said Kai. "She could not have remained hidden from him for long. She is fine. Our focus should be on Tam."

"Agreed," said Jespia. "If we find him quickly, we may be able to minimize the damage enough to save his life; but, he will never be the same."

Kai said, "I can go."

Tieran shook his head. "With the other strikers gone, we need you here." He tapped the desk as he considered his options. He swallowed hard and then looked to Kai. "Send for Connovan."

Farson glared at Rezkin as he boarded the ship. He said, "I hear there was a wedding." Rezkin met his gaze and kept walking. Both strikers followed. "She is upset," said Farson. "I believe she is in her berth crying at this very moment."

"Who?"

"Who do you think? Frisha, the woman you were to marry until two days ago."

"What does it matter? She called it off. Besides, you were the most outspoken against the union. I would think you would be pleased."

"I am not pleased about you marrying the Leréshi queen."

Shezar said, "The marriage is not recognized outside of Lon Lerésh."

"Yes," said Rezkin as he ducked through the small doorway to his cabin. "Nothing has changed, except that I now have an entire army and sizeable navy at my disposal."

"I will grant you that," said Farson. "This will not help matters with Privoth."

"Privoth will get what he wants—only, it will take a bit longer."

"What now?"

"Moldovan has the sword."

Shezar said, "Knowing how much he hates Privoth and that prophecy, he has probably already had it melted down and made into dinnerware."

"Let us hope that is not the case," said Rezkin. "Moldovan is a mage. He knows the prophecy is a farce and is unlikely to feel threatened by it. Gendishen takes it seriously, though, so Moldovan is probably holding the sword for ransom."

Captain Estadd strode through the open doorway and saluted. "Your Majesty, a man is requesting permission to board the ship. It looks as though he intends to stay, but he travels light."

"I will see to it," said Shezar.

Rezkin said, "You stay. Farson, see the man aboard. Bring him here."

Farson glanced between them before leaving. Shezar said, "Do we have a problem?"

Rezkin shook his head. "Not you. *Them.* Neither should be trusted, yet they are both valuable. Keep an eye on them."

"Them? Who is coming aboard?"

The dark-haired man ducked into the room, followed by Farson. He wore a servant's coat but had dropped the air of subjugation. He glanced around the room and nodded "Shezar."

Shezar appeared surprised. "Akris. It has been some time."

"Too long," Akris grumbled. "Who is this?" he said with a nod toward Farson.

"This is Striker Farson."

"Farson? I do not recognize you, and you are too old to be a new recruit. The name sounds familiar, though."

"You have likely read it in the histories," said Rezkin. He looked at Farson. "The accounting of the dead." The remark elicited a scowl from the surly striker.

"Another long-lost brother, then?" He looked at Shezar. "What of me? Am I dead, too, or just forgotten?"

"Do not lay blame at our feet, Akris. You were to remain at your post on Caydean's orders, as were *all* the deployed strikers."

Akris gave a start. "Some were in far more sensitive positions. It would mean capture or death for them to stay too long."

"Indeed," Shezar said, with a hint of sadness. "Roark has gone to recruit those who survive."

"It is true, then." He motioned to Rezkin, who had taken a seat at his desk. "You and Roark serve *him* now. How many others does he have?"

Farson said, "You do not sound as if you are eager to join us, and you ask many questions."

"I am here, am I not?"

"You could be a spy," said Shezar.

Akris glanced at Rezkin. "I saw his *proof*. By the looks of him, I would say there is much he has not disclosed. I saw him put down the queen's guard in the practice yard, and now he bears the title of First King of Lon Lerésh. I am beginning to believe the rumors. He spreads destruction everywhere he goes, yet those who should be fighting him are staunchly loyal. I would not be fit to be called striker if I were not wary."

Rezkin said, "I think you overestimate their loyalty. Most of my allies would kill me if the opportunity arose. The rest are more interested in unseating Caydean at the moment. My appeal ends with his reign."

Akris glanced at the two strikers and then looked back at him. "You are not what I expected. At the palace, you seemed to think yourself quite deserving."

"No one *deserves* to be king, and those who desire it do not fully understand the position."

Akris nodded but appeared suspicious. "You do not seem to think highly of your followers and allies. You believe they will betray you. It speaks of the same madness that is said to possess Caydean."

"On the contrary. Caydean is chaos without order. He is madness. I am prepared for betrayal because it is dictated by the *Rules*: *9, 24, 87, 96, 164,* and *257*."

"You are a striker," Akris said with surprise.

Rezkin stood and rounded the desk. He met Farson's gaze before turning to Akris. "Strikers have honor. *I* do not. Strikers are praised for their service. *I* am feared. Strikers belong to a brotherhood. *I* stand alone. Strikers answer to a master. I *am* the master. Do not mistake me for a striker."

Akris said, "You bear a hardness that is difficult to accept in a man so young."

"The ship is about to set sail," said Rezkin. "You kneel and swear fealty or leave. This is the only time I will give you a choice. If you choose the latter, I suggest you remain in Lon Lerésh and accept your new life."

Akris looked at Farson and then Shezar. His gaze lingered on the lightning bolt that adorned the black and green tabard. He turned back to Rezkin. "You are shrewd. Queen Erisial may have gotten what she wanted, but I fear that somehow you had the upper hand. You may see betrayal everywhere, but I trust in my brethren and in King Bordran. The fact that I am here speaks to my intention to serve you. I will follow you, and you will take me home."

"You do realize, Lord Tieran, that I do not serve you."

"Yes, I know that," said Tieran. His voice was a tad weaker than he would have preferred. "But, you are supposed to serve the king of Ashai. Rezkin is the true king. Since *his* Rez has not been trained, *you* must serve him."

Connovan tilted his head in a manner eerily similar to the way Rezkin did. "That is an interesting tale you weave; but, even if that were true, it does not explain why I should do this for *you*."

"I am Rezkin's heir."

"But not the king."

"Look, Tam is important to Rezkin. If he were here, he would want you to do it."

Connovan chuckled. "If this Tam is important to him, then Rezkin would probably not want me anywhere near him."

"I concede the point, but we need to find Tam. He is Rezkin's best friend."

"Is that what he tells everyone? The Rez has no friends."

Tieran gritted his teeth. "Rezkin is more than the Rez. He is not you."

"Oh, that one is far worse."

Tieran paced behind the desk. He stopped to stare at the disturbing painting and then looked back at the most feared assassin in the world. "Tam has only been apprenticing with him for a few months. He cannot fend for himself—"

"This Tam is Rezkin's apprentice?"

Tieran paused. Connovan's sudden interest triggered equal amounts of hope and concern. "Yes," he said slowly, "he has been training him—well, since they met."

"What does he teach this Tam?"

"Fighting, swordplay," said Tieran. "Other things, too. He makes him read everything we have to read. Tam complains about the boring subjects, and I cannot say I blame him. That is the whole reason we are in this mess." He pointed to his temple. "I told you about the hole in his mind. If we don't get him back soon, he'll die."

The Rez looked at him and grinned. "Tell me about Tamarin Blackwater."

Tieran suddenly worried that he had made a mistake.

On the eleventh day, the sun was well on its way to the horizon as they entered the Straight of Bourdony. They hoped to be back on the Souelian Sea by nightfall. The massive sails were full, and the mages lined the deck to speed their progress. The captain had explained that the surface waters of the Bourdony always flowed eastward into the bay, so escaping was a task. After more than a week out of Kielen, Frisha had finally found her voice.

"How could you?" she hollered.

"Would you care to discuss this privately?" said Rezkin, glancing around them. The crewmen and passengers were staring.

"What does it matter?" she said. "They all know. You married her! You had just gotten through telling me you would probably never marry, if not for *me*, and you go and marry *her*!"

"Again, Leréshi marriages are not recognized outside of Lon Lerésh."

"It doesn't matter! You did it. *You* signed the papers. *You* participated in the ceremony. You—you spent the *night* with her! She is your wife."

"No."

"Oh, always with the lies! Stop lying and admit it!"

Rezkin glanced over to see Coledon watching them along with everyone else. He waved the man over and said, "Please explain to her why I cannot do what she asks."

Coledon crossed his wrists and bowed to Frisha. "Lady Frisha, the king does not refuse in an attempt to deceive you. It is true that Leréshi marriages and claimings are not recognized by the other kingdoms *unless* the man recognizes it outside of Lon Lerésh."

"I don't understand," said Frisha with a pout.

"If our king is in Lon Lerésh, he may speak of the marriage freely. Once he has left Lon Lerésh, he may never speak of it unless he wishes for it to be recognized. If he acknowledges her as his wife even once while he is out of Lon Lerésh, the marriage becomes valid."

Frisha glanced at Rezkin. "How would anyone know?"

Coledon said, "The ceremony contains a spell."

"Ritual magic?" said Wesson.

Coledon nodded, "You do not need to be a mage to perform it. If he acknowledges the marriage, he will be marked and married in truth. It is why he asked me to explain it to you. It would be too easy to slip, and it is difficult to tell what the spell would interpret as recognition of the marriage."

Frisha looked to Wesson. "But spells don't work on him. You said so."

Wesson said, "Do you really want to test it?"

"No," she said rather quickly. She looked back to Coledon. "So, he's really not married?"

Coledon shook his head. "Not outside of Lon Lerésh." Then, he said, "I do not understand. I had heard that you released your claim on him, and you did not claim him at the palace. Please, Lady Frisha, tell me why you are upset so that I may help to remedy it."

Frisha blinked at him through watery lashes. "I-I don't know. It doesn't make any sense. *I* don't make any sense." She glanced around and flushed upon noticing all the people watching her.

Coledon's expression turned sad. "Sometimes a matria does not want a man as consort, but she does not want anyone else to have him either."

Frisha's eyes widened. "Oh no! That's horrible. Of course, I want him to be happy. I would never—" She stopped abruptly as if she had just come to a realization. She turned her mahogany gaze on him. Rezkin said nothing, but he hoped that she finally understood why he could not do as she asked.

He glanced over at Yserria and said, "Where is Malcius?"

"I believe he and Brandt are in their quarters."

"Please fetch him," he said.

Yserria saluted, but her expression soured as she stepped away. Rezkin jumped when something suddenly latched onto his leg, its claws digging into his calf. He glanced down to see an orange-eyed cat staring up at him, its ears laid flat, and its teeth bared. It hissed, then yowled as it released him and shot across the deck. He looked out to sea, but there was nothing.

"Prepare for battle," he shouted. People stared at him in confusion, and he shouted again, "All hands prepare for battle!"

A sudden impact on the starboard side caused the ship to nearly capsize. It listed so far that water sloshed over the railing. Everything not secured to the deck went tumbling toward the sea. Rezkin crashed into an invisible wall just as his feet left the deck, and then Wesson sailed into him. They tumbled into the other side of the ward as the ship righted itself, bobbing in the other direction. Shouts and horn blasts sounded as the ship rocked. Rezkin looked around for Frisha and was glad to see that Coledon had hold of her, and he and Shezar were trying to pull her into the cabin.

Wesson dropped the hastily made ward and was immediately catapulted into the air as something again collided with the ship. He lashed out with a tendril of power, securing himself to the deck as he tumbled. He had never cast the spell before but had seen Xa wield it against Rezkin once. Rezkin had managed to remain aboard but was tossed into the air with the next collision. To Wesson's surprise, he reached out and grabbed the tendril as if it were a rope of substance and not raw power.

People were shouting that men had been thrown overboard, while others hollered about a sea monster, but Wesson and Rezkin could not see anything from where they lay clinging to the rocking deck.

Rezkin shouted, "Can you make this rope into a net? Can you cover the deck with it?"

Wesson thought quickly about the spell, trying to modify it in his mind to meet Rezkin's needs. "Yes, I think so. I do not know how long I can hold it, and you will be the only one who can touch it. Not even I can grab this," he said as he waved his hand through the tendril to no effect.

"Do it. There, to the mainmast," Rezkin said.

Wesson wove the net of power across the deck, and Rezkin grabbed hold of it. He got to his hands and feet and climbed across it as the ship rocked. Men and objects went sliding past, oblivious and unaffected by the net. Once Rezkin reached the mast, he grabbed hold of an actual rope, and Wesson dropped the spell. After tossing one end of a line to Wesson, Rezkin pulled the mage toward him. They both looked out across sea but too late. A massive tentacle whipped through the air, smashing through the mainmast. Wesson kept his grip on the rope and was jerked across the deck as the mast fell. His motion stopped when he slammed against the railing, and he glanced back to see that Rezkin had disappeared.

Wesson scrambled to his feet, securing his boots to the deck of the ship with tendrils of power. As the ship was jarred, he caught sight of Mage Threll at the bow lobbing a fireball at something he was unable to see from his vantage. Climbing over ropes and anything secured to the ship, he reached her just as a monstrous creature reared out of the water. Its tough, bluish-red skin was slick around the giant black eye that stared at him right before it lifted its enormous tentacles. Beneath the flailing appendages was a gaping maw filled with row after row of razor sharp spikes protruding from pink flesh.

His heart threatened to burst from his chest as the spikes descended toward them. Mage Threll cast a spiral wave of flame into the creature's maw. The thing stalled and released a screech infused with a putrid wind but resumed its attack. Wesson knew the end was upon them, and for once permitted a trickle of the macabre joy at his core to breach the surface. He chuckled with mirth as he wove an unfamiliar spell of fire and nocent energy. A thrill drove through him as he cast the dark power. It spread from a single point, an oily black sphere the size of his fist, and each sphere thereafter splitting again and again. The swarm of black spheres struck the sea monster, some sailing past then turning to accost it from the rear. The blobs splattered against the creature's slippery skin and stuck like molasses. Then, they began to sizzle. The creature screamed and its massive tentacles flailed as its skin bubbled and popped in acrid pustules. Wesson laughed uncontrollably as Mage Threll watched in horror.

"No!" she screamed, as she reached into the air.

Wesson's laughter died when he spied the source of her distress. There, wrapped in a colossal tangle of tentacles, was Rezkin. His sword gleamed in the golden-red light of the setting sun as he struggled to free himself from the giant's grasp. Then, he was plunged beneath the frothy waves as the creature dove into the darkening water.

Mage Threll began weaving a spell that Wesson had never seen used in such a way, a web that spiraled outward from the ship and then sunk into the water.

"There," she said, pointing at the deck. "They're beneath the ship. We must do something!"

Before Wesson could respond, the ship began to rise, the hull lifting free of the water high enough to send a shock wave through them when it crashed back down. Wesson and Mage Threll both collided with the deck and then tumbled into the wall that supported the quarterdeck. Wesson looked up at the orange sky and blinked until all the images of a broken mast and sails became one.

His heart leapt as tentacles suddenly surged across the deck. The monster wrapped itself around the ship, and Wesson saw that one of the sinuous appendages ended abruptly in a pulsating amputation that spewed an acrid goo over the planks. He was alarmed that Rezkin was once again missing. Wesson sat up, and just as his head stopped spinning, the warrior came tumbling over the railing on the far side of the deck. Rezkin's chest heaved as he tried to fill his lungs while pulling himself to his feet. He pointed, his sword fisted in a white-knuckled grip, and met Wesson's gaze. He hollered something and then ran across the deck, picking up speed until he took flight, propelling himself from the railing onto the creature's blistered, foaming head.

Wesson played the image over in his mind, trying to figure out what Rezkin had said. There, in front of him, for the briefest moment, it was as if the wind took shape. An unexpected gust smacked into him, and he heard it, Rezkin's words carried on the wind.

"The ships! Demon on the ships!"

His heart pounding, Wesson turned and nearly tripped over Mage Threll. He helped her to her feet, grabbed her arm, and ran dragging her toward the rail. Two silhouettes stood out against the light of the setting sun.

"The ships," he said to Mage Threll. "Rezkin thinks a demon is among them. It must be controlling the sea creature. If we do not destroy the demon, the sea monster will continue to attack no matter how much damage we inflict upon it."

She said, "You saw him? He is alive, thank the Maker."

"You did not?" he said, finally looking at her. That was when he noticed the bloodied matt of hair on one side of her head. Her eyes were unfocused, and she swayed on her feet. "Sit down," he said. "Hold on to this rope so you do not fall overboard."

As she slumped to the deck, Wesson glanced across the angry waves and saw that Rezkin was clinging to a sword buried deep in the creature's hide while he hacked at the beast with a smaller blade. Then, Wesson looked to the two ships. Their sails were stowed, and they had not closed any distance.

"They are holding back," he mumbled, just as the monster grabbed Rezkin and flung him into the air. Rezkin crashed into the frothy water, and the creature turned in pursuit. "He is only buying us time," Wesson said.

He felt sick as the laughter bubbled inside him. He held his breath and then exhaled as he allowed the mirth to ascend. His heart danced to the symphony of destruction that sang within his mind as a spell, bred of chaos, shimmered in the air before him. He grinned, and the thrill of it pressed him into a fit of giggles. Finally, he whipped his hands forward, and he shouted. It was a terrible sound, a sound of anguish and desire. A silent wave of dark energy cut a scar across the water toward the farthest ship. He could see its crew scrambling, as if it might do them some good. Wards began rising along the ship's bow, and Wesson's laughter grew.

The dark wave did not collide with the wards *or* the ship. It shot straight through the hull with no apparent effect. Wesson released another breath. In that instant, the ship imploded, everything within crushed by a mighty force. When the compression reached a maximum, it exploded in a fiery ball of molten debris that rained ash and glass down upon the second ship. Wesson delighted in the wails of pain and fear that reached his ears on a hot wind. He raised his hands to dispatch the second ship, but his arm was pulled down by a firm grip.

Mage Threll used him to draw her weight upward until she was standing beside him. Her face was pale as she wearily pointed toward the frothy water nearer the ship. The sea monster's tentacles had gone slack, and it listed to one side before sinking slowly into the depths. Rezkin floated in the water for a moment, facing the star-speckled, dusky sky, and then he began swimming toward the ship.

Wesson glanced back at the other ship. A gleeful smile threatened at his lips, but he wrapped it tightly with his will and pushed it deep into the dungeon from which it had sprung. It was a struggle, and part of him wanted to let it go, but Mage Threll's firm grip kept him anchored. Then, the aftermath struck him. He heaved into the water as a cry escaped him. He looked at the evidence of his destruction. Where once dozens of men and women had lived, stood nothing but debris. He knew it was unlikely they would find bodies. They would have been crushed and vaporized, leaving behind no evidence that they had existed. Wesson slumped to the ground and buried his head in his hands as he sobbed.

Rezkin grabbed hold of the rope ladder someone had thrown down to him. He dragged himself aboard and stood tall, despite his fatigue. He still felt as if he were fighting for breath beneath the water, but he could not allow the others to witness his physical distress. His sodden armor was heavy after the long battle, and he had lost Kingslayer, but the monster was gone. Rezkin spied Captain Estadd at the helm barking orders. Others scrambled out of his way as he pushed away from the railing and tromped across the deck. They were like ants in a frenzy after someone had stomped their mound, except in one location. Journeyman Wesson sat on the deck with his head buried in his lap, and everyone was giving him a wide berth.

Gazing across the water, Rezkin saw the trail of debris that had once been a ship, and he understood. He glanced at Wesson and then waved to Captain Estadd. He said, "Light the flame."

"What does that mean?" said Mage Threll, who sat beside Wesson, eyeing him warily.

Shezar, who had felt it necessary to hurry over to inspect him, answered in his stead. "They have raised the flag of surrender. We are accepting."

Mage Threll said, "Our ship is in pieces. I am currently holding a ward over a hole in the hull right below us. If it is not repaired before I run out of energy, we will sink. Why would they surrender to *us*?"

"The second ship has been destroyed," said Shezar. "The first is concerned that we will do the same to them." His gaze landed on Wesson. "I doubt anyone has ever seen a ship so thoroughly decimated, and in a single attack, no less."

Rezkin was focused on maintaining a steady breath as his heart calmed. He looked at the tortured mage. "Journeyman, how did you know which ship was carrying the demon?"

Wesson raised his head but would not look at them. "I had no idea. I intended to destroy them both. I decided the closest would be less likely to escape if I destroyed the furthest first."

Rezkin nodded. "That was a well-considered strategy, and your spell was quite effective."

Mage Threll hesitantly reached out and patted Wesson on the back. "That was … impressive. Where did you learn such a thing?"

Wesson shook his head, covering it with his hands again. No one pressed him.

Mage Threll looked at Rezkin. "You were under water a long time. How did you survive?"

Rezkin tilted his head and looked at her curiously. "I was under water, but I was not. At times, it was as if air surrounded me. I thought you had cast a spell."

She shook her head. "No, not I."

Her eyes widened, and Rezkin turned to see what had captured her attention. A river of water that had climbed the ship began to flow across the deck in a narrow stream. As it slipped back into the water on the other side, the deck became dry. What it left behind was the greatest surprise. Rezkin strode toward the item with caution. After close examination, he lifted it from the planks and held it aloft. Blue swirls glinted across a silver edge in the last of the day's light.

He looked toward Nanessy, and she shook her head again.

Captain Estadd stopped a few paces away and said, "The nereids look kindly upon our blessed king."

Rezkin looked at the captain. He sheathed Kingslayer and then surveyed the rest of the ship. He said, "Shezar, find Reaylin so that she may treat Mage Threll before she loses consciousness. Then, see to the hull repair." He looked back at the captain. "What is our status?"

Estadd said, "We will not be going anywhere without a mast. With the help of the mages, we may be able to salvage some of that debris out there for a temporary mend."

"Do we have an accounting of the crew and passengers?"

"You will not like it. Several were injured in the collisions. Others went overboard. We are fishing a few out of the water, but two crewmen are missing, and one is dead."

Rezkin nodded. He had expected worse.

"Ah, there is more. It is about Lord Malcius and Knight Yserria."

Rezkin's gaze hardened. "What is it?"

"They are missing. One of the crewmen remembers them coming out of the cabin just before the first strike. We believe they were thrown overboard, but we have found no evidence."

Rezkin turned to the mages. "Can you search the water for them?"

Wesson waved toward Mage Threll. "That is her expertise."

Nanessy shook her head. "I am holding the water back from multiple leaks, in addition to the ward on the hull. If I were at full strength, I could search the immediate area, maybe fifty yards in every direction, but no more."

Captain Estadd said, "The current is swift here. What sails we have left are preventing us from being pulled back into the bay. If they have been in the water since the onset of the attack, they will be beyond her ability to detect by now."

"That is assuming they are still alive," said Rezkin.

"Well, yes, but I did not wish to say—"

"We should not avoid the truth because we do not like it."

Estadd nodded to the other ship. "We could take that one to look for them."

"No," said Rezkin. "It would take time to transfer ships, and Malcius and Yserria will have been swept that much farther. We also do not have enough personnel to sail both vessels, and the people on the other ship cannot be trusted."

"What do you want to do?"

Before Rezkin could answer, Celise came streaming across the deck. She knelt at Wesson's side and held him in her arms. "My puppy! You were not in the room, and I think you are on the deck in danger, and I am so … um …"

"Frightened?" said Mage Threll.

"Um … I do not know is this the word," said Celise as she hugged Wesson. "I am scream inside my heart."

Rezkin watched as she stroked the battle mage's hair and cooed at him in sweet words and soft tones. Why anyone would genuinely express such weakness for all to see was beyond him, and Wesson did not seem to appreciate the affection. After a few minutes, the battle mage shook her off, claiming he needed to help with the repairs.

Rezkin knew Captain Estadd, who was hollering orders to the crewmen at that moment, was still waiting for an answer. What was he going to do? He doubted Malcius and Yserria had survived the attack, but he felt an obligation to look for them. He had no idea how he would find them, though, considering the size of the bay. It took weeks to cross under ideal conditions; and, by the time temporary repairs were made, Malcius and Yserria could be anywhere.

He said, "Captain Estadd, these temporary repairs, how much can we expect from them?"

The man rubbed his beard and glanced at the broken mainmast. He said, "If the mages are any good, we can limp to port in Ferélle—Havoth, maybe. I would not risk being out any longer than we must. One storm and we will all be swimming with the nereids."

"Very well. See to the repairs. Shezar and Lus will take a team to secure the other vessel. The journeyman will go with them."

"Do you think that is a good idea?" said Mage Threll. "He is very upset."

"You know there are at least a few mages on that ship. He can handle them. I will be in my quarters."

Rezkin entered the cabin and took the steps to his berth. Once there, he searched the entire room and was frustrated when he did not find his quarry. He sloughed his wet clothes and put on a dry set then sat on his bunk. He said into the air, "Bilior. Bilior, where are you?" He stepped over to the porthole and again called, "Bilior!"

He knew the ancient would still be aboard since it seemed to follow him everywhere. He turned from the porthole and nearly collided with a face bearing orange eyes. The tree creature had stretched to Rezkin's height and was staring at him intently.

"Your part of the deal is broken. Two of my companions are gone, and we have not yet secured our sanctuary."

Bilior's feather-leaves shook, and the sound of thrashing limbs suffused the room as he leapt backward. "We are here, and they are there; but safe they be, among the we."

Rezkin felt a shudder of relief. "Where are they?"

"Uspiul did save you, with Hvelia in his embrace. Water to air so that you may live. He did bring your metal scepter, the blade that makes you king of men."

"What are Uspiul and Hvelia?"

"Wind and air, Ancients of Ahn'an they be."

"And they have Malcius and Yserria?"

The katerghen's arms wrapped around his truck, and he shivered to the sound of raindrops on a pond. "With you, not they."

Rezkin felt his frustration rising, and the stone on his chest began to heat. "Then, where are Malcius and Yserria?"

"With the lessers of the sea, they be," said Bilior as he tilted his head curiously to one side.

"These *lessers* are sea spirits, like the nereids of legend?" Bilior looked at him as his leaves twirled in the breeze from the porthole. Rezkin said, "Can they can bring Malcius and Yserria here?"

The creature shook again. "Nay, the sea is strong, the lessers weak. Shift them, guide them, toward the tide. On land they set them free."

Rezkin sat back on his bunk. "The coast is long, and they will not sit still. Even if we found their landing spot, they will be gone." He looked at the curious katerghen. "Those were Ashaiian ships. It was a demon controlling that sea creature, was it not?"

Sounds of lightning and rain echoed around the berth. "Daem'Ahn spread, in human host, Seeking you, in shadow, the shattered light."

"What does that mean?"

Bilior shook in silence and did not explain. He began to shrink, the wooden flesh sprouting fur, the browns and greens turning to a mottled brown and black.

Rezkin frowned. "I do not like it when you take Cat's form."

Then, he thought about what he had said. Why did he care what form the creature took, and why did it bother him that it was the form of his cat? He donned the guise of Dark Tidings, strapping the mask to his belt, and headed toward the main deck. Then, he paused. He had not checked on Frisha. She had been angry with him when he had not sought her after the attack on Cael. He headed back toward her berth and rapped on the door.

"Yes?" Frisha said as she opened it. She looked at him in surprise. "Oh, I didn't expect you. Is everything okay?"

"I thought to inquire as to your well-being," he said.

She blinked at him, and then her eyes began to well with moisture. She abruptly slammed the door. Rezkin stood there confused. Was she angry with him for checking on her? He started to go when the door opened again.

"Wait. I'm sorry. I didn't mean to do that," she said. "I mean, I did, but I shouldn't have. Um, is everything okay?"

Rezkin decided not to attempt to figure her out and instead focused on her question. "No, actually. Malcius and Yserria are missing."

"What!" she shouted as her face drained of color.

He held up a hand, hoping to forestall her panic. "I have reason to believe they will reach shore safely, but we do not know where. We must continue to Ferélle and let them find their own way for now."

Her next expression was suffused with anger, and Rezkin was fascinated with how quickly a person could pass from one emotion to the next. "You *can't* leave them! They're all alone—out in the ocean! They don't have any supplies, and they'll be lost. We must go after them!"

He shook his head. "We cannot, Frisha. The ship is badly damaged. We must get to port where we can make repairs. Malcius and Yserria were swept by the current in the other direction."

"How do you know where they are? How do you know they'll reach land?" she said with tears streaming down her face.

"I cannot explain right now, but I do."

"That isn't good enough, Rezkin. Secrets! Always more secrets. I've already lost Palis, and who knows about my parents and Uncle Marcum and Aunt Adelina and Uncle Simeon and Aunt Pethela. They could all be dead. I can't lose Malcius, too!"

"Connovan said he got Marcum and—"

"Connovan? You trust *Connovan* now? You don't know that he's telling the truth."

Rezkin glanced down the short corridor and lowered his voice. "I used the mage relay in Lon Lerésh to check with some of my people. I do not have any information on your parents yet, but the Jebais and Marcums are together, and they are safe for now."

"*Your people*. What people are those?" She stepped forward, poked a finger at his chest, and hissed, "Thieves and murderers? Malcius and Yserria are *good* people, and you will leave them to die in the sea." The door slammed in his face a second time, and Rezkin was left wondering as to the benefits of checking on her.

14

Malcius awoke to his head being torn apart. It throbbed as the ripping subsided. He shivered, his body frozen, yet his skin felt hot. He tensed as the ripping attacked again and then gasped as ice slithered over his flesh. Then, he began sputtering, ejecting the tiny shards of glass that had filled his throat and dried his mouth as they crunched between his teeth. Crusty flakes stuck to his lashes as he peeled his eyes open. Above him was nothing but blue. The ripping returned, and he braced himself. Cold water sloshed over his chest and up his nose, forcing him to roll over as he coughed into the sand. He swallowed hard, hoping to keep from losing whatever might still be lurking in the empty chamber that was his stomach. His fingers gripped the sand, becoming tangled in red seaweed.

"Ow! Let go of my hair," croaked a feminine voice.

Malcius blinked several times before finally recognizing the image in the sand. "Yserria. Are you well?" At least, that was what he tried to say, but it came out sounding like rocks sliding down a ravine.

"I-I am not sure," she said. "Everything hurts."

Yserria sat up and surveyed their surroundings as Malcius examined her for injury. Her long, strawberry hair had come free of its usual braid and was caked in sand. She had a few bruises and cuts, but most looked too old to have been caused by their current predicament.

"You train too hard," he muttered.

"*You* do not train hard enough," she said as she tried, and failed, to stand.

Malcius helped her sit back up and said, "Just give us a minute to recover, will you? Where do you think we are?"

"I don't know," she said as she pulled her legs to her chest, wrapping her arms around her knees. "I am trying to remember what happened."

Malcius rubbed a sore knot on his head. "We were coming out of the cabin when the ship suddenly lurched. I remember grabbing you, but … I don't know what happened after that."

Yserria stared at the ocean. "Do you think the ship sank?

Malcius could not even consider it, so he said nothing.

"Rezkin will come for us," she said.

"Maybe," he said as he examined his clothes. His overshirt was torn and hanging in pieces, but he at least had both his boots.

Yserria began checking her armor, which seemed to be in good condition, and Malcius wished he had been wearing his when the ship was attacked. She said, "He always says that protecting his friends is his first priority."

Malcius discarded the pieces of his torn shirt. "Yes, but I can also see him saying that we should be capable of fending for ourselves and getting back to Cael on our own."

Yserria looked as if she would argue. Then, she simply sighed. "Yes, he would say something like that." She turned to him, her words forestalled when her gaze caught on his chest. "What is that?" she said.

Malcius glanced down and realized, with relief, that he still had the amulet containing her life stone. "That is none of your concern," he said. "If anything, it should have belonged to Palis, but it is now my curse to bear."

"A family heirloom?" she said as her gaze returned to the sea. "I have none but my father's sword," she said as she patted the scabbard at her hip. "The strikers tell me it is too long and heavy for me, but it is all I have of him."

"Well, now you have that, too," he said with a nod.

Yserria reached up to grasp the torque Rezkin had yet to remove. "Why do you think he insists I wear it?"

Malcius gave her a reproachful look. "You know why."

She smirked. "He does not have those kinds of feelings for me."

Her objection seemed a bit too quick to him, but he decided to let it go for the time being. Instead he said, "Where do you think we are?"

She looked at the sky, squinting into the sun, and then back to the ocean. "We are on the south side of the bay. Since the surface current flows east, we could be in eastern Ferélle or Lon Lerésh. Beyond that, your guess is as good as mine."

Malcius stood and brushed some of the sand from his soggy pants. "Alright, we will travel west. If we are in Lon Lerésh, we can cross the River Rhen and catch the next ship to Uthrel in Esk." Malcius stated the plan with confidence, but he was quaking inside. He had no idea how they would manage any of what he had suggested. His doubts were compounded by the ambiguous look she was giving him. "What?"

"There are three echelons between Kielen and Ferélle. We could be in any one of them. It may be a *long* walk. Also, if we are in Ferélle, we will be traveling the wrong direction."

She sighed and then began stalking down the narrow beach that was lined with forest on the landward side. Malcius collected the discarded remains of his shirt. Rezkin had taught him to never leave evidence of his passing behind. He grabbed a long stick from the brush and followed Yserria. Tall palms and flowering bushes offered shade as they walked. Every once in a while, he found an interesting seashell or piece of coral to collect, using a piece of his shirt to wrap the small treasures. He felt comfort in owning *something* even if he knew the shells to be of little or no value.

His stomach grumbled. "We need to find food," he said.

Yserria kept walking.

"Hey! Did you hear me? I said we need to find food."

She spun, opened her arms wide, and said, "Do you see any food here?"

Malcius scowled. "It would be better to look during the day." He pointed to the forest and said, "There might be fruit—coconuts, maybe." Then, he pointed to the ocean. "We might catch fish."

Yserria put one hand on her hip and pointed to the palm tree. "I've been looking. There are no coconuts on these trees." She then pointed to his stick. "Do you know how to spear fish?"

With his blood heating, he snapped, "No, I have never had the pleasure."

She said, "It is not yet midday. We can walk for a while and hope we find civilization. If not, *then* we will start foraging."

"What makes you think *you're* in charge?"

She stalked over to him and flicked his ear.

"Ow! What the—"

"We are likely in Lon Lerésh—where *women* rule. I outrank you by law.

You are not in Ashai anymore, Malcius Jebai. If you try to act your usual boorish self around these women, you will be lucky to be flogged."

"How is being flogged lucky?"

"Compared to the alternatives?" she said. Then, she turned and once again walked away from him.

Malcius grumbled to himself as he followed. Of all the people in the world, he had to be stuck with Yserria. He would even have preferred Reaylin. At least she could have eased the pain in his head. Yserria only made it worse. He knew, though, that she would likely have died if he were not there—not because of any heroics or skill on his part. No, her life was dependent upon him solely because he bore the life stone that carried a piece of her soul, and Rezkin had forbade him from telling her about it. At least if he did, he would have *something* to hold over her head. He mentally slapped himself for the horrible thought. It would be evil to use someone's own soul against them. He would protect the stone with his life, as Rezkin had asked, and she would never know of the favor he had done for her—no, the favor he had done for Palis.

It was just after midday when Yserria turned toward the forest. Malcius did not bother to ask why since it was obvious. The sand was wet all the way into the forest in a strip about a pace wide. She used her sword to hack at the thicker foliage while Malcius ineffectually whacked at greenery with his stick. He had never ventured from a path into the wild. Even as others had explored Cael, he had remained behind to enjoy the meager comforts of the enchanted palace. He realized quickly that cutting through the forest was far more tiring than walking a cultivated path. He also learned not to walk too close to Yserria since she never bothered to hold the branches she had bent out of her way. It took only two good smacks to the face for him to learn that lesson.

As they walked farther into the darkness of the canopy, the muddy soil turned to a trickle of water, and eventually it became a small pool at the base of a rocky cliff.

"It's very cold, and it smells fresh," Yserria said. "I think it's a spring."

"Does that mean it is safe to drink?"

"It will be safer than dying of dehydration."

"Funny," he said. "Perhaps Rezkin should have made you the fool instead of a knight."

"He may be saving that one for you," she said. "What is your position in his court, again? I cannot seem to remember."

Malcius clenched his teeth. "I am his friend."

"Are you?" she said. "You seem awfully bitter for a friend. If you hold that resentment in too long, it will turn to contempt, which leads to betrayal."

"You overstep, *Knight* Yserria. I am still a count of Ashai."

"I doubt that. Caydean has already replaced your household. Your only chance at being anything is with Rezkin. You had best remember that."

"I do not need *you* to remind me of that." Malcius glanced at the pool of fresh water. He fell to his knees and drank deeply, splashing it over his sun-ripened skin. Then, he sat and leaned against a rock. He glanced at Yserria as she attempted to wrestle her mane into a braid. He had never seen her hair down, but it triggered a memory. Palis had been so excited when he had first seen her running down the corridor of the arena, waving that red ribbon. Malcius had not been able to hear his own thoughts over his brother's ramblings.

He plucked a small white flower from a clump by the pool and twirled it between his fingers. "You did not know me as I was. I suppose you never will. Not now. That man died with Palis." Her expression fell at the mention of his brother. "I do not know who I am anymore, but you surely see the worst of me. I cannot help it. In truth, I have not tried. I am not a bad man, though." He looked up and met her gaze. "I carry my honor in my every breath. Rezkin is my king, and I will follow him wherever he leads, even if it is all for naught." His gaze roved the canopy above them. "It is remarkable, really. I cannot imagine that anyone else could have achieved what he has. He keeps so many secrets, he lies and manipulates, yet I still feel confident that he will strive to do everything he has promised. Is it desperation that drives me to feel that way?"

"I think we all do," she said. "Perhaps that is his true power. He gives hope to the desperate. I sometimes feel like he could fix any problem, no matter how big."

"Except death," Malcius said with an edge.

Yserria looked away. She said, "Do you know how to make a snare?"

"No."

"Come, I will show you. We should gather supplies for now and stay here tonight."

"Perhaps we should move away from the water." At her curious look, he said, "In case predators come for a drink."

She nodded. "I did not think of that." She pointed to a crevice at the top of a pile of rubble. "There."

The crevice was small and uncomfortable that night. Yserria had forbade him from even mentioning propriety as they slept back-to-back. Their mutual foul mood had not been made better by the fact that they had not caught anything to eat before they went to sleep. Sometime near dawn, Malcius's stomach had grumbled loud enough to wake him. As he scrambled down the rocks to check the snares, he woke Yserria, which elicited a colorful diatribe. He was filled with glee upon realizing they had managed to catch three of some small mammal he had never before seen.

"What are they?" he asked upon returning to the pond.

She pursed her lips. "I do not know, but they look edible."

"Excellent," he said, rubbing his hands together. "What now?"

Yserria looked at him and shook her head. "You have never dressed an animal."

He grinned. "One time when we were children, Palis and I put our sister's dress on one of our hounds." Yserria frowned at him, and his smile fell. "I doubt that was what you meant, so no."

She drew her sword and laid one of the small animals on a rock.

"That is a little much, is it not?"

"It is the only blade we have, or are you hiding a hunting knife in your pants?"

Malcius grinned again. "We had best not discuss what I am hiding in my pants."

Yserria turned on him with her sword in hand. "What is wrong with you?"

"What do you mean?" he said.

"You never jest. You do not smile. Are you unwell? Did you eat some berries or mushrooms? If you did, I need to know."

Malcius sat back on a rock and sighed. "No. I do feel a bit lightheaded. I am just hungry. I guess I no longer have the energy to be angry."

Yserria shook her head. "I will talk to Rezkin about wearing you out more often."

"You are an evil witch."

For four days, they walked along the beach, each night returning to the forest in search of food or fresh water. By the fifth day, Malcius's clothes were ragged and his face had sprouted a dark beard. Yserria did her best to brush the tangles from her wavy locks with her fingers, but even braiding it was becoming a challenge. Malcius was glad that they could at least bathe in the ocean or streams to remove the stench. Yserria always led the way, and he was forced to watch her back all day, every day.

As he walked along the beach, Malcius wrapped dried sinew around the end of another small twig. He had used a sharp rock to scrape the twig smooth and sharpen the tip, which he had also hardened in the fire that morning. Yserria had challenged him to make a decent weapon, but he had thought to try something else first. After several failures, he was finally making progress. By the time they stopped to eat that afternoon, he had finished his project.

He walked up to Yserria and said, "Here."

She took it from him and stared at it in confusion.

Malcius huffed. "It is a comb."

She turned her gaze toward him but still said nothing.

"For your hair," he said.

"Ah, yes, I can see that. It is a very nice comb. I just—I thought you were making a weapon."

He scratched his scruffy beard. He wanted to say something, but he was not yet sure what it was. Instead, he said, "I did. We are in Lon Lerésh. Image is power. If we run in to anyone, you need to look good."

Yserria frowned. "You sound like Rezkin. You give a gift and then take it away in the next breath."

"What are you talking about? It is yours."

She tilted her head and said, "Thank you, Malcius. I am sure this will be of great advantage should we encounter any opponents."

Malcius nodded once then sat on a rock and started eating the dried meat he had been carrying in a pouch made from his old shirt.

"Are you feeling well?" she said.

"I am tired, hungry, and too hot or too cold. I smell, I itch everywhere, and I think I have fleas—*on my face*. No, I am not well." He glanced at her. "You seem to be handling things."

She pulled her messy tangle over one shoulder and began tugging at the knots with the comb. "I, too, am miserable. We have no choice, though. We must keep going. Complaining does no good."

"I was not complaining. You *asked*."

"I know," she said as she tugged at a particularly nasty tangle. "I was just saying that I feel the same as you."

Malcius paused in his chewing and looked toward the forest. He glanced back at Yserria who was also staring at the forest. "You heard it too?"

She stood, and he followed, moving through the trees as quietly as possible. About a hundred yards in, the trees gave way to a verdant meadow. Yserria crouched behind a clump of thorny bushes, and Malcius ducked down beside her. There, in the clearing, was a gathering of men and women dressed in all manner of finery—and some not dressed so much, Malcius noted. An open tract was at the middle of the gathering, with targets erected at one end and archers in a line at the other. Spectators sat on benches or stood; and, with each *thunk* of an arrow in a target, they erupted in cheers or jeers.

"We should go back to the beach and avoid them," said Yserria.

Malcius was captivated by one person in particular. "Look," he said, pointing to a man standing on the back of a wagon. "They have ale. *Casks* of ale."

"No," she said. "We can go around. There must be a village around here somewhere."

"It could be anywhere," Malcius said. "I want food. *Real* food."

"And what will you use to *buy* this food and ale?" she said.

"We have been shipwrecked. We will tell them who we are, and they will be generous."

"You are delirious."

"All the more reason to get some food," he replied.

Yserria sighed. "I will go ask some questions. I will not draw as much attention."

Malcius looked at her askance. He waved toward the people and said, "How many warrior women do you see out there? You will draw *all* the attention."

She looked at him quizzically and then dropped her gaze to his chest. She turned away, surveying at the crowd as she muttered. "Not as much as you will get."

He felt his hackles rise and crossed his arms. "What is that supposed to mean?"

She sighed and looked at him. "You will not be dissuaded, will you?"

"No, I am going out there to see if we can get some help."

Narrowing her eyes, she said, "Fine, but you need to stay behind me—and say nothing."

Malcius's blood felt as if it would boil over. "Watch yourself, *knight*. You let this land go to your head."

Yserria quickly knotted her fiery hair atop her head, securing it with the comb he had made her. She said, "In this land, mine is the one that matters." Then, she began skirting the crowd until they were behind the majority of the spectators. They went unnoticed at first, but as soon as they entered the crowd, people began to stare. Malcius started to wonder if she had been right, but his grumbling stomach was persistent.

Yserria stopped in front of a young woman and started jabbering in Leréshi. The woman wore what looked like a single length of grey fabric wrapped around her body, leaving her shins, arms, and shoulders exposed, and a green ribbon was braided through her hair. Upon arrival, Malcius had noticed others with ribbons, ribbons like Celise wore. Now that he was closer, he realized that nearly *everyone* wore a ribbon, even the men, and all in the same place at their temples.

As Yserria stood yammering with the other woman, he noticed that several women who had moved closer were eyeing his hair and openly perusing his body. Some of the men did the same to Yserria, while others refused to turn her direction, only glancing out of the corners of their eyes. Malcius had no idea what was happening. Their behavior made no sense. These Leréshi were crazy.

Finally, Yserria turned to him. "We are near the town of Specra at the western border of the Third Echelon, which is bounded by the River Rhen to the east. We need only travel through one echelon to get to Ferélle."

"Thank the Maker," Malcius said. "How do we get some food?"

Yserria glanced around and shook her head. "I think we had better go now."

"*Why*? These people seem okay. No one and no *thing* has attacked us. It is a better welcome than we had in Gendishen."

"Too late," she said, gritting her teeth.

Malcius followed her gaze to where the crowd was parting to permit a woman who wore a long skirt but had the tiniest scrap of cloth covering her breasts. She was flanked by two large men in armor, each bearing a sword at his hip. "Who is she?"

"That is the echelon," said Yserria. "This archery competition is part of the celebration for her visit." She gave him a pointed look and said, "She is the reason I wanted to leave."

The echelon stopped in front of them, and everyone in the crowd crossed their arms in front of their faces, touching their foreheads to their wrists. Malcius watched as Yserria stepped in front of him. She straightened her back, lifted her chin, and rested her hand on her sword hilt. Malcius was inundated with mixed feelings. He was angry that she thought he needed protecting and ashamed that she might be right. Under Rezkin and the strikers' tutelage, he had become an excellent swordsman, but Yserria was still far better. A lot of people were at the gathering, and they were giving him an undue amount of attention, especially considering his present state.

Yserria stood her ground before the echelon. She could show no weakness.

The echelon, who was nearly a head shorter than she, stopped in front of Yserria. She peered around Yserria to get a look at Malcius and smirked. She returned her attention to Yserria. "*I am Deshari Brigalsi, Third Echelon. Who are you, and why have you interrupted our festivities?*"

Yserria said, "*I am Yserria Rey, Knight of Cael.*"

"*Is that so? I have heard of the would-be Ashaiian king's female knight.*"

"Your *king,*" said Yserria.

Deshari shrugged. "*He is only king of the military.*" She motioned to the guards that had flanked them. "*These are my private retainers.*" With a lift of her chin toward Malcius, she said, "*Who is he? Did you take his sword from him? Did he displease you?*"

"*He is none of your concern. Our ship was attacked at sea. He and I were thrown overboard and swept away in the current. We made it to shore five days east of here. We are trying to get back to Cael. Will you assist us? The king will be generous in his gratitude.*"

Deshari tilted her head and smirked. "*I understand that you have sworn fealty to a* man. *Do you have the authority to offer his money?*"

The woman's syrupy, snide tone grated on Yserria's nerves. Not knowing if it was true, she said, "*He will honor any deal I make.*"

Deshari's gaze dropped to the torque around Yserria's neck. "*Yes, perhaps he will, but we cannot know for sure.*" She abruptly straightened and waved a dismissive hand. "*I have decided. You may go, but I want* him."

Yserria clenched her jaw. "*You cannot have him.*"

"Oh? I heard that you had not claimed a man. He does not wear the ribbon; therefore, I am free to claim him, which I do."

Yserria glanced back at Malcius. "She has claimed you. Do you accept?"

"What? No!"

She schooled her face and turned back to the echelon. "*He does not accept your claim.*" She inwardly screamed as she said, "*I challenge you for him.*"

Deshari smirked again. "*Does he accept yours*?"

"*No*," Yserria said firmly.

"*It is a pity you do not have a champion. He will come with me now.*"

Yserria said, "*I need no champion. I fight my own challenges.*"

A wave of chatter surged through the crowd. The woman's face soured, and she glanced at Yserria's sword. "*Are you the woman who fought in the fifth tier of the King's Tournament?*"

"*The same*," said Yserria.

Deshari glanced back toward the archery targets. "*Then I choose a challenge with the bow. We, in the Third Echelon, are hunters. This is Gemsbrick, my third consort,*" she said as she raised a hand toward the man on her left. "*He is our best archer. He will defend my claim*."

Yserria's gaze flicked to the targets and back to the woman. With disgust, she said, "*You already have three consorts, yet you seek another. You are not only poor in sensibility but also in decorum.*"

With a shrug, Deshari said, "*It is not forbidden. As Third Echelon, I find that my needs are greater than those of lesser matrianeras*."

"*Then you are weak,*" said Yserria. The woman's lips twisted, but she did not take the bait. Having failed to shame the woman out of the challenge, Yserria said, "*You underestimate my resolve and my abilities, Echelon. I have no consorts because I need none to bolster my strength.*"

"*No, you expect your* king *to pay your debts and fight your battles*."

"*On the contrary,*" Yserria said as she raised her voice and gazed over the crowd. "*I am a Knight of Cael. I serve my king by choice. I fight* his *battles, and I claim the spoils on his behalf. I am a weapon at his side, a warrior at his call. My strength multiplies his strength. Through me, you will witness the might of Cael.*" She turned toward the echelon. "*I accept your terms, Echelon, and I challenge you for your seat*."

Deshari's smile slipped. She said, "*I see. We shall discuss the terms of the challenge again. First, you must rest and eat. You will be my guests. Let no one claim that I took advantage of your dire circumstances.*"

"*No,*" Yserria said with all the sarcasm she could muster, "*I am sure no one will say that.*"

Deshari abruptly turned and stalked toward the tents at the other end of the field, trailed by her entourage. Yserria and Malcius were *encouraged* to follow by the guards at their backs.

Malcius tugged at her sleeve. "Wha—"

"Not now," she hissed.

When they reached the encampment, they were escorted to a tent where several servants were scurrying out with what were presumably someone else's personal effects. They both stood in the middle of the tent as people scrambled in and out with pitchers, trays of food, and a couple of small mounds of garments. The whirlwind abruptly ceased when everyone left without having spoken a word to them. Malcius rushed to the table and began stuffing food into his mouth, without concern for etiquette, while Yserria paced over the colorful carpet that covered the grass.

After a few minutes, Malcius paused and said, "Are you not tired of walking? Sit and eat."

She glanced at him and continued her pacing.

"What is wrong with you?" he said.

She strode over to the table and leaned over him. "This is *your* fault," she said, trying to keep her voice down. "You wouldn't stay in the forest. You *had* to come looking for luxuries."

"*Luxuries*? I was starving! We have barely eaten in *five days*."

Yserria eyed the food on the table below her. The savory smell finally overcame her frustration, and she sat.

"Why are you so upset?" said Malcius. "They brought us here and fed us."

Yserria bit into a sweet fruit she had never before tasted and said, "This food comes at a cost."

Malcius looked at the food with suspicion and then said, "What cost?"

"The echelon has claimed you."

Malcius shook his head. "I rejected her claim."

"It does not matter. You are hers."

"Why would she do that?" he said.

Yserria did not look at him as she said, "An attractive, young, virile man with a good sword arm does not go unclaimed in Lon Lerésh."

Malcius started to speak and then paused. "You think I am attractive?"

Yserria rolled her eyes. "She does not know you as I do."

He scowled at her. "What are we going to do? Can we sneak out of here?" He eyed the food. "*After* we eat?"

Yserria sighed. "I challenged her for you."

Malcius abruptly stood. "You cannot claim me!"

"I don't *want* you!" she shouted back. "It means nothing between us. I told her you rejected the claim, which means you would not fight on my behalf. Normally, that would be a problem for a woman without a champion, but I can fight for myself."

"So, it means nothing? We do not have to—um—like Rezkin had to—you know …"

"Not unless you *accept* the claim," she growled, "so do *not* accept it."

"That will not be a problem," he muttered as he sat again. "So, you defeat her champion and I am free, right?"

"No, it is not so easy. I challenged *her*, which means she gets to set the conditions for the challenge. She knows I am a swordswoman, so she chose archery."

Malcius groaned. "Please tell me you know how to use a bow."

"My skills are … acceptable." With a sigh, she added, "The echelon's champion is a master archer. I cannot beat him."

"Then, I am stuck here!" he cried.

"I am *trying* to prevent that. As you pointed out before, image is everything. I took Rezkin's example and made her look weak in front of her people. Then, I challenged her for her seat as echelon."

"You *what*? Why would you do that when you know you cannot *win*?"

"Because the seat of an echelon cannot be won through a simple test of bowmanship. She will have to come up with a new challenge—something more difficult."

"And I am dependent on *you* to win this mysterious, difficult challenge," he said. Malcius grabbed a tankard of ale and emptied its contents. A minute later, he said, "I thought the Leréshi could not prevent a foreigner from leaving, even if he was claimed."

"That is normally true, but we did not get permission to enter the Third Echelon. We are trespassing. She could have us arrested and thrown in the dungeon if she wanted. This torque and the fact that I am a member of House Rey, which currently serves on the queen's council, are probably all that is preventing her from doing so."

Malcius reached for a stack of flatbread and scooped some kind of beige paste onto a dish. "You never told me your family was Leréshi nobility."

"It doesn't work that way here," she said. "My family's house was raised after we visited Kielen because the queen was worried that I would steal her throne."

"Could you?"

She tugged at the torque around her neck. "I probably have the power right now, but it would be suicide. No one lives long in that position, but Queen Erisial has devised a devious plan that might actually work for a while."

A servant ducked into the tent and said, "*The challenge is set for three days hence.*"

Yserria looked at Malcius. "Three days."

15

The air in front of him shimmered like water filled with swirling colors. The colors suddenly merged into jagged lines of sharp, white light, as if it were shining from between the cracks of a broken mirror. The pieces between them began to dissolve, and then he was standing in a luminescent passage. Beyond the walls were fragments of landscapes, as if many worlds had broken apart, the remnants held aloft in smoky clouds. Between the clouds was a wash of stars and colorful dust. As he turned his head, the images shifted to reveal new worlds, each completely unlike the others.

His nerves were on edge as he trod upon the translucent path. He turned, and directly in front of him was a black void. As he stood waiting, a light erupted at its center. It wrapped around him and drew him into the darkness. Then, he was staring at a mirrored wall. Silver eyes stared back at him. The image was not his own.

Rezkin woke to the smell of horse and the ring of a hammer against an anvil. He rolled over and caught himself just before he fell out of the loft. Shaking his groggy head, he tried to remember the face he had seen in the mirror, but all he recalled were silver eyes. Although he had apparently slept deeply, he felt drained. He was also famished. After gathering his pack, he slipped out of the barn and made his way to the road without drawing notice from the farm's few inhabitants. The land was located at the city's edge, so he had not far to go.

Rezkin was glad to finally be alone. Rather than arguing with his companions over his decision, he had simply disappeared. They would be upset, but at least he had done them the courtesy of leaving a note. A few would attempt to follow him, he knew, but he was already far ahead. Each day of his trek, he had passed lines of slaves working in the fields and repairing or paving the roads. Most of the men and women were prisoners. Some had probably been stolen and sold illegally. More than a few were likely refugees, driven from their homes by war, disease, or famine, people like his own.

Bromivah was an old city, older than any in Ashai. The buildings reflected the architecture of a bygone age—one in which artistry and the old beliefs held supreme. Fairies, dragons, gnomes, and nymphs graced the mantles, balustrades, and rooftops. Rezkin thought they glorified the mythical creatures, even honored them, while the more modern pieces tended to idolize the knights who destroyed them. The sharp rooftops and abundance of towers gave the city a vicious appearance, as if it were a gaping maw ready to consume all who entered.

He walked through the open city gates that were manned only at night. The streets were paved, and most of the buildings were constructed of the same grey stone. Some had slate rooves, while others were thatched, but every single one of them had a pole atop bearing a glowing orb. The official reason for the orbs was to allow mages to communicate with each other from anywhere in the city. The orbs also happened to provide the authorities with a method of citywide surveillance, but most of the mundanes were oblivious to that fact.

Rezkin stopped at a stall to purchase a meal and then purchased another. By the time he reached Esyojo Castle, his head had cleared, but he felt lethargic and was still hungry. It was not the first time he had noticed the decrease in his energy since leaving Cael, but only now had it truly begun to concern him. Still, he had fought through worse, and he had a task to complete.

The guards around Esyojo Castle were alert, which was not a surprise. Bromivah was a rough city, and Ferélli officials were always wary of the Adana'Ro. Moldovan would likely be concerned about Adana'Ro stealing the sword back, so it was unlikely he told anyone else where he had stashed it. Rezkin would have to confront the king directly. Given recent revelations, it was sure to be an interesting meeting.

He did not change into the garb of Dark Tidings or the Raven. He did not don the articles of court or those of a king. Rezkin slinked through the castle in his travel disguise—a vagabond. He wore a few armor plates hidden beneath his tunic, and his pack and swords were hidden in an abandoned hovel inside the city that he had passed en route to the castle. His homespun clothes were torn or patched in multiple places, his hair hung loose, and a couple of days' worth of stubble graced his jawline. He needed to make a good impression after all.

Three corridors led to the throne room, one to the main entrance, and two on either side with access to receiving rooms. The corridor and receiving room to the left of the throne room provided passage from the dungeon tower. Those on the right of the throne room were somewhat more comfortable since they were for guests and witnesses. Unsurprisingly, the passage from the dungeon had the least amount of security. Rezkin *removed* the two guards blocking his way into the receiving chamber and then the next two who were waiting within. He dragged the four unconscious men into a dark alcove beneath the tower stairs and left them gagged and bound together. Then, he proceeded through the final doorway.

Moldovan's throne room was grandiose. Like the rest of Bromivah, it was constructed of grey stone and had no windows. It was a dark cavern, the decorative flourishes appearing as fae creatures and monsters dwelling amongst stalactites. Candles or mage lights flickered among them casting eerie shadows in every direction. The room was also devoid of life, save for the guards that stood at attention every five feet along each side of the hall. Moldovan did not hold court. No one entered his throne room without permission, which few received. In fact, most prayed to their gods that they would never see its macabre decor. The chamber's primary function was as a place of conviction and execution, as evidenced by the star-like splay of drainage grooves that radiated from its center into narrow troughs lining the perimeter. On execution day, the outer walls of the castle were literally bathed in blood. Esyojo Castle was the only colorful building in Bromivah.

Rezkin took a moment to focus his *will* and then opened the door enough to permit his entrance. He moved with the shadows around the back of the hall toward the throne and then slithered into the seat. There, he entered a waking meditative state, one in which he split his focus so that his unconscious mind was cognizant of his surroundings, while his conscious mind maintained an air of nonexistence. Then, he waited. The stone around his neck heated, and his drowsiness returned, but preventing the guards in the hall from seeing him became easier. They were not aware of it, but they were becoming accustomed to his presence. He hoped Moldovan appeared before the shift change.

From where he sat, Rezkin realized that every single pair of eyes amongst the mythical creatures was directed at the throne, as if in challenge or judgment. Knowing, now, that at least some of those creatures were not mere fantasies, he felt it a heavy weight to bear. Under their watchful gazes, he had sunk into the swirling colors that suffused the recesses of his mind when the king finally came tromping into the hall. As he strode across the stones, Moldovan brooded, staring at the ground, his arms clasped behind his back, his plush, regal robe swaying around his legs. He made it halfway through the room before he finally glanced up to notice that someone was sitting in his throne. He stopped short and then spun to look at the twelve guards that lined the hall.

"What is this?" he shouted.

The guards shifted as one to see what had disturbed their king. As soon as they saw the intruder, they rushed to surround Moldovan in a ring of swords and spears. Despite their prompt reaction, Moldovan was not satisfied with their blatant lack of awareness. His aged face contorted, and his eyes bulged as he fumed.

"A man is sitting in my throne, and you all just stand there! A filthy beggar —" His rant abruptly ceased, and he turned to look more closely at the intruder. He stepped to the foot of the dais, his guards shuffling around him. Narrowing his eyes, he hissed, "*You*. I know who you are."

Rezkin lounged in the throne with his leg thrown over one of the gilded arms. He rolled his eyes and said, "I would be disappointed if you did not."

"You managed to invade my castle and claim my throne while a dozen of my guards stood here doing nothing, all the while dressed like *that*?" The man took a deep breath and lifted his chin. "I am impressed. You will do well."

"What do you want, Moldovan?" Rezkin said with feigned apathy.

"Should I not be the one to ask you?" He waved his arm around the room. "*You* are the invader."

Rezkin sat up and pretended to admire the gilding on the throne as he spoke. "You know why I am here. You have known for months that I seek the Sword of Eyre. The fact that you insisted I come all this way to retrieve it means you want something."

Moldovan's aged voice cracked as he laughed. "What if I do not intend to give it to you?"

Rezkin shrugged and plucked a stray thread in the seat cushion. "I can take the sword, or I can take your kingdom and *then* take the sword. The choice is yours."

Moldovan grinned. "At least we are in agreement, then."

Rezkin was confused and a little concerned by the king's statement, but rather than show his weakness, he sighed in boredom.

"Leave us," Moldovan said to the guards.

"Your Majesty?" said the guard nearest the throne.

"I said go!"

The guards slowly filed out of the chamber, several glancing back as if to check that their king had not gone mad. Once the doors were closed, Moldovan ascended the steps. He stopped in front of the throne and looked down on Rezkin. He said, "You may drop the pretense. I know you are a cunning and devious man."

Rezkin rose and stared back at the man, peering down into eyes gone pale with age.

Moldovan said, "It is strange to see that face looking back at me. You are your father's son, no doubt, but I would recognize my blood anywhere." He shook his head. "I have met Caydean twice, once as a boy and again as a young man. He was not like his father. He had a darkness in his gaze. I see that same darkness in you. The darkness, I can appreciate. An effective king needs a strong hand and a cold heart. The people will fear you for your ruthlessness and love you for your strength. Make no mistake, they are animals—all of them. They go where you guide them, but if you are weak, they will stray."

Moldovan's gaze became distant, foggy, and confused, as if he were lost. He glanced at Rezkin, as if seeing him for the first time. "Bordran, have you come to claim my daughter?"

Rezkin tilted his head. Just as quickly as the man's mind had left, it returned. Moldovan continued as if he had never stopped. "Thresson was too much like his father. Weak. Unable to do what was necessary. At least, that is what I thought. The fact that *you* are here makes me rethink my opinion of Bordran. He was shrewder than I believed. I always suspected you had survived. Everyone said it was the Ashaiian royal curse, the death of every third child. I *knew*, though. If any blood were strong enough to break the curse, it would be that of Esyojo. I understand, now, why Bordran hid you away. Darkness was not all that resided in Caydean. In him, I saw madness."

Moldovan's gaze turned toward the flickering forms on the walls. "Lecillia was a light amongst these shadows. I had thought to keep her here. I would have sent Merenia in her stead but for Ondoro's insistence. He was a hard man, a worthy king of Ashai. Perhaps you are more like him than your father …" Again, Moldovan's attention drifted for a moment before he continued. "Ondoro, his wife Eyalana and brother Mandrite; my wife Belemnia, sister Erania, and brother Jonish—they are all dead now, have been for some time. I am the last." He looked back to Rezkin. "What of my daughter? I have heard nothing of her in many months. Does Lecillia live?"

Rezkin tilted his head. "She is torn by recent events but seems to be in good health. She now resides in my domain."

Moldovan nodded. "That is good. Perhaps … perhaps I may see her one last time."

Rezkin said, "Give me the Sword of Eyre, and I will make that happen."

His expression hardening, Moldovan pushed past Rezkin and sat in his throne. "Yes, that. You have gained a reputation as someone who can get things done and has no compunctions. You are now a legitimate monarch, *First King of Lon Lerésh.* Never did I think to see the day one of those women took a *husband.*"

Rezkin said nothing, and Moldovan smirked at him knowingly. "I am prepared to recognize your claim to Ashai *and* Cael, and I will give you that worthless sword, but you must first do something for me. You must kill my nephew Boulis and claim the throne."

Rezkin paused as he replayed the words in his mind. "You want me to claim your throne?"

"I am sure it has not escaped your notice that my mind is not as sharp as it once was. It is time for me to step down. Does that surprise you?"

It did. Moldovan seemed the kind of king who would insist on being buried with his throne. Rezkin said nothing, though, and waited for Moldovan to continue, which he did after a moment.

"Ferélle needs a strong king, one who can stand against the likes of the Adana'Ro. I have become a liability, and I will not see this kingdom, which I have ruled over for nearly eighty years, fall into ruin. Bordran was blessed with three sons, while I was cursed to have only two daughters. Merenia, passed away several years ago. Her son Gereshy was killed at the Battle of Ushwick. It has always been my opinion that Boulis was responsible, either by intention or negligence. Gereshy died without an heir, so Boulis will claim the throne upon my death. It is the reason I have refused to die. Boulis cannot be trusted to manage the purse of a miser, much less the kingdom's coffers. Thanks to you, an Esyojo will continue to sit upon the throne. The line will not die with me."

"I cannot sit upon your throne, Moldovan. I already lay claim to three others."

Moldovan stood and faced Rezkin, a light of passion in his aged gaze. "Precisely," he said. "*You* are no king. You are an *emperor*—the first emperor to rule multiple kingdoms on the Souelian. *My* grandson, a King of Ferélle, Emperor of—what will you call your empire?"

Rezkin backed away and searched the dancing shadows. He said, "It was never my intention to create an empire."

Moldovan scoffed. "You expect me to believe that? Prince Nyan was incensed that you stole his bride. When his father refused to hold Ionius accountable, Nyan organized a coup. He has taken half the Jerean army to march on Channería. Since you left, Serret has descended into civil war—something to do with this infamous Raven, who has acquired enough power in Ashai to make things difficult on Caydean and just so happens to support *your* claim to the Ashaiian throne. You have somehow convinced the Leréshi to name you king and already have deals with Ionius and Privoth to recognize you as king of the mysterious Kingdom of Cael. Even a fool could see what you are doing."

Rezkin said, "I have only done what needed to be done."

"Which is why you will succeed in the task I have set before you. It must be you. The line of succession is clear. When Caydean took the oaths that secured him the Ashaiian throne, he was forced to relinquish his claim to Ferélle. Thresson is as good as dead. You are next in line. Boulis threatens your claim. He is your enemy. You will kill him and claim your rightful place as king and emperor."

Rezkin said, "You can keep the kingdom. I only want the sword."

Moldovan grinned. "I am an old man. I have nothing left to lose. I can take the sword with me to the grave. For you, it is all or nothing,"

"First King of Lon Lerésh."

"He is *what*?" said Tieran, his voice echoing through the warehouse.

"That is the latest news," said Captain Jimson. "Rezkin is First King of Lon Lerésh."

"*Did he kill the queen*?" said Tieran.

Jimson cleared his throat. "No, Your Grace, he married her."

Tieran stared at the captain, his heart racing, his mouth hanging open. "That—I cannot—What did you say?"

"It is all over Uthrel," said Jimson. "Every sailor, every merchant, every crier and relay worker—they all say the same. Queen Erisial claimed him as her *husband* and gave him the Leréshi army and navy."

Tieran smacked his forehead. "He is infuriating! He cannot just go and marry the Leréshi queen! What of Cael? What of Ashai? What of *Frisha*?"

"Ah, well, there is no talk of Frisha, Your Grace."

"Will you please stop calling me that? That is what people call my father. You may continue to call me Lord Tieran. No, we have been through enough together, you may call me Tieran, if you prefer."

Jimson shifted. "Yes, Your Grace.

Tieran huffed and kicked a chunk of broken pallet. "What do titles mean anymore? Everyone has gone insane. No one *marries* the Leréshi queen!" He hung his head and then said, "Is there news of anyone else?"

"Only a bit of talk about a female knight of Cael. Nothing we do not already know."

An inkling of hope entered his mind. "Does he recognize the marriage?"

"No one seems to know for sure," said Jimson.

"Well, let us pray to the Maker that he does not."

Beside him, Mage Morgessa said, "I did not think you were much for praying."

Tieran said, "If anyone can force a prayer, it is my cousin. Where is he now?"

"That is also a mystery," said Jimson.

Tieran growled. "We need a relay! This is archaic. Our news is weeks old, at best." He turned to Mage Morgessa. "Are you sure that none of you has the requisite knowledge or power to create one?"

She gave him a disparaging look. "Lord Tieran, we have discussed this a dozen times. King Rezkin brought the supplies from Serret, but none of us knows how to construct one. Since he knew what items were necessary, he is our best bet."

Tieran ran his hands down his face. "If he knows, then why did he not build it?"

"Well, because he is not a mage," she said.

This time he gave her the dubious look.

She raised her hands and said, "I am only telling you what he told me."

Tieran noticed an anxious young man hovering a few paces behind the mage. He recognized the young man as one of Frisha's assistants, but he could not remember his name. "You. What do you want?"

The assistant bowed low and then said, "Your Grace, Trademaster Moyl requests your signature on the final proposals for the Aplin wine deal with the merchant's guild in Uthrel."

Tieran sighed and waved a hand at the young assistant as he looked at Jimson. "See? Frisha was supposed to be taking care of this. It was *her* idea, and she is more adept in trade regulations than she claims." His voice rose as his frustration mounted. "But she ran off to be with *Rezkin*, and *he* married the *Leréshi Queen*!"

A woman was suddenly at his other side. He had not seen her approach. "Your Grace," said Lady Gadderand. "I am quite good with trade. I have run my house's affairs for some time since my dear husband passed away. I would be happy to assist—"

Tieran smiled, but he felt no relief in her offer. "Thank you, Lady Gadderand, but that is not necessary. I will handle it."

The woman barely flinched from the rejection, which only made him more suspicious. She said, "It is most considerate of you to see to these matters, which are far below your station, in Lady Frisha's stead. It did surprise me when I heard she had gone after him. I mean, she had expressed her concerns—"

"You spoke with her," said Tieran.

"Oh yes, at length. She was very upset and confused. I tried to offer counsel, but she would not be reasoned with. I cannot imagine what might have made her think to follow him." She smiled anxiously as she glanced at the others. "Oh, I apologize. My concern for Lady Frisha overtook my sense for a moment. I should not speak of such things in public. Please do keep me in mind if you decide you have more important matters to which you must attend." Before Tieran could respond, she said, "Did I hear you say that King Rezkin is wed?"

~

Tam dozed with his back pressed against the hull. Scant light streamed in from the gaps in the planks above, so he could not see the men and women who shared his fate. He could smell them, though. He, and probably everyone else, had long since given up on dignity. There were no privy breaks. Once a day, they were forced to muck their own filth and carry it up to the deck where it was thrown overboard. In the weeks, or months, he had been on the ship, he had considered following the waste into the sea on several occasions. Others had apparently had the same idea, though, and after the first few jumped, the slavers started chaining them in pairs. Apparently, it was much harder to convince a stranger to end his life at the same time as you.

While they were below deck, the chain that linked him to his partner by shackles around their necks, was fed through a loop on the hull. It was impossible to lie down, but they realized that if one of them stood, the other could lean forward enough to hold his head in his hands while resting his elbows on his knees. The major disadvantage was that if the man standing fell over or passed out, the other would be yanked rather hard by the throat. One man had actually died from a crushed airway, and Tam had chided himself for his envy. In truth, he did not want to die, only he was not sure he could stand living any longer. His head throbbed almost constantly, and he suffered from several nosebleeds per day. He noticed, though, that when he sat in the dark with no distractions, his mind settled to give him enough relief to feel his hunger and thirst. Still, he knew that without the help of the healers that he had been promised, he was doomed to a painful demise.

"*I think we've stopped*," said his partner, Uthey. Uthey had been a mercenary from Gendishen. His company had been wiped out by drauglics, and the slavers had discovered him unconscious on the side of the road. They had decided to capitalize on the find.

Tam roused from his half-dream state. "*Stopped*?" The hull struck something. The ship rocked, and then it struck again.

"*That sounds like a dock*," said Uthey.

Since Uthey was now sitting up, Tam could sit on the bench. "*I am filled with both dread and relief. Where do you think they took us*?"

"*Couldn't say. I lost track of the days. Maybe the Isle of Sand.*"

"*It'll be harder to escape from an island*," said Tam.

Uthey chuckled. "*You think to escape? You'll be dead before you take three steps as a free man.*"

"*I'm not without skills.*"

"*And neither are they. If you decide to escape, do it when I am not tied to your neck.*"

Tam coughed, feeling a tickle at the back of his throat that he knew was blood, since he did not have enough saliva to wet his tongue. He croaked, "*You can die a slave if you want, but someone will come for me.*"

"*Who? Who will come for you? These men take people no one'll miss. If they took you, it's because you were alone.*"

"*I was alone for a reason. My people will come for me.*"

"*Even if they do, they'll not find you. It's not as if the slavers record names and log where you go. If anyone has the will to track you down, the slavers'll know your value. Your friends'll have to pay a fortune to get you back. I doubt you're worth it.*"

Tam tried to lick the salt from his lips, but his dry tongue only scraped against the cracks. He said, "*I am not you.*"

"*No, you are delusional. At least I accept my fate. I could've been torn apart by those lizard monsters, but instead I'll die at the hands of men.*"

"*They are monsters, too,*" said Tam.

"*True, but they're monsters with the keys,*" said Uthey with a shake of his chains.

The grate over their heads was pulled back, and a dark silhouette blocked the sun.

"*Yer comin' out now,*" said the man over their heads. "*Give us any trouble, and we'll make sure ya don't die quickly.*"

"*Monsters,*" Tam muttered.

Yserria blinked as the wind whipped across her face. She looked up at the overcast sky, sighed heavily, and then met the woman's gaze. "No."

"But he is a good man, and he speaks Ashaiian. You see? I have taught him. He even has a touch of the *talent*."

"I have no desire to claim your son, Matrianera Wolshina."

Wolshina clasped her hands before her. "I have saved for this day. I will make you a generous offer."

Malcius said, "Is she offering to pay you to claim her son?"

Yserria scowled at him. "It is a dowry."

The woman nodded as she pointed to a young man hovering at the edge the encampment. "He is handsome and strong."

Yserria could not deny the truth of the woman's words. The man was tall with broad shoulders that supported a well-defined upper body, but he kept his hands in his pockets as he hung his head, only glancing at them occasionally. Looking back at the woman, Yserria said, "Why is he over there? Does he not wish to be claimed?"

The woman fervently shook her head. "No, no! He likes you very much. He is shy. He has difficulty meeting new people, especially a matria of your standing—or is it matrianera?"

Yserria crossed her arms. "It is neither. I am a Knight of Cael, and I have no intention of claiming anyone."

The woman glanced at Malcius. "But, did you not challenge the echelon for this one?"

Yserria pursed her lips. "Yes, but only because she forced my hand."

"Thanks for that," Malcius muttered. "You were perfectly willing to claim Palis."

Yserria rounded on him. "Palis was worth claiming!"

Malcius clamped his mouth shut, glanced at the matrianera, and then stalked off toward the tent. Yserria's blood was boiling. She was angry but not at Malcius. She should not have been so rude to him. She knew he was mourning Palis more than she, but he had been haranguing her ever since Palis's death, and she was tired of the incessant guilt.

Wolshina hesitantly said, "This Palis is another consort?"

As she watched Malcius's retreating form, Yserria replied, "Palis was his brother. He died protecting me."

Wolshina glanced at her son. She bit her lip and said, "If you become echelon, will you stay?"

"No, I serve the king as a member of his royal guard. I go where he goes."

"Then, you will need more protection and someone to keep your house." The woman nodded in the direction Malcius had gone. "I do not think he will do this for you."

"I am capable of taking care of myself," said Yserria.

The woman smiled. "I am sure you are, but everyone needs support." She moved a little closer and lowered her voice. "My son, he is strong and a hard worker, but … he is not aggressive. He is not a fighter. This is why I think you will be a good match. You do not need a fighter." Her gaze flicked to the other people who stared out of curiosity but were respectful enough to keep their distance during *negotiations*. "If he stays here, someone will wish to claim him for champion. He will lose, and he will get killed. Please, I know you are at war, but he will be safer with you than he will be here."

Yserria schooled her features out of respect for the mother's plight. "I am sorry for your troubles, but I will not be guilted into making a claim. This is the fourth time someone has approached me with such a request."

With another pensive glance toward her son, Wolshina said, "I will release him to serve in your household. You need not claim him. Just take him with you." She subtly crossed her wrists in front of her, a pleading gesture. "Please, I will give you his dowry for his care. He will work hard to earn the rest."

Yserria frowned and pointed at the man, causing him to glance her way. Their gazes met, and he immediately dropped his head. She said to Wolshina, "As you said, he is a handsome, strong man. He could easily be claimed as consort in a number of houses even if only to breed and care for the young. Why would he wish to become a servant?"

"Of course, he would prefer to be claimed," she said, "but he would rather become a servant than a champion. Three matrias have already made offers. All three believe he can be trained for combat. He dreads the thought. I beseech you. I know he is only a son, but I love him as if he were my daughter. I wish for him to be happy."

Again, Yserria looked at the shy, young man with golden hair and tanned skin stretched over taut muscle. "A servant?"

"Yes, a servant," the woman said hopefully.

"What is his name?"

"His name is Japa. He is twenty-six years old, and he has been formally educated. His skills are in farming and irrigation. He does not have enough *talent* to be a full mage, but his affinities are for water and earth."

Yserria sighed. "Very well. *If* I win my challenge, I will take Japa, as a servant *only*."

Tears welled in Wolshina's eyes, but Yserria could not tell if they were born of joy or sorrow. The woman grabbed her hands and said, "Thank you! You will not regret this, Knight Yserria. Would you like to meet him?"

Yserria glanced at Japa. "Not now. I must remain focused. Should I win the challenge, there will be plenty of time later. Besides, I think you will need time to convince your son."

"Oh yes, but he will be pleased." The woman crossed her arms and pressed her forehead to her wrists as she backed away. "We will come to you after your victory. Thank you, again."

Yserria returned to the tent she begrudgingly shared with Malcius. Ironically, she had fought to keep him with her. The echelon had tried to make him join her party, but Yserria had insisted he stay with her until the challenge was resolved. The echelon acquiesced, and Yserria wondered if the woman regretted making the claim in the first place. The woman could no longer back out, though, without giving up her seat as echelon.

As she entered the tent, Malcius said, "Well, do you have *another* consort? Are you collecting men, now, like the rest of these Leréshis?"

Yserria lifted her chin. "We have come to an arrangement."

"*Seriously*? You are going to buy that woman's son to-to what? Be your play thing?"

"Lord Malcius!" Her indignation felt less feigned than she had anticipated. In a haughty tone, she said, "That is completely inappropriate. Where is your decorum? Since you are as close to family as I have here, I would expect you to defend my honor, rather than besmirch it."

Malcius straightened as if remembering himself. "I—You are right. That was uncalled for. I apologize."

Yserria gave him a cross nod, then smirked. "Japa is to become my servant, not my consort." She looked at him sweetly and batted her lashes. "Only *you* have that privilege."

Malcius clenched his jaw and said, "I hate this place. You are supposed to meet this challenge tomorrow. Have they told you what it will be? Are they not required to give you time to prepare?"

Yserria's smile fell as her anxiety surged. Her blood soured, her muscles tensed, and her stomach churned. "It is to be a battle."

Malcius frowned. "What kind of battle?"

"A real battle," Yserria said. "We are in the Third Echelon. The Fourth Echelon is led by Orina Goldren, who had already challenged Echelon Deshari for the marshland along the border. Echelon Orina has agreed to split her forces and attack from two equivalent positions. Echelon Deshari's champion will lead his forces against one, and I will lead mine against the other. The winner will be whichever of us is successful in defeating Echelon Orina's forces—or whichever takes fewer losses, if that be the case."

Malcius looked at her in disbelief. "That is absurd. Echelon Orina is Echelon Deshari's enemy. Why would she agree to that?"

Yserria was surprised by his reaction. "Because it is a challenge. Actually, it is three challenges being resolved at once. The echelons often battle. It keeps their troops strong and experienced. They do not go to battle for the sake of destroying each other's forces but to determine a winner."

"You are to fight with weapons?" he said. "And people will be killed?"

"Yes, of course. It *is* a battle."

He threw himself into a rickety folding chair that threatened to collapse with the force. "Who are your warriors?" he said.

"That is the difficult part," Yserria replied. "For this kind of challenge, I would be expected to bring my own forces. Since I have none, the echelon has agreed to allow volunteers to fight with me. It is in her best interest that both battles are won after all. I think it is safe to say that the best fighters will back her champion. She has chosen a different champion to lead the charge. His name is Ifigen. He served in the queen's royal guard before Echelon Deshari claimed him. He has led several successful campaigns against the other echelons since he joined her."

Malcius threw up his hands. "Great. How is this better than the archery competition?"

"Because this one does not depend on my skill alone." She dropped her gaze. "I could not have won the other challenge." Taking a deep breath, she hardened her resolve and looked at him. "I have never led a battle, but I am a Knight of Cael and a King's Royal Guardsman. I have been training with Rezkin and the strikers for months. I can do this. I just need the people."

Malcius shook his head in defeat. "Where is my sword?"

"You may use one of mine," said a gruff voice from the tent's entrance.

Malcius and Yserria both turned to see the intruder. He looked to be in his late forties and was quite fit, despite his limp.

"I am Balen," he said. "I am Wolshina's champion." He raised his hand, and two younger men stepped into the entrance. "These are my sons with my former matria. They are Vannin and Nolus. We have all fought in many battles, and we will fight with you, if you will have us."

Yserria grinned at Malcius. She turned to the men and said, "Please, enter.

I would be honored to have your assistance. I am surprised by your offer, though. I was not exactly accommodating with Japa."

"On the contrary," said Balen. "We are most appreciative of your acceptance. Japa is a gentle man in a warrior's body. To take a life would break him. He will be happy in service to you. I can tell that you are compassionate." He nodded toward Malcius. "It is obvious you do not want this one, but you will personally go to battle to keep him from the echelon because he is your fallen consort's kin." He glanced back at his sons. "The matrias do not often recognize this, but the men of Lon Lerésh honor our bonds. We have spread word of your motives for challenging the echelon. You will not go into battle alone.

16

Rezkin peered at his prey from atop the parapet in the shadow of the building. Boulis was a dour man with short-cropped, black hair and a thin mustache across his upper lip. He wore a bright red suit with yellow frills about the neck and wrists; and his fingers, heavy with golden rings, anxiously gripped a wide-brimmed red hat bearing a large yellow plume. The saber at his hip was sheathed in a gilded scabbard, and he carried a small belt knife encrusted with gemstones. From his shoulders swayed a short red cape trimmed in gold, and his black, knee-high boots were polished to a shine.

Rezkin had been following Boulis for more than a day, and the man had yet to do anything of interest. He had no more reason to kill Boulis than the rantings of an addled old man who was convinced that Boulis had been responsible for his grandson's death. The only truth he had found in the king's claim was in Boulis's money problems. Boulis was, at that moment, in the bailey cheering a sparring match between two soldiers who looked no better than street ruffians. Every bet Boulis had placed had been a losing one, and Rezkin knew this one would be no different. Since Boulis was a betting man, Rezkin wondered if he could entice him into a duel to the death. At least then he would have an excuse to kill the man.

More than anything, Rezkin was frustrated with the disquieting sensation of indecision. Killing Boulis was a means to an end. He should not have needed any more excuse than that. The strikers who had trained him at the fortress would have applauded the plan, but the strikers who currently served him would say it lacked honor. Others of his ilk would have no problem with the task. The Jeng'ri would likely shank Boulis in passing, while the Adana'Ro would use poison or slit his throat in his sleep. With the boisterous crowd, Rezkin could easily have killed the man at any time, yet he waited—he waited for an excuse. He wondered if he could let the man live, perhaps extract an oath of fealty from him, but it would be against the *Rules* to allow an enemy to remain at his back.

Rezkin was also frustrated with Moldovan. If any other monarch were to visit Ferélle, he would not be expected to run about doing Moldovan's errands. To Moldovan, though, this was a test to see if Rezkin was worthy of the crown. Rezkin did not want the crown, though, and he did not serve Moldovan. So, he waited, trying to come up with a better plan. Perhaps he could find the sword on his own. Perhaps he would forget the sword altogether. Only one man stood between him and Cael. Was that man Boulis or Moldovan? Perhaps he should kill them both.

His gaze caught the familiar blonde head weaving through the crowd. Behind it was a darker one, followed by another. Rezkin scanned the perimeter and finally found what he sought. He slinked from the shadow back into the castle. He stalked through the corridor in the new boots and princely garb Moldovan had insisted he wear for that evening's event. It was a sleek, black affair with silver buttons and a gold and silver baldric. The short, black cape had a silver lining, and the Esyojo family crest of two battling vuroles, one silver and one gold, adorned his chest. The silver and gold saber at his hip belonged to Moldovan.

Rezkin rounded a corner, and two guards at the other end of the corridor shouted to two others in an opposite direction before running to intercept him. As they neared him, they slowed and then came to a stop with a bow. Commander Tinen said, "*Your Highness, we respectfully request that you stay with your escort at all times. It is our duty to protect you.*"

Rezkin did not pause as he continued walking. He said, "*How can you protect me if you cannot keep up with me?*"

"*If you will stay with us, we will be more than capable,*" said Tinen.

"*So, I should restrict my movements because of your inferior training?*"

"*I assure you, Your Highness, our training is superior to that of any other kingdom.*"

Rezkin entered an empty office on his right. The two guards followed him, in addition to two more who had joined them. He turned and looked at the commander of his little entourage but said nothing. Tinen waited, but his confusion became increasingly evident under Rezkin's icy stare. After several minutes, Rezkin said, "*Yours is superior?*"

"*Yes, Your Highness*."

Rezkin stepped over to the doorway, reached into the corridor, and grabbed the woman passing by, placing a hand over her mouth to prevent her from screaming. He held her squirming form tightly as he looked at the guardsman. Then, he nodded toward the doorway. "*If your training is superior to that of any other kingdom, then defeat him.*" As Rezkin finished speaking, a man entered the room in a rush. Just before the man met the guards, Rezkin said, "Do not kill them."

The man looked at him, and then the guards were upon him. The woman suddenly stopped squirming as she peered up at him. Rezkin removed his hand from her mouth but kept hold of her.

"Um, Your Majesty?" she said.

"Greetings, Mage Threll," he replied.

Coledon and Brandt hurried into the room on Farson's heels but stopped when they spied Rezkin, who nodded for them to stay back. Then, all four of them watched as Farson battled the four royal guardsmen. The room was too small and heavily furnished to draw swords, and Farson quickly divested the men of their knives. The commander put up a good fight, better than Rezkin would have expected. Farson was breathing heavily and had a bloodied lip by the time he put the last one down. Two of the guards were unconscious, a third was wrapped tightly in the drapery, and Commander Tinen stared up at them from the floor where he lay at the tip of Farson's dagger.

Farson looked at Rezkin and said, "Was that really necessary?"

Rezkin shrugged. "They needed a lesson, and you need the exercise. You are getting slow."

"I think he is getting old," said Brandt.

Farson's look promised Brandt retribution during their next training session. He gave the commander on the floor a warning glare then straightened and sheathed his knife. "Perhaps I am only pretending, to throw you off guard."

"That is absurd," said Rezkin. "You could be infirm and on your deathbed, and I would not drop my guard."

Farson pointed at Tinen, who was glancing between them, waiting for permission to rise. "What did these men do to deserve a lesson?"

Rezkin said, "They thought they had superior training."

Farson shook his head and then stared at Rezkin's head.

"What is it?" said Rezkin.

"You are wearing a crown."

He nodded. "Moldovan insisted. I am to attend court twenty minutes ago."

"Moldovan does not hold court," said Farson.

"He does today."

Farson glanced at Mage Threll. "Are you going to release her or hold her all night?"

Rezkin released the mage, who spun to look at him. She said, "It looks good on you."

"The crown?"

"All of it," she said, her cheeks turning pink.

Coledon looked at him quizzically. "Why did you grab her?"

Rezkin nodded at Farson. "It was the easiest way to get him to reveal himself." Then, he looked down at the commander. "You may rise. Four of you could not defeat one of him, yet you think to protect *me*?"

Tinen's Ashaiian was decent but heavily accented as he spoke. "It does not seem that you need protection from *him*. He is your man?"

Rezkin shrugged and said, "He would kill me if he could."

"Not that you would stay dead," grumbled Farson.

Mage Threll looked at her uncle with disapproval and then cast a spell to wick the blood from his face.

Rezkin turned to Tinen, who was eyeing them all warily. "Gather your men"—he glanced at the unconscious guards—"if you can. We should probably report to the throne room. Boulis will have lost his bet by now and should be there—unless he decided to cast another."

As Tinen moved to unravel the conscious guardsman, Mage Threll said, "Who is Boulis, and why are we going to the throne room?"

"Boulis is the king's nephew," said Rezkin, "and I was supposed to kill him."

"You failed to kill a target," said Farson with surprise.

"Are you sure you were not struck on the head?" replied Rezkin. "Of course, I did not *fail* to kill him. I only failed to see why I should." Rezkin then strode through the doorway and headed toward the throne room.

Farson caught up to him. "This was a request from Moldovan?"

"Yes, in exchange for the sword."

Farson narrowed his eyes and said, "What is your reason for *not* killing him?"

"That is a good point," Rezkin said, but Farson continued to stare at him. Finally, he added, "You would not approve."

"Since when do you care about my approval?"

"Not just you. All of you, my people. Outworlders require a better reason to kill someone than convenience."

Farson said, "So, you are bound by the opinions of others?"

"It is my role as king. Kings should be bound by the will of the people."

"Few kings feel that way," said Farson. "What if a king must make a difficult decision for the good of his people?"

"Then, the king must be willing to suffer the consequences of that decision. This is not one of those times. It is too public. I will not allow Moldovan to seed doubt among my people for his personal vendetta."

Farson did not have time to respond as they filed into the receiving room outside the throne room. The king's seneschal, who had been overly flustered as he paced about the room, urged the guards to open the door promptly. Without another word, Rezkin strode into the throne room. Farson, Mage Threll, Brandt, and Coledon slipped around the side to stand at the edge of the somber crowd, while Rezkin strode to the top of the dais and stood beside the throne.

"You are late," grumbled Moldovan after erecting a sound ward.

"I arrived before Boulis; therefore, I am early."

"He was supposed to be *dead*," Moldovan hissed.

"Perhaps you should take that up with your gods," said Rezkin.

"I expect you to follow through."

"We shall see. I do not serve you, Moldovan. I will determine if Boulis dies by my hand."

Rezkin gazed across the sea of anxious, and even frightened, faces. Their flamboyant dress was in stark contrast to the nightmarish room. The women wore colorful, ruffled, high-collared dresses with sleeves that fell to their wrists and skirts that brushed the floor. The men were dressed in much the same manner as Boulis, and everyone wore large hats, making it difficult for anyone behind the front row to see what was happening. For this reason, the people stood on wooden risers that had been installed along the sides of the hall.

Boulis was not there. After another uncomfortable wait, he finally strode through the far door to the throne room. Upon entering, he appeared genuinely surprised. He peered at the gathered people and then grinned broadly as he nodded toward the spectators while proceeding toward the dais. Upon arrival, he bowed appropriately toward Moldovan and then noticed Rezkin. He appeared perplexed but returned his attention to the king.

"*Your Majesty, I heed your summons*."

"*You are late, Boulis*," barked the king.

"*I apologize, Good King. I was delayed by urgent business.*"

"*Yes, I am aware of your* urgent business *in the bailey. I see you still have your shirt. Is it all you have left of your family's fortune*?" Boulis's face turned scarlet to match his suit, but he refused to look at the chattering onlookers. Moldovan said, "*If you were not so oblivious, you would have realized that you were not the only one summoned.*"

The king stood and looked over his subjects. He lifted his scepter and tapped it on the ground. Then, he and said, "*Today, I abdicate the throne*." He paused to allow the commotion to die, and Boulis's expression brightened. Moldovan held a hand toward Rezkin and said, "*This is King Rezkin of Cael, True King of Ashai, First King of Lon Lerésh, Ruler of the Cimmerian Empire*." The room was completely silent, not a creak or shuffle, as everyone stared at Rezkin. Moldovan met Boulis's startled gaze and said, "*He is the legitimate son of King Bordran of Ashai and Princess Lecillia Esyojo of Ferélle. He is my grandson. By right of succession, I name him King Rezkin of Ferélle*."

Moldovan took his seat as the crowd erupted in a roar of support and disapproval. Boulis stepped forward and shouted, "*Fraud! The king has lost his mind to age, and this imposter seeks to usurp the throne. There were only two princes of Ashai, and he is neither!*"

Rezkin noted that there were more cheers in support of Boulis's position than rejections.

Moldovan said, "*Did you not hear me? A Prince of Ferélle is emperor of three other kingdoms. Esyojo blood, Ferélli blood, rules the Souelian.*"

This time, many of Boulis's former supporters nodded and cheered the king. One man called out, "*Long live the Ferélli emperor!*" and many others took up his cry.

Boulis shouted, "*Do you not think I was prepared for this, Uncle? I knew you would find a way to cheat me of my crown. I will not let the charlatan steal what is rightfully mine!*"

He jerked his arm toward the open doorway, and a man sprinted from the hall into the corridor. A moment later, heavy footfalls and clinking armor could be heard growing louder. The royal guardsmen surrounded Moldovan and Rezkin, several imploring the king to seek safety. Soldiers began filling the throne room at the far end while more of Moldovan's guards filed in from the corridors on either side of the dais, trapping the panicking courtiers between the two forces.

Rezkin turned to Moldovan. "*Where is the sword*?"

"*You think I will tell you now? You will take it and run.*"

"*It will be difficult to find if you die in this mess you instigated.*"

Moldovan grinned at him. "*Then, I had best not die.*"

After Tinen gave his approval, Rezkin's companions pushed their way past the royal guards. Rezkin drew Moldovan's sword and tossed it to Coledon, which seemed to confuse the man, since he was already armed. Rezkin had prepared for Boulis's refusal to accept the king's decision by stashing his belongings where they would be more accessible. He reached behind the tapestry that hung at the back of the throne and withdrew his black blade. Then, he donned the mask of Dark Tidings and waded through the guards, descending the steps to stand at the center of the throne room.

In the eerie voice of Dark Tidings, he said, "I will destroy all who stand against me. I am the storm before the calm, and in that calm is death."

Boulis drew his saber but began backing toward the soldiers as he shouted, "Kill him!"

Rezkin looked over his shoulder to Farson. "They were warned." Then, he met the charge. With every strike, green lightning crackled within the blade. After the first few fell, Rezkin had to pursue his targets, since few stepped forward to meet him. The others were engaged with the king's guard, and armed spectators fought on both sides.

A low two-handed swipe took off one soldier's legs below the knees. Rezkin took the man's head as he fell and kicked it into the face of another just before he stabbed the man through the gut. Then, two soldiers tried attacking at once. Rezkin ducked the swipe at his head and jumped over the one at his legs. He twisted his body as he landed to kick one of the men in the head so hard the man's neck snapped. At the same time, he drew his belt knife and stabbed the second in the kidney. Then, he twisted back to bury the black blade in the man's chest. Dark red blood burbled from the man's lips to spill over the crackling green lightning. Rezkin kicked the man off the blade, turning just in time to miss a mage attack. Tiny sparkles of light slammed into the body of the falling soldier. The sparkles dug into the man's skin and then exploded, causing bloody flesh to splatter all over Rezkin.

He turned, seeking the mage who had launched the attack and found Boulis preparing another. Rezkin drew two throwing stars from his coat. Boulis lost his spell as he was forced to deflect the stars. His next spell was sloppy, and he accidentally took the arm of one of his own men in the casting. Rezkin stepped toward Boulis but was stopped short when a thin stream of fire shot past him to take out two of the soldiers beyond. He glanced over to see Mage Threll give him an apologetic smile. He lobbed another star in her direction. Her eyes widened as the star spun toward her, and then it lodged in the eye of the man behind her. He screamed as he grabbed for the star, slicing his hand in the process. Mage Threll turned, thrusting her hand toward him, emitting a blast of power that knocked him off his feet.

Boulis sent another swarm of sparkling explosives in Rezkin's direction. Rezkin ducked as he raised the black blade, swatting several out of the way, while he snatched a few others out of the air. He looked down at his hand where he held the insubstantial sparks. He could see the tiny spells squirming within them, trying to get out. It was as if they were alive.

Boulis screamed, "*You cannot do that! No, it is impossible! What are you?*" He pointed at Rezkin as he shouted, "*Demon*!"

It was not the first time someone had called him that, and he doubted it would be the last, but Rezkin figured he would know if he were a demon. Rezkin threw the sparks back at Boulis, who erected a hasty shield. A soldier threw himself in front of the would-be king, and Rezkin could not imagine how the man had garnered that kind of dedication from *anyone*. Luckily for the soldier, Boulis's spell was not as effective against armor, and the man was left with only a small, gaping hole in one cheek.

Rezkin moved to advance on Boulis, but the man continued to back away behind his soldiers. Rezkin forced his way through, cutting down anyone who stood in his way, just as he had promised. When he reached the throne room doorway, Rezkin peered into the corridor. More soldiers lined the way.

Brandt stepped up to his side. "Are they with us or against us?"

"I do not know. *They* may not know."

Dark Tidings's eerie voice echoed through the corridor. "*All who stand in my way will die.*"

The soldiers stared at him and then the closest turned their gazes to the floor. Rezkin looked down to see that his clothes were dripping with blood into a crimson pool at his feet, and bloody footsteps marked his passage. The black blade continuously crackled with green lightning, and pieces of flesh clung to his form.

"*Demon*!" shouted Boulis from the other end of the corridor.

The soldiers looked back at Rezkin and hardened their resolve. Then, they attacked. Rezkin waded through them, followed by Brandt, then Farson, Mage Threll, and Coledon, as well as several of the royal guardsmen. Together, they slaughtered every soldier in the corridor. Rezkin led the way through the tower that Boulis had entered. They ran up the stairwell, Rezkin sensing for the use of the *talent* at every landing. Always, Boulis seemed to be above him, so they kept going. Rezkin was the first through the doorway when they reached the top, and he was immediately inundated by a cloud of explosive sparks. He pulled the short cape from his shoulders and used it to sweep the sparks from the air so they would not strike his companions. He balled the cape around the sparks, hoping that his own will was enough to prevent them from exploding.

Boulis had begun to light the signal fire that stood in the center of the platform. Rezkin reached past Farson to Mage Threll. He pulled her from the stairwell onto the platform then pushed her toward the signal fire as he searched for Boulis on the other side. Mage Threll began a spell that caused a fog to form around the signal fire. The fog slowly condensed into rain, and Rezkin was impressed that she had made an actual cloud. His thoughts on the potential uses for a cloud were interrupted by Boulis's scream.

"*You are too late. I will not let you have my birthright. The throne is mine*!" Boulis held in his hands a small clay pot marked with arcane runes. He placed the vessel on the ground and pulled the stopper as he began to recite an incantation. Black fumes spewed from the open container, crawling up his legs. "*H'g'gak shiewei cruikina—*" The incantation was curtailed when a dagger sprouted from Boulis's throat. A horrid screech emanated from the black fumes as they shriveled into themselves. A burst of power knocked everyone on the platform from their feet when the vessel suddenly exploded.

Rezkin pulled himself from the ground and checked that the others were well before approaching Boulis. The man was dead, of course, but Rezkin was always cautious when approaching dead men. After pulling his knife from the man's throat, he gathered the pieces of the clay pot for later examination. He grabbed Boulis by the ankle and dragged him across the platform to the stairwell. The royal guards offered to take the body, but Rezkin refused. He dragged the man the entire way down the tower and then through the corridor toward the throne room. Moldovan had remained on his throne, while the courtiers who were not permitted to leave cowered between the drainage grooves that were carrying blood and body fluids toward the drainage gutters along the walls. Stepping over corpses and splashing through puddles, Rezkin made his way back to the dais where he dropped the body that had been battered nearly beyond recognition.

"*Boulis is dead. Give me the sword.*"

Moldovan said, "*This could all have been avoided if you had killed him in the first place.*"

Rezkin removed his mask and waved around the room. "This was the voice of your people. The dissenters are dead or cower in fear. Esyojo rule is secured."

Moldovan grinned. "*This is why you will rule an empire.*" He stood and picked up his scepter in his gnarled fingers. "*You are an emperor, so I will not ask you to kneel.*"

"*You do not ask me to kneel because you know I will not.*"

The king chuckled. He pulled an amulet from beneath his robe. It had a large garnet set in the center with tapered spirals of gold at the top and bottom. He tapped the scepter to the amulet. He said, "*Duyana espekel umbalai.*" He tapped the scepter to Rezkin's right shoulder, then his left. Finally, Moldovan pressed it to Rezkin's forehead and repeated the incantation. "*Duyana espekel umbalai.*"

The garnet in the amulet began to glow a deep red, as did the scepter. He handed the scepter to Rezkin, then removed the amulet and placed it over Rezkin's head. He said, "*Speak the ancient words.*"

Rezkin considered not saying the words, but after all his troubles, he was not going to walk away without the sword. He glanced at Farson and then said, "*Duyana espekel umbalai.*" The scepter glowed brighter then dimmed as the stone's light grew intense. Finally, the light in both died. Somehow Moldovan looked older after it was finished. The color had faded from his flesh, and his gaze was more distant.

The man looked at Rezkin and said, "*Our family has not ruled Ferélle for so long by chance. Our power sustains us, as it will you. I know you do not intend to stay. You must name a regent, and then take me to my daughter.*"

"*The sword,*" said Rezkin.

"*Yes, yes. You shall have the sword. But you already know where it is.*"

Rezkin tilted his head and realized that he *did* know where it was. In fact, he knew much about the castle, its power, and the history of the royal family that he had not previously known.

Moldovan nodded knowingly and said, "*Esyojo is a legacy, one carried within the king, transferred via the scepter, amulet, and incantation. Now, none but you can wield the enchantments of this stronghold.*"

Rezkin turned to his companions, examining each of them. All were bloody, but most of the blood did not appear to be theirs. Mage Threll looked fatigued. He had seen her watching the impromptu ceremony closely, and he hoped she would be able to explain whatever had just happened. Beyond them, the courtiers clung to each other. While their cries had diminished, their fear persisted as they stood amongst the corpses of their fallen peers.

"Why you four?" Rezkin said, turning his attention back to his companions.

Mage Threll glanced at the others, who did not readily answer. Farson was busy surveying the room, Brandt appeared apathetic, and Coledon naturally deferred to the female. She said, "Coledon speaks Ferélli. You needed a mage, but Journeyman Wesson was not ready, and he is keeping the prisoners in check. After him, my *talent* is most suited for battle." She glanced at her uncle. "The strikers agreed that you would prefer Shezar to remain in charge of the ships, and my uncle thinks he needs to follow me everywhere, besides."

Rezkin glanced at Brandt. He shrugged and said, "I was bored."

Rezkin descended the dais. He looked at Coledon and said, "Kneel." Coledon did so, and Rezkin laid the black blade, still steeped in Ferélli blood, on top of the man's head. He said, "Coledon Anshe, I name you king regent. Stand and claim your scepter."

Coledon blinked up at him in surprise and then stood on shaky legs. He slowly grasped the scepter and looked back at Rezkin. "Why me?"

Rezkin said, "For one, because you are willing to ask that question. Also, you speak several languages, including Ferélli. As the former trademaster of your sister's house, you have valuable experience. Mostly, though, because you are here."

Moldovan barked a laugh and spoke in Ashaiian as the others had. "An

Esyojo with so much power that he passes around kingships like they were water."

Rezkin returned to the dais and faced his grandfather. "It is not because I have power but because people continually insist on inflicting it upon me when I do not desire it."

Moldovan took Rezkin's hand in his own, and Rezkin allowed it, since it was unlikely the former king would attack him at that point. Moldovan held both of their hands side-by-side and said, "Look. Yours is strong. Mine is frail. Some would say it is from age, but I know it is because I bled my strength into this kingdom for nearly eight decades. I have governed with an iron fist, yet few have celebrated my rule. Most no longer hide their whispers that I have lived too long. In you, people find strength and courage. People wish to be a part of something great, even when they cannot find it in themselves. *You* are their greatness."

Moldovan dropped their hands and reached for the arm of one of the royal guardsmen. He said, "I will retire to my bed until you are ready to leave. Remember your promise. I will see my daughter again."

Rezkin turned to the disconsolate spectators and said, "Court is dismissed."

In a unified cry of relief, they ran as one toward the throne room door, some tripping over bodies or slipping in gore. Rezkin then looked at the seneschal and Commander Tinen. "You two will assist your king regent in learning his duties." He turned to Coledon and said, "Rule as I would rule."

Coledon shook his head. "I have been in your company only weeks. I cannot say how you would rule."

"Fairly," said Rezkin. "Come, I have something to show you."

They followed Rezkin, flanked by royal guards, down several flights of stairs to a set of large, wooden doors carved with runes. The guards stopped several paces from the doors and stood at attention along the walls on either side.

Rezkin motioned for Coledon to step forward. "Press the scepter against this," he said, pointing at a rune that looked like a disembodied eye. Coledon did as he had asked, and the scepter and eye glowed red for a brief moment. Rezkin pressed his palm to the door, causing it to swing inward. He led the group into a dark cave. The floor was covered in water, a lake within the bowels of the castle. As Rezkin stepped into the cavernous room, red lights flared in two lines down the center, and they could see that a stone pathway lay just under the surface between them. As they walked down the pathway, varying colors of light began to shine from beneath its glassy surface. Colorful lights and shadows danced across the natural ceiling and walls of the cave, and specks of glowing dust began to twinkle in their midst.

Mage Threll whispered into the dark. "I would never have expected a place so wonderous in this terrifying castle."

"This place is old," said Rezkin, "older than the castle, older than Ferélle."

He stepped onto a small platform in the center. It was just large enough to hold the four of them a few inches above the water. The lights along the pathway winked out, and they were left surrounded by a glowing lake. Rezkin pointed to a groove in the floor and said, "Place the scepter there." Once the scepter was in position, the surface of the lake began to shimmer. There, in the water before them, appeared a map. It was not drawn or painted, but rather an exact image of the city. Rezkin turned the scepter, and the image shifted to show a different place. He brushed his fingers across the crystal at the top of the scepter, and it was as if they were standing in the town, staring down the street. They could see the people moving about. A little girl pointed to an enchanted butterfly made of cloth, a stray dog grabbed a biscuit from a merchant stall, and a woman snagged her coat on a broken cart.

Rezkin said to Coledon, "You may use this to watch over the city." He pointed to a number of other grooves in the floor. "You will find images of other cities in those."

"This is fascinating," said Mage Threll. "I have never heard of anything like it. I could spend the entirety of my life studying this."

"Mages have," said Rezkin. "Only a few are permitted the knowledge to use it. No one knows how the lake works. They know only how to use it. They create new orbs to spread in other cities, but none have been able to reproduce the lake itself. I believe this predates man. It is a remnant of the Ahn'an."

"How do you know so much about it?"

Rezkin furrowed his brow and stared at the water. "It is as if the ceremony awoke something in me—a memory that is not my own. I know things now that I did not before, but it is as if I have always known them."

"Spells do not usually affect you," said Farson.

"It was not Moldovan's power. He only activated it. This is much older."

Rezkin peered into the dark water that was intermittently painted with swirling light. He pulled the Dark Tidings mask from the tie at his belt and secured it over his face.

"What are you doing?" said Mage Threll. "You are not going in there. You just said that it holds ancient power that *can* affect you."

Rezkin glanced her way and then stepped off the platform. His stomach met his throat as he instantly plummeted to the bottom, as if falling through air to collide with the ground. Before he struck, in what was sure to be a deadly crunch, a liquid blanket wrapped around him, slowing his descent. He breathed deeply through the mask as he slowed to a stop, and the aqueous fabric held him aloft while he searched for the bottom. His boot touched the hard rock, and the fluid grip released him. Rezkin steadied himself and looked around in the darkness. Lights swirled in the distance and sometimes closer. He could feel the water surrounding him, dampening his movements, but he trod over the rock floor as if held down by a weight. As he searched for the sword, he took care to avoid the light. In those dark waters, amongst the lights, it began to feel as if he were in a dream. It was reminiscent of the meditative trance he entered in lieu of sleep. After minutes or hours, he no longer knew, he began to hear music. As the music grew louder, more light surrounded him. He spun, looking all around, and found no way to avoid them. They closed in on him until he was immersed in light.

Rezkin began to feel calm, the same soothing tranquility that inundated him at Caellurum. His persistent hunger began to subside, and the ache of fatigue was vanquished, replaced by a clarity he had not realized had been missing. The small Caelian stone around his neck heated, but Rezkin was captivated by a figure in the water. At first, he thought it was distant, a vague outline of a person moving toward him. Then it reached out and touched his face, and he realized the being was much closer.

The watery figures began to take shape, some of them appearing feminine, while others were masculine. *Nixies*, he thought. They surrounded him, perhaps by the dozens. They chittered like ripples in a creek. It sounded like laughter. They stroked his face and hair and tugged at his mask. Then, they began to pull in earnest. His arms were wrenched behind him, and they swept his feet from beneath him. Tackling him to the ground, they snapped his head back and forth as they pulled at the mask. Rezkin kicked and twisted as he struggled against the insubstantial beings. The stone around his neck began to radiate heat. One of the nixies reached for it and pulled back with a shriek.

The water was suddenly filled with tiny bubbles, and the nixies backed away. They kept their distance and watched the bubbles pensively. Rezkin scrambled to his feet and stood in the center, knowing he had no strength or power to fight them. The song changed, and the bubbles began to take on a shape of their own. A woman's figure shimmered in the water where the lights bounced off the spherical surfaces of the bubbles that composed her. She reached for Rezkin's mask but did not touch it. She tilted her head and reached again. Then, the bubbles shifted to produce a new form, one with whom he was familiar. It was a treelike creature with feather-tipped twigs atop its head. The bubble form shifted again to resemble a sword but not the Sword of Eyre. It was Kingslayer. The form shifted again to resemble the woman.

Rezkin remembered what Bilior had told him about the other ancients. He was in the water, but this creature was made of air. He said, "Hvelia?" The sound escaped the mask in a globule of bubbles.

The being tilted her head and then reached for the mask again. Rezkin's heart raced as he grasped its edge. Even if this was truly the Ancient of wind, there was no guarantee she would be amicable. There was a chance that Bilior had been lying about their deal. Rezkin took a deep breath and then pulled the mask away. A stream of bubbles instantly covered his face. He secured the mask to his belt by feel, and when his vision cleared, Rezkin was astonished. There, in the depths of a black lake in a dark cave, was an entire underwater world he had not been able to see through the enchantments on the mask. The nixies appeared more substantial, with individual features and expressions. Many of them jumped in excitement and cheered as they clapped each other on the back and hugged in celebration of some achievement.

Creatures Rezkin had never seen nor heard tell of, some larger than a horse, swam past, some disappearing into the branching caves. Rezkin finally inhaled, his mouth filling with bubbles. They abruptly coalesced and filled his airway and lungs. It was a strange sensation, but he was glad to not be drowning. Then, he saw her. Swimming toward him was not some insubstantial nixie but a real woman. When she drew closer, he realized that she was not human. Her pale, seafoam-green eyes were far larger than those of a human, her cheeks narrower, and her cheekbones sharper. Her thin mouth was set above a pointed chin. Long, ash blonde hair floated in the water around her head, from which he could see the protruding tips of pointed ears. The entirety of her skin sparkled from the tiny, translucent scales that covered it down to her waist where the scales grew larger and darker over the length of a long, sinuous fish tale. She was one of the fabled merfolk, and in her hands was a sword—the Sword of Eyre.

Rezkin reached out and stroked a strand of the mesmerizing woman's hair.

She blinked at him curiously and then stroked his own. She was fascinating, but she was not the woman from his dreams. He grasped the sword. The water abruptly wrapped tightly around him, and his entire world became a rush of bubbles and rough currents. His ears throbbed and then popped as he ascended, and he gasped as his head breached the surface.

Rezkin's companions shouted and reached for him, pulling him onto the platform. He lay there for a moment, staring at the shadows dancing among stalactites on the ceiling. After taking a deep breath, he pulled himself to his feet and then looked down at the sword. So much trouble he had endured to gain this worthless blade. It was not worthless to Privoth, though, and that was what mattered. His ears popped again, and he realized that buzzing sound was his companions talking to him.

"What?" he said.

Mage Threll said, "You were down there forever. You are not even wearing your mask! How did you not drown?"

Farson said, "Perhaps he did, and his body refuses to accept it."

Rezkin frowned at his former trainer and then said, "We have the sword." He glanced back at the water almost longingly. He gained his feet and turned toward the walking path that lit as he approached.

Farson's voice held a hint of laughter as he said, "You lost your crown."

Rezkin brushed his hand across his head and realized that Farson was right. He did not care for the crown anyway. He was halfway across the walkway when Mage Threll gasped. Rezkin turned to see what had elicited such a reaction. He followed her gaze to a glinting object in the water. A feminine hand with slender fingers covered in tiny, sparkling scales held his crown above the water. He took the crown with one hand and held her hand with the other. She grasped his hand in return as he peered past the surface into her green gaze. Then, she slipped into the depths and was gone.

As Rezkin left the cave, he felt a loss, as if a part of him had been left behind. He glanced at his hand and found that some glittery flecks remained. It was a small token, but it was one he realized he wanted far more than the crown. He also realized that he longed for Cael.

17

Yserria bristled as she approached the echelon's tent. The battle had been delayed until they could reach the staging ground; and, after having traveled north for two days, she was supposed to be in the midst of preparing for it. She was, instead, needlessly summoned to speak with the echelon while the woman broke her fast in comfort. Yserria did not wait for an invitation to enter. She had been summoned after all. She was not going to give this woman the power to make her wait. Yserria stalked through the opulent travel accommodations to the small table that held an assortment of preserves, breads, and cream.

Deshari's smile was affable, while her tone held only contempt. "*Would you care to join me? These are some of the finest preserves the Souelian has to offer. This one is from Ferélle, but perhaps you prefer a taste of home? I have an Ashaiian mint-fig. I am not entirely sure what a fig is, but I do enjoy the taste.*"

"*What do you want?*" Yserria said.

Deshari motioned to a chair. "*Please, sit down. I do not care to strain my neck looking up at you.*"

"*No, your neck should feel great as you watch me go into battle.*"

Deshari laughed. "*I would never watch such barbaric sport. No, I shall enjoy the company of Gemsbrick, while you are dallying in the field, and shall be ready to celebrate our success upon your return.*"

"*You wish for my return?*"

"*Of course. I do want to prevail over Orina after all. I have no concerns that you will fare better than my Ifigen. He is a seasoned commander and is familiar with the style of Orina's champion Carthano.*"

"*Then what do you want?*" said Yserria.

Deshari placed her butter knife on her plate and said, "*Very well, to business. I wanted to give you a chance to withdraw the challenge. There is no need to risk your life when we know that you have no intention of staying to rule as echelon. You cannot retain the position from afar. It will be pointless.*"

"*I will withdraw my challenge for echelon if you withdraw your claim for Lord Malcius.*"

She tipped her goblet back and said, "*Well, you know I cannot do that. It would appear weak. My adversaries watch closely. Many covet my position.*"

"*After today, you will no longer have that problem,*" said Yserria.

"*You fancy yourself a wolf, but we both know you are a mere pup. Without the weight of that torque and support of your master, you and your house would have no standing in this queendom.*"

Yserria said, "*He is not my master. He is my king and yours as well. He chose me because I can fight for him, not so that he may fight for me. If you have nothing more to say, I must return to my preparations. I go to win a battle today.*"

Deshari pursed her lips, so Yserria stood and then stalked out of the tent, heading toward the staging ground. When she arrived, she was surprised to see that her force had grown to nearly double what it had been at dawn. Several dozen men ceased their chatter and stood at attention. As one, they saluted her, not the formal bow given a matrianera, but a one-armed, fisted salute of a soldier. Yserria nodded and said, "*Thank you for volunteering for the battle challenge for Third Echelon. I am honored by your gift of service. It is time to solidify our plan of engagement. As you were.*" The men relaxed and returned to their preparations as Yserria looked for Balen.

She found him going over plans with Malcius. For Malcius's sake, she spoke in Ashaiian. "The echelon is worried. She tried to get me to withdraw my challenge."

"As she should be," said Balen. "The echelon likes to think her consort a military genius. He is a brutal warrior and a good leader, but he has always depended on his second to devise the plan."

"How does that help us?" she said.

Balen grinned. "I am his second."

Yserria smiled. "That is good news. I am unfamiliar with the terrain, my opponent"—she thumbed over her shoulder—"my men—pretty much all of it. I am depending on your experience and guidance."

"That will make you a good general," said Balen.

Yserria nodded. "Rezkin says it is important to recognize your followers' strengths and capitalize on them. He says that I should not believe that I can or should do everything better than everyone else."

"This Rezkin sounds like a wise man. Is he your trainer?"

"Yes, he is my king—and yours."

"I had heard rumors, but I did not believe them all. I did not realize you were so close to your king."

Yserria's face flushed. "We are not close in the intimate sense, if that is what you are implying."

"I should say not," said Malcius. After seeing her frown, he said, "What? I am trying to defend your honor, *as you asked.*"

She blinked in surprise. "Oh, um, thank you, Lord Malcius."

Malcius crossed his arms and nodded once, then looked at Balen who seemed utterly confused. Balen shook his head and then withdrew a map. He explained how he thought Ifigen would conduct his battle and then covered his own plan. Since Deshari was defending her claim to the land, she had the privilege of choosing the battle site. She and Ifigen would each be defending their own small hill. The Fourth Echelon's forces would be attacking from the north, and a small tributary bounded the hills to the south.

Yserria pointed to the river bend on the western flank of her hill. Ifigen's hill was not adjacent to the river. "Can they use this to flank us?" she said.

Balen shook his head. "That would be difficult. The river flows in the other direction."

"Could we use it to flank them?"

He rubbed his chin. "It would be a good plan, but we do not have enough men."

"Orina knows that," Yserria mused. "She knows that my force is smaller than Ifigen's. She would not expect us to split the few we have."

"Because it would be suicide," said Malcius.

"Maybe not," she said. "Is this map accurate?"

"Very much so," said Balen.

"Then, look. Our hill is steeper on the northeastern side. This means that

Orina will not be able to attack us from due north. It will force her to move slightly to the west, but there is a rise here. Her troops will be closer to the river, but they will not be able to see our unit in the water until it is too late."

Balen nodded. "What you say is true, but we still need more men."

Yserria placed her hands on her hips and said, "How can we get them?"

"Perhaps a demonstration. Some of the men are not convinced that you can fight."

She huffed. "I made it to the second round in the fifth tier at the King's Tournament."

"You would probably have made it to the third if Rezkin had not defeated you," said Malcius.

She glanced at him, uncertain if he were chiding her. He appeared sincere, so she said, "Thank you."

He furrowed his brow. "For what?"

Balen said, "It is true, then? You are the female swordmaster who was at the King's Tournament?"

Yserria paused and then lifted her chin. "Yes, I am the swordmaster."

"I see. This is why the echelon chose archery instead of the sword."

Malcius said, "What kind of demonstration did you have in mind?"

"Never mind," said Yserria. "I know what will do."

Malcius and many of the warriors who had committed themselves to her cause followed Yserria as she stalked to the center of the encampment. Others stopped what they were doing to investigate the commotion. She turned and faced her men, bowed, then turned to face the gathering crowd of onlookers. She bowed again and drew her father's sword, holding it in front of her, the tip toward the overcast sky. Then, she began to move. Her form was graceful, but her motions strange to Malcius. After the first few passes, some of the men began to clap. Others joined them, and after a minute, Malcius was surrounded by an intense cadence of long and short claps. Every so often the men would root as one, a barking sound that complimented the patterned claps.

Malcius leaned over to Balen and said, "What is she doing? I have never seen a sword form like that."

"It is not a sword form. It is a sort of ritual, a dance but with meaning. It is only performed by the royal guard upon a queen's death or crowning, or when the army goes to war. It is meant to provoke dedication and instill strength. I do not know how she knows the dance, but she must be a swordmaster if she is capable of performing it without killing herself."

Yserria tossed the sword into the sky, allowing it to flip, end over end, before catching it. She then swept it behind her back and did the same. Each time she caught the sword, she performed some acrobatic that might have even impressed Rezkin. Malcius became more anxious with each turn, and his sense of relief when it was finally finished was surprising.

To Balen, he said, "Her father was a royal guard. He taught her the sword."

Yserria ended with a flourish, and the crowd erupted in cheers. Men and a few women came to speak with her, and Yserria urged every one of them to join her force. Some of them accepted immediately, while others said they required time for consideration. After she had spoken with the majority, she rejoined Malcius and Balen.

Balen shook his head. "It is a risky move, but we *might* have enough to pull it off."

Malcius looked at Yserria and said, "May I speak with you privately?" They walked a short distance to where they could still be seen but not heard. He said, "You do not have to do this. Let me be your champion. I will go to battle in your stead."

She scoffed. "What are you talking about?"

"Look around you, Yserria. This is a *real* battle. People will die. You need not risk your life on my account. I will fight the battle for my own freedom as your champion."

"You cannot be my champion," she said. "I have claimed you. You could fight as my champion in any challenge except the matter of the claim. For this matter, you would need to accept the claim, and we would be required to consummate the bond before witnesses."

"I thought that was only for marriages! I thought that anyone could fight as your champion."

"Anyone can, *unless* I have claimed him. Then, we must complete the bond. It does not matter if it is for husband or consort, although the requirements for a husband are more—*intense*."

Malcius's thoughts were thrown into chaos as his heart raced. Palis had lost his life to save Yserria. He could not just let her walk into a battle and get killed. Why had he never considered that before? He needed to keep her safe. He said, "Would it be so terrible? It is certainly better than dying."

She slapped him. Malcius raised a hand to his stinging cheek. The shock of it woke him from his panic. "What—"

"You are a horrible person, Malcius Jebai."

"But—"

"What I do with my body might be acceptable here in Lon Lerésh, but anywhere else, I would be a ruined woman. Do you hate me so much that you would sentence me to a long life of loneliness?"

"No, I—"

"And, you have no faith in my abilities as a warrior. I have trained hard for this, and I am capable. I risk my life to keep you free, and this is how you repay me?"

Yserria stalked away, and Malcius was left wondering what in the world had just happened. Balen strode over as he watched Yserria storm off toward the staging ground. He said, "I know not what you said to her, but I think you are lucky to have gotten away with a slap. She looks furious enough to win the battle on her own."

Malcius groaned and followed her through the crowd. Some of the men laughed at his misfortune as he passed, while others offered their condolences. He was so preoccupied by the attention that he nearly ran into a hulking man who stepped in front of him. The man grabbed hold of his shirt as he lost his footing, preventing him from further embarrassing himself by falling onto his rear.

The man said, "I am Mage Dolinar. I will fight at your side."

Malcius looked up at the dark-skinned man, obviously of Pruari descent. He was one of the largest men Malcius had ever seen, and his voice rumbled like a war drum.

Malcius grasped the man's hand. "I am Malcius of House Jebai. I thank you, but I must ask why? You have only seen me make a fool of myself."

Dolinar grinned, his broad smile lightening the mood. He slapped Malcius's shoulder and said, "It looks like you need the help."

"He is not wrong," Balen said with a smirk.

Mage Dolinar turned and pushed Malcius toward the staging ground. He waved a hand toward the men and said, "We have all been in similar situations with our matrias. Well, perhaps not exactly yours. Most of our matrias depend on our strength as champions for physical challenges. Your matria is a she-wolf. She readily bares her claws and teeth, but I think she would not be satisfied with a docile man."

"She is not my matria," said Malcius.

"No, but she will be once she defeats the echelon's champion. You are a lucky man."

"You seem confident that we will prevail."

"I am a truthseeker."

"You can see the future?"

Dolinar laughed. "No, that is not a talent I bear. I see things as they truly are. Knight Yserria is worthy of her title. Her confidence is genuine. The echelon fears her."

"So, you chose the side you think will win?"

"I choose the side that I desire to win. I do not care for the echelon. She is devious, always scheming. It hurts my eyes to see so much deception, but it is most common in women of power in our queendom. The only way to gain power here is to take it, and the support of their peers is crucial. The good are eventually corrupted of necessity. That one, though, she shows her true self. It is most refreshing."

Malcius followed Dolinar's gaze. Yserria was standing at the war table speaking with Balen's sons. A ray of light shined through a crack in the clouds to glint off the torque around her neck. Malcius said, "Perhaps she can afford to be true because she is backed by one more devious than the rest."

"You speak of your king?"

"And yours," Malcius said, meeting the man's dark gaze.

"Hmm, it is not wise to speak of royalty with such disdain."

"He would not deny it. I think he prides himself in the effort, but he seems to feel no pride—or anything, for that matter."

"You know him well?"

Malcius glanced at Yserria. "I once called him friend."

"But no longer?"

"You ask many questions," Malcius replied.

Dolinar shrugged. "It is my talent. I seek to understand the things I see. I do not believe you reject your king."

Malcius kicked a rock. "No, I do not reject him as my king. As a friend—it is complicated. I have blamed him for all our troubles, and I depend on him to solve them." He glanced at Dolinar's knowing gaze and shook his head. "I guess, inside I know he is not responsible, yet I trust he will make amends, regardless." He growled in frustration. "I just—I cannot let go of the anger."

Dolinar nodded. "When I was young, my father was killed in a challenge. I blamed our matrianera for a long time even though she was not responsible for his death. It was easier to blame someone I cared about, someone with whom I felt safe, than the true enemy that frightened me." Dolinar briefly crossed his wrists and said, "If you will excuse me, Malcius Jebai, I must confer with my comrades."

As Dolinar walked away, Balen said, "He is a wise man. You would do well to heed his words."

Yserria shaded her eyes with her hand. The clouds had dissipated by late morning, and the sun shone bright over the battle field. Echelon Orina's troops were scattered around the base of the hill to the north, the largest group toward the west, as she had predicted. She did not look to the south where Balen led the second unit down the river.

"Are you sure we can trust them?" said Malcius.

"We have no choice," she replied.

"Balen seems a decent fellow, but these people are conniving. He admitted that he is Ifigen's second. What better way to sabotage us?"

"What does it matter?" she said. "If he betrays us, then we lose. If he were not with us, we would have no troops, and we would still lose. If he is with us, at least we have a chance at winning."

"You should have let me lead the second unit."

"He is more familiar with the terrain and the men."

She saw his frustration in his dark glare and clenched jaw. He said, "Where do you want me then, *matria*?"

She scowled at him. "Go wherever you want."

He lifted his chin and said, "Then, I shall stand beside *you*."

The first horn blared, and the troops on both sides began to move into position. Yserria found that her men were well accustomed to the challenge of battle and required little encouragement or direction. She spied Ifigen on the far hill. He was pacing back and forth in front of his men, presumably delivering some inspiring speech. Yserria had no such speech. These men did not know her, nor did they care much for her cause. Most of them probably fought because they relished the battle.

She walked along the front line, then turned and raised her voice. "*You do not know me, so to ask you to fight for me would be less than inspiring; but, you do know Echelon Deshari. If we win, you need no longer concern yourself with her.*" Her gaze roved over their faces. None cheered, probably out of fear of what might happen to them should they lose, but a fire lit within their hungry gazes. She grinned. "*We fight to secure our survival, and we fight to destroy our common enemy. We fight as one, as a pack. We fight as wolves*."

This time, the men rooted. It was the same cadence they had chanted during the dance, and it was inspiring. Their chant grew louder, and even those on the adjacent fields turned to stare. The second horn blared, and the battle began.

The front line of Orina's troops pushed forward, ascending Yserria's hill. They hid behind large shields attached to logs on wheels, each pushed by half a dozen men up the slope. Ifigen's archers cast the first volley of arrows at the men climbing his hill, but Yserria waited. After two volleys on the adjacent hill, the frontline infantry rushed from behind the shields to attack Ifigen's forces.

Yserria returned her attention to her own battle. When Orina's front line was nearly to the top, she raised a signal flag. Her men abruptly shifted into a grid with large gaps between the files. Dolinar cast his spell, and dozens of boulders from the other side of the hill began rolling forward between the columns. Yserria gave the signal to the archers, who aimed high so that their arrows would drop behind the shields to strike the men pushing the logs. The arrows struck just as the boulders tumbled down the front slope, crashing into the shields. With no one to hold them, the logs plummeted backward, rolling over and dragging the men behind them. Some of the men were able to escape the shields before they were crushed, and Yserria's infantry met them with force.

Just as Yserria was beginning to feel confident, a fierce wind began swirling atop the hill, capturing shields and shoving her troops into one another. Dozens of small fireballs, none large enough to kill but certainly large enough to cause damage, were cast toward the crest where they were whipped up by the wind. The fire spread, and the fireballs struck at random. During the commotion, Orina's forces gained ground. They began to swarm the hill.

Yserria could hear the pounding of hooves, but she could not find their source. Suddenly, the illusion dropped, as if a curtain were drawn back, and a small cavalry unit plowed through their lines. She called to one of her mages, a life mage who was already in the midst of casting a spell. The horses suddenly reared and began thrashing against nonexistent restraints. As the confused horses ran amuck, her archers and pike men took down their riders.

After striking down an infantryman who had been unlucky enough to top the hill, she turned to Malcius. She grabbed him by the collar and pulled him away from the man with whom he was engaged. After running her sword through the man's ribs, she turned to him.

She held the signal flare out for him and said, "Lead the charge!"

"What? Me? Now?"

"Yes, now! Go!"

He grabbed the flare, and Yserria watched his back as he cut his way to the front line. He activated the purple orb that propelled itself into the sky, setting phase two of their plan into motion. Yserria's troops descended the hill, leaving a gap in the line to the west. She was depending on Deshari's duplicity, certain the echelon had been feeding her opponent information. Orina would know that Yserria had little experience and would expect her to make novice mistakes. Sacrificing the high ground enticed Orina's troops, and the poorly placed line gave them an opening. Orina's champion took the advantage, his troops filing into the gap, segregating Yserria's men and acquiring a pathway to summit.

Balen's men did not appear. No charge from the rear, no final rout. He had abandoned her. Yserria's heart plummeted into her stomach, and she looked for Malcius. He was there in the fray, deep in the thick of it, determined to drive the enemy into the rear forces that were not coming. She hurried to the crest of the hill and scanned the other hill to see how Ifigen's troops fared and was shocked. His hill had been overrun, and Orina's forces had been diverted to *her* field.

Dolinar ran up to her, breathing heavily as he leaned on his knees. He was bleeding from several gashes, and his armor was hanging from one shoulder.

"*Echelon Orina has broken the terms of the challenge. She was not satisfied to wait and see if you would fail. She seeks to overthrow Echelon Deshari.*"

"*I see that. Where is Balen*?"

He pointed toward the base of the rise along the river. "*There, Echelon Orina's troops are now nearly double, and he was forced to engage much farther back. If he had not been there, though, we would already have been overrun.*"

Yserria had to think fast. What would Rezkin do? Something unimaginable, she was sure. "*Gather the mages*," she said. "*Move the river*."

He looked at her as if she were mad. "*You wish for us to do what? That is impossible*."

"*No*," she said, pointing to the gentle slope of the ridge along the hill's elongated western flank. "*The saddle there is low, and the rock beds dip away. You can see where they have already slumped. With a bit of power, you can force them to slide on their own. It will dam the river and open a passage through here. The field below will be flooded. Orina's troops will be decimated.*"

"*And some of our own,*" said Dolinar.

"*We will sound a retreat right before you act. We will save as many as we can, but if we do nothing, all of them will die.*"

"*I am an earth mage. I know this land. What you ask—I do not believe it can be done.*"

"*We cannot know until we try; and, if we do not try, we will never have another chance.*"

Dolinar nodded and then sprinted off to gather the few mages at their disposal. Yserria gripped her sword, whispered a prayer to the Maker, and then descended into the turmoil, fighting her way toward Malcius. The grass on the slope had been ripped and churned, and the topsoil had become loose. With every precarious step, Yserria slashed and ducked. She used her body weight to send more than one enemy tumbling down the hill and tried to catch a few of her own men who might have shared the same fate. She finally caught up with Malcius, and without discussion, the two fell into the partnered combat they had been taught. Guarding each other's backs, they fought until those in their immediate vicinity were dead, then moved farther along the line.

After what felt like years, Yserria heard a resounding *crack* followed by a massive rumble. The ground shook beneath their feet, and soldiers on both sides paused in fear of what was to come. She looked for the signal, but there was no sign for retreat, so she kept fighting. Several minutes later, there was another blast, this one louder. This time, the ground's trembling was accompanied by the roar of rushing water.

Yserria screamed, "*Retreat!* Retreat!"

She grabbed Malcius and began dragging him up the hill as they swatted away those in pursuit. The water blasted past, only paces below their position. As it tore through the hill, it took with it chunks of soil. The slope on which they sought refuge began to fall into the churning muck. With masses of earth eroding beneath them, Yserria and Malcius ran for the steeper high ground of the eastern flank. As they gripped an outcrop for support, Yserria looked over the battleground. Most, but not all, of her troops had made it to higher ground. The lowland was a swath of churning, grey water seeking its way back toward the riverbed. Across the river, on the other side of what had been the western flank of her hill, Balen and his men fought the last of their enemies on a low rise over the empty tract where the river had previously flowed.

Yserria breathed heavily and motioned for Malcius to follow. They crested the hill and found the mages lying in the grass in varying states of well-being. Yserria slid down the slope that had once been slight and came to a stop next to Dolinar, who lay back staring at the sky. She looked up at the life mage whose name she could not remember. "*Good job with the horses*."

The woman waved her hand in dismissal. "*It was nothing compared to this*," she said with a wave toward the cliff that fell into the new path of the river.

Looking down at Dolinar, Yserria said, "*What is wrong with him*?"

The woman said, "*He overextended his power. He will be ill and disoriented for some time, but he will be fine once he regains his power*—if *he regains his power*."

"*This could be permanent?*"

The woman shrugged. "*Sometimes. At least he is not dead.*"

Malcius said, "*Death might be preferable to this.*"

The woman smiled faintly and stroked the braid at Dolinar's temple. "*I am sure he will recover. Dolinar is strong.*"

"*You are his matria?*"

With a nod, the woman said, "*We are members of the echelon's household. She will not be pleased that we fought for you.*"

Yserria stood and said, "*You need not worry about that. Deshari is no longer echelon. I have won the challenge. Now, I must issue another.*"

She mounted the rise and then stalked down the hill with determination, skirting the water to the east. As she marched, those of her troops who could stand gathered in her wake. Malcius hurried beside her.

"What are you doing?" he said.

"I must challenge Orina."

"For what? We have won. We can go now!"

"She broke the terms of the challenge against the Third Echelon, which is now me. If I do not challenge her, I will appear weak and lose standing."

"*What do you care*?" said Malcius. "We. Can. Leave."

Yserria stopped to face him and pointed back to the men and woman who had followed her into combat. "They fought for nothing more than a respect for my motives and the promise of a better echelon. Orina has proven to be without honor. If I leave the echelon in disarray, she will claim it and place one of her ilk in the position. If I abandon these people now, they will have fought for nothing." Yserria began walking again toward Orina's encampment on the other side of the valley. "Right now, Orina is weak. Her forces are destroyed. She cannot defend herself against a challenge."

When they arrived, Orina's servants were rushing to pack her belongings. Yserria stopped outside the echelon's tent and called to her. "*Orina Goldren of the Fourth Echelon, I am Yserria Rey of the Third Echelon. You have violated the covenant of challenge against the Third Echelon. On behalf of my people, I challenge you for your seat!*"

A blonde woman in a slinky green dress and beige sandals stepped out of the tent. She carried a folding fan that she used to cool herself as she stood nonchalantly looking at the crowd.

"*I am Echelon Orina Goldren. You cannot challenge me. My arrangement was made with Echelon Deshari Brigalsi.*"

Yserria raised her sword toward the woman. "*I have won her seat in challenge. I am now Third Echelon, and I am here to hold you accountable.*"

Orina's eyes widened. "*Deshari said nothing of a challenge for her seat. She said the challenge was for a claim on a foreigner.*"

Yserria grinned. "*Then, she lied. She tried to take my man, and I challenged her for her seat in return. That is irrelevant, though, as it has no bearing on your actions.*"

Orina straightened. "*Her forces were split, and there was unrest in her camp. I would have been remiss not to take advantage of the situation.*"

"*I do not believe you were unaware of the challenge for her seat. It was no secret. You thought to destroy us both and claim the echelon.*"

A scream emanated from the tent, and a woman came running out, nearly colliding with Orina. Orina turned and screamed at her retainers. "*You were supposed to keep her quiet, you idiots!*"

"*She kidnapped me!*" screamed Deshari. "*In the middle of a challenge. It is not permitted! The challenge is void.*"

Yserria said, "*No, Deshari. I completed the challenge. I prevailed against her forces*—both *units, whereas your champion fell.*"

Deshari's face paled. "*Ifigen is dead?*" She looked at Orina in horror. "*You said nothing! You would not even permit me to mourn my consort?*"

Yserria said, "*You plotted against me, Deshari, and Orina plotted against you. Now, I will take both your echelons.*" Yserria met Deshari's stricken gaze and said, "*You nipped at the wolf's heels, and the wolf bit back.*"

Orina glanced around as if searching for something—or someone. "*I need a champion,*" she shouted. She looked to one of her sodden men who had been lucky enough to survive the flood. He was a hard-looking man with scars across his bare chest. He shook his head. She looked to another, and he too refused. She called out, "*Whosoever serves as my champion will become first consort to the echelon.*" No one stepped forward.

Yserria sheathed her sword. "*You have failed to produce a champion. Your seat is forfeit.*"

"*On behalf of what house do you claim the echelons?*" said the man with the scars.

Yserria paused. She could not claim the echelons under House Rey or the power would go to her aunt. She had to claim them for herself.

"What is it?" Malcius whispered.

"They wish to know the name of my house."

He stared at her for a moment and then said, "Palis."

She glanced at him to see if he was serious. He motioned for her to proceed. She looked at him again, uncertainly, then turned back to the crowd, "*I claim the Third and Fourth Echelons under House Palis.*"

18

Tam and Uthey, together, followed the rest of the prisoners through the passage. It was the first daylight he had seen in over a week after being held in the dark cell of the cave near the docks. A few times a day, a guard would walk past their cell carrying a torch. Twice each day, someone opened their cell to toss in food, which was already rancid half the time, and a couple of buckets of putrid water. That was all the light they had seen. In those brief moments, Tam had estimated about thirty people shared his cell. Sometimes he heard them whispering or crying in the dark, but most kept quiet. Sometimes they stood, and sometimes they sat, but they never moved about. Their bodies had been forsaken to the darkness, their minds trapped within the confines of their imaginations. Tam had wondered if he would ever see the sun again.

He squeezed his eyes shut against the brightness. The sharp pain behind his eyeballs nearly dropped him to his knees. He stumbled on the sandy path, but Uthey pulled him to his feet—not out of kindness or concern. The slavers had few rules: 1) do as they say, or you will be tortured or killed; and 2) whatever happens to your partner, happens to you. Uthey was looking out for his own neck. Tam flinched when a rock collided with his temple. He blinked up toward the top of the passage. The walls were made of posts as thick as his arm, tied together with rope and covered in canvas. A walkway had been constructed along the top on the other side, and guards paced back and forth watching their progress. Filthy children laughed as they threw rocks and dirt clods at the prisoners from above.

Tam searched the figures around him as he dragged his feet through the sand. He recognized many of the prisoners as those who had been trapped in the ship's hull with him, but there were also others. It was not surprising that many faces were missing. A handful had died before they had even reached port. Several others had died in the cell. He had been forced to sleep next to a corpse for two days before the guards finally came for the bodies. What had made it all the worse was that he had spoken to the woman. He had assured her that they would find a way out of the mess. He supposed she *had* found a way out.

A sharp pain shot through his head, and stars swam before his eyes. Sometimes he envied the dead.

"*What is wrong with you*," whispered Uthey.

"*I have a hole in my mind*," he mumbled.

"*You mean in your* head. *It's called your nose, and you're bleeding from it.*"

Tam wiped his nose. Considering the amount of pain, he was surprised there was so little blood. He closed his eyes for a moment, allowing Uthey to pull him along, and concentrated on his breathing. He blocked out the sounds as best he could, and the pain began to subside. It struck again when he opened his eyes, but it was not as strong as before.

As they neared what he thought to be the end of the passage, they were suddenly assailed with streams of cold water. Guards and a few water mages stood atop the wall tossing buckets or casting streams over their heads. Tam shivered but was grateful to get rid of the filth. The water stopped too quickly, though, and he realized that he was still covered in filth, only now it was wet filth. They marched forward again, the passage opening into an appalling market. Instead of carts and stalls filled with goods and food, row upon row of cages filled with men, women, and even children lined the paths. Some of the cages contained dogs or more exotic species. Merchants, traders, and other wealthy sorts strolled down the rows, taking notes and asking questions of the slavers. As Tam and Uthey were shoved into a cage, he realized that these people saw no difference between the prisoners and the animals.

"*What happens now?*" he said.

"*Now, they will wait for someone to buy us,*" said Uthey. "*If we're lucky, we'll go to a plantation. We don't want to end up on a ship or in the mines.*"

"*I don't intend to be a slave for the rest of my life. We need to escape.*"

"*How do you propose we do that?*"

"*I can pick the lock on the cage. We can open some of the other cages to create a distraction. If we make it to the docks, we can stow away on a merchant ship or steal some clothes and pretend to be sailors.*"

"*And what about these,*" said Uthey as he lifted the chain attached to their necks.

Tam eyed Uthey's collar. "*Do you think they're enchanted?*"

Uthey narrowed his eyes as he looked at Tam's. "*Don't see any runes. They've got a place for a key.*"

"*I might be able to pick those, too,*" said Tam. "*I'll need a couple of pins. Something thin and sharp but strong.*"

They searched the cage for anything of use. The sides and top had bars made of thick iron. The ground was sandy, but more bars lay only a few inches deep. Tam was glad a roof lay over the bars, even it was made of old, rotting boards. One of the slavers walked up and smacked a cane against the bars, eliciting a jarring ring that smacked Tam right behind the eyes.

The slaver said, "*Kunduta bundunana. Niheshet kwafugarana.*"

Tam looked to Uthey, who shrugged and said, "*I don't speak Verrili.*"

The slaver said in Gendishen, "*You need not bother. You cannot escape.*"

"*My people will come,*" said Tam. "*You have made a mistake in taking us.*"

The man laughed, sun-darkened skin stretching tight over his sharp cheekbones. "*You Gendishen are all the same. You think too highly of yourselves. You are no one now. Your people, if you have any, will not find you. If they come looking, maybe we will throw them in a cage, too.*" He cackled at his own joke as he walked away.

As Tam and Uthey waited out the day, two more pairs of prisoners joined them. One of them was a young woman who looked terrified. The man she was chained to pulled her into his lap as he lounged against the bars. He ran his fingers over the bare flesh of her arms and neck. Her dress had been ripped down the front, and she held it together where it had been hastily tied in knots.

The man looked up at Tam and grinned. "*At least they gave me a consolation prize.*"

Tam looked at the woman. "*Do you know this man?*"

She blinked at him, then cried, "I don't know what you're saying. I don't know what anyone is saying."

"You're Ashaiian?" he said.

The woman's face lit, and she smiled for the first time. She struggled to climb out of the man's lap to get closer to Tam. "Please, tell me what's happening. Where are we?"

"My name is Tamarin Blackwater. I'm also from Ashai. What is your name?"

"Malena."

"Malena, I believe we are on the Isle of Sand. They intend to sell us for slaves."

She shook her head vigorously. "But, I didn't do anything wrong! I'm not a criminal. I was visiting my sister and her husband in Jerea, and these men came in and took us. I don't know what happened to her. Why did they take us?"

"Are you aware that King Caydean has started a war?"

"With Jerea?"

"With *everyone*. Ashaiians are no longer safe in the other kingdoms. We are refugees."

"They must let us go home," she cried.

He shook his head. "It is not safe there, either. Caydean has declared war on his own people. He has arrested or killed over half the noble families and their retainers. Most of the commoners have been drafted into the army or forced to work in support of the army." Seeing her horrified expression, he said, "But, there is hope. The True King of Ashai has established a new kingdom—the Kingdom of Cael. All refugees are welcome there."

One of the other prisoners laughed. With a Channerían accent, he said, "The True King? The Kingdom of Cael? They are myths. No such place exists. You look for saviors where there are none."

Tam scowled at the man. "It does exist. I've been there, and I serve the True King. He will come for me."

The man laughed again. "*You*? This True King, the savior of Ashai, will come for *you*?" He looked at Malena. "Do not listen to him. He has lost his mind."

Tam pointed to his head. "I haven't lost my mind," he hissed. "There is a hole in it. They put it there while I was *on Cael*."

The others shared a knowing look. Malena's face fell, and tears welled in her eyes. Tam leaned forward to grasp her hand. "I'm not mad, and I'm not lying. When we escape, I will take you there."

Her smile did not reach her eyes. "Thank you," she said, as she patted his hand. "That is kind." By her patronizing tone, Tam knew she did not believe him.

That night, the slavers did not vacate the market. They gathered around fire pits at the intersections, eating and laughing. The prisoners had not been fed that night, and Tam's stomach burned. Worse than the hunger was the thirst. After weeks in the ship's hold and another in the dark cave, he knew that if they did not escape soon, he would be too weak to try.

"*They do it on purpose, you know.*"

Tam rolled his head toward Uthey. "*Do what?*"

"*Keep us hungry and thirsty. Keep us weak.*"

Tam wondered if he had spoken his thoughts aloud. "*So that we can't escape?*"

"*Nah, they've got that under control,*" Uthey said with a lift of his arm and jingle of the chain. "*They think if we're miserable, we'll be thankful to our new masters when they feed us. We're less likely to give them trouble. You can't be grateful for what you have unless you know how much worse it could be.*"

Tam said, "*Maybe that works for some, but I remember how much* better *it can be.*"

"*Then you've lived a blessed life. I guess being a king's man'll do it for you. Yeah, I heard your nonsense. I don't speak Ashaiian, but I understand a bit of the trade language. I got the gist of it. I don't care if you're mad, so long as you don't get me killed.*"

"*I'm not mad,*" said Tam. "*I need to find some healers. The mages cast a spell to put a hole in my mind so that I can learn things faster. If they don't close it soon, I'll die. It's probably too late as it is, but I'm not ready to give up.*"

"*That'd be a neat trick—having things spill into your mind. I don't believe you, but even if I did, it wouldn't matter. You're not going to find any healers. From what I hear, Verril doesn't have many—only a few for the king and court. No way there's any around here.*"

Tam growled in frustration. "*You don't believe me? A few months ago, I didn't speak a word of Gendishen.*"

Uthey shrugged. "*Maybe you did, maybe you didn't. Maybe you're a fast learner. Why don't you do us a favor and learn Verrili. That'd be somewhat useful.*"

"*That's the problem. I don't choose what I learn. It all just flows in—all of it! I didn't notice at first. The hole was smaller, maybe. Lately, I can feel it.*

Everything goes in, but it's a mess. I can't sort through it. It's tearing my mind apart. It's why I get these headaches and nosebleeds."

"*I think you've got a tumor. You know what that is? My cousin's friend's sister's mother had one. She went to a healer. He said it's where a lump grows in your brain that doesn't belong there. It makes you think all kinds of crazy things. Gives you headaches and nosebleeds, too.*"

"*It's not a tumor,*" said Tam.

Uthey shrugged again. "*Of course, you would say that. You have a tumor.*"

The next morning, they were marched through the passage again. After visiting an open pit where they could relieve themselves *without* privacy, they were lined up for inspection. Men and women peered into their mouths and ears and poked them as nearly every inch of their bodies was examined. Tam was glad they had at least been allowed to wear clothes even if his boots had been taken. The prisoners who resisted were beaten, and those that did not live up to the slavers' standards were taken away, their partners reassigned. After being thoroughly humiliated, the prisoners were returned to their cages. The others who had shared the space with Uthey and Tam were still there, but an additional set of strangers had been added to the cage that was smaller than a horse stall.

After a while, a commotion erupted farther down the lane. The hoots and hollers moved closer, and Tam peered through the bars to find the source. A couple of men were walking alongside a cart pulled by a donkey. The cart was piled high with slop. Tam's stomach grumbled, and where before he would never have considered eating what looked like a tavern's refuse, he was now elated to see such a bounty. The cart stopped in front of their cage, and one of the men used a bucket to scoop out some of the slop. Then, he threw it into their cage through the bars, not even bothering to open the door. The prisoners descended on the rubbish like rabid animals, Tam included. He briefly worried that Malena would go hungry until one man tried to claim her score, and she bit him. Tam sat cross-legged with his stash in his lap, shoving chunks of old cabbage and hard biscuits into his mouth.

Uthey said, "*Who's the woman?*"

Tam gave him a questioning glance.

With a nod, Uthey said, "*That's not something a man buys for himself.*"

Tam glanced at his wrist. It seemed like a terribly long time ago, but he had once sat outside a horse stall on a ship talking with a beautiful, sweet girl named Netty. She had woven the small bracelet from horse hair and hay. As he looked at it now, he found a few golden strands that must have belonged to her.

He dabbed the crumbs that had fallen on his pants, refusing to lose the tiniest morsel. He said, "It's a trivial thing, a minor token—a gift from someone I had thought to court. Then, I realized she was far above my station, and it would never happen."

"*So, you fancied a real lady. Can't imagine one giving out bracelets made of grass and hair. Who was she really? The weaver's daughter?*"

Tam scowled at him. "*You're right. She isn't a lady. She's a princess.*"

Uthey laughed. "*Of course, Kingsman, you would think to marry a princess. Mayhap your princess will sew you a new suit and clean your boots, too. I almost envy you your tumor. You may be crazy, but you dream a pleasant life.*"

Tam picked up a small, mushy potato covered in sprouts. He took a large bite and was thankful for the moisture, despite the bitter taste.

Uthey leaned over and whispered, "*You need to take more.*"

Tam's chewing was made more difficult by the dryness in his mouth, but he finally swallowed and said, "*I took my share. Everyone needs to eat.*"

Uthey nodded toward the newcomers. "*The skinny ones won't make it anyway.*" He looked back at Tam. "*Your eyes are innocent, and you smile too much, but your body is fit. You might be useful in a fight. You need to stay strong.*"

"*I've seen my share of trouble,*" said Tam. "*Had some run-ins with bandits, took out a few slavers when they came for me, and I was in Skutton at the time of the attack on the King's Tournament.*"

"*Hmm, I might've caused a stir when they took me, as well,*" said Uthey. He nodded toward the others. "*I've noticed something about the pairings. It doesn't seem random. The woman and that man—they're both the good-looking sort, a bit soft. Nobles like that kind of thing around their estates.*" He nodded to the next pair. "*Those two are scrawny. Not sure what good they'll be. Those two over there are strong.*" He looked back to Tam. "*I think they put us together for a reason, and I doubt it'll be a plush plantation for you and me. We'll need to keep each other's backs where we're going.*"

"*Where's that?*"

Uthey shrugged. "*Don't know, but it's sure to be full of men like us.*"

One of the larger men, a curly-haired fellow with a flat nose, said, "*Hey, what're you two going on about over there*?" He looked to the others for support. "*They're talking about us. They're plotting something*."

Malena's partner pulled her into his lap. "*Come here, darlin'. Best keep you out of their way.*" Malena pushed and kicked at him, but he held strong as his hands started to roam her body.

Tam said, "*Stop it! You leave her alone or—*"

"*Or what?*" The man lifted his chin toward where the slavers lurked. "*Remember, what happens to me, happens to her.*"

"*Only if they think we've been causing trouble. If you die of natural causes, she gets a new partner.*"

"*Natural causes*?" The man laughed. "*You think to starve me to death? Maybe wait 'til I die of old age*?"

"*Ain't none of us gonna die of old age,*" muttered Uthey.

"*All the more reason to have a little fun before I go*," said the man.

Tam stood and looked back at Uthey, who grumbled but followed as he stepped across the cage. The others stood as well, in anticipation of a fight. The woman scrambled out of the man's lap and backed away the length of her restraint. Tam faced her partner with determination. The big man who had voiced his discontent moments before stepped up to Tam's left. Tam elbowed him in the stomach and then backhanded his temple, sending the man crashing into his partner, and causing the two of them to fall into the other men. Ducking a swing from the woman's partner, Tam thrust his open palm in the *V* below the man's sternum, just as Rezkin had taught him. He felt the small bone break away, and he knew he had used enough force for it to have punctured something vital. As the man doubled over, Tam backed to his side of the cage. He gave the other men a warning glare, and Malena's partner slid to the floor holding his abdomen. Tam retook his seat, and Uthey followed.

The gasping man looked at him with fury in his eyes and said, "*When I catch my breath, I'm going to make you pay for that. Then, I'm going to make her pay for it, too*."

Tam met the man's dark gaze. "*You'll be lucky to see the morning. Either way, you'll not be in the mood to bother her*."

Uthey looked over at him and grinned. "*You will do well in a fight, so long as you don't kick the lion.*"

A bubble of laughter broke through Tam's misery as he thought of how Rezkin might respond. He said, "*I* am *the lion.*"

. . .

Tam awoke the next morning to a squeal. Malena said, "He's dead. By the Maker, he's dead." She yanked the chain around her neck as if it might fall away with the effort. "Get it off me." She gripped the bars and screamed for the slavers. "Help me! Get him away! He's dead." Her frantic gaze darted around the cage. "I can't be chained to a corpse!

Uthey nudged Tam and said, "*You killed him with one strike. I was standing right next to you, and I barely saw it.*"

Tam was also a little surprised. Rezkin had told him the technique could kill a man, but he had not truly expected it to work. His muscles began to tighten with anxiety as Malena's cries finally caught the attention of their captors.

"*What is it? I will make you suffer if you waste my time,*" said the nearest slaver. He was a gap-toothed man with long, stringy hair gathered into multiple messy braids. Shells and other small trinkets were tied into the locks as well as his plaited beard.

"Please," said Malena. "My partner is dead. Please take him away."

The man looked at her, but he did not appear to understand her words. Tam said, "*That man is dead. He should be removed before the rest of us succumb to his illness.*"

Another man approached, this one bearing a large stick Tam had seen him use to beat people, sometimes even other slavers. "*What is happening here? What trouble have you caused now, Fiero*?"

Fiero pointed into the cage. "*I've done nothing, Ipon. One of the prisoners is dead.*"

Ipon opened the cage, and dragged the dead man out, pulling Malena with him. He looked the corpse over and said, "*No blood. No marks. Did you give them water?*"

"*Same as the others,*" Fiero said, waving to the other cages.

Ipon pointed to Malena. "*What is she doing in there?*"

"*We were holding the two of them for Lady Askiva.*"

"*I know that, you idiot. Why is she with the men? Lady Askiva will not want her if she arrives with child.*" He pointed to the dead man. "*I'm holding you responsible for this, Fiero. His price will come out of your pay. You lose nearly as many as you sell. If I didn't keep constant watch over you, we would have none to sell at all.*"

"*That's not true, Ipon. It's not my fault. These are Barbarus's slaves.*"

"*Gah, you blame Barbarus. If you were one of the other men, I would beat you senseless.*"

"*But you know his are always half dead when they arrive.*"

"*I can't argue with that, but you should know that means they need extra care when they get here. How did I get stuck with an idiot for a son? Put her with the women and get rid of this one.*" As Ipon walked away, he shouted, "*And give them extra food and water.*"

Uthey leaned over. "*What did they say?*"

Tam glanced at him in annoyance. "*Weren't you listening? They think he died of thirst. They're going to move her with the women and give us more food and water.*"

Uthey's gaze followed Fiero as he dragged away the body. He said, "*How did you know what they were saying*?"

"*I'm not deaf,*" Tam said.

"*That's obvious, but they were speaking Verrili, and so were you.*" Then, Uthey smacked Tam on the back. "*You've done us a service. My thanks, friend.*"

Tam was uncomfortable being thanked for killing a man—at least, not only because they would receive extra food and water. He had done it for Malena, and she had been separated from them. He supposed it was better for her to join the women. He felt a drop of moisture on his hand and looked down. His nose was bleeding again. Then, it was as if a light burst before his eyes.

The port city of Havoth was in an uproar as Rezkin rode through the streets. He was surprised by the size of the fanfare, considering the event had only been planned and implemented in the little more than a week that it took to establish order in and return from Bromivah. Rezkin rode toward the rear of the procession, surrounded by royal guards and soldiers, while Moldovan's coach was in the lead. It was a symbolic gesture, the ushering in of a new king. Farson and Mage Threll rode at his sides. The sounds of horns, pipes, and drums, and colorful scarves and shiny objects lobbed by jugglers filled the air. Acrobats twisted and flipped along the flanks, and amongst them, and Rezkin caught sight of a pair of blue eyes staring at him from behind a red mask.

Mage Threll erected a sound shield around the three of them, and then she and Farson fell into a discussion, with Rezkin silently existing between them.

She said, "You never told me he was a legitimate prince of Ashai."

"I was not aware," replied Farson.

"You knew."

"I suspected. What does it matter to you?"

"It would have made the choice to follow him easier."

"You made that decision on your own."

"Yes, but I would not have been so conflicted."

"You did not seem *conflicted* when you ran off with him against my wishes."

Rezkin saw her glance at him out of the corner of her eye. He continued to survey the crowd, giving the appearance that he was not listening, even though he would have needed to be deaf not to hear them.

"I did not run off with *him*. I was running with the escapees."

"You knew I was near and that I would come for you. You also knew I had forbidden you to go near him."

She glanced at Rezkin again, and her expression turned to resolve. "You are glad I did. Besides keeping me safe, you desire nothing more than to be at his side."

Farson did not answer, nor did he meet her accusatory gaze.

Rezkin said, "He desires only to keep me in his sights. He watches for weakness."

Mage Threll turned to him. "You know that is untrue. He is depending on you to fix Ashai—and, I suppose, every other kingdom you have claimed."

Farson muttered, "They would not need fixing if he would stop claiming them."

Nanessy ignored her uncle and spoke to Rezkin, "At this point, you are the only one who can do it."

Rezkin said, "If chaos reigns, someone will step in to seize power and instill order. My participation is unnecessary."

"Your *participation* is necessary to ensure that it goes in our favor."

He finally looked at her. "Who is to say that it should?"

She appeared surprised. "What do you mean?"

Rezkin returned his gaze to the crowd. "Your uncle knows me. He knows what I am. He does not believe I am worthy of kingship, yet I now bear several crowns. These people call me emperor. Perhaps *I* am the enemy you should seek to destroy."

Farson glanced at him, but Mage Threll was having none of it. "You are not the one using demons to do your dirty work. It is spreading. It was a demon in the tower, was it not?"

Rezkin said, "I believe the demon was housed in the vessel. I killed Boulis before it could possess him."

"Then what happened to it?"

"I would assume that, without another willing vessel, it returned to H'khajnak."

She said, "I would prefer not to *assume* anything with regard to demons. How did it get here in the first place? I doubt Boulis had the power or knowledge to summon it."

Farson said, "I doubt he had the courage."

"No," replied Rezkin. "He waited until the last minute. He had hoped to gain power without it. Someone else was behind the demon."

When they arrived at the docks, Moldovan made a show of boarding *Stargazer* with all the pomp and circumstance due a departing king. Rezkin felt that by agreeing to wear the impractical attire, he had fulfilled his duty; but, Moldovan had been disappointed, desiring to bedeck Rezkin in such royal fashion as to make movement practically impossible. As it was, he wore an outfit similar to the impromptu coronation attire, except that the king's amulet hung around his neck, and his short cape had been replaced with a long, black cloak lined with soft, black and silver pelts.

Rezkin offered an obligatory wave toward the crowd then turned to examine the ship repairs. *Stargazer* was in top condition. Beside him, Moldovan said, "I took the liberty of having your ship repaired. The shipwright said he had never seen such damage, and the other vessel had virtually none, yet they surrendered."

"That's because the third ship was obliterated," said a female voice from behind him.

Rezkin turned to see Reaylin standing there with a hand on her hip.

Moldovan narrowed his eyes at the young woman wearing the panels of a healer's apprentice over warrior's armor. He said, "I shall be intrigued to hear the tale."

Reaylin glanced at Moldovan curiously then turned to Rezkin. She looked him up and down and smiled suggestively. "You look better than ever. I don't see anything that needs healing, but that doesn't mean I can't make you feel better."

Rezkin said, "I am well, Reaylin, how is Frisha?" He had learned his lesson. He was supposed to check on Frisha—always.

Reaylin rolled her eyes. "I don't know. Why are you wearing a crown?"

Rezkin glanced at Shezar who had joined them for the briefing before returning to the Ashaiian ship. They had renamed it *Sea Devil*, in recognition of its tumultuous past. Shezar said, "We did not know how much to tell them, so we said nothing."

Rezkin turned back to Reaylin. "This is King Moldovan—"

"*Prince* Moldovan," the former king said. He grinned and said, "Somehow, just saying it makes me feel a bit younger." The old man looked up at Rezkin and said, "But, you have my permission to call me grandfather."

Reaylin's eyes were wide as she glanced between the two of them. Rezkin said, "Have my belongings moved. *Prince* Moldovan may take my quarters."

Moldovan said, "Nonsense. You are the emperor. We must ensure that everyone remembers that." He frowned at Reaylin. "Have my belongings placed in one of the other berths. I will make it a priority to teach your people how to show their emperor proper respect."

Reaylin glanced at Rezkin. "Emperor?"

Rezkin turned to Moldovan. "This is Apprentice Healer Reaylin de Voss. She is … a friend. She need not observe the formalities"—he looked back to Reaylin—"so long as she continues to adhere to her oath." Then, he said, "Do as Prince Moldovan requests, and send for Frisha."

Reaylin bobbed her head and strutted away, swinging her hips a bit more than necessary.

A few minutes later, Frisha strode up to them. She glanced at his attire but did not ask. She said, "Welcome back."

"Are you well?" he said.

She nodded. "Yes, as well as can be. Why?"

He said, "I felt it important to inquire as to your well-being."

She blinked at him and lifted her chin. "Oh. I am well, thank you. You don't need to check on me all the time."

He said, "You were upset when I did not."

"Well, yes, but that was before, and nothing has happened since you disappeared." She narrowed her eyes at him. "How many did you kill this time? Any new wives I should know about?"

Moldovan looked at Rezkin. "Another *friend*?"

"Yes."

Meanwhile, Mage Threll stepped forward to confront Frisha. "Perhaps you should ask how many he *saved* this time."

Moldovan glanced at Mage Threll. "You seem to have many female *friends*." With a grin, he said, "My grandson does an Esyojo proud."

Frisha looked at Moldovan for the first time. "Grandson?"

"Lecillia's father," Rezkin said and then turned to gaze over the crowd gathered around the dock. He searched for blue in a pool of red, but she did not make it easy. The ebb and flow of the crowd was like a wave, and suddenly she appeared in the midst of a group of women as they briefly parted. He met her gaze and then stepped to the top of the gangplank, holding out his hand. The woman sidled forward, her black cloak catching in the breeze to reveal a formfitting red dress. The end of the matching scarf she wore over her face fluttered in the breeze. Her movements were reminiscent of a serpent as she flowed toward him. She took his hand, and her eyes held a smirk behind her veil.

Frisha was used to Rezkin's attention wandering. He always watched the crowds, but she was not prepared for the odd display that happened next. It was as if he had been looking for someone, and then she appeared. By her dress and sensuous movements, Frisha first thought the woman a Leréshi. Then, she saw the eyes, and her blood turned to ice. She recognized that woman. As Rezkin led her toward the cabin, the woman glanced her way. Her eyes held a glint of laughter, and Frisha wanted to slap her as much as she wanted to run and hide.

The man Rezkin had introduced as his grandfather chuckled, an aged, wheezing sound. "Yes, that one is an Esyojo."

Frisha swallowed her bile as she watched them enter the cabin. She said, "That woman is not his lover. At least, I don't think she is. I don't know anything anymore, but she is just as likely to die in there as she is to live." When she turned back to Moldovan, he was staring at her, his aged gaze calculating.

"Who are you?" He stepped closer. "You are too familiar with your king. You scold him, yet you fear him."

Frisha raised her chin. "I am Frisha Souvain-Marcum. I am Rezkin's friend." She paused and then added, "We were to be married, but I … I called it off."

"You? To be queen? Then, you and I shall become well acquainted. I wish to know the woman my grandson chose to wed."

"As I said, we are no longer betrothed."

"Why? Why would you sacrifice your position? You would be empress."

"Empress?" she said weakly.

Moldovan chuckled as his manservant came to lead him to his berth.

After the two men walked away, she was left standing with Farson and Nanessy. She looked to Farson questioningly.

"Moldovan abdicated to Rezkin. He is ruler of multiple kingdoms now. That makes him an emperor. He has named his empire Cimmeria."

Finding her voice was difficult for Frisha at that moment. It came out soft and shaky. "He said he would give me *every* kingdom if it was what I desired. I thought it an exaggeration, a romantic gesture. I thought his sweet words too good to be true." She blinked away her tears. "It *was* too good to be true. It was never meant to be romantic." She laughed without mirth. "To him, a gift of an empire is just as practical as a scarf." She pulled the filmy, green fabric from her neck and balled it in her fist as she fled to her berth.

Nanessy looked to her uncle. "Is she equating a scarf with an empire? I fail to understand why she is upset."

He said, "Frisha knows that Rezkin would take her back if she asked. She has had to choose between being a queen—or *empress*—and being loved."

"What do you mean?"

"She wants Rezkin to love her. He does not."

Nanessy felt terribly guilty for the sudden thrill that caused her heart to flutter. "I thought—I mean, he seemed to—"

Her uncle gave her a knowing look. "He is *incapable* of love."

She flushed. "No one is incapable of love."

"He *is* no one," said Farson.

She frowned at him but said, "Love can grow in time. Minder Finwy says that love can heal the darkest of souls."

"He has no soul to heal," said Farson. He growled in anger, "We destroyed it." He took a calming breath and shook his head. "I admire her for her decision. I believe most women would not have had the strength to reject such an offer."

Nanessy thought about Rezkin standing there in his regal suit and cloak, with the gold and silver crown atop his raven-black hair. She considered the way he moved, like a predator after his prey as he wielded the power of kings.

She saw his icy blue eyes, so full of intelligence and cunning, the knowledge of ages glinting from above a heart-stopping smile. She said, "If she has the man she loves, and he treats her well, perhaps it does not matter that he does not love her in return."

Her uncle frowned at her sadly and then left her to her fantasies.

The woman entered his berth ahead of him. She had come into his domain *alone*, and he would not give her the chance to test her skill. Rezkin allowed her to inspect the space, and then she returned to face him in the center of the room.

"We will not be overheard?"

"The room is enchanted. No sound will leave here."

"Then, no one will hear my screams?"

"If I choose to kill you, you will not have time to scream."

The secrelé smirked as she reached up to remove the veil. "That was not exactly what I had in mind. No, you are a single-minded man, and yours is not like that of most men." She ran a finger along the crease between her breasts and said, "Would you, *could* you, ever let down your guard to lay with me?"

"That would be folly," he said.

She had a husky laugh. "Yes, it would."

"What do you want?" said Rezkin. "You have Oledia. I have the sword. Our business is concluded."

"Is it?" This time she looked at him uncertainly. "The great mother was concerned that you might have been a little perturbed that we did not have the sword for you. She thought you might consider another visit—one less pleasant."

"There was nothing pleasant about the last one."

She glanced down and smirked. "For you, perhaps. I, for one, enjoyed the show."

"If she was so concerned about my seeking retribution, why did she not send you to reacquire the sword for me—or at least let me know you did not have it?"

"We could not have gotten the sword. We tried to discover its location, but Moldovan never told anyone where he hid it. In truth, the great mother did not expect you to be successful in your endeavors. We did not believe you to be the Riel'gesh. That is why I have come and why I have revealed my face."

She knelt on the floor and then slowly drew eight throwing stars from where they were hidden about her person. Each one, she laid around her, and he knew they represented the points of an octagram, an eight-pointed star. From a pocket in her dress, she withdrew another veil, one Rezkin recognized as belonging to the great mother. The secrelé positioned the filmy fabric around her in a circle and then opened her palms toward him.

"I, Arethia, tasked to speak on behalf of the great mother and the Adana'Ro. We follow the path of Riel'sheng, and we recognize you as the Riel'gesh. Your will is our will. Our swords are your swords. Our bodies are your bodies. We serve you in life and follow you unto death."

Rezkin looked down at the woman, frustrated yet pleased. Having the Adana'Ro at his disposal would be useful, but he did not feel comfortable with their belief that he was more than human. He said, "I did not ask for this."

"Yet, it is given," she said, for once without a hint of humor.

When Tam awoke, it was night—either that or they were in a cave, because no light seeped in between the cracks of the boards. The absence of the jarring and creaks of the wagon's skirmish with the rutted road was what woke him. Day after day was a monotony of dreamy hazes, and every night was a waking nightmare as he struggled to hold on to the memories of a better life. Ilanet—had he known her or was she a dream? He ran his finger over the bracelet on his wrist. He could not have made it for himself. And Frisha. Sometimes she was a little girl chasing him through the yard with ribbons in her hair. Other times, she was a grown woman staring dreamy-eyed at a vicious god. Had he known a god?

The door opened, and Fiero growled at them to get out of the wagon. After hours of sitting in one position, stuffed between the other filthy prisoners, Tam stood on shaky legs that cramped with the effort. He clenched his teeth against the pain. It was not as bad as the headaches, which, for the moment, had subsided. He felt better in the dark, especially when it was quiet.

Uthey tumbled into him as he stepped out of the wagon, and Ipon struck them both with his stick for causing trouble. Tam felt no anger toward Uthey for inciting Ipon's ire. It was pointless to hold a grudge when the next time it would likely be his own fault. As one of Ipon's men lit the fire with his *talent*, Ipon ordered the prisoners to relieve themselves in the bushes. Once that was done, they were made to walk in a line, circling around the fire again and again. Afterward, they jumped for a while, then did sit-stands and push-ups.

They received more food than at any other time since his capture. Ipon said he would get more money for them if they were strong when they arrived at the quarry, enough to make it worth feeding them.

The quarry. It was the last place anyone wanted to go. Worse than the caves, worse than the ships, the quarry was the opening to the hells, the pit of despair—or so Tam had been told. He could not imagine it being worse than what he had already suffered. He and Uthey leaned against each other's backs as they filled their mouths with mush they scooped from their bowls with their fingers. Tam bit down on what he kept telling himself were raisins or seeds. He cared little about what he ate, so long as his stomach no longer ached with hunger.

"*Is it time?*" whispered Uthey while Ipon berated Fiero for the troubles of the world.

Tam nodded. "*Tonight. I overheard them talking earlier. We arrive tomorrow, so if we're going to do it, it has to be tonight.*"

"*Have you discovered who has the key?*"

"*No. It has not come up.*"

Uthey eyed the other men. "*We could force them to unlock one of us.*"

"*They only unlock the dead.*"

Uthey nodded. "*At least we would know who has the key.*"

"*I'd rather kill the slavers and dig through their pockets.*"

"*You and me both, but they have mages and weapons.*"

"*I am the weapon,*" said Tam. "*Rule 233.*" His thoughts and memories abruptly aligned around a central figure. Rezkin. He knew Rezkin. *Oh.* Rezkin was Frisha's dark god. *No*, Tam thought, *not a god. A man. Maybe.* Rezkin was a conundrum, but Rezkin would come for him.

"*That's a ridiculous rule,*" said Uthey. "*A man with a sword and knowledge to use it will win against a man without one.*"

"*You don't know my king,*" said Tam.

Uthey silently chuckled. "*Neither do you, but if it keeps you sane, then you are welcome believe whatever you want.*"

To the other side of Tam was a Leréshi sailor named Mogalay, who knew a bit of Gendishen. He said, "*When this king of yours comes to save you, you will introduce us, yes? Maybe he can take us with him to your secret island, and we can all be claimed by princesses.*" A few of the men who spoke Gendishen laughed. Others never laughed even if they spoke the language. Tam was glad that Uthey laughed often.

He turned to Uthey. "*How do you laugh*?" Uthey gave him a strange look, so Tam nodded toward the slavers. "*With all of this? With the hunger and beatings, with the chains and blisters, with no choices in your life, how do you laugh?*"

Uthey stared at the fire for a long time and finally said, "*Every moment is a bubble of sorrow in my chest. The bubbles build up to weigh heavily on my heart. I must release them, or they will crush me from within.*"

Tam stared at him, and then he laughed. Tam laughed, and Uthey laughed, and many of the other men laughed. Ipon stormed over to scold them, and they laughed harder. They all lay down with welts that night.

A few hours later, Tam reached over and shook Uthey. The man's snoring ceased, and they both lay still to make sure the lookout had not seen.

"*Where is he?*" whispered Uthey.

"*I don't know. He went into the woods over there and hasn't returned. We should go now.*"

They glanced behind them to see Ipon and a couple of the other slavers fast asleep. Another lookout was stationed on the other side of the wagon, but he would not be looking their way. Tam kicked Mogalay and gave him the signal. Mogalay woke his partner and then the next men in the line. Uthey, being closest to the tree line on the side opposite the slavers, led the way crawling on hands and knees. Tam glanced back to see how many followed and note whether the others might alert their captors. When he turned back, he was met by a pair of black eyes. Slavering lips pulled back to reveal sharp pinkish-white fangs.

Ahead of him, Uthey yanked the chain, but Tam refused to budge. He remained frozen, hoping Uthey would not panic when he finally saw the creature. The beast that looked like a cross between a cat and a wolf took a step forward, and Tam felt its hot breath sweep over his face. The beast suddenly lurched, and Tam realized that Uthey had kicked it in the side.

"*What is it?*" Tam said.

"*A vurole*," said Uthey as they tried to stand, partially tripping over each other in their haste.

The vurole abruptly pounced on Uthey, who screamed as the creature latched onto his arm. Tam jumped on the vurole's back, reaching around its thick neck to grasp the chain that bound him to his partner. His fingers brushed the metal, and he almost fell off the creature as he reached for it again. Gripping the heavy coat of the squirming beast with one hand, he stretched as far as he could reach to grab hold of the chain. Once within his grasp, he wrenched the thick links around the vurole's throat and threw his weight backward. The vurole released Uthey's arm, and Tam held tight as the creature twisted and bucked like an untamed stallion. His muscles were locked with fear and determination. The creature slammed into a tree, smashing his leg, then rolled to scrape him from its back. A rock dug into Tam's shoulder, but he gritted his teeth and held tight. He knew that if he let go, he would die. It lurched to its feet and tried to bite Tam's leg where it was tucked tightly against the beast's side, but with Uthey's weight on the other end of the chain, the beast could not reach. Eventually, the vurole's movements slowed, and it stumbled, partially trapping Tam beneath it. Tam held the chain with all his might even after the creature ceased to breathe.

Uthey gripped Tam's shoulder. "*It's dead! Come, we must seek safety.*"

Tam shook his head without words as he clung to the beast. Uthey growled as he bent to heft a large rock with one ruined arm. He slammed the rock into the vurole's face until it was no longer recognizable. Only then did Tam let go. He glanced at the surrounding chaos. The entire camp had been swarmed. The slavers fought with weapons and *talent* while the slaves were torn apart or scrambled for hiding places. Several had closed themselves in the wagon, but they would not open the door to admit others, so men climbed each other to huddle on the roof. The vuroles moved in to surround the wagon, and Tam and Uthey were left to fend for themselves.

Tam tugged Uthey toward a downed slaver and grabbed the man's sword. By the lack of blood on the blade, he figured the man had never had the chance to use it against the creature that killed him. Tam pushed Uthey out of the way as a vurole jumped at him. He stabbed the beast under the ribs just before he was yanked off his feet by the chain around his neck. Another vurole had grabbed Uthey by the leg and was dragging them both toward the forest. Tam dug at the collar, trying to breathe, and he suddenly knew how the vurole he killed had felt. The vurole loped around a tree, and the chain became wrapped with Tam and Uthey on opposite sides. Uthey screamed as the creature savaged his leg, frustrated by its lack of progress. Tam blinked away the spots in his eyes and coughed as he gasped for air. He rolled onto his side and felt something hard jabbing his rib. To his relief, the sword had caught in a tear in his clothes. He grabbed the hilt and stumbled toward the creature. It abruptly released Uthey's leg to try another attack, and Tam stabbed the beast through the throat. Blood spewed over them both as the blade ripped through flesh.

Tam breathed heavily as he glanced toward the campsite. The slavers would likely succeed in fighting off the remaining vuroles, so he figured this was their only chance to escape. He surveyed Uthey's wounds, then ripped a strip off the bottom of his shirt and quickly wrapped the man's leg.

He said, "*Can you run*?"

Uthey gritted his teeth. "*I'll run to the hells and back if I must.*"

Uthey exhaled heavily a few times, and then Tam helped him to his feet. Tam threw Uthey's good arm around his shoulders and, with Uthey holding his injured arm to his chest, they ran. Progress was slow in the dark forest, but they were driven by knowledge of the fate that awaited them if they were caught. After a few hours, their path was abruptly truncated by a steep ravine. The bottom could not be seen in the dark, but they could hear rushing water.

"*Which way do we go?*" said Uthey.

"*I don't know. We need to go east. Maybe we can board a ship in Ferélle.*"

"*We'll not be safe in Ferélle, either. The enslavement of criminals is legal there.*"

"*But we're not criminals,*" said Tam. "*We were kidnapped illegally!*"

"*They'll not believe us. We should go west to Pruar. No slavery, and it's closer.*"

Tam looked to the sky for direction, but the canopy blocked most of the view. "*Which way is west*?"

Uthey blinked upward and shook his head. "*I can't tell.*"

Tam glanced back at the ravine. "*The river should flow toward the sea, right*?"

"*Maybe. According to the maps, Verril has many streams and rivers coming off the Drahgfir Mountains in the south. Some flow mostly east, others west, some go straight north. I couldn't say which way it goes.*"

"*Alright,*" said Tam. "*We can't stay here. Do we go upriver or down*?"

Uthey shook his head. "*No, I'll not be responsible for us getting caught.*"

"*Okay, we'll toss a stick.*"

"*Sounds fair.*"

Tam picked up a small stick with a knob on one end. He glanced at Uthey. "*We follow the knob.*" Uthey nodded, and Tam tossed it into the air. From there, they traveled downriver.

19

Malcius stepped off the ferry and could not have been gladder to be on foreign soil. Japa came next, pushing the small wagon that contained Yserria's trunk and their traveling packs. Eight guards, four from each of the echelons, followed, and then Yserria. She passed the line of guards that waited on her without rolling her eyes, but Malcius knew what she was thinking. She had severely protested the need for guards, but the influential matrianeras of both echelons insisted that she needed them. Malcius had decided they were all spies and assassins.

"Come on," said Malcius. "The docks are not far."

Japa said, "First Consort, perhaps we should seek lodgings for the echelon. The longer we wait, the more difficult it will be to find a place in the event that no passage is available."

Malcius scowled at the man. "I have asked you not to call me that. You are probably right, though. Is anyone here familiar with Esk?"

One of Yserria's guards, Noko of House Linoni of the Fourth Echelon, said, "I have been here many times. It would be my honor to seek shelter for the echelon."

Malcius said, "Very well. You and Japa find an inn. The rest of us will head to the docks." Everyone nodded, but no one moved. Malcius sighed and rolled his eyes. He looked to Yserria and said, "By your leave, Echelon."

Yserria glanced at the others. She waved her hand and said, "Yes. Go. Do what he said."

She sidled up next to him and muttered, "It is like having children. I must tell them to do *everything*."

"That is what it means to have servants at your call," said Malcius. "Eventually, they will learn your preferences and disposition and start taking care of those tasks on their own."

As they began walking south along the road that followed the river to the docks, she said, "I do not intend to have them that long."

Malcius glanced at the guards who followed them. A few spoke Ashaiian, but most did not—or so they claimed. He said, "You are now the head of two echelons. You had best get used to them."

Yserria said, "Queen Erisial will not permit me to retain that kind of power. She already feels threatened by the perception of strength I bear through Rezkin. I doubt she will allow me to keep one echelon, much less two. Besides, I am committed to serving Rezkin as a royal guard. I do not have time to administer an echelon."

"Rezkin collects influence," said Malcius. "He will probably value your position as echelon more than as a guardsman. It seems that most Leréshi overlook the fact that he is their king. As echelon, you can *encourage* your people to accept him."

After a minute, she said, "You are very good at politics—at least, in the way people relate to each other—outside of Lon Lerésh, that is. Rezkin would benefit from your counsel."

"Rezkin has little need of my counsel. It is I who have benefited from knowing him. I guess you could say that he helped me put my life into perspective. At first, I did not comprehend his desire to befriend Tam, nor did I understand his interest in Frisha. Dark things exist in this world, though, and loyalty and dedication are more valuable than titles."

"I am surprised to hear you say that," she said.

"My whole life has been wrapped in politics. Every word, every action has been judged as a reflection of my house. I accepted this with the understanding that everyone else was enduring the same scrutiny. It was important to make waves only when such was your intention. I had thought Tam and Frisha uncouth and lacking in culture and propriety. I realize now that they were being *genuine*, with no concern for house politics. They wear no masks. Mage Dolinar said something that made me realize the same is true with you."

Yserria glanced at him but did not respond. Eventually, she said, "Rezkin wears a mask."

"But was that not the point?" he said. "No one knew who he was. He could have been anyone. He forced us to recognize him for his skill. His mask is overly intimidating, but it need not be. His achievements speak for themselves."

She did not look at him as she said, "I have not heard you speak so highly of him since Palis died."

Malcius had no response, and he was saved from thinking of something when they encountered a massive crowd. Everyone was attempting to shuffle toward the docks, which, according to their guards, were still several blocks away.

A female guard named Ptelana stepped forward. She was a dark-skinned Leréshi woman from the Third Echelon who had considerable skill with the bow and spoke fluent Ashaiian and Ferélli. She said, "By your leave, Echelon, I will discover the reason for this gathering."

"Yes, please do," said Yserria.

Ptelana stepped into the crowd, and they watched as she questioned several people. When she returned, she said, "A new king has been crowned in Ferélle. His fleet is to arrive today. One man claimed the new king is the emperor of Cimmeria."

"I have never heard of Cimmeria," said Malcius.

"Nor have I," said Yserria.

"Perhaps we should avoid him," said Malcius. "He could be in league with Caydean. If not, he may be seeking to take advantage of the unrest on the Souelian."

Ptelana looked at him and said, "One woman said she had heard a rumor that he is the king of Lon Lerésh, but she did not believe it."

Yserria and Malcius grinned at each other. Yserria said, "Should we dare to hope?"

Malcius crossed his arms. "If anyone could take over another kingdom and start an empire, it would be Rezkin."

"We must find out," she said. "We need to get through this crowd."

Ptelana grinned. "You may leave that to me, Echelon." She crossed her wrists, pressing them to her forehead. "By your leave." Then, she disappeared into the crowd.

~

Slender fingers slipped into the clear water. They slapped the surface, spraying water into the air. An echo of soft laughter flitted on the breeze, and then the entire world was a rush of watery bubbles. Distorted blobs of green and brown danced back and forth in the light above, and below was only murky darkness. A figure in the dark, a shadowy silhouette, slowly drew closer. It entered the sphere of light, the farthest it would travel in the water, and became brighter, clearer. A halo of white hair swayed with the current, obscuring the view. Then, silver eyes emerged from the swath. A pale hand reached forward, the fingers uncurled, and a light blue crystal lay nestled in the palm.

Rezkin was not sure what had awoken him, but he was almost certain it had been his stomach. Although he had slept the entire night, he still felt drained. He knew he would feel somewhat better after he had eaten. With a glance at his time dial, he realized he had eaten a full meal little more than an hour before. His legs wobbled as he tried to stand, so he sat back and took deep breaths as he began running through a list of causes. Had he been poisoned? Had he encountered a toxin? Did he have an infection? Was he ill? He opened his eyes to find a plum taking up his entire field of view. It was nearly touching his nose. Rezkin shifted to see the plum's bearer, and large orange eyes blinked back at him.

"Power spent is power lost. Power gained is power tamed," said the craggy, lilting voice.

Rezkin eyed the piece of fruit. He knew that a fae gift was never what it seemed. He said, "What is the price?"

Bilior glanced at Rezkin's chest where the stone had grown hot beneath his shirt. The sensation occurred more frequently of late, such that the stone was warm most of the time. The katerghen said, "The price, the cost, mistrust, beware." His limbs cracked as they curled in on themselves. "It is paid."

Rezkin wondered if the ancient had somehow weakened him so that he would be beholden to the creature's will, but he took the plum anyway. He examined the surface with a critical eye and a sniff. It smelled sweet, and the dots of moisture clinging to the taut, purple-black skin brought to his attention a thirst that had been overshadowed by the hunger and fatigue. He used a knife to cut into the plum as he glanced at Bilior. The katerghen's gaze shifted anxiously between his face and the plum. Inside was the juicy pink and yellow flesh of normal plum, except that it had no pit. Rezkin's stomach grumbled again, and he glanced at Bilior. The katerghen's anticipation was palatable. Rezkin licked a drop of juice from his finger and waited a few minutes. When he felt no ill effects, he finally braved the fruit. His hunger overtook him, and he consumed the entire plum within seconds.

Bilior stretched out on the floor and propped his head on a twiggy arm. He watched as if waiting for a show. Nothing happened. Rezkin shook his head as he got to his feet. Suddenly, the room was filled with colors. Bilior was composed of the brightest colors Rezkin had ever seen. They swirled across his woody flesh in a chaotic dance of eddies and waves. The walls were drab and dim, and the muddled browns barely moved within them. He looked down at himself. He was nearly as bright as Bilior, but his colors appeared shattered, like a vessel of colored glass that had been broken and pieced back together a thousand times. He began to hear a hum, a distant melody. It grew louder the longer he listened. It was a tune with which he was familiar. It was the music of his meditation.

Rezkin glanced down at the katerghen who looked pleased as his leafy feathers danced to the cadence of the music. In that moment, it was almost as if he understood the katerghen's native language. The secret was just beyond his grasp. He wondered, if he focused long enough, might he learn it? His hunger abated, he felt energized, determined. Rezkin put on the guise of Dark Tidings, strapped on his swords, hooked the mask to his belt, and strode toward the door. He glanced back to the katerghen, but Bilior was gone.

Once on deck, Rezkin was amazed by the vivid dance of hues that pervaded the world. Living things shined the brightest to his eyes, while those that had once been alive appeared dim. Objects that had never lived did not swirl with colors, but rather radiated varying amounts of light. In combination with the sun, it was rather overwhelming. He blinked several times, hoping the previously hidden lights of the world would fade. He focused his eyesight, as if trying to see through a fog. After a few minutes, the lights became less intrusive. He knew not whether they had changed or if his mind had begun to accept them.

Striker Akris strode up to him. "Are you well, Your Majesty?"

Rezkin looked at the striker, whose colors appeared different from his own. He wondered if the patterns had meaning. "All is well," he said. "Do you have a report?"

"Yes. This city was alerted of our impending arrival, and a large crowd has gathered at the docks. The governor has issued an invitation, and we have received a request for a meeting with a Leréshi echelon."

"Which echelon?"

"The missive says the third *and* fourth."

Rezkin nodded. "I anticipated a shift in power after Erisial's daring move. Who is it?"

"House Palis," said Akris. He looked thoughtful and then said, "Was that not the name of Lord Malcius's brother?"

"It was," said Rezkin. The tension between his shoulders released. He had not realized his level of concern over Malcius and Yserria's disappearance until that moment, but he now knew that at least one of them had survived. He said, "Bring them aboard."

Less than an hour later, Yserria and Malcius boarded *Stargazer*, accompanied by their entourage. Frisha pushed past everyone to fling her arms around Malcius while Rezkin greeted Yserria.

"You look well, Echelon."

Yserria shook her head. "It was a difficult time, and *he* made it worse with his obstinance, but we prevailed in the name of our king."

Malcius grinned. "She said that she would show them the might of the Kingdom of Cael, and she delivered."

Frisha reached up to tug at Malcius's hair. "What is this?" she said, fingering the red ribbon.

Malcius huffed and snapped at Yserria. "Why did you not remind me to remove this? I cannot believe it has been there all this time." Then, he looked at Frisha and said, "Some despicable woman tried to *claim* me as consort, so Yserria was forced to challenge her. It was the Third Echelon—Ah!" Malcius suddenly winced and held his hand to the side of his face. "It burns!" he hollered.

"Malcius!" yelled Yserria. "I told you to never speak of that! We agreed that *I* would tell the story!"

"What does it matter?" he said as he turned to her. "I was only saying what happened."

Frisha inhaled sharply and slapped her hands over her mouth as she got a look at Malcius's face. Alarmed by her reaction, Malcius ran his fingers over the skin along the right side of his forehead down to his cheekbone.

"What is it?" he said. "Was I stung by a wasp? Is it bad?"

Frisha looked to Rezkin, who stared at Malcius with apathy. Upon noticing

Frisha's pleading gaze, he said, "What? I can do nothing about this. They are now married."

"No!" screamed Yserria. "No, I did not ask for this. It's not right!"

"You claimed him. That was a statement of willingness on your part. He just recognized the claim outside of Lon Lerésh. The ritual spell has run its course."

"What are you talking about?" said Malcius. "What ritual spell? And, what is this about our being married?"

Frisha looked to Rezkin. "Is there nothing that can be done?"

He shrugged. "Men have tried for centuries to undo the binding. The ritual is very old. It gains power with time and use. Malcius bears Yserria's mark. A like one will adorn her face by the end of the day." He looked to Malcius. "Within Lon Lerésh, you are recognized as her consort. Anywhere else, you are now her husband." He paused, then said, "You realize that she is still my ward. Since you did not ask permission to marry her, I have the right to challenge you to a duel to the death." Malcius's face paled.

Frisha fisted her hands on her hips and turned to Rezkin. "Don't be cruel. This is not a joking matter."

"You think I jest?" he said then turned back to Malcius. "Yserria's mark will prevent you from entering into another union, so you two will have to work things out."

Yserria rounded on Malcius. "*You*! This is *your* fault. Again! You were forbidden from speaking of it. You agreed! Why do you never listen? Always, you are running your mouth."

"*My* fault? Why did you not tell me this would happen?"

"I thought you *knew*! You agreed not to speak of it—*ever*." Yserria stormed away, but Malcius followed her into the cabin, presumably to continue their argument in private.

"I can't believe that just happened," said Frisha. She looked up at Rezkin. "I am glad you never speak of it, and I'm sorry for berating you. It still doesn't change what happened, though."

Rezkin could tell from the pain in her eyes that she would probably never forgive him. A pain struck him in the chest as he decided it was better for her since he would never be able to give her what she wanted. He knew the pain he experienced was one of loss. He had felt it long ago at the northern fortress. He had felt it with Palis's death, and he had felt it when Malcius and Yserria had disappeared. What he did not understand was why he felt it now. Frisha had not died or disappeared. She was still his friend, and she was standing right in front of him, yet he still felt that he had lost her somehow.

He said, "You should gather your things. You will be moving to the other ship for your return to Cael."

"You are not going with us?" she said.

"No. I must complete the deal with Privoth."

As she walked away, he glanced back at the other ships. The former crew of the Ashaiian ship had been imprisoned in Havoth; and the ship, renamed *Mystic,* had a primarily Ferélli crew. Two Ferélli warships, *Atlandisi* and *Vispania,* now escorted *Stargazer* as well. Farson and Shezar were busy figuring out what to do with Yserria's entourage, so Rezkin summoned Akris. He said, "Move unnecessary personnel to *Mystic*. Prepare it and *Vispania* for a return to Cael. After we have resupplied, *Stargazer* and *Atlandisi* will land at Fort Ulep. From there, we will head straight for Drovsk."

Akris left to carry out his orders, and Rezkin turned to the other two strikers. He waved to the captain to join them. "Moldovan wishes to meet with the governor to assure him this was not a hostile takeover. Assign him a Ferélli guard so that it will not appear that we are forcing him." To the strikers, he said, "One of you follow and remain hidden as backup. Return as soon as the meeting is concluded. We are leaving as soon as the ships are reorganized and resupplied."

"No shore leave, then?" said Estadd.

Rezkin looked at the captain. "A secret war is already being waged. Enemies are being recruited and have been placed. It is unlikely that we have encountered so many demons by coincidence, yet I doubt we were being targeted. I believe it is because they are already so profuse. Demons and spies may even be aboard this ship. It is best to assume that, aside from Cael, no port is a friendly port."

After he saw that everyone was performing their duties, Rezkin went to look for Wesson. The mage was in the storeroom hunched over a crate he was using as a table. Broken pieces of pottery were scattered over its surface, a few having spilled onto the floor, and an unblemished specimen was at the center of his focus. Rezkin watched as Wesson designed the structure of a spell, then laid it over the pot. He then cast another at the broken pieces. The shards began to rattle and shift, moving closer to each other and fighting for space. Then, the undamaged pot began to shake, a hollow sound escaping its open mouth. It abruptly shattered, spilling its pieces on top of the others.

"No!" Wesson cried as he buried his hands in his curly locks. He glanced up at Rezkin and said, "I *must* put it back together. If I can tear it apart, I should be able to put it back together."

As he began frantically gathering the pieces of both pots, Rezkin moved to crouch at his level on the other side of the crate.

"Journeyman Wesson, you cannot put the Ashaiian ship back together, nor can you recreate the people. They are lost. You must accept that."

Wesson blinked at him. "I *know* that. But, I must find balance. For the sake of my sanity, I must be able to *fix* things, not just destroy them."

Rezkin stared at the broken pieces with his enchanted eyesight. Although they lacked the swirling colors, their broken disarray reminded him of his own colors of shattered glass. He noticed that the pottery shards still possessed the same glow as the pot when it had been whole. He said, "The pieces have not changed, only their arrangement, their relationship with each other. Before, they possessed a synchrony of purpose, a design; whereas now, they are fragmented, without purpose, and without order."

Wesson looked at the pieces. "Yes, I see what you are saying."

Rezkin said, "Some people might prefer them this way."

"Why would anyone want broken pottery?"

"Because now they can be shaped and combined in any way you want."

"Like a mosaic?"

Rezkin picked up a piece glazed with blue and white designs, turned it, and then placed it on the crate. He added another and then another. After a few minutes, he sat back and examined the design.

"It is beautiful," said Wesson. "It looks like a star."

Rezkin tapped the crate. "It would not have been possible had the pieces remained in their original state."

Wesson looked at the pieces sullenly. He said, "But it will never again be a pot."

Rezkin motioned to the open crate beside them. "Does it need to be? We have more pots."

"But I have no use for this," Wesson said, motioning to the mosaic. "A pot is useful."

"Then make it into something useful," said Rezkin. "Perhaps, with time, you will learn to create things anew. Perhaps you will even learn to fix them. You should not punish yourself for your ignorance, so long as you continue to correct it."

Wesson still looked at the pieces with disappointment but muttered, "How did you get to be so wise?"

Rezkin said, "I do not know if I am wise, but I think differently than most." He lifted one of the pots from the crate and set it next to the mosaic. He pointed to the pot and said, "This is most people." Then, he pointed to the mosaic and said, "This is me. Perhaps someday you will fix me, too."

Wesson looked up in surprise. "But you are amazing how you are!"

Rezkin grinned and watched as the meaning dawned in the mage's eyes.

"Oh."

Rezkin tilted his head and settled a sword on to the crate. "Now, I need you to look at this."

Wesson lowered his face to peer closely at the weapon. He said, "It is a sword."

"I know," said Rezkin. "It is the mythical Sword of Eyre."

Wesson looked at the sword again. He lifted it from the crate and turned it in every way. "It is only a sword. It is not even enchanted—not in any way. It contains no mage materials. There is nothing special about it. It would be impossible to set it aflame for any length of time."

Rezkin nodded as his suspicions were confirmed. The prophecy of the Sword of Eyre was a fraud.

Frisha looked in the mirror. For the second time, a stranger stared back at her. "Do you think it's too much?"

Celise laughed. "This is very not much. You look pretty, but we can have more?"

"No, it's enough. It's just that I don't recognize myself. My eyes look huge and bright, and my lips—do you think it sends the wrong message? I know most of the ladies at court wear face paints, but I never—"

"You must stop this worry," said Celise. "You are not to be queen, but we still want to have status, yes? We must *impress* them. If we look to have … um, this is the word for knowing we are good?"

"Confidence?"

"Yes, we must look to have confidence, and they will think we are important. Trust me. This is how it is done. We must hurry."

"What's the rush?" said Frisha.

"We are almost the last to leave the ship. It is not good to be last. This shows a worry that we are not good enough to be ahead of others. To be first is to be too eager. We are at a good time now."

"She has a point," said Moldovan. Frisha jumped, not having noticed him standing in the doorway. He said, "I have decided to escort you down the gangplank. A lady should never go it alone."

Celise's expression fell. "My Wesson is not here to be escort."

Moldovan smiled, the wrinkles around his mouth and eyes becoming craggier. "Then I shall have the pleasure of escorting two beautiful women."

Frisha watched her feet as she descended the gangplank since she did not want to make a fool of herself by falling into the water. When she looked up, she was confronted by a stern-faced high lord with every reason to be angry. They stared at each other, he the judge and she the accused. Finally, his expression softened, and he said, "I am glad to see that you are well."

Frisha smiled, but his attention had already moved on to the old king at her side. After Tieran introduced himself, he said, "Do I know you? You look somewhat familiar."

Moldovan's expression was hard. He said, "Lord Tieran Nirius, I met you only once, I think. You would have been a small boy then."

Frisha said, "This is King … ah, I mean *Prince* Moldovan of Ferélle."

Tieran's brows rose, and then he stepped back and performed a courtly bow. "Greetings, Your Highness. I have the honor of offering you Cael's finest hospitality—such as it may be. I must apologize in advance. Ours is a young kingdom, and the accommodations will not meet the standards to which you are accustomed, but we will do our best to address your every need."

Moldovan raised his chin and looked down his nose at Tieran in judgment. Then, he winked at Frisha and said, "*That* is how royalty should be addressed." He turned back to Tieran. "Thank you, I humbly accept your gracious hospitality, Lord Tieran—or is it prince? Were you not named heir presumptive?"

Tieran's grin appeared forced. "Well, we have not yet worked out the system of titles and holdings. Lord Tieran will do for now."

Moldovan nodded and said, "I did not come for the comforts. I came to see my daughter."

"Of course, I will escort you directly."

"No, you stay and enjoy the company of these lovely ladies." He pointed to the personnel running around the dock in newly designed palace livery. "I would be glad to have one of these servants show me to her."

After Tieran called over a servant to escort Moldovan, Frisha said, "This is Celise, daughter of Queen Erisial. She is … ah … a friend? … of Journeyman Mage Wesson's."

Celise's joy was bright enough to fill the dock as she said, "Yes, I have claimed sweet Wesson as my first consort. It is a pleasure to meet you, Lord Tieran. Frisha has said much of you to me."

Tieran glanced at Frisha. She released an uncomfortable laugh and said, "Oh, you know, just the little things—nothing serious. I've been telling her about our projects and some of our experiences trying to govern together." He said nothing, at first, only staring at her with eyes the color of the ocean far beyond the influence of land. She shifted under his silent gaze.

"Yes, I understand," he said. "It is the little things we often find ourselves pondering. I think, sometimes, that they are thieves, stealing importance from other matters." Frisha was not sure how to respond, but it became unnecessary as he turned his attention to Celise. He performed a small bow, glanced at the blue ribbon in her hair, and said, "We are honored that you have joined us, Matria Celise." His gaze darted to Frisha before he looked back to Celise and said, "We have heard only rumors of the events that took place in your queendom. I shall be most grateful to hear an accurate telling."

Frisha pursed her lips. "What you heard is probably true. Rezkin married the queen and became king of Lon Lerésh. Moldovan abdicated to Rezkin, so now he's king of Ferélle, too, which makes him emperor of an imaginary place called Cimmeria, and Cael and Ashai are supposed to be a part of it."

"It is true, then? Rezkin *married* Queen Erisial? Does he recognize it?"

She huffed. "No, and believe me, we would know if he did. Malcius accidentally recognized Yserria's claim, and now they're married."

His eyes widened. "This is going to be an interesting story, but it will probably best be told when you are both rested. I shall escort you to your quarters."

As they walked through the corridors, Celise stared in awe at the mesmerizing enchanted palace, reminding Frisha of her first time walking the halls. Eventually, Celise said, "I hope my Wesson will recognize my claim. He did not accept it, but I will show him that it is good."

Frisha said, "Why did you choose Wesson?"

Celise grinned. "He is not a warrior. He is not scary."

Frisha looked at her sideways. "You know that he completely obliterated an entire warship?"

Tieran turned to her. "He did what?"

Celise bobbed her head. "Yes, but he did this with Mage Threll, and we were in the water. It mostly sank, I think. He was saving us with his power. He is not a bad dangerous." Frisha started to correct her but then decided to let her think what she wanted about Wesson. She seemed very happy, and Frisha only hoped Celise did not suffer when she realized the truth.

Celise was placed with Ilanet, who had moved rooms when Frisha went missing. She offered a slight protest since she wanted to share a room with Wesson. It was decided that the two of them could discuss that once he returned. Tieran turned to Frisha as the door closed. He said, "I just realized that we seem to be collecting princesses."

Frisha laughed. "Royals, in general."

He chuckled and then said, "Perhaps you would join me after you are rested? We have much to discuss."

"Of course."

Upon arriving at Fort Ulep, Rezkin's entourage was met with a mixture of forced deference and poorly concealed hostility. The ten stone men had been moved to the center of the village that had grown around the fort. They had been arranged in their original circle with a stone pillar at the center. Their names and ranks had been engraved on the pillar, and a garden of red solanias, perpetually blooming vimaral flowers, had been planted at their feet.

Rezkin stepped up next to Wesson who was staring disconsolately at the display. He said, "They may yet wake."

Wesson did not take his eyes from them. "I have never known you to engender false hope."

"The spell was experimental. We do not know its long-term effects. Therefore, hope and condemnation are equally valid. One of them, however, is counterproductive."

Wesson drew his eyes from the memorial to look at Rezkin. "You do not think I should be held responsible for this?"

Rezkin tilted his head. "You *are* responsible for this, but that does not make you guilty. If you feel remuneration is necessary, then ensure this does not happen again by helping to defeat the real enemy."

Wesson said, "Caydean was not responsible for this, so what enemy am I to fight?"

Rezkin looked to the memorial. "The face was different, but the enemy was the same. Hate. It is a senseless emotion that induces strife wherever it persists."

"How am I supposed to fight *hate*?"

Rezkin looked back to him. "Defeat all those who wield it."

"Then, are we not the same as them?"

Rezkin said, "I do not hate my enemies. I merely recognize the need for them to be silenced in whatever manner is fitting."

He gathered his reins and mounted one of the Ferélli rockhorses they had brought with them. The rockhorses were sturdy beasts well suited for the rugged desert terrain of Ferélle. Unlike the Gendishen reds, they were not particularly fast, but they were hearty. Wesson followed, mounting his own mare, and they rejoined the cavalcade that was waiting for them on the road that led east to Drovsk. Many of the townsfolk and soldiers gathered to watch the procession in silence, their thoughts expressed by their heated glares.

The commander at Fort Ulep had assigned a unit to escort them, which contained four purifiers. The eclectic party of Ashaiians, Ferélli, Leréshis, and Gendishen traveled east. The one group that was absent was the mages with the exception of Wesson. While he had proven himself capable of fending off the purifiers, he was not sure he could do the same for anyone else. There was also the high probability that Privoth would gather a larger force to attack him this time. The Gendishen with whom they traveled continued to blame Rezkin and Wesson for the fate of their comrades, despite the fact that, since their last visit, authorities had received more reports of drauglics attacking in small numbers.

By day, the groups spread out to keep an eye on each other, but at night the camp was strongly segregated by nationality. Rezkin sat by the fire surrounded by an assortment of guards. Almost everyone was a potential threat, particularly Yserria's Leréshis, since Erisial had upset her entire culture by marrying him, and the only way to get rid of Erisial was to kill him first. He was surveying the group when something caught his attention. For the briefest moment, it appeared that tiny people danced within the fire. He blinked, and they were gone.

While the brilliant colors associated with Bilior's fruit had disappeared, Rezkin still felt energized. He was becoming restless from lack of activity after sitting in the saddle for days on end, so he decided to go exploring. His first challenge was to disappear from a camp in which it was the duty of nearly every pair of eyes to remain on him. He decided he should probably tell someone that he was going, or the factions would start a war between them when they realized he had disappeared. He looked around to decide whom he should tell that would not cause them to follow. He settled on Malcius. He made the excuse that he needed to speak with Malcius in private about his union with Yserria but instead explained he was going for a stroll and would return by dawn. Then, to Malcius's dismay, he slipped away.

Rezkin slithered through the tall grasses of the vast Gendishen plain toward a copse of trees in the distance. They appeared as a dark stain in the otherwise pale landscape, but he was inclined to explore them, either through some inexplicable pull or because they were the only item of any interest in the area. The trees along the perimeter looked young, but as he walked farther into the forest, they grew old and craggy, their gnarled branches bent and twisted in unusual ways. The canopy had grown thick, blocking sight of the stars and moon, but the wooded depths were lit by a soft blue glow from an unknown light source that seemed to emanate from everywhere. The walk through the copse that should have consumed no more than fifteen minutes had claimed hours of his time. Just as Rezkin thought to turn around, he spied a break in the trees. Within the clearing was a massive boulder as large as a two-story inn. A clear pool rested at its base, fed by a trickle of spring water that flowed from a fissure in the floor of the opening to a cave.

Shadows cast by the flickering light of fire flitted across the walls of the cave.

Rezkin crept closer, listening for sounds of the cave's occupants. The hollow gale of air passing through chambers began to produce a melodic tune, a familiar one. He stepped lightly along the watery path into the cave. It branched in several directions, but the other paths were dry, so he followed the water to its source. When he arrived, he saw only a small puddle in the middle of an empty chamber, and he realized a detail he had been missing. The water was flowing *into* the cave, *into* the puddle that began to rise in a thin stream beyond the level of the stone in which it sat.

The shadows shifted, and Rezkin noticed that the light source had moved. He turned to find two flames the size of his palm burning over a pile of leaves and sticks on a rock ledge. The flames merged into one and then split again. They morphed into little figures that danced around each other as if putting on a show. Eventually, six smaller flames erupted from the debris. The tiny flames created a ring around the larger two, dancing and spinning to the music of the hollow melody. The ground began to shake, a massive rumble that caused rocks to fall from the ceiling and walls. Rezkin was about to dart for the exit when a stone monster stepped out of the wall beside it. A large serpent slipped into the room through the space between the stone monster's feet. As it coiled in the center beside the somewhat man-shaped pillar of water, it began to morph into a tree-like creature he recognized.

Bilior blinked up at him from where he crouched low on the ground, but he said nothing. Rezkin glanced at the other beings, the elementals he assumed were Ahn'an.

"Why have you brought me here?"

Bilior tilted his head to look at him sideways. "The paths be open, among them you walk. We listen."

"I do not understand."

Rezkin glanced away as a rumble emanated from the stone monster, followed by the sound of bellows as the wind whipped through the fire. When he looked back, Malcius was staring at him.

"What is this?" Rezkin said in alarm.

Malcius ran a hand down his own face and said, "This aura is better suited for discussion. You do not always understand me." He glanced at the stone monster and shrugged. "You do not understand *them* at all, so I suppose I should be content with what I have."

"You sound like him," said Rezkin.

"We had best make this quick. His aura is more difficult to hold since he does not possess the power. Someone opened the pathways. You stumbled onto one when you left the human camp. We guided you here so that you would not get lost."

Rezkin glanced around the cave. "I am not in my realm?"

Malcius pursed his lips. "You are in a pocket of your realm, one only those with great power can access. The pathways lead to many realms and many such pockets. He who opened them is inexperienced and dangerous. You are not the only one who may stumble onto a path."

"You mean other people could be getting trapped in these realms?"

Malcius shook his head. "No. They are not open to all. You must possess the right power to travel the pathways. But, other *things* may pass between worlds. What is more concerning is that we cannot sense the power used to open them."

"What does that mean?"

"We are Ahn'an, composed of Mikayal and Rheina. We cannot sense the power of Nihko."

"So, someone wielding the power of Nihko opened them? You mean a demon."

"Most likely, but the Daem'Ahn cannot leave their realm alone. They must be invited into this one by a host. This one is close."

"A possession. How can we determine who is possessed?"

"The Ahn'tep are composed of all three of the Ahn. You, the humans and other creatures of this realm, are Ahn'tep. They have this power, some more than others."

"The Sen," said Rezkin.

Malcius tilted his head. "The Blessed of Nihko have more than most."

"Not all humans are Sen, though. Can others sense the demons? The mages, perhaps?"

Malcius shrugged. "Theoretically, yes. We do not know human spells. We cannot help you with this." He glanced at the others. "It is the reason we made the deal. You are supposed to provide the army."

"*These* are the other Ancients?" said Rezkin, glancing at the others who watched him intently. Malcius nodded toward each of them. "Hvelia," he said of the debris strewn wind. "Uspiul—" indicating the humanoid figure made of infinitely flowing water. "Liti and Itli, you have met," he said of the little fire dancers Rezkin had first seen inside a Caellian crystal. "The large one is Goragana," Malcius said, looking toward the towering rock giant.

Rezkin bowed to each of them. "I am honored." He turned back to Bilior. "I have amassed the armies of two kingdoms, but if the threat is as great as you believe, it will not be enough."

"They come," Malcius said before his form began to melt. "Our deal is almost complete. We wait. Call should you need the power"—Bilior crouched and bobbed up and down—"power of life, earth, wind, and fire. In thoughts and senses, a focused sign."

Goragana groaned as he stepped away from the entrance. Rezkin looked at the Ancients one more time before stepping back into the night. When he emerged, he was standing at the edge of his camp exactly where he had left.

Malcius turned to him. "This is not fair, Rez. You know the others will blame *me* when they cannot find you, and I must tell them that you left."

Rezkin glanced at the campsite where everything appeared calm. "No one noticed my absence?"

"Oh no, you came up with a good enough excuse. Using my predicament with Yserria was a low blow." He huffed. "How long do you intend to be gone?"

"What are you talking about? I have just returned."

"You jest? Perhaps you should be the fool and not the emperor."

Rezkin tilted his head to peer at the sky. It appeared that no time had passed since he left the camp. He said, "Is that how you speak to an emperor? I think you do not take my position seriously."

Malcius shook his head. "Probably more than *you*. You rack up titles and act like it is just another day. I think you would rather I speak to you honestly than stand on formality"

Rezkin grinned at him. "You are beginning to understand. Married life is having a profound effect on you." Rezkin strolled back into the camp with Malcius on his heels.

"That is not funny, Rez. You, the jester. What has gotten in to you?"

"Outworlders often jest," he said. "I believe it is a way to form personal bonds. If you truly do not appreciate it, I will cease the attempt."

Malcius glanced at him and sighed. "No, it is better than being serious all the time. You are an emperor. Someone with such great power should have a sense of humor."

Rezkin tilted his head. "Then, I shall continue my pursuit of the art." He turned toward his tent as he said, "Perhaps you should, too."

Malcius's head jerked toward Rezkin. "Wha—Hey!"

Rezkin entered his tent then slipped out the gap in the back. Farson was standing there with a scowl. "What?"

"You disappeared."

"You followed us."

"Yes," said Farson. "I am not an idiot. You have no interest in Malcius's marital status. Where did you go?"

"To the edge of camp. I was with Malcius."

Farson shook his head. "I mean when you disappeared."

Rezkin looked at him curiously. Had Farson somehow detected his passage? He said, "What are you talking about?"

"You told Malcius you were going to leave. Malcius turned around to throw a tantrum, and you started walking through the field. Then, you vanished—*completely* vanished. Next thing I know, you are standing right in front of Malcius again. Where did you go, and how did you get there?"

"You are mistaken. It was a trick of the light. Your eyes were confused by the dark."

"Does this have to do with the cat?"

"The cat?"

"Yes, the cat that shows up before a demon attack."

Rezkin paused to consider. He decided that it was probably best to alert someone else to the danger. "Perhaps. I have reason to believe one or more demons or otherworldly creatures could be near."

"I will not ask why you know that since you are obviously averse to sharing. How do we know who the demon is?"

"I do not know, yet. It would be best to discuss it with Journeyman Wesson."

"What if *he* is the demon?"

"Then, it would probably be a moot point, considering his level of power. Keep your eyes open for suspicious activity."

Farson looked at him with incredulity. "Have you *seen* our convoy?"

20

Tam pulled at the long, green stalk, but when it would not budge, he began digging the root out of the soil with his fingers. He brushed the dirt from it as best he could and then picked up a rock and began smashing and grinding it into another rock. He worked quickly as he knew they were out of time. He grabbed the stack of assorted leaves he had gathered and crumbled them into the root paste.

"*I should boil this*," he said, "*but we don't have time, or water, or a fire.*"

"*You think that will work? Where did you learn it?*" said Uthey.

Tam glanced over his shoulder, pausing to listen for danger. Hearing nothing suspicious, he went back to grinding. Once everything was mixed together, he scooped up a glob and smeared it into the bite wound on Uthey's arm. Then, he moved on to the man's leg. Finally, he said, "*From a master healer of the mundane.*"

Uthey chuckled. "*Was he a king, too*?"

"*The same. I mean, he wasn't king at the time. He was just a traveler we met in a tavern. I didn't think I was paying attention when he talked about plants, but*"—he pointed to his head—"*it's this hole. I'm remembering things that happened long ago as if they happened yesterday.*"

"*Hmm, a remedy invented by a tumor. This stuff'll probably kill me.*"

Tam felt the man's fevered skin. "*You'll die anyway.*"

"*Good to know*," said Uthey.

When he was done applying the paste, Tam scraped the remainder onto a large leaf and folded it over to fit in his pocket. Then, he smeared the rock with fresh deer dung, turned it over, and buried it.

"*Why did you do that?*"

"*To throw them off if they have dogs. They'll track the scent.*"

"*Good thinking, but I don't think anyone's coming after us. It's been ... I don't know ... days, weeks? Probably most of them were killed in the attack. The rest will have sought help or gone to the quarry.*"

"*Someone is coming. Can't you feel it?*" said Tam. His gaze darted about then he looked back at Uthey with urgency. "*It's in the wind. It sounds different.*"

"*You're bleeding again,*" said Uthey.

Tam absently wiped his nose and then realized he had used the hand smeared in dung. He glanced up again. The wind had changed. It hummed in synchrony with the pounding in his head. "*We have to go,*" he said.

He helped Uthey to his feet, and they stumbled through the forest along the riverbank. It was well past midday when they came to a low point where the bank disappeared, and they trudged across a sandbar to the river's edge. Tam lagged behind to the extent their chain would allow to cover their tracks, and Uthey was in no condition to argue. They drank and bathed, and then Tam reapplied the paste to Uthey's wounds.

The former mercenary said, "*I think I'm feeling a bit better. The water helps.*"

Opening another pouch made of leaves, Tam examined the last of the previous day's berry harvest. He handed half of them to Uthey then unceremoniously shoved the other half into his mouth.

Uthey said, "*This might be our last meal. We should savor them.*"

Tam watched the river. Did it look normal? He said, "*I don't plan on dying.*"

Uthey tugged at the collar shackle. "*Well, when I die, you can cut off my head.*"

"*You're not dying, either,*" said Tam. "*Besides, I no longer have a sword with which to remove your head.*"

"*Yes, your slippery fingers,*" said Uthey.

"*If you hadn't fallen over the ravine, nearly yanking my head off, I wouldn't have dropped it.*"

"*It was not my fault that I lost my balance due to the fever,*" said Uthey.

"*No matter,*" said Tam. "*We will rid you of the fever soon enough.*" Then, he lurched to his feet and dragged Uthey from the sand. Wiping their tracks as they shuffled along, he pulled Uthey back into the forest on the other side of the sand bar. They had walked a few dozen feet into the thicket when Tam tugged Uthey down to crouch behind the undergrowth.

"*What are we doing?*" said Uthey, "*I thought* I *was the one who was supposed to go mad from fever.*"

"*Sh,*" hissed Tam, and then he pointed toward the river.

A boat came into view. It carried only nine soldiers, but it was followed by at least a dozen more like it. The soldiers pulled the boats onto the sand bar and then set to making camp. Tam watched them for a few minutes and then motioned for Uthey to leave. They hurried deeper into the forest, trying to make as little sound as possible. Once they were far enough away, Tam allowed Uthey a moment to catch his breath.

Uthey looked at him and said, "*What are Ashaiian soldiers doing this deep into Verril?*"

Tam said nothing as he listened to the wind and trees.

"*Maybe they're here to rescue you,*" said Uthey, his chuckle becoming a wheeze, but he continued to jest. "*Maybe it's your king.*"

"*They do not serve my king,*" said Tam. "*They are the enemy—for now.*"

They both jumped at the sound of branches crackling behind them. When they turned around, they were confronted by three grinning men in armor bearing weapons. One stepped forward as two more appeared behind them.

"*What do we have here?*" said the leader.

"*Looks like two escaped slaves,*" said one of his men.

Uthey whispered, "*What are they saying?*"

Tam realized the men were speaking Verrili. He knew he could not defeat them all. If Uthey had been well, they might have put up a fight; but, as it was, any protest would end in pain and suffering.

"*I think we made a mistake,*" he said in Gendishen.

Another man with broken teeth, who also spoke Gendishen, said, "*I'd say you're right.*"

The man nodded for them to move. After another ten paces through the forest, they reached the edge of the tree line where the land dropped off a cliff. It looked to be more than a hundred feet to the base. At the bottom was a massive pit where hundreds of slaves were pushing carts, hauling rocks, and breaking boulders. Some disappeared into caves in the sides of the cliffs, some were whipped as they worked, and others were thrown into a smaller pit for the dead.

The man with the broken teeth leaned over Tam's shoulder so that Tam could smell his putrid breath as he spoke. "*Welcome to the quarry.*"

There was only one way in and out of the quarry, and it was by a platform on the other side of the pit that was raised and lowered with ropes. Once Tam stepped off the platform onto the rugged detritus, he knew he would have to find a way to escape. He was practically as far from Cael as he could get—on the complete opposite side of the Souelian. No one knew where he had gone. No one had witnessed his kidnapping; and even if they had, no one in Uthrel would talk. To his friends, he had just disappeared. In the unlikely event that someone tracked him to the Isle of Sand, they would never know where he had been sent afterward. He would be trapped in the quarry for the rest of his short life. There was no way Rezkin could find him. Not even the Rez, himself, would find him.

~

"I've found him," said Connovan, and Tieran looked up with a sigh of relief.

"Where is he?"

"He was taken by slavers to the Isle of Sand," said Connovan. With a mischievous grin, he said, "Perhaps I should go after him."

"No," said Tieran, a little too hastily. "Rezkin should return soon. He will decide what to do."

Connovan tipped his head. "I leave it to you; but, remember, many do not survive the Isle of Sand. He will eventually be sold, if he has not been already. The longer we wait, the harder it will be to find him."

Tieran exhaled heavily. "Tam is strong. We must have faith that he can hold out."

Connovan tilted his head in the same unnerving way he had seen so many times from Rezkin. "Perhaps he is, perhaps not. If he fails, he was not worthy of his *apprenticeship*. Testing Rez's pet is not *your* motivation, though." His tone shifted to accusation. "You have orders to keep me from leaving."

Tieran sat back and tapped his finger on the desk. He forced himself to meet Connovan's predatory gaze. He said, "I was not supposed to allow you off the island. I permitted your trip to Uthrel due to the exceptional circumstances."

"Permitted? You practically begged." A small silver knife appeared in Connovan's hand. He spun it over his fingers, seemingly without effort. "If I desired to leave, you could not stop me."

Tieran sucked in a breath. He felt a shift in the space around him as if something was there but just out of sight. He said, "No, but *they* can."

Two of the shielreyah materialized, one beside him, the other next to Connovan. The former Rez's gaze traveled the length of the vaporous warrior. He said, "I was not aware they respond to your call."

Neither was I, thought Tieran.

"We respond to the will of the *Spirétua Syek-lyé,*" said the one closest to Connovan. Tieran thought his name was Cikayri, but he found them difficult to tell apart.

"He is not here," said Connovan.

"He is everywhere," said the Cikayri. "You will not leave Caellurum. You will not harm the kin of the *Spirétua Syek-lyé*."

Tieran scowled at Connovan. "You were considering killing me?"

"Of course not," said Connovan. "Maiming, perhaps—just a bit." He glanced at the shielreyah next to Tieran. "These *things* do present a challenge. Still, they can be fooled. I heard about the attack. People were kidnapped. People died." He glanced at the one next to him again. "They are not infallible." Connovan stood and performed an unnecessary courtly bow. He paused as he was about to speak. Then, he said, "You really should decide on a title. People do not know how to formally address you."

Tieran grumbled, "Must we lean so heavily on titles?"

Connovan said, "You are not sounding like yourself, Lord Tieran. So many years of your father's teachings spoiled. Has being labeled a traitor caused this destruction? It is such a little thing, really."

Gritting his teeth, Tieran said, "My father did not seek to make me a great man. He only wanted to make me like him. Rezkin has shown me a better way."

Connovan nodded. "I believe he has, Lord Tieran. The question is *why*?"

~

When Frisha lay down, she thought she would never be able to sleep. As it was, though, she slept soundly through the evening, night, and half of the next morning. She wiped the sleep from her eyes then washed and combed her hair before reapplying the face paints as Celise had shown her. She then headed to the king's office in hopes of finding Tieran. She opened the door to find him slumped over the desk.

"Are you busy?" she said.

He lifted his head. "I am excogitating."

Frisha's face flushed. "Uh, sh-should I give you some privacy?"

His slack jaw and furrowed brow expressed utter confusion. Then, he laughed and shook his head. "It means to think through or figure out something."

Frisha huffed, her face heating again. "That is a ridiculous word. Why did you not say that in the first place?"

Tieran picked up the book that lay open on the desk, turning it so she could see the title. *The Inviolable Mind: A Guide to Tactical Supremacy*. "I read it in here," he said. "I have been lax in preparing for my duties and am now making up for lost time. Do I sound more astute?"

"It makes you sound pompous."

"Ah, we do not want that." His gaze traveled over her, and she shifted uncomfortably. He said, "Are you rested?"

She smiled. "I think I slept too much, but I do feel the better for it."

He nodded. "Shall we walk, then? Perhaps the garden will be a welcomed respite after so many weeks at sea."

"That sounds pleasant," she said.

They spoke of his struggles and the decisions he had made while she was away, and she told him the story of their voyage as they strolled along their usual routes through the gardens. The plants had grown much in her absence. Tieran had even cultivated his own plot that had all the herbs Frisha's mother had grown at home. She asked if he would not mind sitting there for a while as she enjoyed the familiar scents.

"There is something I need to tell you," said Tieran, "and you are not going to like it."

She laid a hand on his where it rested on the bench. "Please, I cannot take any more bad news right now. Can it wait?"

"I think you will be angry with me for not telling you sooner."

"Is there anything I can do about it?"

He swallowed hard as he met her gaze. "No, there may be nothing to be done about it."

She glanced at the garden. "Then Rezkin will fix it."

Tieran looked away. He said, "I wish *I* could fix it. I feel so inadequate at times."

"It's not your fault, Tieran. Rezkin was trained for this. It is his life's purpose." She met his gaze and said, "You have a different purpose."

He laughed. "I wish I knew what that was."

"And I, mine," said Frisha. "Perhaps that is why he has such clarity. He knows exactly what he is supposed to be doing."

"I think he has no idea what he is doing. He just makes it up as he goes."

Her brow furrowed. "Considering who he is, that is even more frightening."

They sat in silence for a while. Questions hung in the air like a thick blanket—all the subjects they had not yet broached. Finally, she said, "I called off the betrothal."

He appeared uncomfortable but not surprised. He said, "I suppose having your betrothed marry another woman would give one pause."

She shook her head. "No, before that. Sometimes I wonder if he would have accepted her deal if I had not. Still, I would not change my decision. He is not the man I thought him to be. I think I have accepted who he is, for his sake and that of the kingdom, but he is not the man I wish to marry."

"You would be empress," said Tieran.

"But I would not be loved."

Tieran looked surprised. "You think he does not love you?"

"He said as much."

He was silent for a while as he appeared to struggle with something. He said, "I think he does, but he is not aware of it. I think he does not know what love is because he has never been given any. At least, not before he met us."

"I have considered that many times," she said. "While we were gone, I learned things about him—things I cannot forget."

"More than what Connovan revealed?"

She nodded. "I have tried to connect it with what I thought I knew of him, and I cannot. I think he is truly different people—or no one, as Connovan said. I realized that I only love a part of him, and I do not think it is the biggest part. Who he truly is, in every aspect—I do not love that man."

She looked up to find Tieran staring at her. He pulled a kerchief from his pocket then reached over and gently wiped the paint from her lips.

He said, "You do not need it." He took a deep breath and met her gaze. "I did not notice at first. I was so wrapped up in myself—in the usual customs—

that I could not see the natural beauty before me. I have struggled for some time now. I am dedicated to my cousin, and I will remain loyal to him, always; but, he does not deserve you. He showed me that you are driven and brave, that you are honest and trustworthy; but, I see something he does not. You are passionate and deeply romantic. You offer your heart to people and plead with them to do the same.

"Rezkin opened my eyes to who I was and who I should be, but you opened my heart. I was distraught when you disappeared. I even thought to take a ship and go after you, but everyone assured me that you were safe with Rezkin. The truth is, you have never been safe with him. Your heart is open and bleeding, and he does not see. I am no longer the man I was when we first met. I hope that you can learn to see me as the man I am struggling to become."

Frisha was struck speechless. She wondered if she were truly still asleep in her room. Perhaps she had not yet left the ship. The herbal scents were real, though. She reached up to touch his face. He was real. He lifted his hand to grasp hers and then pressed a kiss to her fingertips. Then, he moved closer, and she did not move away. She asked herself why she was not moving, then realized she *wanted* to be close to him.

"I don't understand," she said. "You were so upset when I told you I was having doubts about Rezkin. You were pushing me to stay with him."

He held his hand to her face as he stroked her cheek. "I was angry but not with you. I loved you even then, but I am loyal to Rezkin. I was wracked with guilt for wanting you, but I feared what would happen if you left him."

"What would that be?"

"This," he said as he leaned in and pressed his lips to hers.

Her belly fluttered, and her skin flushed with heat as a thrill surged through her from deep within. She wanted *him.* She wrapped her arms around his neck, pressing her breasts to his chest and kissed him with the passion she had kept bottled up for so long. They stayed like that, locked in each other's arms for an eternity wrapped in a few short minutes. Tieran eventually pulled her arms from his neck and backed away. She made to follow, but he pressed his fingers to her lips, stalling her, then trailed them along her jaw to rest his palm on her neck. She knew he could feel her wildly beating pulse, but she felt no shame in it. They were both breathing heavily.

He said, "We must stop, or I will dare go too far. I do not want that for you."

Frisha's heart sank, and it must have shown on her face.

He shook his head. "Do not get me wrong. I *want* to, but I want this to be right between us. I wish to court you properly in hopes that, someday, you might do me the honor of becoming my wife."

Frisha struggled to find words, and then a terrible thought struck her. She said, "Rezkin."

Tieran's face scrunched in pain. "That is not what I had hoped to hear."

"No! I mean, what if he does not approve?" She shook her head vigorously. "I have seen him angry. I do not want that directed at you."

Tieran exhaled in a rush. "I have considered that more than is good for my sanity. In truth, I am petrified, for I may not survive the encounter. You are worth it, though. I would face an army of elven wraiths to keep you at my side."

Wesson was relieved when the procession stopped to water the horses around midmorning. His rear was sore from riding for so many days after spending the majority of the past couple of months on a ship. Besides that, it seemed the entirety of Gendishen was devoid of shade, and although the autumn breeze was cool, the sun was still scorching. He wiped his forehead and looked up at Rezkin. "I have no idea where to begin."

Rezkin handed him a leather pouch, which Wesson discovered contained pottery shards. Rezkin said, "These are the remains of the vessel that housed the demon in Ferélle. It is covered in runes. I thought it might shed some light on the subject."

"You were carrying these around with you?"

"I did not want to risk losing them, so I kept them in my pack."

"I see." Wesson picked up one of the pieces, rolling it over to examine the runes. He said, "I think … I think I have seen something like this before, a long time ago. I once found a vessel with similar markings. It was empty but whole. I did not know what to make of it at the time. I could be wrong, though. I was young. Maybe it was just an unusual design."

"What can you tell us about this one?" said Farson.

Wesson scratched his head and tugged at an errant curl. "There was one other place I have seen similar markings." He glanced at Farson. "You have seen them, too." Farson and Wesson both looked at Rezkin.

"*What*?" said Rezkin.

"It was the first time we were in Ferélle, when we met the Adana'Ro. Just as you walked through the ward that Mage Threll and I constructed, we caught a glimpse of markings nearly covering your body. It was rather obvious at the time due to your state of undress."

"It is true," said Farson.

"They were *these* markings?" Rezkin said in alarm. Although he had heard people call him one often enough, he did not want to be associated with demons.

Wesson shook his head. "I cannot say for sure. It was only a brief flash. I think they were not exactly the same but perhaps written in the same language."

Rezkin said, "Connovan told us the markings on my skin were made by the Sen to document the events of death and resurrection, or retrieval, as they called it; but, according to the histories, the Sen were forbidden from performing demon magic. The Sen are said to derive their power from Nihko, Goddess of Death and the Afterlife. It is Nihko's power than binds our souls to our human vessels. Demons are the product of Nihko and Rheina, and they reside in the realm of H'khajnak. In order for them to enter this realm, they must be bound to a vessel. Perhaps these runes bind them to the clay pot in the same way that the shielreyah are bound to Caellurum."

Wesson nodded. "That would make sense. Perhaps this is where I went wrong with the stone men. I crafted the power into a spell that I attached to their persons, but spells are sometimes fickle when attached to living beings because we are in a constant state of change. These runes would not change, so they would hold the spells better."

"How would you do that?" said Farson.

"Well, as is said to have happened with Rezkin, they could be tattooed on, or branded, or scarred. One could be temporarily drawn in ink, chalk, or stain."

"What about blood or feces?" said Rezkin.

Wesson looked at him sharply. "Yes, but that would also invoke blood magic. Contrary to popular belief, blood magic is not always restricted to the use of blood. It could be any part of a living creature: blood, hair, feces, saliva …"

"The drauglics' ukwa was covered in feces. I did not think it strange at the time since that is supposed to be typical of their kind."

“The feces could also have been covering more permanent marks,” said Farson. “Did Healer Aelis or Boulis have any marks?”

“I do not know if anyone checked,” said Rezkin. “I doubt anyone thought to look.”

Wesson said, “It would be helpful if I had some runes to study—besides these, I mean.”

“If we kill another demon host, then you shall have some,” said Rezkin.

Wesson shuffled his feet and cleared his throat. “I was thinking about, perhaps, someone more—*alive*—and more available.” He stared at Rezkin hopefully.

“You mean *me*?”

Wesson shrugged.

Farson glanced over to the rest of the cavalcade and said, “It is time to go. People are getting either too comfortable or restless.” He nodded toward one group that appeared to be having a particularly heated exchange. “I believe the Leréshis and Gendishen are about to wage war.”

For the rest of the trip to the capital, they did not discuss the demon issue, although they alerted their close companions to maintain vigilance and report anything strange. As they rode into the city accompanied by the unit from Fort Ulep, Wesson pulled up beside Rezkin. He said, “I think it is the purifiers.”

Rezkin glanced at him. “Why do you say that?”

“I feel much negativity from them. Every time I look at them, I become furious.”

“That is to be expected, regardless. They commit genocide against your kind.”

“Perhaps we could check them for runes.”

“I doubt they would allow that.”

“You could *encourage* them.”

Rezkin raised a brow at him, and Wesson felt a tiny bit bad for suggesting it. No, he decided, he did not feel bad about it at all. He said, “Perhaps if we tell them we are looking for demons, they will consent.”

“They will more likely just point to you.”

Wesson glanced back at the four purifiers riding toward the rear of the procession. He mumbled, “Perhaps we should kill them anyway.” He turned back to find skepticism in Rezkin’s gaze but no judgment. Wesson said, “They have been trying to attach their leashes to me the entire trip." Glancing back, again, he said, "Look, now there are two more."

Rezkin said, "You knew that would happen when you insisted on coming."

"If I were not so strong, I would be dead already—burned at the stake like all the other innocent mages. How can these people not be demons?"

"It is easy to blame the horrors and injustices of hate on demons, much harder to credit our fellow human beings. We do not like seeing such terrible defects in ourselves. The irony is that demons do not act out of hate or contempt. They are begotten of chaos, and it is that which they seek to spread in the same way that we often seek order. It is simply their nature."

"So, you are saying humans are *worse* than demons."

"Only in their motives," said Rezkin. "The results are the same, except that demons wield power most humans cannot defend against."

"You know a lot about demons."

Rezkin nodded. "I have been learning much about the old gods, about how we fit into their design. The Ahn'an, the Ahn'tep, and the Daem'Ahn have a fascinating history, and it has been insightful."

"I have heard none of this from the priests of the Maker," said Wesson.

Rezkin said, "Since Minder Finwy has insisted on following me everywhere, you are in luck. Perhaps we should discuss the matter with him on the return trip."

Wesson glanced back at the minder who was riding a little too close to the purifiers for his taste. Then, he glanced at Yserria and Malcius as he turned back around. The two always rode side-by-side, but he had not seen them speak in days—at least, no more than the occasional snide remark. Yserria had been simmering ever since the bond mark appeared on the side of her face. She had asked Wesson to examine it at least a hundred times; and, every time, he obliged. Still, he knew of no way to break it short of death.

Their procession was led to the palace, rather than the council's overgress. Wesson's hackles rose as they approached. Two lines of purifiers, at least twenty of them, were stationed along the path. He knew they were all there for *him*. As soon as they were within range, he felt their tendrils of power testing him. It was not a full-on assault, but he knew that if any of them succeeded in attaching a binding spell, they would swarm him.

Rezkin glanced at him and said, "You have my approval if you wish to make an example of some of them."

Wesson fancied the thought but said, "That might start a war."

"Privoth knows there is more at stake here than a single mage. Then again, the purifiers are emotionally charged zealots, so you could be correct."

When they reached the steps to the palace, the entire procession dismounted. Wesson, Farson, Malcius, Yserria, and Brandt all wore the hoods, tabards, and black face paint as they had the first time they visited. Rezkin and his entourage were escorted through the palace doors. They did not have far to travel. They entered the throne room along with Minder Finwy, who said he was there to bear witness on behalf of the Temple, two of Yserria's guards, and two Ferélli. The rest remained in the receiving hall or in the palace yard with the horses and supplies. Rezkin became suspicious when he noticed that none of the courtiers were in attendance. The council members were seated on benches along the walls. Armored guards stood between the benches, and two dozen purifiers filed into the room behind them.

Privoth sat on his throne, a drab monstrosity, roughly carved from stone and nearly reaching the ceiling. The leader of the purifiers, who had been so embittered by Wesson on their last visit, stood to the king's right. Rezkin walked the path between massive stone pillars that were topped with huge bowls of flaming oil.

He stopped at the foot of the dais. "Greetings, King Privoth. I have returned to conclude our business."

Privoth gripped the arms of his throne and looked at him with a scorching gaze. "Did you bring it?"

Rezkin held out his hand, and Farson stepped forward. The striker removed the silky wrap and handed the sword to Rezkin. Holding it high for everyone to see, he said, "I have brought the Sword of Eyre, thereby fulfilling my end of the bargain."

Privoth stood from his seat and descended the steps. He took the sword from Rezkin and examined it as if expecting to discover a fake. He grinned and announced, "This is the Sword of Eyre." The councilors clapped as Privoth walked back to the foot of the stairs. Privoth then turned and said, "Kill them."

Every armed person in the room abruptly drew their weapons. Rezkin said, "We had a deal, Privoth—the sword for Cael."

"You think I would give you a piece of my land—*King of Lon Lerésh*? You think I would share my land after you ally yourself with those, those *women*? And, King of Ferélle! You think to walk into *my* throne room and steal away my crown for your empire as you did Moldovan's?"

"I never desired Moldovan's crown, nor that of Lon Lerésh, nor *yours*. I only require Cael," said Rezkin, "and, as we agreed, I will use it to take back Ashai."

Privoth shook with anger as he said, "You have plenty of land for your precious refugees, yet you still seek to take mine!"

"It matters not how much land I possess. We had an agreement. You will fulfill your part of the bargain."

Privoth's smile was ruthless. "No, I shall watch you die."

As Privoth's guards moved in, the councilors began to shout at Privoth to make his men stand down. The councilors appeared genuinely confused, but Rezkin thought they likely desired only to escape from the room before blood was shed. Some tried to leave, but the exits were blocked and barred, so they huddled near the benches and in the corners of the room. The guards advanced on Rezkin's people, who had formed a perimeter defense with Minder Finwy and Wesson at the center, the latter engaged in a battle of wills with the purifiers. The others had orders to defend Wesson if he could not defend himself. Ptelana drew her bow and was the first to attack. She released several arrows, taking down two purifiers and a guard before the swordsmen reached them. She repositioned herself in the center of the circle with the minder and Wesson and continued firing arrows into the fray.

As they had practiced, Rezkin's unit ebbed and flowed, expanding and contracting the ring as one side or the other was pushed back. The doors at the front of the throne room shook, and then the pounding ceased as more swordplay could be heard on the other side. As the enemy fell, fresh troops swarmed into the room through the side doors. It appeared to Rezkin that Privoth had prepared his entire army for battle. It was only a matter of time before his people were overwhelmed.

Rezkin shouted to his people to close the circle as he rushed forward to meet Privoth. He was merciless as he cut a swath through the guards. Many of them ran rather than confront him. Privoth tossed his precious Sword of Eyre to the ground and drew his own two-handed longsword. He met Rezkin's charge with fire in his eyes. Their blades clashed, green lightning crackling within the black blade. Privoth was on the defensive as Rezkin pushed forward, forcing the king up the steps. Once at the top, Privoth dodged Rezkin's strikes by ducking behind the throne. Each time Rezkin struck at him, the king dashed behind the stone monolith and then returned with a strike or thrust of his own. Meanwhile, guardsmen continued to attack Rezkin from behind. He sliced one man across the throat and then stabbed another through the gap in his brigandine. After making a pass at Privoth, he gutted another guard, then began backing down the steps. With Privoth playing mouse behind the throne, he had the chance to implement his backup plan.

"You run, you coward!" called Privoth. "Your people already begin to fall!"

Rezkin would not be baited into turning his back to check on his comrades. He had already seen that two of the Ferélli guards and one of the Leréshi had been struck down. Yserria held her side as blood dribbled over her fingers, and it looked as if Malcius had been struck in the head. Farson bled from a few minor cuts, and Wesson and Minder Finwy had blood splattered over their faces, source unknown.

After fending off the few soldiers near him brave enough to attack, Rezkin sheathed the black blade and bent to retrieve the Sword of Eyre. One soldier thought to take advantage of Rezkin's position and lost his legs. As he straightened, Rezkin summoned his focus. He had learned at an early age to protect himself from mage attacks using his focus shield and had even extended it to another person within close proximity; but, he had never attempted to shield someone from across a room. He formed the shield in his mind, a mental exercise that had not been required since forming one had become second nature. Then, he pulled the shield from the potential, as he had been taught, and cast it toward Wesson.

"Gah," Wesson shouted as the shield struck him.

Rezkin did not have time to see the shield's effect, if any, but he assumed it had been of some benefit when an explosion suddenly rocked the rear of the throne room. He held the sword out to his side and hummed to the sounds of wails and shouts and crashing stones. He hummed the tune of the wind, the sound of the swirling light.

Call should you need the power, power of life, earth, wind, and fire. In thoughts and senses, a focused sign. Bilior's words echoed in his mind. He focused. He imagined his standard—the raven gripping a green lightning bolt. But, he knew, somehow, that was not right. His focus shifted, and he saw the rainbow of colors, his colors, shattered and pieced together in a mosaic.

Then, he felt the tug. Something had listened. Something was responding. He searched his mind for the source of the tug, and he saw them. Tiny flames danced all around his mind. He held his hand in the air, reaching toward the bowl of flame on the nearest pillar and *pulled* with his will.

A drop of fire spilled over the side of the pillar, then another. Throughout the throne room, fire began to drip from the torches and sconces. Little candle-flames, perhaps hundreds of them, skipped across the floor toward him. They slithered up his legs, so that he appeared to be on fire, and then danced down his arm toward the sword. The little flame elementals gathered along the blade and dug into spaces in the metal that Rezkin could not see but knew to be there through his connection with the fae creatures.

With the sword aflame, Rezkin stalked toward the dais. Privoth backed away in a feverish panic. When Rezkin reached the top of the steps, he realized the sounds and commotion had ceased behind him. He raised the sword over his head and thrust it into the seat of the throne. It sank a third of the way into the stone, and the flames enveloped the entire sword as he backed away. Rezkin turned to survey the room, all the while keeping track of Privoth. Everyone was in stasis, staring either at him or the sword—except for his small unit in the center that breathed heavily as they stood ready to defend themselves.

Rezkin looked back to Privoth and pointed to the flaming sword. "There is your prophecy, set in the stone of your own throne. If you want it, you must claim it." He looked to the councilors and then the soldiers. "Cael is *mine*." He turned his hard gaze back to the councilors. "A deal with Gendishen is a deal broken. Your kingdom is without honor and cannot be trusted." He then descended the dais, gathered his people, and stalked out of the throne room.

Wesson stared at the evidence of his presence. All of the purifiers were dead, most having been crushed by fallen pieces of the ceiling and outer wall. He had not meant to kill them. He could not even be sure that he was responsible. Something had struck him, something strange that had blasted past his shields. In an instant, the purifiers' attacks against him had been nullified. It was as if he had been splashed with cool water after spending the day sweltering in the desert. It was then that his power had gotten away from him. All the spells he had been preparing, all the attacks he had tried to cast and failed, escaped at once in a messy ball of power that had rocked the palace, blasting a hole through one corner and causing the ceiling and part of the wall to cave in on top of the purifiers.

He was not terribly upset about killing them, which *did* upset him. In a way, they too had been victims. Most of them had probably been stolen as children and trained to believe that the very power that made them special had turned them evil. Wesson was so busy stewing in his thoughts that he did not notice the man in the open passage outside the throne room. Something pricked his senses, and he turned to see Reader Kessa hurrying down a side corridor. She screamed, and he glanced in the direction of her wide-eyed gaze just in time to see a black, vaporous serpent shooting toward him. Mage Kessa threw herself in front of him, taking the brunt of the attack. A gut-wrenching shriek tore from her throat as her skin blackened and bubbled. Tiny tendrils of smoke lashed at Wesson's sleeves, burning through them with ease.

Wesson looked to the source of the attack. At the other end of the open corridor was the leader of the purifiers. His appearance had somehow changed. He looked angrier, darker, and more foreboding. His gaze was consumed in blackness, and his twisted lips sneered with hateful glee as he lobbed another attack. Wesson thrust a simple shield toward the mass of black vines twisting through the air toward him. Some of the vines were destroyed, but others persisted. He quickly constructed a net of the whip-like tendrils he had learned from Xa but added his own touch using nocent power and fire. The net streamed forward, the black strands lined in flame. When the destructive spell collided with the demonic power, it produced a burst of nauseating energy. Wesson doubled over trying not to retch, while others around him were unsuccessful. When he glanced up, he was surprised to see that his net had not been consumed in the impact, but instead swept down the corridor to envelop the purifier. It burned a hashed pattern into his skin, shredding his clothes and tearing flesh from bone.

The possessed man did not stop, though. He raised a fist dripping with bloody flesh and pointed to Wesson. A half-dozen soldiers rushed forth from a vaporous cloud behind the purifier, fully armed and ready to attack. Their eyes were black voids, an effect not unlike that of Rezkin's mask. Wesson thrust a stream of fire at the men, but their charred bodies continued. Suddenly, Yserria, Farson, and Malcius jumped into the fray, slicing and chopping at the soldiers, who did not succumb to their injuries until collapsing from loss of blood.

The purifier remained standing, preparing his next attack, and Wesson was worried the others might be struck. He formed a small orb in the air in front of him. The orb grew larger as he fed power into it. A bit of earth, a little water, a dash of fire, and a whole load of nocent—the orb appeared as a bubble of ink larger than his head. He mentally sucked in his power and then released it, blasting the orb forward. Too late, he realized that Rezkin had prepared his own attack. As Rezkin's black blade swept around to take the purifier's head, it collided with the orb. It looked as if the blade had sliced through water, somehow dragging the inky blackness with it. The green lightning within the black blade bled out and crackled within Wesson's spell. As the blade cut through the purifier's body, the lightning snapped through the air with a black cloud forming around both the purifier and Rezkin. When the cloud dissipated, the purifier had been vaporized, and Rezkin's entire body was crackling with green lightning.

Wesson's king and emperor raised his icy gaze toward him from the other end of the corridor, and it was as if he could see into Wesson's very soul.

Wesson blurted, "Ah … sorry?"

Rezkin shook his head and walked away.

21

Wesson knelt at Master Reader Kessa's side. She gripped his sleeve as she sought his gaze. Her lips wagged, but no sound emerged through the pain.

He said, "Hold on. Rezkin will help you. He will know what to do."

She reached up and gripped the pendant that hung from the thin, gold chain at her throat. With a tug, it came loose. She pressed the small, gold disk into his palm.

He shook his head. "No. No—"

"You must. You … can … defeat him."

"I can defeat who?"

She never answered. In fact, she never drew another breath. As Wesson struggled to contain his sorrow, Malcius pulled him to his feet and guided him toward the cavalcade.

Malcius said, "You nearly killed our emperor."

Wesson looked at him blankly.

Malcius said, "After all of this? That would have been a terrible ending to our story."

Wesson laughed through his tears, and Malcius patted him on the back.

About an hour into their journey home, Wesson pulled his horse up beside Rezkin.

"How did you do it?"

Rezkin glanced at him. "Do what?"

"How did you put fire on the sword? It is impossible, yet you did it. I need to know how."

Rezkin's roaming gaze never stopped, and Wesson wondered how he never exhausted of being on constant alert. Rezkin said, "I recalled a conversation I once had with Malcius and Brandt about naming swords. Brandt mentioned that he had read about spirits becoming trapped in the metal of a blade."

"Yes, I have heard of it, but no one has ever actually *seen* one."

"I knew we could not put a spell on the blade, but I thought perhaps to imbue it with a spirit—one of fire."

"An *elemental*?" Wesson felt a thrill. He had never seen an elemental. Few had. "You *called* to an elemental, and one came?"

Rezkin said, "You saw the little flames."

Wesson's heart thudded with excitement as he said, "*Those* were elementals? There were dozens of them."

"There were exactly two-hundred and eighty-three," said Rezkin. "It is the number required to maintain the flame on the sword. I am not sure how I know that, but I must eventually release them."

"How did you call nearly *three hundred* elementals? How did you call *any*?" He shifted uncomfortably under Rezkin's icy stare.

After a prolonged silence, Rezkin turned to Farson and said, "The journeyman and I will ride ahead."

Farson said, "That would defeat the purpose of the escort."

"We will stay within sight. He and I need to have a discussion."

"Then stay here and use a sound ward."

Rezkin gave the striker a pointed look. "And risk someone reading our lips?"

Wesson watched the exchange with fascination. The dynamic between Rezkin and his former trainer, who apparently wanted to kill him, was intriguing; but, he wondered if the enmity was sincere. At times, it seemed as if Rezkin trusted the striker more than any other, and Farson rarely declined the chance to assist or offer advice. Still, Wesson felt a thread of mortal danger lay just beneath the surface of every exchange.

"I am going with you," said Farson.

For the slightest moment, Wesson thought Rezkin looked his age, a younger man, one in need of support. It lasted no more than a breath, and then he wondered if he had seen it at all.

"Very well," said Rezkin. "The strikers will need to know anyway."

Wesson watched Farson's reaction as carefully as he had Rezkin's. Whenever Rezkin included Farson with the other strikers, a glimmer of pride shimmered in his eyes. Wesson wondered if it was because Farson had missed being a striker or because Rezkin recognized him as such.

Once they were a few dozen paces ahead of the rest of the cavalcade, Wesson erected the sound ward around them. Rezkin glanced at him as if reconsidering then said, "I had hoped this matter could be resolved swiftly and without effort beyond what I already had planned. Circumstances have changed, and it has become evident that the enemy is several steps ahead of us."

"You mean Caydean?" said Wesson, hearing echoes of Reader Kessa's final words.

"Perhaps," said Rezkin. "Caydean is certainly part of it, but I do not know if he is the source." Turning to look at him, Rezkin said, "I knew about the demon threat before the first attack."

Wesson was not surprised. Rezkin always knew more than he shared. He said, "Why did you not warn us?"

Rezkin furrowed his brow, and Wesson wondered if it was a natural expression or an affectation. "I did not know if the threat was real at first. My source was not particularly reliable." He glanced at Wesson. "It was one of the fae."

"You have met one of the fae?" Wesson did not know why he was so surprised, considering Rezkin's connection to the elementals.

Rezkin nodded. "I made a deal with one."

"You did *what*?" blurted Farson. "Perhaps you are not so immune to power after all. I cannot see you doing something so inane otherwise."

Wesson agreed with the sentiment. He said, "If you have the poor luck to encounter one of the fae, you are never, *ever* supposed to make a deal. They are tricksters and manipulators. It is one of the first rules you learn as an apprentice."

"I know that," said Rezkin, "but circumstances were dire."

Farson said, "Do you know how many *Rules* you broke? What could possibly be important enough to risk making a deal that could mean your life—or your freedom for *eternity*?"

Rezkin met the striker's challenging gaze. "The safety and welfare of my friends, of a shipload of refugees, of an entire *kingdom* of refugees. I was observing *Rule 1*, which supersedes all others." He glanced at Wesson. "Truth be told, I am not certain he would have allowed me to leave the forest if I had not accepted."

"Then his powers affect you?" said Wesson.

"Yes, and while he has implied that I *may* have the power to fight him, I do not know how. I am at his mercy every time he shows himself. He is *always* near, yet I cannot find him."

Wesson's eyes widened. "The cat."

Rezkin shook his head. "The cat is just a cat. The fae is called a katerghen, more commonly known as a forest nymph, and he is a shapeshifter. Sometimes he takes the form of the cat so as not to draw suspicion. You should know that he can also mimic people. Somehow, he takes on their auras and draws from their memories. The first time I met him, he was you, Journeyman."

"He was able to fool you?" said Farson.

"I recognized something was wrong quickly, but I had not considered fae involvement. What is more important is that he told me demons were coming, that they were a threat to all life, and that they were coming from Ashai."

Farson said, "So, you made a deal for information?"

"No, the information was given freely in order to convince me to accept the deal. He promised a kingdom of safety for my people."

"Cael," said Wesson.

"Yes, that is how I knew to go there."

"And what must you give in return?" said Farson.

"An army."

"For what?"

"To fight the demons. It seemed a reasonable deal, considering I already intended to build an army to fight Caydean, who is most likely the source of the demons."

"And if he is not?" said Farson.

"Then we would need to fight the demons anyway. You see? The deal only works in my favor."

"Except that you did not need to involve yourself in this at all," said Farson. "You could have left Ashai. Without a master, without the oaths, you could go off to do anything you want."

"This is my purpose, Farson. It is what I want."

After an uncomfortable lull in the conversation, Wesson said, "You have not explained the Sword of Eyre."

Rezkin gave Farson a warning look and then said, "It turns out the katerghen with whom I made the deal was one of the ancients."

"An *ancient*? A *real* ancient, one of the five? The first and oldest of its kind?"

"Yes, but there are actually six ancients. There are two for fire—unless it is one being that is split in two. The katerghen is the ancient of life."

"You have met them *all*?"

"Briefly," said Rezkin. "I did not know it, but when I made the deal with the katerghen, he was speaking on behalf of the ancients, on behalf of all fae in this world."

Farson said, "That means if they had reneged on their deal, *you* would be the master of the fae."

"Yes. If I fail, I will serve them for the rest of my life, however long that may be."

"They have already delivered," said Farson.

"Not exactly," said Rezkin. "They promised *safety*. *All* of our people must remain safe until Cael is ours. If even one of them dies, the ancients will have failed."

"But we have already lost people," said Wesson.

"I believe the deal only applies to the people who were aboard the ship when I made the deal. All the people who have died joined us later."

Wesson checked off his mental list, and he realized Rezkin was right. "That is the reason you are so determined to keep Cael, and that is why the elementals came when you called."

"Precisely," said Rezkin. "And, I have already amassed the armies and navies of two kingdoms, plus my *forces* in Ashai. The problem is, I do not think it will be enough. The demons already infest these lands. As I said before, it is no coincidence that we have encountered so many. If I deploy the armies of Lon Lerésh and Ferélle to Ashai, those kingdoms will be left defenseless."

Farson said, "While you have been taking over criminal underworlds and kingdoms, you have also been engaged in this whole other war between fae and demons without our knowledge. Is there anything else?"

Rezkin tilted his head. "A demon opened the pathways to other realms. They are closed now, as far as I know, but other magical creatures may have entered this world."

Farson stared at Rezkin with resignation. "Is that all?"

Rezkin shook his head and said, "Not that concerns you at this time."

Farson said, "You felt that a war with *demons* and *fae* did not concern us until just now!"

"I never said it did not concern you, Farson. I kept it from you because I do not trust you. Let us not forget that you intend to kill me."

"And me?" said Wesson.

Rezkin turned to him with cold eyes. "I hardly know anything about you—far less than anyone else I keep in close company. The fact that I permit you your privacy and do not require your fealty demonstrates my level of respect for you."

Farson looked at Wesson in surprise. "You have not sworn fealty to him?"

Wesson shook his head.

Farson looked to Rezkin. "He has a greater chance of harming you than anyone I have encountered. Why would you risk that?"

"Because he would not give it," said Rezkin.

Farson looked at Wesson.

Wesson did not know how to answer the unspoken question. He was averse to swearing fealty to anyone, but was it not expected and required to swear loyalty to one's king?

Rezkin said, "Journeyman Battle Mage Wesson is bound to no one, as it should be. I recognized the need long before I learned of my ancestor's motive for creating the Rez. That knowledge has affirmed my belief."

"You leave him unbound on purpose? To kill you?" Farson said incredulously.

Rezkin's cool blue gaze fell on Wesson. "He knows he may not survive the encounter. He will not attempt it unless it becomes absolutely necessary."

Wesson had never asked why Rezkin did not require his fealty. Rezkin's persistent faith in his skills as a mage paled in comparison to the faith he had placed in him as a person.

~

"It's here," said Frisha.

Tieran turned from the window that overlooked the sea. He had been wondering if the sea they saw from the tower was the same one as below. Since he had not seen the ship arrive, he still could not be certain. "Are you ready?" he said.

"No."

Tieran rubbed her arms. "You know how he is. He sees everything. He will know."

"Maybe. I think he's kind of oblivious about relationships. It turns out every time I thought he was being romantic, he was just being practical or performing his *duty*."

He hooked a finger under her chin and lifted her face so that he could look into her eyes. "Do not judge your worth by his inadequacies. You deserve happiness … and romance. I intend to give you both."

Frisha smiled at him. "You have changed so much, Tieran Nirius."

His smile fell. "I feel like I am betraying him."

"He doesn't love me."

"Neither of us can say how he truly feels."

"Maybe not, but that is what he wants me to believe, and I have accepted it." She laid a hand over his heart. "You are not second choice, Tieran. I know I could have him if I wanted, but I choose you."

He kissed her—a soft, lingering kiss. Then, he said, "Shall we walk in the garden one last time before he kills me?"

The pit in his stomach that had begun to gnaw at him on the last leg of the voyage started to ease as soon as he set foot in the warehouse. It was further proof that he was somehow tied to Caellurum. It was a weakness that he would need to address sooner than later. If he was to wage war, he would need to leave the island without becoming ill. His people were on the island, though, and he was supposed to be king. Hoping to please *one* of those people, he recalled that his first directive was to check on Frisha. She had said he no longer need do so, but Frisha was fickle.

Manaua informed him that Frisha had left the corveua near the gardens, so he headed there after settling his belongings in his room and checking on Cat. Apparently, since Frisha had stowed away on the ship, Ilanet had taken responsibility for Cat's care. He would be having a talk with her later.

As he rounded the last turn in the path before reaching the garden, he heard laughter, both feminine and masculine, and it was coming closer. Frisha came bounding out of the garden with Tieran in pursuit. He grabbed her hand and spun her into his arms. Rezkin noted their flushed skin and heavy breathing, both of which could be explained by a run. The glowing smiles were less characteristic of post-run expressions for these two, and the dilated pupils and warm embrace were evidence enough. He cleared his throat, and they both glanced his way.

Frisha pushed Tieran away, seemingly in a hurry to put distance between them, and Tieran backed up a pace, as if he intended to run. Rezkin raised an eyebrow, daring him to try. Tieran swallowed hard and said, "Rezkin, g-greetings. I am glad to see that you made it back in one piece."

Rezkin turned his gaze to Frisha. She bit her lip timidly then lifted her chin and stepped closer to Tieran, taking his hand in hers. Tieran quickly disengaged and stepped forward, protectively placing Frisha behind him. "Look, Rez, ah, we need to discuss, ah, *this*."

Rezkin had seen enough. It felt as if he had been stabbed in the heart again. He knew it was not coincidence that both times it had been a woman. Frisha peered around Tieran's back. He met her pleading gaze and said, "Happiness looks good on you, Frisha." Then, he looked at Tieran. "And you, Cousin."

Tieran looked at him with suspicion. "You are not angry?"

"Why would I be angry?"

"Well, because, you know … she and I—"

"Have you treated her as a lady?"

"Yes! Of course."

Rezkin glanced into the tree about ten paces away for confirmation. Xa was stretched out on a branch, lounging against the trunk as he whittled a small stick into nothing. He shrugged and said, "It has been a rather boring show."

Frisha shrieked. "Have you been spying on us?"

Xa said, "I am *do'riel'und*. I go where you go."

Frisha balled her fists and stomped her foot. "No! Absolutely not! You are invading my privacy!"

Xa shrugged again. "You must get used to it." He finally looked at her. "Besides, for your precious *propriety's* sake, you are not supposed to be alone with him. Think of me as your chaperone."

Frisha's face flushed as she glanced at Tieran, who had the decency to appear abashed.

Rezkin started to leave, but Tieran bounded forward. "Really, Rezkin. You approve? You would give us your blessing?"

"For what am I giving my blessing, Tieran?"

"We wish to be married." Then, in a rush, he said, "Not now, mind you. After an acceptable period of courting."

Rezkin glanced at Frisha, who looked genuinely hopeful. He said, "It is as it was always meant to be."

Tieran furrowed his brow. "Are you saying you *planned* this?"

"I said nothing of the sort," replied Rezkin. He wanted to leave. He needed to call a training session with the strikers—immediately. "Is there anything else?"

Tieran stared at him for a moment, then seemingly woke and said, "Yes."

"Well, what is it?"

"Uh, if you were not angry before, you will be now." Tieran glanced back at Frisha apologetically. "Tam went missing several weeks ago. I know you told me not to let him leave the island, but I sent Connovan to find him. I could think of no one better suited to the task, besides you. He found a trail, I guess. He said that Tam was taken by slave traders to the Isle of Sand." Rezkin stared at Tieran as dozens of scenarios flashed through his mind. Tieran said, "Connovan offered to go after him, but he seemed a little *too* interested in Tam." He glanced back at Xa. Then said, "Considering who he is, I thought it best to wait for your return. I am sorry if I made the wrong choice. I had no idea what to do."

The stab wound to Rezkin's heart felt as if it had been ripped open, and the stone resting on his chest had heated to nearly unbearable. He inhaled deeply and focused on shattering his feelings, replacing them with the vast emptiness that had become so familiar during his training. He said, "Tam is likely already dead." He turned to leave, but Frisha ran up and blocked his way.

She had tears in her eyes, but she appeared furious. "You can't know that! You have to go after him."

Rezkin said, "If not, then he is already mad and will be dead soon enough."

Frisha said, "Tam is strong. He can handle it. He'll survive."

"Perhaps, if it were just the slavers, but he had what you might call a medical condition. If it was not treated weeks ago, then it is too late. He is dead."

"What medical condition?" she said with a hiccup.

"That is no longer important."

"Yes, it is!" She shook her finger in his face. "You said *Rule 1* is to protect and honor your friends. Tam is your *best* friend. You have failed. You *must* go after him."

Rezkin felt empty as he looked at her. He said, "I have a war to wage. I cannot be everywhere at once."

"Your BEST friend, Rezkin!"

"I will send a striker to confirm his death and retrieve his body, if possible. Will that make you happy? This is the kind of thing for which they are trained."

"No! Not good enough. It has to be *you*. *You* are the best, and *you* are responsible for his welfare. If you cannot take care of your best friend, then how do you intend to care for an empire?"

Rezkin looked at Tieran. In that moment, he had an overwhelming urge to kill his cousin, and he did not know why. He looked down at Frisha, and he knew he had failed to bury his anger when it escaped in his voice. "I never wanted an empire. I did all of this for *you*—for you and *him*."

"Then find *him*!"

Rezkin stared into her deep brown eyes, red and watery with tears. He turned to a very pale Tieran. "You are in charge of the war. I am going to search for a dead man."

"What? Wait, Rez ..."

Rezkin stormed away before they could assail him again. Just before he reached the corveua, he felt a sharp sting on his neck. His arm felt heavier as he reached up to pluck the tiny, feathered needle from his neck. His first thought was that Connovan was up to his tricks. He furrowed his brow as he spun the dart between his fingers. He had never seen anything like it. The feathers looked exotic, and the miniscule needle was engraved with runes that seemed familiar, but his mind was becoming foggy. He stumbled through the corveua, and his last thought was a call for the shielreyah.

EPILOGUE

"*It worked (eager),*" she said, peering at the prostrate man from her perch in the rocks.

"*Too quickly, (cautious)*," said Entris. "*He is almost completely drained. It may succeed in killing him (concerned).*"

"*Then our presence here will no longer be necessary, and we can go home (impatient).*"

He said, "*We must deal with this (determined).*"

"*So, is he, or is he not (impatient)?*" she said.

Entris's emerald eyes glinted in the waning light when he glanced at her. "*I would have said no, except the poison worked (confused). What does his aura say (curious)?*"

She shook her head. "*I cannot tell. I have never seen one so utterly destroyed (disgusted).*"

"*Perhaps it is because of the Daem'Ahn. I have never seen such a possession (curious).*"

She drummed her fingers on her blow tube. "*The Daem'Ahn complicates things (frustrated).*"

"*We will not engage unless he survives (decisive).*" Entris looked at her. "*For now, we watch and wait. How shall we pass the time (playful)?*"

Rezkin will return in *King's Dark Tidings,* Book Five

CHARACTERS

Rezkin - Warrior, King of Cael, True King of Ashai
Pride - Rezkin's horse, battle charger
Malcius Jebai - First son of Count Simeon Jebai, Rezkin's friend
Wesson Seth - Battle mage
Brandt Gerrand - Heir of House Gerrand, friend of the Jebais
Zankai (Kai) Colguerun Tresdian - Ashaiian striker loyal to Rezkin
Yserria Rey - Rezkin's royal guard, swordmaster
Minder Finwy - Priest of the Maker in Channería, Minder Barkal's assistant
Farson - Rezkin's former trainer
Palis - Malcius's younger brother
Jimson Bell - Ashaiian Army captain, friend of Rezkin
Brell Millins - Sergeant in the King's Army (Ashai)
Frisha Souvain-Marcum - Rezkin's Girl Friend, General Marcum's niece.
Tieran Nirius - Heir to House Wellinven
Privoth - King of Gendishen
Ionius - King of Channería
Myer Lour - Officer at Drovsk blockade
Fyer Volt - Soldier at Drovsk blockade
Gurrell Yuold - Former chieftain of the Eastern Mountains men
Myerin - Eastern Mountains tribe warrior
Auria - Eastern Mountains Viergnacht Tribe Mother

Olfid - Auria's husband
Orin - Leader of the White Crescent mercenary company
Kessa - Master Reader from Ashai; captured by Privoth
Tamarin Blackwater - Rezkin's apprentice and friend
Jespia - Healer
Ondrus Hammel - Life mage
Hilith Gadderand - Former thieves' guild leader
Drascon Listh - Ashaiian soldier, Second Lieutenant
Aplin Guel - Apprentice life mage
Ilanet (Netty) - Princess of Channería
Morgessa Freil - Elemental mage; earth and fire
Shiela Jebai - Malcius's sister
Tresq Abertine - Viscount from Sandea
Master Connovan - Fisherman who saved Mistress Levelle
Mistress Levelle - Woman in mourning
Lecillia - Queen Mother of Ashai
Fehrwin - Urhyus's son; Third King of Ashai
Urhyus - Coroleus's son; Second King of Ashai
Geneve - Captain of the Marabelle
Reaylin de Voss - Healer, warrior from Ashai
Oledia - Queen Erisial's daughter (Lon Lerésh)
Erisial - Queen of Lon Lerésh
Matrianera Gereldina - Woman to whom Yserria's torque once belonged
Matrianera Telía Anshe - Blonde who helps escort the travers to the Leréshi palace
Matrianera Vielda - Middle-aged Leréshi truthseeker
Celise - Young woman from Lon Lerésh
Nayala - Matrianera of House Tekahl (Lon Lerésh)
Banen - Nayala's first consort (Lon Lerésh)
Heylin - Nayala's second consort (Lon Lerésh)
Dayleen - Matrianera in Lon Lerésh
Paksis - Telía's mother
Ienia - Yserria's mother
Yenis - Yserria's aunt
Serunius - Erisial's consort
Coledon Anshe - Warrior who wants to be claimed by Yserria
Akris - Striker working for the Channerían ambassador in Lon Lerésh

Morlin - Man who attacks Celise
Jennia Leyet - One of Queen's Council; Morlin's matrianera
Mik - Leréshi palace guard
Ger - A palace guard
Bruthes - Captain of the Guard of Lon Lerésh
Dorovick - First Consort for House Jesqueli
Hyenth - First Consort for House Mierette
Naltis - Telía's consort
Hvelia - Ahn'an Ancient of wind
Uspiul - Ahn'an Ancient of water
Deshari Brigalsi - Third Echelon
Gemsbrick - Deshari's champion; master archer
Orina Goldren - Fourth Echelon
Moldovan Esyojo - King of Ferélle
Ondoro - King of Ashai (Bordran's father)
Eyalana - Queen of Ashai (Bordran's mother)
Mandrite - Bordran's brother
Belemnia - Moldovan's wife
Erania - Moldovan's sister
Jonish - Moldovan's brother
Merenia - Moldovan's second daughter
Gereshy - Merenia's son
Boulis - Erania's son
Moyl - Trademaster (Cael)
Uthey - Former mercenary from Gendishen
Wolshina - Leréshi matrianera who wants Yserria to claim her son
Ifigen - Deshari's champion; former royal guard
Balen - Wolshina's champion
Vannin - Balen's son with former matria
Nolus - Balen's son with former matria
Tinen - Commander of Rezkin's Ferélli royal guard
Carthano - Orina's champion
Dolinar - Mage; Pruari descent; Truthseeker
Malena - Woman in cage on the Isle of Sand
Fiero - Slaver in market on Isle of Sand
Ipon - Slave master in market on Isle of Sand
Lady Askiva - Verrili noblewoman

Barbarus - Stave trader who captured Tam
Arethia - A secrelé of the Adana'Ro
Yerlin Tomwell - Life mage
Mogalay - Leréshi sailor held captive with Tam
Noko Linoni - House Linoni; Fourth Echelon; Yserria's guard; male
Ptelana - Dark-skinned Leréshi woman; Third Echelon; archer; Yserria's guard
Cikayri - Shielreyah
Entris - Mysterious person on the hill

DEFINITIONS

Stargazer - Rezkin's ship
Ictali - small, white creatures on Cael
minder - priest of the Temple of the Maker
Collectiare - head of the Temple of the Maker
Purifiers - zealots who hunt mages
White Crescents - mercenary band in Gendishen
overgress - a pantheon in Gendishen
Ahn - Gods
Ahn'an - fae (beings composed of the power of only two gods: Mikayal and Rheina)
Ahn'tep - beings composed of all three gods: Mikayal, Rheina, and Nihko
Daem'Ahn - demons (beings composed of the power of only two gods: Nihko and Rheina)
Rheina - Goddess of the Firmament, the Realm of Life
Mikayal - Goddess of Death, the Afterlife
Nihko - God of the Soul/War
Chiandre - the soul's connection between the physical vessel/body and the Afterlife
Shielreyah - eihelvanan warriors who gave up their spirits to guard the citadel
Drauglics - wild; vicious semi-intelligent creatures
Ukwa - drauglic leader

Dergmyer - Gendishen officer's rank roughly equivalent to a major.
Myer - Gendishen officer's rank roughly equivalent to a captain.
Fyer - Gendishen officer's rank roughly equivalent to a sergeant.
Vimaral plants/animals - plants/animals that have been modified with magic
Marabelle- passenger ship purchased by Rezkin for Cael
Adana'Ro - assassins of Ferélle
Ro - the innocent as defined by the Adana'Ro
Ruk - those who walk in darkness as defined by the Adana'Ro
Matria - a woman who claims a consort in Lon Lerésh
Matrianera - the head of a house in Lon Lerésh
Vuroles – wolf-like desert creatures that hunt in packs
Echelon - governor of a province in Lon Lerésh
Nixie - fresh water spirits, Ahn'an
Mystic - Ashaiian warship that surrendered
Atlandisi - Ferélli warship
Vispania - Ferélli warship
solanias - perpetually blooming vimaral flowers in a variety of colors

ABOUT THE AUTHOR

Kel Kade lives in Texas and has most recently served as an adjunct college faculty member, inspiring young minds and introducing them to the fascinating and very real world of geosciences. Thanks to Kade's enthusiastic readers and the success of the *King's Dark Tidings* series, Kade is now able to pursue the completion of a Ph.D. in geosciences (presently A.B.D.) and create universes spanning space and time, develop criminal empires, plot the downfall of tyrannous rulers, and dive into fantastical mysteries full time.

Growing up, Kade lived a military lifestyle of traveling to and living in new places. These experiences with distinctive cultures and geography instilled in Kade a sense of wanderlust and opened a young mind to the knowledge that the Earth is expansive and wild. A deep interest in science, ancient history, cultural anthropology, art, music, languages, and spirituality is evidenced by the diversity and richness of the places and cultures depicted in Kade's writing.

NOTE FROM THE AUTHOR

I hope you enjoyed reading this fourth book in the King's Dark Tidings (KDT) series. Please consider leaving a review or comments so that I may continue to improve and expand upon this ongoing series. Also, sign up for my newsletter for updates or find me on my website (www.kelkade.com), Twitter (@Kel_Kade), or Facebook (@read_KelKade). Rezkin will return in *King's Dark Tidings* Book Five.

Printed in the USA
CPSIA information can be obtained
at www.ICGtesting.com
LVHW091531151223
766290LV00031B/471/J